MEAN LITTLE PEOPLE

PAIGE DEARTH

Dirt On The Author

Born and raised in Plymouth Meeting, a small town west of Philadelphia, Paige Dearth was a victim of child abuse and spent her early years yearning desperately for a better life. Living through the fear and isolation that marked her youth, she found a way of coping with the trauma: she developed the ability to dream up stories grounded in reality that would provide her with a creative outlet when she finally embarked on a series of novels. Paige's debut novel, Believe Like A Child, is the darkest version of the life she imagines she would have been doomed to lead had fate not intervened just in the nick of time. The beginning of Believe Like A Child is based on Paige's life while the remainder of the book is fiction. Paige writes real-life horror and refers to her work as Fiction with Mean-ing. She hopes that awareness through fiction creates prevention.

Connect With Paige

Find all of Paige's books on Amazon

Sign up for new book releases: paigedearth.com

Follow Paige At:

Facebook: facebook.com/paigedearth

Instagram: paigedearth

Goodreads

Twitter: @paigedearth

More books by Paige

Home Street Home Series:
Believe Like A Child
When Smiles Fade
One Among Us
Mean Little People
Never Be Alone
My Final Breath

Rainey Paxton Series:
A Little Pinprick
A Little High

For my daughter, the love of my life, the holder of my heart...you inspire me.
Mom

~

For my friend George. You stood up for me without fear, guided by truth. Your uncompromised integrity and ethical compass have made a profound impact on my life. You're the best kind of person, one who takes a staunch stand against bullies. I will always remember and be grateful for what you did for me. You are a good friend.
Morning George.
Love, Fred

~

For my Linda. Listen honey: You stood by me when everyone turned their backs to me. Our love runs deep for each other, which has always been, always will be and will never change. Thank you for standing by me.
Turtle

Acknowledgements

To all those who have been bullied or are being bullied: may you find the peace you so deserve, and know that you are not alone. Be brave. Find the strength within you to overcome, to become the great person you were born to be; it's the best retribution.

Love and gratitude to my kinder, softer half, my husband, Remo. Your drive to help me live my dream is nothing short of amazing.

My deep gratitude to Jaime Levine for pushing me to finish this book. This novel would have been gathering dust on a shelf if it weren't for your honesty, persistence and words of wisdom.

Many thanks to all the people who continue to read my work—without all of you, my dream would be nothing more than a bunch of lonely words.

For all of the book bloggers and reviewers, I would still be hidden in the darkness if you hadn't shined your light on me—thank you all so much!

Big E, I love you!

COLDHEARTED

Someone once told me that I was coldhearted. They believed it. I didn't.

Kids learn how to cope. Bullied kids find that special superpower inside that pushes them to survive. They wear masks on the outside for the world to see, but inside they are raging, struggling to experience normal.

Bullied kids face fear every day. They are beaten by words or actions—both cause pain; both leave scars. Eventually, they build a strong armor around their hearts that thickens over time.

Bullies yell. They strike out with angry words and tight fists. Bullies grow puffy. They need power to feed their powerless existence.

Though they rarely know it, the bullied are stronger than their enemies because they have the courage to face their demons every day and seek deep within themselves to find the serenity they so deserve.

Bullied children often replace pain with numbness; fear and anger with indifference; chaos with peace. They find a way to move on—sometimes they seek revenge; sometimes they become feared.

Someone once told me I was coldhearted. They were wrong.

I suppose they've never been bullied.

~Paige Dearth

The Beating Path

Seven-year-old Tony Bruno feared the dark hands of death were reaching for him. His small feet pounded against the hot pavement as he tried to get away from the boys chasing after him.

In midstride two of the seven-year-old boys snatched Tony by the back of his worn-out T-shirt. His arms flailed spastically. He tried to make contact with his small fists. One boy got angry and yelled, "Knock it off, Bruno, ya little queer."

Tony was dragged through the trash that lined the sidewalk.

"Leave me alone," Tony cried in a high-pitched voice.

"Shut up, Bruno. I swear if ya open your mouth again, we'll kill ya," Vincent snapped.

Tony twisted and pitched against the boys. He fought with everything he had in him, but he was no match for the kids who used bullying as an after-school activity.

Tony's eyes fixed on his surroundings as if he were seeing them for the first time. He looked into the open lot, taking in the small patch of trees and overgrown grass. On either side of the lot were brick buildings with broken windows that revealed the lifeless blackness within. Vines clung to the exterior as if they'd grown there from the inside out. Tony never walked between the buildings. It was taboo. This place scared him. This was the place where monsters lived. He'd heard the groan of drunks coming from deep inside the cavity of the broken-down buildings when he'd walked by months before with his mother.

Tony fixated on his mother's words now.

"There are googamongers that live in that place. Do ya know what a googamonger is?" Teresa had said.

Tony had shaken his head, scanning the trees and buildings, waiting for a humanlike creature to come after him.

"They're real big. Bigger than your father. They got long claws for fingers and real pointy teeth. They like to eat children 'cause every time they eat a kid, they grow stronger. So you keep your skinny ass outta there."

Tony was paralyzed with fear thinking about the googamongers. He kept fighting against his tormentors, but they dragged him deeper into the forbidden lot. Vincent and his friends forced Tony into the shadow of a small grouping of trees. Tony peed himself, imagining the googamongers watching him, getting ready to eat him. His stomach turned with a wispy emptiness. Tony made one final attempt to free himself and got one arm loose. Vincent punched Tony in the gut, and a few seconds later, Tony's head slammed against a large oak tree.

Vincent poked his index finger into Tony's sternum. "Give us all your money."

"I ain't g . . . g . . . got no money." Tony stared into Vincent's rich brown eyes through the jet-black hair that fell in front of them.

Frankie grabbed Tony around the waist and threw him to the ground. Then he pulled Tony's T-shirt over his head and threw it off to the side.

"Look!" Frankie stood over the boy. "Bruno peed himself."

The boys stood in a circle around Tony and laughed.

Vincent turned to his best friend, Patton. "Grab the bucket we left in the grass."

Patton stared for a moment as if he was trying to read Vincent's mind. He jumped up and down and clapped his hands together. "Yeahhhhhh," he sang as he ran into the tall grass.

Patton raced back to the noisy circle of boys. Vincent pulled the old plastic clothesline they had stolen from the neighbor lady they called Mrs. Mean. He handed the line to Patton, who threw it over a tree limb while another boy turned the bucket upside down.

A few minutes later, Tony was standing on the bucket with the plastic cord around his neck. His fingers clawed at the cord with frantic desperation. His body shook. In the heat of the day, Tony's teeth chattered. He couldn't think. His mind went blank. While Tony didn't comprehend the possible consequences of the boy's actions, he felt he was in grave danger.

Vincent looked at Tony and smiled. "He looks just like that cowboy in the movie. They hung 'im from a tree; then one of the guys kicked the horse he was sittin' on, and the guy fell off. He was swingin' by his neck. It was so cool—his legs were movin' like he was ridin' a bike, and he was twitchin' and stuff."

The energy in the small group of boys was a blend of morbid curiosity and fear of the unknown. Tony's motions were jerky. His tongue stuck to the roof of his mouth. The more his fear showed outwardly, the higher the energy level rose through the circle of boys.

"I need to go home," Tony cried. "My ma will be lookin' for me."

"You'll go home when we say ya can," Patton hissed. Then he picked up a long stick and whacked Tony on his bare back. The rough, bark-covered branches dug into his tender flesh and left bloated, red welts.

"Wow! Let me try that," Vincent said, picking up a branch and slashing it across Tony's abdomen.

Tony continued to pull at the cord around his neck. Each time one of the boys whacked him with a stick, he flinched, and the rope tightened. After a short time, Tony's muscles went limp, and he welcomed the numb feeling inside his head. His eyelids drooped, and he stopped fighting. His shoulders flopped forward, and his head hung. With a lack of oxygen, death crept upon him, bringing him the closure he longed for.

"Hey! What the hell are ya boys doin' over there?" A male voice boomed.

Vincent turned and saw a delivery truck driver at the edge of the lot; he was coming toward them.

Vincent screamed, "Run!"

The boys took off in different directions, but Patton hesitated for a moment and kicked the bucket from under Tony's feet before he took off.

The cord was just long enough so Tony landed on his tippy-toes, but the initial fall tightened it around his neck, jarring him awake. Tony tried to suck in a breath, and when nothing came through, his panic heightened, and he lost his balance. He lost his battle against the strangling cord. His windpipe betrayed him, and the lack of oxygen comforted him again.

The deliveryman reached Tony right before he slipped out of consciousness. He lifted Tony's small body and held him on his hip, as though he were a toddler. The man quickly loosened the rope around Tony's neck. Tony gulped air into his lungs, and the bluish color in his face shortly returned to normal.

"What the hell happened here?" the deliveryman said. He pulled a knife from his pocket and cut the cord.

Tony rubbed his neck with his fingertips. He looked around with a pinched expression. Then he remembered. "Vincent and his friends followed me. And . . . and . . . they made me come here and . . ."

Tony sobbed from the memory that rushed into his mind.

"OK, big guy. What's your name?"

"Tony."

"Well, I'm Mac. Let's get ya home. Where's your shirt?"

Tony looked around the tall grass in a daze. It was gone. Carried off by Patton.

"Forget the shirt. Ya all right?"

Tony nodded.

"Ya think ya can stand?" Mac said, placing Tony on his feet.

Tony wobbled at first but then gained his footing.

"Where do you live?"

"Over that way," Tony said, pointing in the direction of his row home.

Mac slowly walked Tony to his house and stood at the front door with him.

"Everything will be fine," Mac said and softly rapped on the front door.

"What the hell did ya do now?" Tony's father, Carmen, yelled when he flung the door open.

"Nothin'," Tony replied timidly.

Carmen looked at Mac, whose mouth hung open.

"What the hell are ya starin' at, and who are ya, anyway?" Carmen barked.

Mac adjusted his stance. His legs locked at the knees and his chest pushed forward. "I just found your kid being hung from a tree. A group of boys was hurtin' him. Those boys ain't got no scruples. Your son almost died."

"My son almost died 'cause he ain't got no backbone. Now, go on and deliver your packages. Stay the hell outta other people's business."

Mac stared at Carmen for a moment. Then he bent down and looked into Tony's eyes. "You take care of yourself. Stay away from those boys. Ya hear?"

Tony nodded. "Yeah, I wish they'd just leave me alone."

"Oh, for cryin' out loud! Get the hell in this house before I give ya another beatin'."

Tony knew from Carmen's squinty eyes that his father was having a worse day than normal. For a passing moment, Tony wished that he could go live with Mac. He didn't want to face his father, not alone, not again.

After Carmen slammed the door, he turned to his son. His eyes pored over Tony's gangly body, and he bent slightly at the waist to look closely at the purple mark that the cord had left around his neck.

Carmen's upper lip lifted. "Where's your shirt?"

Tony sniffled, his fear ignited by his father's venomous stare. He took a few steps backward and crossed his arms over his abdomen.

"I asked ya a question, boy."

"The kids stole it from me."

"Why did ya let 'em steal it?"

"I didn't let 'em. They made me."

"That's 'cause you're a little weasel. Ain't got no man in ya."

Carmen grabbed a handful of Tony's thick brown hair and pulled his head back to look into his son's green eyes. "You're pathetic. Go to your room, and don't come out till I say so. While you're up there, I want cha to think about how much ya embarrass me. I swear your ma cheated on me with another man, 'cause ya ain't no son of mine. Look at ya! Covered in all those scratches and bruises. The sight of ya makes me sick. Get outta my livin' room before I slap the shit outta ya."

Tony gimped up the steps as quickly as he could manage and shut his bedroom door gingerly. He pulled on a clean T-shirt and lay on his bed, waiting for his mother to come home. He rubbed his arms and legs with open hands. Pulling the blanket from his bed, he wrapped himself tightly and waited. He put his hand up to his forehead, expecting it to be on fire, but it was cold and clammy.

Then his bedroom door flew open. He sat up quickly, and the blanket dropped to his sides when he saw the belt in his father's hand. Carmen's hand lifted into the air, and the belt came down on Tony with a hard crack. The beating went on for several minutes, and when it stopped, Tony lay in a ball wishing the boys had killed him.

Chapter One

Tony's father, Carmen, had been placed in a Catholic orphanage after his mother died when he was barely three years old. The nuns who ran the facility had believed in the saying "Spare the rod; spoil the child." When Carmen turned six, his father brought him back home after marrying another woman. But his stepmother, with three children of her own, didn't take to Carmen. She complained about his appearance and lack of manners. Over time, Carmen's father beat him, trying to make his son into what his new wife wanted. But the more beatings Carmen withstood, the greater the anger the child stored inside. Many days of his childhood, Carmen walked around with black eyes or bruises on his body. Immediately after graduating from high school, Carmen was thrown out of his home and out of his father's life.

Carmen took a job as a roofer. He hated the labor-intensive work, feeling like it was below him, and a year later, after marrying Tony's mother, Teresa, he was hired by a large rigging company in Philadelphia, where Tony's family lived.

Teresa and Carmen had met in high school. Teresa had followed in her mother's footsteps and had become a seamstress at a small bridal shop.

Ten years into Carmen and Teresa's rocky marriage, with two kids, Carmen was laid off from his job and fell into a deep depression. To ease his sorrows and worries, he let his casual drinking become excessive, sloppy, and repulsive. The neighborhood watched the transformation, and he became a big joke to those who knew him. Because his rigging skills weren't in high demand, Carmen couldn't figure out what to do to earn a living.

Teresa bore the brunt of Carmen's anger over what he considered a failed life. Tony remembered the first time his father had struck his mother. One neighbor had just left the house after dropping off pants for Teresa to hem.

"Why do ya have to let the neighbors in here?" Carmen had growled.

"Because I'm tryin' to earn some extra money. What kind of question is that?"

"It's the kinda question a man asks when his wife is actin' like some sniveling beggar lookin' for a couple of dollars. Look at cha—ya look ridiculous wit' that measuring thing hangin' around your neck, kissin' that bitch's ass so ya can make a couple of dollars."

"Well, if ya got a real job, maybe I wouldn't have to take in side work," Teresa had fired back.

Tony had been lying on the floor in front of the television with his sister, Macie, who was three years younger than he was. He pretended like nothing was wrong, but Carmen's anger escalated, and his father rose from his worn-out recliner. He thudded over to Teresa and punched her hard in the belly.

"Stop it," Tony cried.

Like a grizzly bear drawn to a new noise, Carmen turned toward Tony and took a few steps in his direction.

Teresa grabbed on to Carmen's shoulder, and he flung her off.

"You little bitch. Don't cha ever try and get in my way," Carmen yelled. He grabbed Teresa's arm and twisted it behind her back, sending her to her knees.

"Carmen, stop! Please stop!"

"That's where ya belong, on your knees suckin' me off."

As Carmen let go of her arm, he grabbed a handful of her hair, and she rose to her feet. Carmen put his face close to hers.

"Now get in the fuckin' kitchen and do your fuckin' job before I break both of your arms."

Teresa was crying as she looked over at Tony, with Macie wrapped in a tight embrace. "Come on, Tony. Come help me in the kitchen."

Tony cautiously walked by his father with Macie behind him. Her small arms were fastened around her brother's waist. As Tony slunk by his father, Carmen jabbed him in the temple with his thick fingers.

"Get the fuck outta my sight. I can't stand any of ya."

Tony pulled Macie toward his mother as she started for the kitchen. When they were alone, Teresa grabbed her children and held them tightly.

"It's gonna be all right," Teresa said in a low, shaky voice.

"I'm scared," Tony said. "What if Dad hurts us real bad?"

Teresa looked into her son's eyes. "I'm scared too, baby. We just gotta keep 'im happy. That means doin' what he says and stayin' outta his way."

Teresa swallowed hard. "Just make sure you're a good boy."

"But I didn't do nothin', and he hit me in the head just now."

"That's 'cause ya was lookin' at him. Don't even look at 'im no more. Not when he's mad like that."

"Why can't we just go live with Grandma?"

"'Cause her and Grandpa don't need our problems. We just gotta deal wit' 'em on our own."

Now, as he lay on his bed nursing the welts from his father's beating, Tony rubbed his face with his hands. He kept looking toward the doorway for his father to appear while his mother started dinner. The room closed in on him until the small space made his breathing ragged. *What are we going to do now? How can I help my family?* Tony thought.

Chapter Two

The day after the hanging incident, Tony crouched low in the corner of the brick building in the schoolyard. His arms were crossed over his head to protect himself. The schoolyard was filled with children, playing and laughing, several watching him from a distance. The teacher and her aide stood across the long stretch of blacktop, unable to see through the crowd of rowdy second graders to where Tony was being bullied.

"Get away from me," Tony whimpered.

"You're such a dork. Maybe if we kick your butt again, we can knock the dork outta ya," Vincent said. Five of Vincent's friends stood around in a semicircle, egging on the harassment.

Vincent laughed wholeheartedly, and then he kicked Tony in the leg. Instinctively, Tony grabbed the spot where Vincent's sneaker had landed, and Vincent smacked him on the top of the head. Tony put his hands up to cover his face, but Vincent didn't let up. He kept on slapping and kicking Tony until all of his own rage was spent.

"You're an idiot, Tony. Ya ain't even smart enough to be in school. Ya should just stay in your house and never come to school," Vincent said.

"Maybe we can hang him again," Patton said.

Vincent smiled. "Would ya like that, Bruno? Gettin' hung again?"

Tony hyperventilated. Tears stung his eyes. He held his breath and curled his hands into tight fists. He feared the boys; he feared his father. His life had become lightless. He felt as though he were in a deep, dark, wet hole filled with sticky hatred.

As Tony's anguish escalated, he could no longer hold back his wails of sorrow. The group of boys watched him for a moment; then they walked away, satisfied. Tony lay in a fetal position on the pavement, wishing that someone would come to his rescue.

After several minutes, Tony sat up cautiously and looked around, embarrassed. Groups of children on the playground stood motionless, watching him. Several small clusters of children were giggling and pointing. Others wore faces of relief, happy that Tony's fate was not their own.

In kindergarten and first grade, Vincent and his friends had stuck to verbal assaults. But now, in the second grade, they had become physically abusive with Tony, turning their teasing into torment.

Tony was scared to move but even more worried the boys would come back and make good on their promise to hang him again. He got to his feet and walked slowly toward the door that led into the building.

"Hey, Tony," Brian, another second-grader, said in a friendly tone, approaching him. "Here, do ya wanna drink?"

Tony turned toward the boy. He watched Brian for a moment; then a smile played on his lips. Tony's throat was dry. He looked at the condensation on the soda can and imagined the cool liquid sliding down his scratchy throat.

"Thanks a lot, Brian," Tony said, reaching for the can.

Tony put the can to his lips. The liquid splashed over his tongue; then, as he swallowed, he tasted the dirt.

Tony choked on the contents and spit the foul mixture onto the ground.

"You're such a moron," Brian taunted, as the other kids laughed. "You're so easy to pick on," he added.

Tony fell silent. His head hung, and his shoulders drooped forward. He walked fast toward the doors of the building. He wanted to get inside, to hide from his peers.

Miss Cassidy, Tony's teacher, scanned the schoolyard, and her eyes stopped on Tony. She rushed over to him as he gripped the door handle.

"Tony, what happened to you?" Miss Cassidy asked. Instinctively she gently touched his red cheek. Then she discreetly wiped away the saliva and dirt stuck on his chin.

"Nothin', Miss Cassidy," Tony said, his voice barely audible.

"Nothing, huh? Well, it doesn't look like nothing to me. Come on. Let's go inside and rinse your face with cold water."

Miss Cassidy looked around and spotted Vincent and his friends gawking at her. She lifted both eyebrows and pinched her lips together at the moment that Vincent made eye contact—a sign to let the boy know she was onto him. Miss Cassidy took Tony by the hand and led him into the building.

Once they were alone, she knelt down and placed her hands on Tony's shoulders. "Were Vincent and his friends picking on you?"

Tony shook his head slowly, but he wouldn't make eye contact.

"Are you sure?" she pressed.

Tony nodded. He thought about snitching, but the bees buzzing around in his belly reminded him there would be consequences.

"How did you get that bruise on your neck? It looks like someone was choking you."

"I ran into somethin' at my house."

"Tony, are you telling me the truth? Is there something you need to talk about?"

"No, Miss Cassidy. Can I go to the bathroom?" Tony said.

Inside the boy's bathroom, Tony looked at himself in the mirror. He was repulsed by the hollow person who stared back at him.

"You're a dork," he said out loud. "Everybody hates ya. Why can't ya fight back?"

Tony's impulse was to bust the mirror to pieces and smash the pathetic reflection that glared back at him, judging him.

"I hate ya," he said to his reflection. "I wish ya would disappear. Nobody likes ya. Not even your father."

After a few minutes, Tony washed his hands and purposely took his time walking to his classroom. Every second in the hallway was time away from the mean kids. He opened the classroom door and stepped inside. The room fell silent; then several children snickered.

"Wah! Wah! Wah! I want my mommy," Patton bellowed.

Tony wrapped his arms around himself as if he could ward off the cutting words and scathing stares that sliced through him and settled in the center of his heart.

"Patton! You stop that this instant," Miss Cassidy said.

Patton looked at Miss Cassidy innocently. "What? I didn't do nothin'."

"I want you to go straight to the principal's office," she demanded.

Patton smiled at his friends but didn't move out of his chair.

"This instant!" she yelled, surprising everyone, including herself.

As Patton slid past Tony, he whispered, "You're gonna be real sorry for this, ya stupid jerk."

Tony cringed and edged his way to his seat. He walked through the aisle of second graders cautiously. Only a few feet from his desk, one boy stuck out his foot and tripped him. Tony flew into the desk of one of the popular girls. She looked at him sympathetically at first, but realizing the other kids were watching her, she quickly pinched her nose with her thumb and index finger and turned away.

"Ew," she said, pushing Tony away from her, "you smell bad, and you're ugly."

The other kids laughed, and Tony wished he could disappear, be invisible.

Finally sitting at his desk, Tony gazed at Miss Cassidy as she lectured the class about how to treat each other. Her voice was a constant buzz of white noise in his ears as she droned on about the importance of kindness, an alien concept to him. Tony's thoughts wandered to his father. Carmen would never let people push him around; Carmen had mocked Tony for being weak since the bullying began in kindergarten. The thought of going home with more bruises boosted his anxiety. His heart thudded in his chest; he could feel every heartbeat. Tony knew his father would "give it to him" when he saw Tony's swollen lip. It was the same cycle of insanity. After his peers beat him down, he would stand before Carmen for judgment. Meanness and cruelty seemed inescapable.

When the last bell of the day rang, Tony hurried to the bus and sat in the front seat behind the bus driver. As Vincent and his friends entered, they poked, slapped, or pinched him on their way to the back of the bus. When they arrived at his bus stop that day, he ran as fast as he could until he was rushing through the front door of his house.

Teresa looked up from her sewing machine. "What's the rush? Hey, come over here—let me take a look at ya," she said.

Tony walked over to his mother, and she lifted his chin.

"Those no-good little shit stains do this to ya again?" Teresa asked.

Tony nodded.

"Go upstairs and wash up before your father gets home."

Tony hesitated. "Ma, Dad's gonna be real mad when he sees me, huh?"

Teresa closed her eyes and lowered her head. "Don't get all worked up. Your face will get more swollen, and then for sure your father will know ya got an ass whoop...Those boys were pickin' on ya again."

To Tony's delight, his father didn't make it home before he'd gone to bed that night. As he drifted off to sleep, he imagined being the strongest boy in the world and hurting every single person that had hurt him.

Chapter Three

"Tony! Get your ass downstairs, boy!" Carmen screamed.

Tony jolted out of a deep sleep and rushed out of bed. He pulled on the jeans he had left on the floor from the day before. From the top of the stairs, he looked down at his father, who was waiting for him. An icy chill ran up his spine as he hurried down the steps.

"You gotta be kiddin' me? Look at ya. You're a mess. I don't wanna claim ya as my goddamn kid. If ya got outta bed earlier, you'd been able to brush those monster teeth and wash that goop outta your eyes. You disgust me, boy."

Tony walked into the kitchen and kept his eyes glued to the green-and-yellow linoleum floor. He told himself every night before he went to sleep he would wake up before Carmen screamed his name. He had even asked his mother to wake him or buy him an alarm clock, but she had warned that Carmen would have both of their asses for spending unnecessary money. Carmen expected the boy to wake up on his own, and that meant that he needed to program his brain.

"Pick up your feet when you walk. What's wrong wit' cha? You're too lazy to lift those cinderblocks off the ground. Nah, that's right, ya rather drag them around like an ape," Carmen commented.

Tony could tell his father was in an especially bad mood. His words seemed to grind out from deep within his throat, releasing a steady growl the way a dog's insides rumble before letting out a real bark. Tony sat in his chair at the table, and Teresa put a bowl of cereal in front of him.

"What's wrong wit' your face?" Carmen asked.

Tony looked over at his mother, who quickly looked away.

"Don't look at your ma. I asked ya a question, boy. What the hell happened to ya?"

Tony gathered enough courage but was still too scared to make eye contact. "A couple of kids were pickin' on me at school. I couldn't stop 'em. There were lots of 'em and only me."

Carmen mimicked in a high-pitched tone, "There were lots of 'em and only me. I don't care if there are fifty of 'em. If they mess wit' ya, fight the hell back. You see this shit, Teresa? You're raisin' a little pansy over here. Look at 'em. He can't even look me in the eye when he talks. How did ya get to be so damn wimpy?"

Tony's eyes burned with angry tears. He knew that crying would only infuriate his father more, but he couldn't prevent them from spilling over.

"Oh, for Chrissake, get a goddamn grip on yourself. You're cryin' like a little girl. You cry more than your little sister."

Tony stood up from the table and pushed his chair back. "Why are ya always yellin' at me? It ain't my fault. I don't do nothin' to make the kids pick on me. Besides, I never learned how to fight."

Carmen glared at Tony. "Ya listen here—fightin' ain't somethin' ya learn; it's just somethin' ya just know how to do. It comes from bein' born in the city. Ya should know how to protect yourself, and ya ain't gonna do that by lettin' some little punks kick your ass all the time. Ain't ya got no man instincts? What are ya, a girl?"

"Carmen, please, let's have a nice breakfast," Teresa said softly, trying to smother the burning embers just waiting to ignite. "We shouldn't encourage Tony to fight."

Carmen pushed up to the edge of his chair, his face next to his wife's. Teresa shrank away from him.

"Encourage it? You're damn straight I encourage it. I welcome it. How do ya think I feel havin' the kid that everyone picks on? It makes me look like shit in front of my friends."

"I'm sorry, Carmen."

"Damn right you're sorry. You're a sorry excuse for a woman is what cha are."

Tony looked down into his soggy cereal. It reflected how he felt on the inside: heavy, mushy, and drowning, with no escape from the murky place in which he lived.

Carmen watched his son. He wanted to break him.

In a low, deep voice, Carmen said, "When I was in school, I was the guy that everyone feared. Now I've been given a boy who ain't got no guts. Ain't got no fight in 'im. I wish ya was never born."

Carmen's cruel words made Tony's heart weep. Now he knew for sure that his father hated him.

Chapter Four

After school that day, Tony noticed the warm weather had arrived. It was a reminder that summer was on its way, and Tony looked forward to being away from school.

"Ma, I finished my homework. Can I go outside?"

Teresa smiled softly. "Yeah. Don't go too far, and stay away from the place where the googamongers live."

Tony cringed thinking about the haunted lot a couple of blocks away. Tony grabbed his basketball off the living room floor and ran to the front door. He rushed out onto the sidewalk. Outside, the heat of the sun made Tony's muscles feel limber. He looked up and down the block, and seeing no other kids, he felt safe. He dribbled the basketball in front of his house. Tony pretended he was a famous basketball player as he raced up and down his block, bouncing the ball.

"Tony Bruno just did the impossible," he said aloud, pretending to be the sports announcer. "This kid from South Philly is the best we've ever seen." Tony was running and waving at the brick buildings on either side of his street. He was looking up into the sky, pretending it was filled with fans going wild over him, accepting him, making him feel liked and special.

Tony pretended that he was dodging his opponents, making his way to the net. He stopped and dribbled the ball a couple of times. Lost in his fantasy, he turned to his right to pass the basketball to his teammate. Tony halted, as though he'd been slapped in the face. He looked around him; there was no one to pass the ball to, and he felt crushed by loneliness.

Tony scanned the block frantically, hoping that no one had watched him. He felt ridiculous thinking he could ever be great at anything. He put the ball under his arm and slowly walked back to his house, feeling so alone. When Tony was by himself, he felt invisible. When he was with his peers or father, he was the center of attention, the human trash can to dump their frustrations into.

Tony pulled the screen door open and walked inside, letting the basketball roll into the corner of the room.

"Back so soon?" Teresa asked.

"Yeah. There ain't nobody to play wit'."

"Come over here," Teresa said, gesturing to the spot next to her.

Tony cuddled up to his mother. She put her arm around him and kissed the top of his head.

"Ya know, Tony, sometimes kids are just mean...just mean little people. They don't know ya like I do, 'cause if they did, they'd be standin' in line to be your friend. I wanna ask ya somethin' and want ya to tell me the truth, OK?" Teresa said.

"Sure," Tony said in a sigh.

"Were ya ever mean to any of those boys? Did ya ever say somethin' to 'em to piss 'em off?"

Tony looked into his mother's face. His brows were taut and his jaw locked tight. Adrenaline infused with a hefty dose of annoyance burned through him. He stared at her for a few seconds. Her eyes were warm, ready to receive anything he might admit to her. He could see she wasn't blaming him for being bullied. Her warm brown eyes caressed his bruised ego.

"I don't know what I did, Ma. I think about it all the time. I remember the other kids didn't like me in kindergarten 'cause I was quiet. The other boys told me to play wit' the girls all the time. It wasn't that I didn't wanna talk wit' 'em—I just like to listen more than I talk, that's all. Then it just got bigger, Ma, and nobody wanted to be my friend. I don't know how to stop it 'cause I ain't never figured out how I started it. It just sorta happened."

Teresa pulled him closer and ran her fingers through the thick carpet of hair on his head. "Son, someday this will all be behind ya. Right now, it feels like the only thing in the world that matters. I'm tellin' ya as sure as I'm sittin' here that you're gonna grow up and be a big and powerful man. Even bigger than your father, and he's pretty big." She paused and smiled at her son. "Here's the thing I want ya to remember: someday when you're on top of the world, ya gotta remember how these little pricks made ya feel. You understand what I'm tryin' to say?"

"Yeah, you're tellin' me don't ever be mean to nobody for no good reason. Right?"

"That's exactly right," Teresa said.

"But how come Dad is mean to me for no good reason?"

"All your father knows is that his father was hard on him when he was your age. All he knows how to do for ya is to be hard."

"Is that how come he's always pickin' on me and says everything I do is wrong? Just 'cause his dad did it to him?"

"Yeah, Tony. It's his sick way of toughenin' ya up," she explained.

"Yeah, well, I hate his way of doin' stuff. It makes me pissed off. Besides, he picks on you too."

Teresa stroked the top of Tony's head, and he relaxed into her. Tony contemplated what his mother had told him. He wanted to believe that someday everything would be different for him...he needed to believe his mother. It was the only spark of hope left in him.

Teresa stood up. "Tony and Macie, put on your shoes. We need to run down to the Italian Market. I gotta get some ground beef for dinner. I wanna get back here before your father gets home."

Tony hurried to get his shoes on. He loved going to the Italian Market; it was one of his favorite places in South Philadelphia. The three of them walked briskly to the market, and Teresa chatted the entire way.

At the market Tony stood by his mother's side.

"Hi, Harry," Teresa said to the butcher. "Ya got any cheap ground beef?"

"Sure, Teresa. Got some in the back. Only a couple of days old, but still good if ya cook it today."

"I need a good deal on it," Teresa yelled after him.

"Ya always do," Harry said.

When Harry came back with the almost-rancid meat, he and Teresa got into a conversation about the sad state of the Philadelphia Eagles. While they were talking, Tony spotted three men walking on the sidewalk. They swaggered past the vendors, who waved and smiled at them. Everyone knew the men. They were the Mafia men. Tony watched them, fascinated. He had seen them in the Italian Market before. They weren't afraid of anyone. They were the men everyone feared.

Teresa looked down at her son and followed his gaze.

"They're mobsters, Tony. We don't want nothin' to do wit' the Mafia. Quit staring at 'em before ya get us in a load of shit."

Tony smiled. Even my ma is scared of those guys. It was written all over her face. Her jaw was set hard, and she wouldn't even glance in their direction. Tony wanted to be just like those men. A guy people respected. A man no one would ever pick on. Tony wished as hard as he could that he could be just like them someday.

One mobster glanced into the butcher shop and saw Tony watching them. Tony's breath caught in his chest, but he couldn't look away. Then the mobster gave him a slight nod of the head, and Tony had his very first feeling of acceptance.

Chapter Five

The summer between second and third grade started like every other for Tony...alone. He sat on his porch steps and daydreamed. He played with his sister, Macie, but she wasn't very much fun since all she wanted to do was play with her dolls. He had just finished playing war with his small green army soldiers when the screen door to his house opened.

"Tony, the new neighbors are movin' in next week. I want cha to clean up this porch. We don't want the new people thinkin' we're slobs," Teresa said.

"Wow! New neighbors? Do you think they have a boy as old as me? Wouldn't that be great, Ma? Maybe we could be friends."

Tony cleaned the porch with enthusiasm, filled with hope. He whistled tunes while he emptied boxes and swept away leaves from the previous winter.

The following week Tony sat on his porch every day waiting for the new family to arrive. By Wednesday, he was deflated and lumbered into the house.

"Ma, are these people ever gonna move in? I been waitin' all week," Tony whined.

"Ya need to be patient. Delores—you know, the lady who does my hair? Well, she said they're movin' in tomorra."

First thing on Thursday morning, Tony sat on his porch steps. It wasn't until after ten that a moving truck and a brown car pulled up to the curb. Tony watched intently as a family of five stepped onto the sidewalk, they all looked up at their new home. There were three kids: a teenage girl, a young boy, and a toddler. Tony rushed over to the family.

"Hi, I'm Tony. I live right there," he said, pointing to his family's row home.

The mother said, "Well, hello, Tony. We're the Abellis'. This is Rosemary, Marco, and the baby of the family, Aida. I'm Mrs. Abelli, and this is my husband, Mr. Abelli."

"Nice to meet ya. What grade are ya in?" Tony asked, concentrating on Marco. The young boy had blond, curly hair and wide-set blue eyes. He was a little taller than Tony but thin as a rail.

"I'm goin' into third grade," Marco said.

"Yeah? Wow! So am I. Ya wanna play?"

Marco looked at his mother, "Can I, Ma? Pleeeease."

Mrs. Abelli smiled. "Yeah, go ahead. But don't ya go anywhere else without me knowing."

Marco turned to Tony. "What do ya wanna play?"

The two ran off, and it was as though they had known each other for years. They played together for a few hours until Tony's mother stepped onto the front porch to call him in for lunch. Tony and Marco ran up the block to where Teresa was waiting.

Teresa crossed her arms over her chest and gave the boys a smile. "Well now. Who's this?"

"This is my new friend, Marco. He just moved into the Donatis' old house," Tony said, breathlessly.

"Oh yeah. I heard ya's was movin' in today," Teresa said, glancing at the moving truck.

"Can Marco eat lunch wit' us today?"

"Sure. But first ya gotta go ask your ma if it's OK."

A few minutes later, Tony and Marco rushed through the door. Teresa looked up to see the two boys, and relief washed over her.

"You can call my ma Mrs. B, and that's my little sister, Macie."

Macie gave the boys a crooked smile and buried her face in Teresa's skirt, which made the boys laugh.

"I bet you two are hungry from all that playin' ya did. I boiled some hot dogs and opened a bag of chips for ya," Teresa said.

As soon as the boys finished lunch, they rushed back outside into the sun. They were racing down the block to see who was faster.

"I'm really havin' fun. I'm glad ya moved in," Tony admitted.

"Me too. I always have fun. In my old neighborhood, I had lots of kids to play wit'."

"We got lots of kids around here, but there ain't too many that play on our block," Tony said.

Over the next couple of weeks, Tony and Marco were inseparable. On the Fourth of July, Tony talked his mother into taking the two of them to the fireworks at a local baseball field. Teresa sat with friends from the neighborhood, and the two boys sat on a blanket at the edge of the field. They were lying on their backs looking up at the stars.

"When I grow up, I'm gonna be an astronaut," Marco said, gazing at the clear sky, lit up by the bright moon and stars.

"Wow. That's cool. I don't know what I'm gonna be yet. I wanna be somethin' really great," Tony said.

"Why don' cha be an astronaut like me? We could go into space together," Marco said.

"Nah. I can't do that. My ma wouldn't want me goin' off in a rocket ship; she'd be scared somethin' bad would happen to me. Besides, I wanna be able to have a gun. Maybe I'll go in the army," Tony said.

"A gun? Yeah, that would be really cool. Maybe I'll go in the army too. Did ya ever shoot one?" Marco asked.

"Not a real one. Just a cap gun once. But I wanna shoot a real gun. Did ya ever shoot a real gun?"

"Nah. My parents don't believe in guns. They say if there weren't so many guns in the world, there wouldn't be so many robbers and bad people," Marco said, rolling his eyes.

Tony propped himself up on his elbow. "Man, look at all the people here."

Marco looked around and smiled. As they were taking in the crowd, the people seemed to part, and Tony saw Vincent and his friends heading straight at them.

"Ain't ya the new kid?" Vincent asked.

"Yeah. I'm Marco."

"Why ya hangin' out wit' the freak?" Vincent asked. Patton and the others were standing next to Vincent snickering, an act that Marco picked up on quickly.

"Who, Tony?" Marco said.

"Yeah, don't cha know everybody hates 'im and wishes he would die?" Vincent said.

Tony's blood pressure rose quickly, and he couldn't contain himself. He didn't want to lose Marco as a friend.

"Shut up, Vincent! Me and Marco are best friends, and he don't care what ya gotta say about me."

Vincent leaned over and flicked Tony in the forehead. Tony's hand covered the pulsing sting. Everyone was staring at him, even Marco. Tony wanted to jump to his feet and run.

"Like I was sayin', ya better think 'bout who you're hangin' wit' unless ya just like bein' around losers," Vincent said.

Marco sat stunned into silence. As Tony sat next to him on the blanket, he thought about how much he liked Marco. In fact, Tony thought Marco was great, but he noticed that Vincent and his friends made Marco jittery. Tony knew the mean boys would give his new friend trouble too.

"I don't know what you're talkin' about," Marco managed to say.

"You'll see when school starts. Ya better ditch this creep now before it's too late," Vincent warned.

Humiliated in front of his new friend, Tony choked out the words lodged in his throat: "I hate you, Vincent. Why don't you leave us alone? I hate all of you." He looked over to Patton and the other boys.

"Oh, look, fellas, the baby is gonna cry again. If your ma wasn't sittin' over there, we'd show Marco how easy ya are to beat up. I told ya, Marco," Vincent said, turning his attention to the other boy, "ya better lose this mamma's boy unless ya wanna end up just like 'im."

Vincent and his friends turned and walked away, but he stopped abruptly and looked back at Marco.

"Ya wanna come to the snack bar wit' us?"

Marco watched Vincent for a moment. He was already terrified of the small gang of boys and definitely did not want to be one of the kids in school who got picked on. He was torn between his loyalty to Tony and wanting to fit in.

"Sure. Come on, Tony," Marco said.

"No way. Not him. He ain't comin' wit' us. If ya wanna hang wit' us that means ya need to leave the little freak here," Vincent said.

Tony looked at Marco. His eyes pleaded with him to stay and not give in to the bullies.

"Come on, Marco. Stay here. We can go to the snack bar by ourselves," Tony begged.

Marco could feel Tony's pain. He wanted to tell him that everything would be fine, but the fear of being an outcast in his new school overshadowed any compassion he had for Tony.

"I'll go get us somethin' and bring it back. We can share it," Marco said, as he stood and walked away with Vincent and his friends.

Tony sat on the blanket, speechless. His guts felt like he was on a roller coaster, and a wave of heat rushed to his chest. Tony watched with bitter sadness as Marco disappeared into the crowd of people. He lay back on the blanket and closed his eyes. He didn't want to cry, but the tears pushed against the inside of his eyelids until they leaked their way through. He rolled onto his belly and covered the back of his head with his hands, trying to conceal his emotions and get control of the heavy sobs that were taking over. Tony's insides quivered, and he willed himself to be calm. He took heavy, snorting breaths through his nose. As his anger grew, it pushed aside his feeling of abandonment, and his crying halted.

Tony peered up into the bleachers where his mother was sitting; her head was bowed. Even from a distance, he knew she was crying.

"I'm sorry, Ma," he said to himself.

Tony's body jerked upright as the first of the fireworks burst overhead. He watched them without seeing their beauty. His heart was broken, and his mind was numb, lost in his solitary misery.

Chapter Six

The next morning Marco knocked on Tony's front door. Teresa looked at him through the screen door.

"Hi, Mrs. B. Is Tony home?"

"Yeah, he's here." Teresa paused. "I guess ya can come in."

The edginess in her voice caused Marco to hesitate, but he stepped into the house anyway.

"So what happened to ya last night, Marco? Ya was hangin' wit' Tony, and all of a sudden ya walked off wit' some other boys and left him alone."

"Sorry, Mrs. B. They're my new friends. I meant to come back and share the candy I got wit' Tony, but we started playin' kickball, and I forgot what time it was, and then..."

Teresa raised her hand up. "Good friends don't do that to each other, Marco. Maybe next time you oughta think about how you're makin' someone else feel. Huh? How's that sound?"

Tony had been standing at the top of the stairs the whole time his mother spoke to Marco. He was happy she was "giving it" to his so-called friend. When it got quiet, Tony made his way down the steps.

"What do ya want, Marco?"

"I came to see if ya wanna play. I'm sorry 'bout last night. Are you mad at me?" Marco said, following Tony into the kitchen.

"Yeah, you were a real jerk. Why did ya leave like that?"

"I don't know. I just wanted to make some more friends."

"Well, me and those guys don't like each other. They're mean, and I hate 'em," Tony spat.

"Just 'cause you hate 'em don't mean I have to hate 'em."

"Whatever, Marco. Someday they'll turn on ya. That's what they do, ya know—they only like each other."

Tony pulled a box of cereal out of the cabinet and grabbed two bowls. He handed one to Marco, and they sat at the kitchen table and ate breakfast in silence. Tony contemplated telling Marco about how Vincent and his friends bullied him, but he was worried that if Marco knew the whole truth, he would be too afraid to remain his friend. So Tony decided less was better.

"We're still friends, right?" Marco said, breaking the silence.

"I guess so."

The remainder of Tony's summer was spent playing with Marco and exploring around their neighborhood. In late August, their adventures had led them to the open lot between the two haunted buildings where Tony had almost died.

Marco ran into the tall grass, but Tony froze on the sidewalk.

"Come on, Tony. What are ya waitin' for? Ya scared or somethin'?" Marco teased.

"Googamongers live in there. My ma told me all about them. They eat kids."

Marco's shoulders went up, and his eyes grew two sizes.

"Googamongers?"

"Yeah, they got big teeth and claws for fingers," Tony said.

"Aw, come on, Tony. Your ma was just tryin' to scare ya."

"Bad stuff happened to me here a while ago. I ain't goin' in there."

Marco wanted to press the issue. He wanted to see if the googamongers were real, but Tony turned and walked away.

Marco looked up into a window of one of the abandoned brick buildings. He would have sworn he saw someone looking back at him. A stab of fear ran through him.

"Who cares about that stupid place anyway?" Marco said, running after Tony.

By the end of August, Tony and Marco had forgotten about what happened with Vincent and his friends. The summer had been the best of Tony's life. The two boys played and explored. They shared their infatuation with a couple of the young girls who lived on the block, but that was more to show off for each other. Before they were ready, the summer was gone, and it was time to start the third grade.

"I can't believe we gotta go back to school tomorra," Tony said, while they were taking a break from playing war, a game where two enemies hid from each other and the first one to douse the other with his water pistol was the winner.

"Yeah, I know. I hate school," Marco said.

"Yeah, me too. And I gotta see all those jerks again," Tony said.

"Ya know, Vincent and his friends ain't so bad, Tony. Maybe ya should give 'em a chance."

"Nah. I hate those guys. They're mean. Anyway, I hope we're in the same classes. That would be cool," Tony said, quickly changing the subject.

Tony had butterflies in his belly that night knowing that he'd be back in the clutches of the bullies when school started the next day.

Chapter Seven

After Tony and Marco got onto the school bus the next morning, Marco proceeded to the back, while Tony hesitated and stayed close to the driver.

"Come on," Marco said. "There's an open seat back there." He pointed to the seat in front of Vincent and his friends.

Tony stood still for a moment and then decided to see what would happen. Maybe if they like Marco, they'll like me now since he's my best friend, Tony thought.

"Hey, Marco," Vincent said.

"Hi, Vincent."

"What the heck are ya doin' back here, Bruno? Go sit up front wit' the girls, ya little weasel," Patton barked at Tony.

Tony looked at Patton for an extended moment.

"Take a picture, ya freak—it lasts longer," Patton mocked, throwing a pencil at Tony's head.

Tony's body went rigid. He suddenly felt nauseous. His instincts told him to get away from the boys quickly. Tony whispered to Marco, "We better go back up front."

As if Marco hadn't heard what Tony had said, he plopped down in the seat and stared up at Tony.

"Get outta here, lame brain!" Vincent yelled at Tony.

Tony made his way to the front of the bus and sat by himself. It wasn't long before he felt the spitballs hitting him in the back of the head. After the sixth one lodged itself in his thick mane, Tony turned around for a quick look at the boys, and when he did, he saw Marco laughing. Feeling betrayed, Tony stood up in the middle of the aisle.

"I hate all of you. I hope someday people are mean to you. Then you'll know how it feels," Tony yelled.

Vincent and the other boys laughed harder. Marco laughed halfheartedly but didn't stand up for his friend. Tony's face was bright red, and his hands were shaking out of control. He felt as though a volcano were inside of him on the cusp of erupting.

Suddenly, the bus driver, a middle-aged woman, pulled off to the side of the road. Marge got out of the driver's seat. She gently put her hand on Tony's shoulder. "Take your seat."

Tony did as he was told, and then Marge marched the rest of the way down the aisle to Vincent and his friends.

"Ya know, boys, it ain't nice to treat people mean. Ya shouldn't pick on anyone. I'm sure it makes that little guy feel real bad," Marge lectured.

"We ain't pickin' on him. He just started yellin' at us," Patton argued.

"I know exactly what cha did. I have two eyes and two ears. I use all of 'em. Don't pretend like ya didn't egg 'em on. Now, just leave 'em alone before I report ya to the principal. Is that what cha want on your first day of school? I bet your parents wouldn't like that, now would they?"

The boys stared at Marge with blank expressions. She turned and walked up the aisle toward her seat. Marge paused and whispered to Tony, "Don't let those jerks get the best of ya. No matter how scared ya might be, always make 'em think ya ain't afraid."

Tony looked up at Marge. "I don't wanna be left out no more."

"Sometimes bein' left out is better than bein' let in. Remember that," Marge said.

"Easy for you to say. Ya ain't the one gettin' picked on."

"You're right. I ain't. But I do know that when ya had enough you'll do somethin' that makes 'em stop. Let me tell ya somethin' important: in life there are lots of lousy people. Ya got two choices when ya meet those kinds of jerks: eat or be eaten. I see that fire in your eyes. Be brave."

As Marge took her seat, Tony felt a small rush of power. For a split second, he felt free, as if all of his troubles had been erased. It was a great feeling. Tony hoped that he could hang on to the good sensation. Just like Marge said, I will be brave, he thought.

When the kids got off the bus at school and Marge drove away, Patton kicked Tony in the ass, and he did a belly flop onto the sidewalk.

"Keep it up, Bruno, and I'll kill ya," Patton said.

Tony got to his knees and quickly stood up. He watched the group of boys walk away. When Marco looked back over his shoulder at Tony, he was laughing. In that moment, Tony's sudden feeling of bravery turned to despair. The summer was over, and he was alone once again.

Chapter Eight

L ater that afternoon, when Marco went to Tony's house to play, Tony confronted his so-called friend.

"What do ya want?" Tony said when he opened the front door.

"To see if ya wanna play," Marco said.

"Why do ya wanna play wit' me at home and then treat me like crap in school? I saw ya laughin' with Vincent and the other guys."

"I don't know. I guess I don't wanna get picked on. I don't want everyone to hate me like they hate you."

"Well, you're a big ass, Marco."

Marco looked down at his sneakers with shoelaces from his father's old work boots, flushing with shame.

"Sorry, Tony. Do ya wanna play or what?"

Tony considered his options. He could stay inside and do nothing or go with Marco and have fun. Giving in to his desire to feel normal, Tony followed Marco outside. They were playing dodge ball when Vincent, Patton, and two other boys walked up the block toward them.

"What are ya doin', Marco?" Vincent asked.

Marco's face turned blood red. "Nuttin'."

"Why are ya playin' with the little mutant?" Vincent said.

"Well...well, he begged me to play dodge ball wit' 'im, and I figured I could hit 'im wit' the ball real hard and probably knock 'im over."

"Hey, I like that idea—give me the ball," Vincent said.

Vincent threw the ball and hit Tony in the face. The five boys, including Marco, raced down the block after Tony, throwing the ball at him.

"You jerks!" Tony screamed, as he gripped his bleeding nose. "I hate all of you. Especially you, Marco."

"Why don't ya run in and cry to your mommy?" Marco screamed.

Tony stopped running and caught the ball that Patton had aimed at his gut. Tony couldn't take his eyes off of Marco. In the pit of his stomach, he felt his guts twist. The strong urge to punch Marco in the face was almost too much to hold back. He threw the ball at Marco, and it bounced off of his thigh.

"Ya throw like a girl," Marco said. "That didn't even hurt."

Tony walked quickly back to his house as the boys yelled after him. He startled Teresa when he slammed the door behind him.

"Tony, what happened? Why ya bleedin'?" Teresa said.

"I don't wanna talk about it. I just wanna be left alone. I hate everybody. I just want to kick all their asses." Tony stormed up the stairs, intentionally slamming his foot on every step, imagining he was stomping on the heads of all the boys who made his life so miserable.

Teresa followed him a few minutes later and sat on the edge of Tony's bed.

"Honey, ya can tell me what happened. It'll be good for ya to tell someone."

Tony rolled onto his side, putting his back to his mother.

"It's the same ole thing, Ma. The other kids just give me a hard time." Tony rolled over and faced her. "Now Marco is makin' fun of me too."

Tony looked at his mother intently. Teresa's face reddened, and her eyes glittered as if someone was holding a match against them.

Teresa tried to hold back her emotions, but she couldn't. "Marco is a little rat. He better not come knockin' on our door again. I'll give that little shit a piece of my mind and then walk over to their house and slap the hell outta his mother for raisin' someone wit'out a heart."

"No, Ma. Promise me ya won't do that. If he tells the other guys, then it'll give 'em somethin' else to tease me about. Do ya promise?"

Despite her overwhelming need to set things straight, Teresa nodded.

Teresa tousled Tony's hair. "How 'bout if I make ya a snack?"

Tony shook his head. "I ain't hungry. I feel sick to my stomach, and my brain hurts."

Teresa felt his forehead to see if he had a fever. Tony pushed her hand away.

"I ain't got fever. I just wanna be left alone."

Even though all the boys had bullied him horribly on his first day back to school, Marco's disloyalty had gotten into his craw and planted a knot of resentment.

After Teresa left Tony's bedroom, he lay flat on his back and put his hands under his head. He replayed the scene that had happened a short while ago, and his fury escalated. The muscles in his calves tightened, and his lips pinched tightly together. He'd been dealing with Vincent and his friends for years, and now he realized with certainty that Marco had become one of them.

Chapter Nine

It was Easter time, and Tony was about to make his First Holy Communion, one sacrament he would go through as part of being raised Catholic.

For the special occasion, Teresa had made Tony a white suit. When he came into the kitchen, dressed for church, Teresa's hand covered her mouth, and tears sprang to her eyes.

"Look at you. You're so handsome," Teresa said.

Carmen looked up from the bacon and eggs he was eating. "He looks like a faggot."

Tony looked down at himself, quickly becoming self-conscious.

"Stop it, Carmen. You're bein' mean," Teresa said.

Carmen dropped his fork onto his plate and glared at Teresa. "Ya wanna start the day like this?"

Teresa gave Carmen a worried look. "No, Carmen. I'm sorry."

Teresa turned her attention back to Tony. It was his special day, and she didn't want Carmen to ruin it. "Tony, I left some flowers on the front seat of my car. I got 'em so you can leave 'em as a gift to the Virgin Mary. Run out and grab 'em 'cause we're driving to the church in your father's car."

Tony's morning had started happily until his father had spewed his menacing words, like an angry fire-breathing dragon. Feeling defeated, Tony sauntered down the front steps, making certain not to scuff his new shoes that his mother had bought him. Teresa's car was parked at the end of the block, and Tony walked to it while he played his father's comment repeatedly in his head. All he wanted to do was rip off the white suit and go back to bed, hide under the covers, and never come out.

When Tony reached the car, he unlocked the door.

"Oh, look at the fairy in his white outfit," Vincent's voice shrieked. The voice ripped through Tony's already dreary thoughts.

"Leave me alone, Vincent. I make my First Holy Communion today," Tony said, thinking that would mean something to him.

Vincent sneered at him. "Ya look like an elf that fell into a bottle of bleach."

Vincent and his friends laughed, but Tony opened the car door. He wanted to get back to his house quickly. He reached in and took out the flowers. He shut the car door and turned around to face the group of boys.

"Oh man, look at 'im. An elf with flowers," Vincent teased. Then he hurled a stone at Tony.

The stone, intentionally covered in mud, hit Tony in the center of his chest. He looked down at his shirt and suit jacket, which was now splattered with wet brown earth.

"You asshole!" Tony screamed.

Tony threw the flowers to the sidewalk and grabbed Vincent by the throat. The two boys hit the ground with a thud. Tony was on top of Vincent, and as his anger boiled over, he punched Vincent in the face over and over. Tony grabbed Vincent by the throat again and slammed his head into the concrete. Try as he might, Vincent wasn't strong enough to overcome the power of pure adrenaline holding Tony's body prisoner.

Soon after the fight began, Tony felt himself being lifted off of Vincent. His eyes pivoted around him as he tried to focus. He was swinging and kicking as Teresa held him in midair by his waist.

"Maybe next time you'll think twice about pickin' on Tony. Looks like ya got your butt whipped," Teresa said to Vincent.

Vincent was lying on the ground where Tony had left him, crying. His friends stood over him, all of them too shocked to say anything.

Once Teresa got Tony back into their house, she sat him down and came back with a cold, wet cloth. She gently wiped his face off. Dressed for church, Carmen descended the stairs and stood motionless as he stared at his son.

"What the hell happened?" Carmen demanded, assessing the condition of his son's suit.

"There was a fight," Teresa commented casually.

"Jesus Christ, Tony. Ya let this happen on your Communion day? What the hell is wrong wit' ya, boy?"

Teresa put her hand on her hip. "He kicked that little bastard's ass."

Carmen almost smiled. "Oh yeah? Well...good! It's about time. How bad did ya beat 'im?"

Tony looked at his mother. He had no idea. All he could remember was being angry. Then something inside of him had snapped...the rest was a blur.

"That boy is gonna have some bruisin'. I had to pull Tony off of 'im. He was goin' wild, slamming the kid's head into the cement and everything. Kid's face was bleeding too."

Tony looked down at his hands...blood was on them. He had barely any memory of what he'd done to Vincent. The only thing he could remember was the overwhelming urge to kill him.

"Well, well, well," Carmen said. "Looks like we have more to celebrate today than God. For once in your life, ya didn't act like some sniveling little girl."

Tony glared at his father, resentful that the first compliment he ever received from him was swarming in criticism.

Tony looked away from Carmen. There is nothing, not even my rotten father that can destroy my one and only victory.

Chapter Ten

After Tony's fight with Vincent, the mean boys lost interest in Tony. Vincent and his gang thought Tony was nuts and wanted to stay as far away from him as possible. Vincent had a black eye and swollen lip from his encounter with Tony. None of the other boys wanted to get a dose of the ass whooping Tony had given to Vincent. That one act had shifted all the power, and because of it, Tony had spent the next three days at school worry free. He was even asked by some of the less popular kids to sit with them at lunch, but Tony refused. He preferred to be alone now. Yet, instead of eating lunch in the bathroom, Tony found a seat at an empty table in the corner of the cafeteria. For the first time, Tony didn't mind eating lunch alone; peace had replaced loneliness, and power had replaced weakness.

The following weekend Teresa asked Tony to run down to the local grocery store four blocks away to buy some items she needed. Tony had purchased the items and was a few blocks from his home when he noticed a kid sitting on porch steps up ahead. As he got closer, he could hear an older voice screaming from inside the row home. When Tony got to the house where the boy was sitting, the kid looked up at him.

Realizing it was Vincent, Tony paused. "Do you live here?" he said.

Vincent's face was twisted, a mixture of fear and anger. He nodded.

"Vincent! Ya dirty fucker! Get your ass inside, ya little bastard," the older voice boomed.

Vincent stood and walked away from his home. The screen door banged open, and a seventeen-year-old came rushing onto the porch. Vincent picked up speed and ran. The teenager chased Vincent to the end of the block, gave up, and walked back to his house.

"What the fuck are ya staring at?"

Tony took a step backward. "Nothin'."

"You friends wit' my little piss-ass brother?"

Tony shook his head.

"What's your name?"

"Tony. What's yours?"

"Richie. I'm Vincent's older brother. Hey, ain't ya that kid that kicked Vincent's ass last week?"

Tony nodded.

"Good. Good for you. My brother is a little asshole. Steals my shit, ya know?"

Tony shrugged.

"Well, if ya see the bastard, tell him to get the hell back here. The longer he waits, the worse I'm gonna give it to 'im."

Tony remained silent and walked back to his house. As he passed an alleyway, he glanced in. He saw Vincent leaning against the wall, trying to catch his breath.

"You all right?" Tony said.

Vincent looked over at Tony, his face wet with tears.

"Yeah, I'm fine."

"Ya don't look fine. Your brother is lookin' for ya. He said if I see ya to tell ya to go home."

Vincent kicked the brick wall.

"I hate him! I hate Richie, and I'm not goin' home."

Tony was confused. His emotions were playing at odds. He wanted to help the boy with his pain, but Vincent had also been the source of his own pain for several years. Tony stepped closer to Vincent.

"Your brother, Richie, give ya those marks on your arm?"

Vincent rubbed his forearm, as if he could erase the finger marks that lingered like haunting purple shadows over his flesh. "Yeah."

"He always do stuff like that to ya?"

"Yeah, he's a jerk-off. I was only four when my dad died. After that, my ma had to get more jobs. She's got three jobs now. She told Richie he's the boss since he's older. He's been hittin' me ever since my ma started workin' so much."

Tony felt a connection. "My dad hits me."

The boys fell silent. Tony was thinking about Vincent's circumstances, seeing him in a new light. He never would have imagined that Vincent was picked on.

"Um...ya wanna come to my house? My ma baked cookies today," Tony said.

Vincent nodded. "Why ya bein' nice to me?"

Tony shoved his hands in his front pockets and smiled. "Dunno. I figure I already kicked your ass, so I ain't got nothin' to lose." Tony grew serious. "I guess I know how ya feel. I mean, it sucks bein' picked on and beat up all the time."

"Yeah." Vincent felt suffocated in the vine of shame that strangled him in a tight embrace.

When they walked into Tony's house, Teresa looked up from her sewing. She recognized Vincent as the boy Tony had beat up on his communion day.

"What's he doin' here?" she said.

"It's OK, Ma. Vincent and me are gonna have some cookies."

"Oh yeah? So now all of a sudden you're bein' friends wit' Tony?" she asked Vincent.

Vince shrugged. "I'm sorry," he mumbled.

"Yeah, you're sorry all right." Teresa grabbed Tony by the shoulder. "Why ya hangin' wit' this kid? Ya sure he ain't usin' ya like Marco did?"

"Nah. It's all right. I invited him to come here. Vincent's big brother hits 'im. He ain't got nowhere else to go."

"Oh. I see," Teresa said, softening the tone of her voice.

"Well you two go ahead and have some cookies. Don't let me find out you're screwing wit' Tony again. Ya hear?"

"Yeah, Mrs. Bruno," Vincent said obediently.

"Call me Mrs. B."

Teresa listened intently as the two boys chatted in the kitchen and munched on cookies. It seemed odd to her, but Tony and Vincent got along as if they had always been friends. She felt a stroke of happiness ripple through her body. Teresa made the sign of the cross and softly whispered, "Please, God, don't let this kid be cruel to my son, or I'll break his fuckin' neck. Amen."

Chapter Eleven

The next day, when Tony got onto the bus, Vincent waved him into the back.

"Hey, Tony," Vincent said, "ya wanna sit wit' me?"

"Sure."

"Hey, what the hell ya doin', Vincent? We don't want Bruno sittin' wit' us. Did ya forget he kicked your ass?" Patton taunted.

"Shut up, Patton, or I'll smash your face in," Vincent said through clenched teeth. "Tony and me talked, and now we're friends. Anybody got a problem wit' that?"

"I gotta problem wit' it, and so do the rest of the guys, right?" Patton said. He looked to the other delinquents in his group, and they all nodded.

"Yeah, well, too bad. If ya got a problem wit' it, ya can go sit up front wit' the girls," Vincent said.

Marge, the school bus driver, kept an eye on what was happening. Something had changed for Tony. But still, just to be certain it wasn't a cruel prank, she monitored the boys until they got to school.

"Tony, I wanna talk to ya a minute," Marge said, as Tony was about to leave the bus.

Tony sat in the front seat behind Marge until the bus was empty.

"So now you're friends wit' those boys?"

"Nah. I'm only friends wit' Vincent. The other boys still don't like me, and I think they ain't gonna like Vincent no more 'cause of it."

Marge took a sip of the cold, stale coffee she had bought before she started her bus route. Her nose wrinkled up, and she stuck her tongue out. Marge abandoned the coffee and turned her attention back to Tony. "Ya listen to me real good. Those little brats ain't nothin' but trouble. If you're friends wit' 'em, I want ya to know that. I see 'em stealin' and pushin' the other kids around. Ain't never gonna turn out to be respectable men actin' like that, ya understand?"

"Yeah, I ain't like that, though. I'm only gonna stand up for the things that are important to me. I ain't never gonna steal from people for no good reason. I'll only steal if we need extra food or somethin' like that."

Tony's face turned bright red. He hadn't meant to admit that to Marge; it had slipped out. But Marge listened with mild amusement. Tony was such a stoic kid, seemingly older than his nine years.

"Well, it ain't good to steal from nobody, but I'm talkin' about the kids ya go to school wit'. Some of 'em, their parents got a little more and some a little less, but you're all in the same place when it comes to not havin' everything you need. You're a good boy, Tony, and I want ya to stay that way. Ya got a good heart. Ya be nice to people, got it?"

"Got it, Marge. I gotta go before the bell rings."

"OK, Tony. Ya have a nice day now."

Tony got off the bus, and seeing Vincent, he headed over to where his new friend was waiting.

"What did she want?"

"Uh, she just wanted to see how my ma was doin'. That's all," Tony lied.

The two boys were disrupted by a crowd that quickly gathered in the far end of the schoolyard. Tony and Vincent rushed over to see what was happening.

"Knock it off!" Marco screamed at Patton and two other boys.

Patton stepped closer and slapped Marco in the head. As Tony looked on, watching Marco, it was as if he was looking at his old self. His blood rushed to his chest, and he dashed between Marco and Patton.

"Leave 'im alone, Patton. You're always pickin' on somebody," Tony said.

Patton pushed Tony in the chest with both hands. "Oh yeah? What are ya gonna do it about it?"

Tony balled his hand into a fist and socked Patton in the face. Patton was momentarily shocked but quickly regained his wits. He grabbed Tony by the collar and punched him. The two boys hit the ground hard, both swinging at each other. Once Tony started to lose his battle, Vincent dove in and pulled Patton off of him.

"What's your problem, Vincent? Tony your girlfriend now?" Patton said, breathlessly.

Unable to control his temper, Vincent punched Patton in the face, and he dropped to the ground in a heap. Tony got up and walked up to Marco. "See, it ain't so nice bein' picked on and havin' no friends. You're lucky I helped ya this time, Marco, but that's it."

Tony and Vincent walked slowly to the front of the school.

"Why did ya go and do that?" Vincent asked.

"'Cause it wasn't a fair fight. I'm sick of all this crap. If someone does ya wrong, then ya fight. It's stupid to fight for no good reason."

Vincent stopped walking and gawked at Tony.

"That's the stupidest thing I ever heard."

Tony laughed. "Yeah, well, that's just the way I feel."

Tony wasn't certain how he felt about anything. He hoped that one day he would figure it all out. A lot had changed rapidly in his small world. Tony wanted to live up to the standards that his mother and Marge preached to him. However, there was something in his blood, a hidden desire, a force that made him feel out of control.

Chapter Twelve

B y the time Tony was in seventh grade, he had left the scrawny, scared boy behind. He was the biggest kid in his class. Tony was tall, and lifting weights had made his muscles hard and thick. He and Vincent were like brothers. They did everything together, and Vincent had become like a second son to Teresa. Carmen's cruel behavior remained intact, always keeping Tony on edge. Tony never knew when his father would fly off the handle for no good reason and beat him or his mother. The older he became, the more responsible Tony felt for allowing his father to continue his torment.

Tony finally stood up to his father the day Carmen took his anger out on Macie.

"Macie, go get the newspaper off the porch," Carmen ordered.

"But I'm in my pajamas," she whined.

Carmen inched up to the edge of his seat. "What did I just tell ya to do? Does it look like I give a shit what you're wearin'? Go get the goddamn newspaper. Now!" Carmen growled and slapped Macie on the top of her head.

Tony heard the exchange from the kitchen, and his stomach rumbled and dropped. I have to protect Macie at least, he told himself. Tony walked out into the small living room and glared at his father, an act that got Carmen's attention.

"What the hell are ya lookin' at, ya little prick?" Carmen sneered.

"Nothin' much."

Carmen stood and removed his belt. "Who do ya think you're talking to, boy?"

Tony stood firm—he didn't move; he didn't blink; he stared at his father with pure hatred. He could feel his hands shake, and he placed them firmly on his own hips. Carmen stared back with hatred in his eyes, as if he wanted to beat the hell out of Tony.

"Tony?" Teresa said, breaking her son out of his trance.

Tony looked over at his mother. "You stay wit' Macie; I'll go get the newspaper," he said to his mother in a serious tone.

Tony came back inside a few seconds later and threw the newspaper at his father's feet. Carmen jumped up out of his chair. "That's it! I've taken enough shit from ya. Ya think you're some badass now? Is that it? Well, let's see how bad ya really are."

Tony stepped closer to his father; at five foot ten, Tony was almost as tall as Carmen now. "Ya know, Dad, maybe you oughta act like you care. It ain't all about you all the time. Don't ya think we're sick of puttin' up with all the stuff ya dish out? We're sick and tired of ya pushin' us around and beatin' on us."

Carmen punched Tony in the side of the face and then followed up with a kick to his groin. He stood back, a twisted smile playing on his mouth as he admired his work. Tony was in a ball on the floor holding his crotch, rocking back and forth. Satisfied, Carmen grabbed the newspaper and took it up to his bedroom.

"Tony, why do ya instigate 'im like that? Ya know he's an asshole. There ain't nothin' that's gonna change that," Teresa whispered.

Tony was gasping. He focused his mind on breathing, but his anger boiled deep in his throat like hot lava. "He's a dick, Ma. Dad's a big dick. He's been pickin' on me since I was little, and I hate his guts."

"Listen here, Tony. I know what you're sayin'. I know ya hate what your father does to us, and I hope someday, when ya find the woman you're gonna marry, that ya treat her like a queen. Ya remember how your father makes ya feel if ya ever think about bein' mean to your kids. That's the best thing ya can do," Teresa said.

"That's not the best we can do. Why don't we leave here and go live somewhere else? Why do ya wanna stay here wit' 'im?"

"Your grandparents would never approve of me runnin' out on your dad for gettin' slapped around—they'd say that ain't no good reason. Besides, we ain't got nowhere else to go. Where would the three of us live? I don't make enough money from my job for us to be on our own," Teresa said in a hushed voice.

"Well, I hate 'im, and as soon as I can move outta here, I'm gonna," Tony stated and stomped out of the room.

Teresa knew that Tony was right. She'd been raised with the idea that a husband and wife stayed together through thick and thin. Her parents would have never supported such a silly decision, and Teresa had abandoned thoughts of leaving Carmen years ago. It was true that Carmen beat Teresa, but her father had done the same thing to her mother. Her parents were still together, and age had mellowed them. Teresa had always believed that the same fate was awaiting her.

A few hours later, after Carmen left the house, Tony sat next to Macie and stroked her thin, limp hair. Macie wasn't at all like Tony. Her eyes were closely set, her nose was too big and her nostrils spread across the sides of her small face. She was curled up against his leg. Turning his full attention to his mother, Tony noticed the deep lines around her eyes and mouth. The years hadn't been good to her—the worries about money and her children and enduring the relentless poor treatment at the hands of her husband were taking a toll. Tony saw it all now, and he vowed to himself that someday, if he ever got married, he would be nothing like his father.

Chapter Thirteen

It was Tony's first day of eighth grade. He hated school and would have preferred to wander the streets of South Philadelphia than to sit in a classroom listening to his teachers drone on about a bunch of things that happened a hundred years ago.

Tony and Vincent had just entered their homeroom class and taken their seats. The teacher was mumbling through the roster as the children recited, "Here," at the sound of their names.

Before the teacher could finish his roll call, the principal showed up at the classroom door with a boy standing next to him. The boy was shorter than Tony, with dark-brown hair and eyes the color of honey. His olive skin revealed his Italian heritage. Tony elbowed Vincent.

"What?"

"Look, don't we know that kid from somewhere?"

Vincent flicked his pencil back and forth between his fingers, pretending he would hurl it at the kid. "Yeah, he sorta looks familiar. Where ya think he's from?"

"Dunno. What's with the dress pants and button-down shirt? He looks like he's ready to go to church or somethin'," Tony said.

Vincent waved a dismissive hand. "How the fuck do I know? Maybe he's a fuckin' momma's boy. All I know is he looks weird."

It was almost noon when the bell rang indicating it was time for lunch.

"It's about time. I'm starvin' over here," Tony said, trailing the other teens toward the cafeteria.

Tony and Vincent sat at a table alone eating their lunches. They were talking about their weekend plans to hang out in Packer Park and the possibility of scoring a feel from two girls that liked them.

"Yeah, I heard Rita will give a guy whatever he wants if ya tell her she's pretty," Vincent joked.

"She ain't just pretty—she's Miss fuckin' America if that'll get me laid," Tony said.

The boys were interrupted by a crowd of teens from the other side of the cafeteria who had gathered in a circle. They were yelling and laughing. Most of the girls huddled together in a corner with their hands covering their mouths. Tony and Vincent bolted over to the circle of boys. In the center was the class bully, Rex; his oversized teeth, slightly bucked and crooked, were clenched together, accentuating his protruding forehead and clown-like nose. Rex was ugly inside and out, the type of kid that adults want to clobber for acting unruly in public. Rex sat on top of the new boy, alternating his slaps on either side of the kid's face. The new kid was bleeding from just below his right eye and his nose. Rex, oblivious to the damage he was doing, just kept pounding away at the boy, as though if he kept it up long enough, the kid would dissolve and become one with the beige speckles of the dreary old tile floor.

"Open your fuckin' eyes and watch me kick your little bitch ass," Rex screamed.

"Whoa," Tony said, pulling Rex up by his shirt.

"Stay the fuck outta it, Tony," Rex yelled.

"Who the hell are ya yellin' at?" Tony's annoyance was apparent.

The other boys stopped cheering when they saw Tony curl his hand into a fist and land the first punch on the side of Rex's face. The boy dropped to the floor next to the new kid.

Tony turned to the new kid and extended his hand to help him up. The new kid's adrenaline was pumping, and he was angry as hell. He reached for the napkins on the table next to him to sop up the blood on his face and dripping from his nose.

"Goddamn, fucking idiot," the new kid stated.

Tony and Vincent snickered.

Tony watched the new kid. "Yeah, Rex is a total douchebag. He starts shit where there ain't none. What's your name?"

"Salvatore," he said.

"Oh yeah? Good to meet ya, Sal."

"No, my name is Salvatore, not Sal," he said. Salvatore brushed the dirt off of his clothes. "What are your names?"

"I'm Tony, and this here's Vincent."

"Why ya so proper and shit?" Vincent asked.

"I'm not proper, but I was brought up well, and I'm expected to act that way." Salvatore's father had told him this a million times over the years.

"Oh yeah? I guess we ain't been brought up well then," Tony said, giving Vincent a sternum poke.

Salvatore brushed his hair back in place. "How come you call yourself Vincent instead of Vinny? Isn't Vinny more South Philly?"

"It ain't 'cause I was brought up well and shit. It's 'cause my ma is a Bible beater who thought if everyone called me Vincent, after Saint Vincent de Paul, I'd grow up to serve the poor just like the saint did. But one day when I was little, I told my

48

ma, 'We are the poor, so why do I have to be servin' poor people?' My ma, she's a good lady, but she beat me half senseless with a really big wooden spoon she uses to stir her tomato sauce wit'. She screamed, 'Vincent, you goddamn sonofabitch, if I ever hear ya talk about what ya ain't got, I'll beat the livin' hell outta ya. There are people worse off than you are, and ya better do what's right, by God.' She scared the holy shit outta me, and ever since I make sure people call me Vincent, and, if I got any change to spare, I give it to one of the bums that live on the street. But I ain't usually got any leftover money."

Salvatore laughed at Vincent's story. "OK. Then I'll call you Vincent." He turned to Tony. "And is Tony your real name?"

"Nah, my real name is Antney, but my ma calls me Tony."

"You mean Anthony?"

"Yeah, Antney, like I just told ya."

"Why doesn't your mom call you Anth...Antney?"

Tony pushed his thick black hair from his forehead. "Well, I was named after my mother's sister's husband. Anyway, my uncle Antney hooked up wit' another girl when my aunt was pregnant wit' my cousin. When my aunt found out, she left his ass in the dust when she was six months pregnant. After she left 'im, my grandparents didn't talk to my aunt no more 'cause she was supposed to stay married no matter what. Anyway, my mother got really mad. I mean, everyone loved my uncle Antney, but she said, 'No son of mine is gonna have the same name as that no-good, lying, cheatin' ass-wipe.' So she told me, 'From now on your name is Tony.' I told her, 'OK, Ma, but I like Antney better.' Her face crunched up, and her top lip lifted so I could see her teeth and shit. She looked like some kinda demon from another planet, and I thought she was gonna kill me or somethin'. So I said, 'Yeah, Ma, I think I like Tony better.'"

The boys stared at each other for a moment.

"So ya wanna meet up after school?" Vincent asked.

"For what?" Salvatore asked.

"What do ya mean, for what? To hang out wit' us," Tony explained. "We usually go down to the Italian Market after school. Some of the vendors let us help close their stands. They let us take home the food they're gonna throw out."

"Oh, well, that sounds interesting," Salvatore stated. "I mean, I don't think my mother would appreciate me bringing home food that was going to be thrown away, though."

"Oh yeah? You rich or somethin'?" Tony asked.

"I guess so. I mean, my dad has plenty of money to buy us everything we need."

"Yeah? That's cool. We ain't never knew nobody who had plenty of money. What's that like?" Tony asked, as Vincent stood next to him nodding.

"I don't know what it's like. I guess it's like nice. I never thought about it."

Tony cocked his head to one side. "What's your dad do?"

"He's a businessman."

"What kinda business does he have?" Tony asked.

"The kind of business where he makes a lot of money. I don't know."

Salvatore was guarded. He was perplexed by Tony and Vincent's obsession with money.

"Maybe your dad can teach us how to be businessmen," Vincent said, hopeful.

"I guess he could. I don't know. My dad hasn't ever met anyone I know. I never really had any friends in my old school. Never had any when I lived here before either," Salvatore explained.

"We thought we knew ya," Tony said. "So you lived here before. Did we know ya?"

"No, I didn't really talk to the other kids. We moved away from here when I was six."

"No wonder we don't really remember ya. We thought we seen ya before, though. Where did ya move from?" Tony asked.

"We just moved here from New York."

"New York, huh? What's it like there?" Tony asked.

"It's like New York. There are lots of people and things to do. They have really good restaurants, and my mom took me to see Broadway shows. I miss it already."

"So ya gonna meet us later?" Vincent asked.

"I doubt my dad would let me. I have to go right home after school."

"All right, well, it was good meetin' ya again. Try to stay away from that asshole over there," Tony said, pointing to Rex.

Salvatore nodded. "Sure. Thanks."

Hearing the bell ring, Tony and Vincent walked out of the cafeteria.

"I like Salvatore," Tony said. "He didn't even seem bothered that Rex beat his ass. I remember when you were an asshole and picked on me all the time. I was scared shitless."

"Yeah, I told ya I'm sorry a hundred times for that. Ya know, I like him too. There's somethin' about 'im. He's weird, but he's got balls."

As Tony tried to take his math quiz, his thoughts went to Salvatore. Tony had always wanted to be fearless, but he never seemed able to escape the darkness of his home. But the new kid, Salvatore—he wasn't afraid of anything.

Chapter Fourteen

One month after school had started, Salvatore's father, Johnny, called him into his home office.

"Why do you keep coming home with bruises on your face? I know someone is picking on you. Who is this boy that keeps kicking your ass?" Johnny said.

"Some bully named Rex."

"Why don't you fight back?" Johnny asked.

"I tried that, Pop. This guy is way bigger than me." Salvatore knew he sounded defeated, and he didn't want to disappoint his father.

"No one beats up on a Morano. Does this boy know who I am?" Johnny yelled.

"Why would he know you? The kids in my class hardly know me. Besides, someday I'm going to be just like you, and then they'll be sorry. Mom says I'm going to be really big and strong when I get older. Then I'll show them all. I promise."

Johnny Morano thought about it for a moment. His boy was right. Someday Salvatore would be a man to be feared. Johnny still had no intention of sitting idly by and watching his kid get beat up day after day.

"From now on Big Paulie will pick you up from school. Nobody messes with him..."

"No, Pop. You can't do that. I have to learn how to defend myself. Big Paulie can't be with me all the time. I want to take karate lessons. That way I can defend myself."

Johnny reached for his cigar, cranked the wheel on his Zippo lighter, and sucked on the unlit tip until a thick cloud of smoke spilled out of his mouth, "OK. We'll get you karate lessons then. But I'm telling you right now that this is going to stop. No kid of mine is going to be picked on by some rundown piece of street trash."

Salvatore felt a sense of victory. It wasn't that he was afraid of Rex. In fact, he hated the guy and vowed to himself to get even with him someday. "I'm going to tell Mom that you said I can take karate lessons." As he turned to leave his father's office, he glanced over his shoulder. "Don't worry, Pop; I'm going to take care of this."

Johnny Morano nodded. When he was alone in his office, he thought back to his own youth. He'd been raised by strict Catholic parents. Johnny had loved his mother and father, but they'd stifled his ability to have any fun. Eventually, he grew resentful and rebelled against their strict ways. In junior high school, he joined a street gang, and as they took over the streets of his New York neighborhood, it was Johnny who emerged as the ringleader. He always devised ways of getting even with the other gangs. When he was seventeen, Johnny beat another teen in the head with a rock. The teen died, and Johnny threatened that if anyone snitched on him, he would kill them too. This single act put Johnny in line to become a made man in the Bonanni family.

After Salvatore was born, Johnny moved his young family to Philadelphia for a year where he was sent to work out a deal with the Philadelphia crime family. When he moved back to New York, it wasn't long before Johnny rose through the ranks of the Bonanni family, eventually landing himself as a consigliere and later, the underboss. As the second in charge to the Bonanni boss, Johnny was as ruthless and powerful as they came. Then, after Conti, the boss of the Philadelphia family was gunned down, and he was asked to step in as the new boss of the Philadelphia family. His life of violence and coldblooded retaliation had paid off. His thoughts shifted back to his son. Salvatore was much different than he was as a teenager. But he knew his son was fearless, and that gave Johnny great promise for the future.

Chapter Fifteen

O ver the next couple of days, Johnny Morano had Big Paulie drive him to Salvatore's school, and they'd sit at a distance in the car watching. On the first day, they saw Salvatore getting picked on by Rex and some of his friends. None of the other kids stepped in to help. On the second day, when Johnny couldn't watch his son be beaten up anymore, he grabbed for the door handle of the car, but Big Paulie put his hand on Johnny's shoulder.

"Look."

Johnny watched Tony and Vincent sprint toward the rowdy teens. They pushed their way through the crowd until they were standing on either side of Rex. Vincent grabbed both of his arms from behind while Tony hammered him in the abdomen with heavy punches. When Rex could no longer stand on his own, Vincent let him drop to the ground and kicked him.

"What did we tell ya 'bout pickin' on people littler than ya? What are ya, hard of hearin'?" Vincent yelled.

Vincent turned to Rex's three friends, who stood on the side with rage in their eyes.

"Ya thinkin' 'bout fuckin' wit' us? Is that what's goin' on in those pea brains of yours? Ya better think long and hard before ya do, 'cause once ya cross us, your ass is ours," Vincent threatened.

Tony and Vincent walked to Salvatore a few feet away. "Ya all right?" Tony asked.

"Yeah, I'm fine. Someday, I'll get even with that bitch; don't worry," Salvatore said, seething.

"Oh, look, Vincent, he talks shit like we do. Who woulda thought?"

Tony patted Salvatore on the shoulder. "Look man, ya seem like an all-right dude. Ya just need to keep away from that asshole. Ya know what I'm sayin'?"

"Yes, I do know what you're saying. But I won't back down from him. He can beat on me all he wants because I'm not afraid," Salvatore declared.

Tony and Vincent exchanged amused looks. Salvatore was so small they felt like giants standing next to him. In a few seconds, they busted out laughing. "We ain't laughin' at ya Salvatore; we're laughin' wit' ya."

Initially Salvatore was enraged at the duo's fit of laughter. But after he watched them for a moment, he realized they meant no harm. They had stepped in twice already and stopped Rex. Finally, Salvatore broke down and laughed with them.

"You guys want to go get a cheesesteak? My treat," Salvatore offered.

"Sure we do," Vincent answered.

As the three teens walked toward South Street, Johnny sat in the car watching.

"My boy may have found himself a couple of new friends, Big Paulie," Johnny said.

"Yeah, it looks like he did. You wanna follow them to be sure?"

"Yes."

Johnny Morano, the godfather of the Italian mob, watched his son for the rest of the afternoon. The three boys got along well. He and Big Paulie watched Salvatore laughing wholeheartedly; it had been a long time since Johnny had seen his son so happy. It made him feel good. Then he realized he'd found an answer to his problem—two answers, to be exact.

Chapter Sixteen

"Hey, boys. Come over here," Johnny yelled from the car window the next afternoon.

"What the fuck does this guy want?" Vincent whispered to Tony.

Tony and Vincent slowly crossed the street to Johnny's car.

"What are your names?" Johnny asked.

"Who wants to know?" Vincent responded.

"I'm not going to hurt you. I just want to know your names," Johnny repeated.

"We didn't do nothin'," Tony said, feeling nervous.

Johnny smiled bitterly. "What are your names?"

Tony had the familiar twist in his gut. He wanted to turn and run, but instead stood by Vincent's side. "I'm Tony, and this is Vincent."

"My name is Johnny Morano. I'm Salvatore's father, and this is Big Paulie."

Tony bent down lower so he could eye up Big Paulie, who lived up to the term big.

"Oh, yeah, you're the businessman. Salvatore told us 'bout ya. What do ya want from us?"

"I have a proposition for you."

"A prop-a-what?" Tony asked.

"I have a business deal for you. I'm going to pay you to watch out for Salvatore. I'll give you ten dollars each a week. For that, you will make sure that no one fucks with my son."

"I don't know, Mr. Morano—ten bucks a week doesn't seem like much to be somebody's bodyguard," Vincent said, remembering that Salvatore's father was rich. Vincent's boldness made Tony nervous. He didn't want to lose a chance of earning ten dollars a week.

Johnny rubbed his chin and glanced at his friend. "What do you think, Big Paulie? How much do you think a bodyguard is worth?"

"I think ten bucks a week is damn good. Hell, I would've killed somebody for ten bucks when I was their age."

"Well, that was a long time ago, Big Paulie. Maybe these boys are right. How about if I pay you each twenty dollars a week?" Johnny offered.

Tony's stomach gurgled. He felt apprehensive and on guard, but twenty dollars a week was a lot of money.

Vincent quickly extended his hand to Johnny through the car window. "It's a deal."

"Good. Very good. Just be certain that you boys don't disappoint me. I don't like to be disappointed...ever," Johnny said, making eye contact with one and then the other.

Johnny liked how Tony squirmed at his threatening tone and the seriousness in his voice.

"We won't," Tony said flatly.

After Johnny and Big Paulie pulled away from the curb, the boys turned to face each other.

"Twenty bucks a week," Tony said.

"We're fuckin' rich," Vincent yelped, grabbing Tony by the shoulders.

"Yeah, well, just remember what Mr. Morano said...we can't fuck this up. I think the guy was real serious 'bout that, Vincent."

"I know. But we're gonna be great at this bodyguard shit. Maybe when we grow up, we can be bodyguards to famous people. We'll be the best bodyguards that ever lived," Vincent exclaimed.

"Yeah, maybe. I ain't so sure this is a good thing. Mr. Morano seems like a real mean man. Maybe we should tell 'im that we ain't gonna do it," Tony said, feeling anxious that they would be unable to fulfill their promise.

"Ya worry too much. All we gotta do is make sure that asshole Rex doesn't beat up Salvatore. Why do ya always get so nervous all the time?"

"'Cause if I get caught doin' anythin' wrong, my father will kill me. Besides, I wanna do good stuff for people."

"This is good stuff," Vincent countered. "We're protectin' somebody who needs our help."

The boys walked down the block in silence. Tony could feel to the depth of his soul that something was wrong and he should walk away from the deal, but he didn't want to disappoint Vincent, and he pushed his feelings of dread aside.

Chapter Seventeen

Tony and Vincent followed Salvatore everywhere. And, after a few days, Salvatore thought they were up to something.

"Why are you two always following me around? What gives?"

"We ain't followin' ya. We just like hangin' out. We was thinkin' that we could hang out after school today. Ya know, take a walk down to the Italian Market and all. Whata ya say?" Tony asked.

Salvatore looked at the ground and blushed. "Yeah, sure, I guess so. I'll need to stop home first and let my mom know where I'm going." His father had been encouraging him to find some friends, and Salvatore wanted to please him.

"Sure, that ain't no big deal. We'll come wit' cha," Vincent offered.

"No, that wouldn't be a good idea. I, I, um, I can't really bring friends home with me. My parents won't let me bring anyone they don't know into our house, especially my dad."

"No? Why not?" Tony asked, his earlier feelings of fear gripping him.

"Well, because my dad is very protective about his privacy."

"Protective? Why?" Tony asked.

"He just likes to be sure that he knows the people who come into our house. That's all."

"All right, so we'll wait outside then," Vincent said.

"Yeah, OK, I guess that'll be fine."

Salvatore went to his last class of the day. But instead of listening to the teacher lecture, he thought about his father. Shortly after his tenth birthday, his father had sat him down in the living room of their New York brownstone.

"Salvatore, you might start hearing things about me, and I want to explain what I do in the best way that I can. You see, a long time ago, there were a group of men who lived in Italy. It was on Easter day when a French solider grabbed a young, married Palermo woman from the crowd of people gathered to celebrate the holiday. The solider began to bother the woman...touch her where he shouldn't have. When the woman's mother found out what happened to her daughter, she ran through the streets of her small town screaming, 'Mia figlia, mia figlia!'

That means "my daughter, my daughter." The Sicilian men gathered together to protect the women in their small town. First, they killed the French soldier who touched the young woman. Then the men killed all the French soldiers they could find until the French finally left them alone. This story traveled through the other small towns of Italy, and other Sicilians came together and killed French soldiers. In Italy, mia figlia signaled to the Sicilians it was time to go to battle."

Johnny paused, gauging whether his young son understood what he was telling him. To Johnny's delight, Salvatore wanted to know more. "Then what happened?"

"Well, then these men became a part of a secret society. The men who belonged to this society, well, they made a promise to protect each other and their families. Now, they all understood that to do this would mean they'd have to steal and maybe even hurt people. So, you see, I'm a part of that secret society of men that started a long time ago. There are times when I have to do things that the police don't like and even say is wrong. What's important is that you stick by me and never tell anyone what goes on in this house or things you might hear me talk about. The secret society calls this the code of silence. Now, if anyone asks you questions about me, all you have to do is tell them that you've never seen or heard anything, because as my son you will also be part of the secret society when you get older. This is how we protect our family. Do you understand?"

"What happens if someone breaks the code of silence?"

"They are punished. Severely punished, and sometimes so are their families," Johnny said.

Johnny studied his son's face. "What is it? What's bothering you?"

"If these guys protect each other and their families, then why would you punish them?"

"Because each man knows that protection is only provided if he remains loyal to the family. If he doesn't, they must pay for their defiance."

Salvatore stared at his father, and another thought slammed into his brain. "I'm scared, Pop. Do you think the police are going to come here and ask me questions? What if they arrest me for lying or something?"

Johnny smiled. "You don't have to worry about the police. Nothing is going to happen. I'm telling you this just in case one day, when you are much older, you are asked to tell the police things about me or the society we belong to."

Salvatore nodded apprehensively, still unnerved by the possibility of having to lie to a policeman. He pushed his anxiety aside and looked up at his father. "What's the name of our society, Pop?"

"The Mafia."

Salvatore tilted his head, and his nostrils flared. "Why is it called that?"

"Remember I told you about the mother who ran through the streets of Italy screaming mia figlia? Well, many years later, Italians in America pronounced it

Ma Fia, and so our society became known as the Mafia. But remember, the name of our society doesn't mean as much as what we stand for."

Salvatore nodded, leaned over, and hugged Johnny. He was too young to fully understand what it meant for his father to be a high-ranking member of the mob. He believed his father was a great man. Salvatore felt very special that Johnny had confided in him. Johnny and Salvatore had shaken hands to confirm the vow of silence between them. This had made Salvatore feel grown up and a deeper part of his father's life.

When the last bell rang indicating the end of the school day, Salvatore's thoughts were interrupted, and he rushed outside to look for Tony and Vincent. He saw them sitting on the sidewalk and hurried over to them. "Are you guys ready to go?"

The two boys looked up from the bug on the pavement they had been tormenting for the past couple of minutes. "Yeah, we're ready," Tony said, getting to his feet.

"What will we do at the Italian Market?" Salvatore asked.

"We'll walk around and talk to the vendors. Ya know, just hang out and see what's happenin'. We just sorta go wit' the flow when we're there," Vincent explained.

It was almost four o'clock by the time the boys made it to the Italian Market on Ninth Street. There were three city blocks of row homes that had been converted into storefronts with tables of food and goods on the sidewalk. The colorful awnings, narrow passage, and vendors yelling out their solicitation for business on the sidewalk made it feel like a third-world country. Shop owners set up their produce, cheeses, and fresh-caught fish in wooden boxes. The smells melded with an overarching scent of fresh-baked bread and cakes. The Italian Market symbolized the culture of the city, a combination of food and in-your-face manners.

When the boys approached the first street vendor, the man looked the boys over, and his gaze settled on Salvatore.

"How ya doin'?" he asked.

"We're doin' real good, Pete. This is our new friend, Salvatore," Tony answered.

"Nice to meet you, Pete," Salvatore stated politely.

"Hey, ain't ya Johnny's boy?"

"Yes..."

"Well, here then. Go on and pick out one of those peaches. These here are the best batch I got all year."

"Can we have one too?" Vincent asked.

"Sure, ya can. Let Salvatore over here pick one first, though."

The three boys looked at each other and smiled.

"Go on, Salvatore. Pick one quick 'cause we ain't got all day. We got a lot of ground to cover," Tony said.

The vendor plucked the peach that Salvatore picked out of his hand. "Let me just go wash that for ya. I'll be right back."

A few minutes later, Pete returned and handed the peach back to Salvatore.

"What's wrong wit' ya, Pete?" Vincent asked. "Why ya actin' all crazy and shit? How come ya ain't washin' our peaches too?"

Pete smiled at Salvatore. "Tell your father I said hello, will ya, Salvatore?"

"Yeah, sure, I'll tell him. Thanks for the peach, Mister..."

"Pete, you can call me Pete."

"Right. Thanks for the peach, Pete."

"Sure, Salvatore. Anytime ya wanna good piece a fruit, ya come and see me. Ya hear?"

"Ah, come on already. What the hell is this? You're actin' really weird, Pete. Let's go, Salvatore, before he tries to make ya a fruit salad," Vincent taunted.

As the boys walked away, Tony talked at top speed about how Pete had treated Salvatore. But for Salvatore this treatment wasn't any different from the treatment he got from the men in New York who knew Johnny was his father. They were, after all, either a part of or beholden to the Mafia.

"Hey Salvatore, what's your father do again?"

"He's a businessman."

As they continued to walk the rest of the block, a few men Tony had seen in the market with his mother approached them. Tony froze when he realized these were the mobsters his mother had warned him about.

"How ya doin', Salvatore?" one man said.

Tony stared wide-eyed with his mouth hanging open.

"I'm good, Angelo. Is my dad here?"

"Nah, ya know he don't like to come here too often." Before Angelo turned to leave, he said, "I'll be over your house later. See ya then."

It was then that Tony knew exactly who Johnny Morano was and that Salvatore's father was a mobster. He became even more nervous about the business deal he'd entered into with Johnny and wondered if he had the courage to go through with his promise to protect Salvatore.

Chapter Eighteen

T he next night the boys were walking to South Street looking for something to do. They had cut through an alleyway, and out of nowhere, five boys jumped out from behind a Dumpster. It took a moment to recognize them as boys from their school. Rex ran at Salvatore and punched him on the side of his face.

Tony and Vincent were attacked before they could react. Two of Rex's friends jumped on Tony and forced him to the ground and kicked him. Tony fought back, and Rex piled into the fight. Vincent was losing his own battle against the other two boys, who were on top of him smashing his head face first into the broken asphalt.

A short distance from where Tony and Vincent were being assaulted, Salvatore sat up slowly, reached under his pant leg, and rushed toward Rex. Before any of them knew what was happening, Salvatore had an eight-inch, serrated knife pressed against Rex's throat.

"You think I'm afraid of you? I'm not. I've been waiting for you to come after me at just the right time," Salvatore said, his voice steady and commanding attention.

Rex held his arms out and his hands in the air. "OK, you win. You gotta knife, so ya win. Let's go, guys. Leave these assholes alone."

Salvatore slowly removed the knife from Rex's throat, but held it in a combat position just the way Big Paulie had shown him. "I want you to remember something, Rex. The next time you think about fucking with me or my friends...well, let's just say I suggest you think twice. You may not know it, but I come from a family that doesn't like to be bullied."

Rex held Salvatore's cold, hard eyes for a moment, and the blood in his veins ran cold. His entire body turned icy. Rex noted Salvatore's rigid body and unblinking eyes. Salvatore was dead serious.

After Rex and his friends left the alley, Salvatore rushed over to Tony, who was groggy. Small moaning sounds escaped from his throat. Vincent hobbled over to Tony and Salvatore.

"Tony? Tony? What the fuck? Tony, you OK?" Vincent said in a scared voice.

Tony slowly sat up and looked from Salvatore to Vincent. He was confused. His eyes were swollen, and he couldn't see clearly, but he knew he'd just witnessed Rex's reaction to Salvatore...or was it a dream?

"Tony. It's Salvatore and Vincent. Are you all right?"

Tony slowly nodded. "What the fuck just happened?"

"Christ! This little fucker pulled a blade on Rex. Threatened to cut him open," Vincent said.

"I thought I saw something like that. I remember seein' Rex. Looked like he was gonna shit his pants," Tony said wearily, looking up at Salvatore.

"Where did ya get the knife?" Tony asked slowly, his speech still impaired.

"A friend gave it to me. Showed me how to use it too just in case I ever needed to defend myself," Salvatore explained.

"Oh yeah? What friend?" Vincent asked.

"Just a friend."

When Tony's head cleared, Vincent and Salvatore helped him off of the ground and walked him back to his house. They had just stepped inside the house when Teresa bolted up from the sofa.

"Oh, dear God, what the hell happened to him?" Teresa screamed when she saw his bruised and bloodied face.

"It ain't nothin', Mrs. B. Some kids we go to school wit' beat us up when we weren't lookin'," Vincent said.

"It ain't nothing? Vincent, I'll slap the livin' shit outta ya. Don't ya give me none of that it ain't nothin' bullshit. Look at my boy. He's bleeding." Teresa rushed from the room to get towels and peroxide to clean him up.

As Teresa reentered the living room, she eyed up Salvatore. "And who the hell are you?"

"My name is Salvatore. It's nice to meet you, Mrs. Bruno."

"Just call her Mrs. B," Tony said, as he tried to dodge the towel his mother was shoving at him to clean up his face.

"It's very nice to meet you, Mrs. B."

"Where the hell did ya find this one?" Teresa asked.

"He used to live here, but then he moved to New York, and now he moved back here," Vincent said.

Teresa nodded as she fussed over Tony, cleaning his wounds.

"Ow, Ma, that hurts," Tony said, pulling away from his mother.

"Tony Bruno, ya better sit still, or I'll give ya somethin' to complain about. Ya want these cuts gettin' infected? Now stop whining so I can fix ya up. Ya boys are always findin' trouble. What's wrong wit' the two of yas?" Teresa looked at Vincent.

"But, Mrs. B, we were surprise attacked and..."

Teresa raised her hand in the air, and Vincent fell silent.

"Yes, Mrs. B," Vincent said with respect.

Teresa lifted her head and looked at Salvatore. "What's your last name?"

"Morano."

Teresa stopped dead in her tracks and was plagued with worry. As she realized that Salvatore's father was the head of the mob, her limbs went limp.

"You boys better get home. It's getting late," Teresa said.

When Vincent and Salvatore left, Teresa sat on the sofa next to Tony.

"Ya know who that boy is?"

"Yeah, Ma. I know. He's a kid I go to school wit'."

"He's not just a kid from your school. That is Johnny Morano's son. Do you know who his father is?"

Tony nodded. "He's a mobster. Right?"

"That's right. He's a mobster, and they are dangerous people. They kill people for no good reason. Do ya understand?"

"How do ya know they kill people?"

"'Cause I know! I don't want ya hangin' out wit' that boy. I don't want Johnny Morano anywhere near ya. Do you hear me?"

Tony shrugged. "But he's my friend, Ma."

"Any son of Johnny Morano's is no friend to my son. Ya won't get nothin' but trouble hangin' out wit' him."

"Salvatore ain't like that, though. He's a good friend."

"Ya listen real good. Ya stay away from that boy. If I find out you're hangin' wit' 'im, I swear to the Baby Jesus I'll break your fuckin' head. It's for your own good."

When Tony lay in his bed that night, he got jittery about being friends with Salvatore. He liked him a lot, but after the knife incident, Tony realized that maybe his mother was right about Salvatore and the mob. Maybe they were to be feared and he should stay as far away from Salvatore as possible. Then he saw himself as weak, remembering how the other kids had avoided being around him because they feared getting picked on. No, Tony thought, I'm not gonna be one of those people. Salvatore is my friend and will stay my friend, no matter what my mother thinks.

***

Back at the Morano house, Johnny and Big Paulie sat on the leather sofa in his office.

"How did it go?" Johnny asked.

"Salvatore did real good, Johnny. He did everything just like I taught him to do."

"And you were ready?"

"Yeah, me and Crazy Bobby were standin' by. We didn't need to do nothin', though. They never even knew we was there. Ya woulda been really proud of Salvatore."

"What about his friends?"

"Those two boys couldn't believe what Salvatore had done. I think the three of them will be friends for a long time," Big Paulie said.

"Good, very good. My son is finally becoming a man. He needs to retaliate against that punk, Rex. Do you think he's ready?"

"Yeah, Johnny, he's ready. Salvatore ain't afraid of no one. He's just like his old man."

Johnny Morano smiled broadly. At Salvatore's age he'd already been part of a street gang—that's where he'd learned to act out and take revenge against anyone who threatened to harm him. Now it was Salvatore's turn to show everyone what he was made of.

Chapter Nineteen

It was one week after Johnny had first hired Tony and Vincent to protect Salvatore.

"Boys," Johnny yelled from the car window.

Tony and Vincent walked over to the car, and Johnny held out one twenty-dollar bill for each of them.

"Nah, we don't want no money, Mr. Morano," Tony said. "Salvatore is a...he's a good friend."

Johnny paused and smiled at the boys. "Oh yeah, tell me about being good friends. Does it have anything to do with your busted-up face?"

Tony shoved his hands into the pockets of his worn jeans and shifted back and forth from one foot to the other. He debated about how much he should share with Mr. Morano.

"He, uh, helped us when these guys jumped us, so we don't want no money from ya. Salvatore is a good guy. The three of us watch out for each other now. Thanks anyway," Tony said, wanting to get away from Johnny quickly.

Johnny shifted his gaze to Vincent. "Are you sure I can't pay you?"

"Nope, just like Tony said. Salvatore is one of us now—he helped us out all right. We can't take no money to be friends with somebody we like."

"OK. Well, I'll tell you what. I'd like the two of you to come over to my house for dinner tomorrow night. I will tell Salvatore that I want to meet the two boys that he's been hanging out with. He will ask you to come for dinner. Now, don't utter a word to him about anything we've talked about. I don't want him to know that we have already met. Do you both understand me?"

Vincent nodded, but Tony didn't respond.

"What? Are you turning down my invitation?" Johnny asked, glaring at Tony. His voice was solid, pushy, and the boy cringed.

"No. Course not. I gotta, you know, ask my ma first."

"Well, you tell your mother that you've already accepted the invitation and it would be rude not to show up. Do we understand each other?"

Tony nodded.

"I'll see you tomorrow night, then." Johnny gave a flick of his wrist, and Big Paulie drove away.

"What the hell's wrong wit' ya?" Vincent said. "We both know Johnny Morano runs the mob. Are ya lookin' to get us killed or somethin'?"

"I don't know about all this, Vincent. I don't think we oughta be hangin' at Salvatore's house. Once my ma found out he was Johnny's kid, she said I ain't even allowed to be friends wit' 'im no more."

"So now ya gotta do everything your ma says? Just tell her you're comin' to my house for dinner. She ain't never gonna know."

Tony lowered his head, focusing on a crack in the sidewalk. He was scared to be around Johnny Morano, even though he liked Salvatore. He was also worried that if he didn't go, Vincent and Salvatore would become close friends and he would have no one.

"All right, I'll go, but I'm tellin' ya, Vincent, somethin' don't feel right."

Vincent nodded, and the two boys raced toward the entrance of the school as the bell for homeroom rang. Tony sat in class unable to shake the awful feeling from his body. He suddenly felt as though he was once again in a situation he didn't know how to get out of.

Chapter Twenty

"Now listen. My mother doesn't like rude people, and my father demands respect," Salvatore instructed as they walked to his house after school the next day. "In fact, it's the first time my father has ever asked to meet any of my friends. Don't screw this up. Just act normal...if that's possible."

Tony laughed. "Act normal? Vincent don't know nothin' about actin' normal."

"Hey, fuck you, Tony. I know how to act normal. What the fuck is normal anyway?"

"Normal means you can't curse and act like fools," Salvatore chided.

When the boys walked into the Morano house, they stopped short in the foyer.

"Holy fuck," Vincent said breathlessly, looking around the enormous entryway and staring up at the six-foot, round chandelier that hung in the middle of the vaulted ceiling above their heads.

Salvatore cast a scathing look in his direction for cursing.

"Sorry," Vincent muttered.

Tony and Vincent followed Salvatore as they walked through the pristine home, following the delicious aroma of homemade tomato sauce and garlic bread. They stood in the oversized kitchen behind Salvatore.

Tony watched Alessandra Morano closely as she moved about the room. She was a small, thin woman. Her brown eyes were warm, but there was also a hint of sadness to them.

***

Tony couldn't have known that Alessandra and Johnny's marriage had been arranged by the head of the Bonanni family. They had been introduced at a wedding and had only gone on half a dozen dates. Within three months, they had been married. Alessandra had felt the burden of marrying a stranger on their wedding night.

"Come to me," Johnny had said when they were inside their hotel suite.

Alessandra walked hesitantly and stood before her new husband.

Johnny ran his hands over her breasts, and Alessandra began to cry.

"Now, now. There's no need to cry. This is our wedding night. Let's get you out of that dress," Johnny said, lust welling up inside of him.

Johnny slowly unbuttoned her dress until it slipped off of her shoulders and fell to the floor. A mound of satin and lace wrapped around her feet. Then he studied her body, circling her like a tiger about to eat its prey.

"Take off your bra."

Alessandra slowly unfastened the hooks, but held the material over her breasts.

"Take it off, Alessandra. I want to look at you." His voice was steady, emotionless.

Alessandra let her bra drop to the floor, and Johnny gently took her wrists and pushed them out to her sides. Her breasts stood firmly in front of him.

"They are beautiful, Alessandra." He bent slightly and took one of her breasts into his mouth. His tongue circled her nipple lightly, and she felt a slight stirring.

Johnny pulled her close to him and ran his hand down the small of her back. He kissed her softly, gliding his tongue across hers. Alessandra was petrified, and yet, there was a burning desire for him to continue. Johnny slid one hand into the back of her underwear, and pulling away from her slightly, he ran his other hand down the front of her stomach and slid his fingers inside of her. Alessandra was a virgin, and while it felt good, she also felt violated.

"Yes, Alessandra, that's it," Johnny whispered in her ear.

He stepped away from her. "Take off your underwear."

Alessandra was mortified and humiliated. She stared at him.

Johnny took Alessandra by the hand and led her over to the sofa. He sat down and rested his head on the large cushion as she stood over him.

"Go on. It's your duty as my wife. I want to look at you naked."

With trembling hands, Alessandra slid her lace panties past her thighs. She knew about sex but now that the moment had arrived, she was scared.

Johnny took in all her curves. He had been aroused by Alessandra being a virgin, but now as she stood in front of him with her silky, smooth skin, he couldn't hold himself back any longer. He led her into the bedroom, where they stood facing each other.

"Take my clothes off, Alessandra," he instructed.

Her fingers felt as though they weren't attached to her hands, and she clumsily undid the first two buttons of his shirt.

"No. Undress me slowly."

Alessandra wanted to punch her new husband. She wanted to run from the room and never see him again. She had imagined her first time would be special and romantic, but Johnny's words and actions made her feel cheap and dirty. When she finished undressing her husband, he took her over to the bed.

"Lie down on your back," he said.

Alessandra did as she was told. Her arms were crossed over her chest, and her legs were bent at the knees and locked in a shut position.

"Arms by your side, Alessandra. A man wants to see his wife."

She uncrossed her arms and laid them on either side of her.

"Yes, that's it," he said, playing with her nipples.

Alessandra blushed. She wanted to put her clothes back on and go home to her parents. The urge to flee was gnawing at her.

Johnny was still standing over her. He ran his hands over her body from her breasts down to her knees. "Spread your legs."

Alessandra, overcome with panic, shook her head.

"It's not a question, Alessandra. Spread your legs."

When she still refused to budge, Johnny pressed her legs apart. Alessandra lay on the bed, arms and legs spread wide open, feeling filthy and ruined. The sight of his erect penis frightened her. She hadn't expected it would be so ugly.

Johnny got on top of her, not able to hold himself back any longer. He thrust himself into Alessandra, and a sharp sound dislodged from her throat as he took her virginity.

When Johnny was finished, he rolled over and fell asleep. Alessandra stayed awake all night reliving her "first time," and in the early-morning hours, she assured herself that the next time would be better. But her wedding night had stolen a piece of her, and the sadness lingered in her eyes years later.

As the years went by, Alessandra learned to adapt to her marriage and even found she enjoyed having sex with her husband. Johnny had always been good to her, and, for the most part, had given her everything her heart desired. Over time she grew to love Johnny, and she was madly in love with her children.

***

Tony hadn't taken his eyes off of Alessandra since he entered the kitchen. He saw her grace and beauty, yet there was something missing, some ghost that lurked behind her kind eyes, and he instantly had a stab of sympathy for the woman.

"Mom, these are my friends, Tony and Vincent."

Alessandra Morano put the lid back on the pot of tomato sauce and walked over to the boys. "It's very nice to meet both of you. I hope you like raviolis. It's Salvatore's favorite meal."

Tony nodded and stepped forward, his hand extended. "Nice to meet ya too, Mrs. Morano." Tony was nervous, and his sweaty palm and high-pitched voice didn't go unnoticed by Alessandra.

Alessandra smiled. The boy was nervous, and she understood why. Johnny could make or break a person's life, and she knew that Tony sensed this.

"Well, come in and sit down. We will be eating in about ten minutes."

Alessandra turned to her daughter and gently placed her hands on the child's shoulders. "This is Salvatore's sister, Gianna." The beautiful nine-year-old gave them both a smile. Tony and Vincent smiled and gave Gianna a nod.

Alessandra nudged Gianna. "Go tell your father that Salvatore and his friends are here."

A few minutes later, Johnny Morano walked into the kitchen with a thick, lit cigar dangling from his mouth. "Now, who do we have here?"

"Pop, these are my friends from school, Tony and Vincent."

"It's very nice to meet you boys. Come now and have a seat. Mrs. Morano is almost ready to serve us dinner," Johnny said, as if Alessandra wasn't in the room with them.

Tony and Vincent played along, shaking Johnny's hand, pretending they'd never met. Johnny Morano watched them closely. He could see that Tony wasn't comfortable being there and Vincent was too comfortable for his liking. But something about Tony didn't sit well with Johnny. Maybe it was because the boy was too scared and nervous. Johnny liked people who were sure of themselves and didn't care for the sniveling types.

After dinner Alessandra sent the boys to pick up a few groceries at a convenience store a few blocks from their home. Tony was happy to be out of the Moranos' house. After purchasing the items on Alessandra's list, the boys stepped outside and were confronted by Rex. Rex was holding a steak knife in his hand and pushed it toward Salvatore.

"You and me, Morano. What cha gonna do now that I got the knife?"

"Hey, Rex, we don't want no trouble," Tony said.

Rex's eyes riveted to Tony as he spoke. In that split second, Salvatore pulled his knife from under his pant leg and stuck it into Rex's chest. Acting quickly, Salvatore pulled the knife from Rex's body and ran. On pure instinct Vincent followed him.

Tony was glued to his spot. He got on the ground next to Rex and put his hand on the wound, trying to stop the bleeding. At that moment, a customer walked out of the convenience store.

"Hey, what are you doin', boy?" the man yelled.

The man grabbed Tony and pinned him to the pavement while the store owner, now outside, looked after Rex.

"I didn't do nothin'. Let me go."

"I saw exactly what you did," the man said, looking into Tony's face. "I know who you are...I know your no-good father. You're stayin' right here until the police come, you piece of shit."

Panic stricken, Tony jerked and heaved his body until he broke free. He jumped to his feet and ran as fast as he could to get away. By the time he reached the Moranos', he was shaking violently. Tony banged on the door, and it was quickly opened by Salvatore.

"What happened to you? Why didn't you run?"

"Ya stabbed the guy, Salvatore. I couldn't just leave 'im there. I think ya killed 'im."

Johnny came barreling into the foyer and pulled Tony inside with one hand. His face was flushed and his nostrils flared.

"What have you done? Have you brought the police to my home?"

"N-n-no, Mr. Morano. We was just comin' out of the store when Rex..."

"Shut up! You're a stupid boy. Let me tell you what's going to happen. You're going to get the fuck out of my house and go straight home. If the police come to visit you for your utter stupidity, and you say one word about my son, I will kill you and your entire family. Do you understand me?"

Tony looked to Vincent for support, but he lowered his head, scared that Johnny would turn on him too.

"I understand," Tony said, tears streaking down his face.

"Go! Get out. There is nothing more here for you."

Tony made his way home in the shadows. He took the dark alleys and less-traveled roads to avoid the well-lit streets. As he walked into his house, Teresa looked up from her sewing.

"Where were ya?"

"I told ya, I was eatin' at Vincent's."

"No, ya didn't. Vincent's mother called here. You're lying. Where were ya?"

Before Tony could answer, there was a knock at the door. Teresa pulled the door open, and on her porch stood two broad-shouldered Philadelphia police officers.

"Officers? Can I help ya?"

"Yes, ma'am. Are you Mrs. Bruno?"

Teresa nodded.

"Is your son Tony Bruno?"

Chapter Twenty-One

At the sound of his name, Tony vomited on the living room carpet. Teresa stared at the police officers as if they had spoken to her in an unknown language.

"Ma'am, is Tony Bruno your son?"

"Yeah."

"Is he here now?"

"Yes."

Teresa spread herself in the doorway like a linebacker.

"Ma'am, you need to let us in. We have a warrant to arrest your son."

"That ain't possible," Teresa said.

One policeman gently took Teresa's arm and led her into the home. Tony was on his hands and knees, hyperventilating.

"Are you Tony Bruno?"

Tony looked over at the policemen, and he retched again.

"OK, son. Now take it easy. I'm Officer Malloy, and this is Officer Campbell. We have a warrant for your arrest. I want you to stand up slowly."

Officer Malloy grabbed Tony under the arm and helped him to his feet.

"OK, I need you to put your hands behind your back."

Tony obeyed, and he panicked as the cool metal of the cuffs fastened around his wrists.

"How old are you, Tony?"

"Thirteen," he said in a trembling voice.

"All right. Officer Campbell and I are taking you to the police station to ask you some questions." He turned to Teresa. "Do you have a lawyer?"

Teresa shook her head. "Why are you takin' my boy? What's he done?"

Officer Malloy swallowed the lump that had formed in his throat. Tony looked at the cop with a sorrowful expression.

In a low, soft tone, Officer Malloy answered, "He's suspected of murder."

"What! No! Not my boy. Not my Tony. Please leave him here wit' me. He ain't perfect, but he ain't no murderer. I swear," Teresa cried.

"Ma'am, I understand your grief. I would suggest that you contact a public attorney. The court can give you the information that you need."

"Where are you takin' him?"

"We'll take him to the Philadelphia Police Station, where he'll be processed and moved to a facility for youth offenders," Officer Malloy stated. "He will only be kept at the station for a short period of time, less than six hours, before we move him to a juvenile detention placement."

With his hands behind his back, held in place by handcuffs, Tony walked toward his mother. Teresa grabbed him lightly and kissed his cheek.

"It'll be OK, baby. Don't cha worry; they'll find out this is all a big mistake," Teresa said.

Chapter Twenty-Two

As Tony rode in the back of the police car, his head felt as though it were filled with a thick liquid. His rapid thoughts of what would happen to him escalated his fear. This made it impossible for him to think clearly. Tony couldn't imagine what it would be like to go to prison for a crime he hadn't committed, and his belly felt like it was filled with boiling acid. His new, unknown reality terrified him. Johnny's threat played over in his ears, and nothing made sense. Would Johnny really kill me and my family? Tony had heard what people said about the mobsters . . . they were ruthless murderers who took what they wanted at all costs.

Inside the police station, Tony looked around him, his eyes wide and his heart erratically pulsing in his chest.

Officer Malloy took Tony by the arm to a room where he was photographed and fingerprinted. Then he was placed in a solitary holding cell where he couldn't see or hear anyone. Tony looked around him. The gray block walls matched the darker gray floor. The fluorescent lighting overhead was covered by a metal cage. There was a small cot bolted to the floor in the corner, and the cell door had a narrow opening where Tony could peer out into the empty hallway.

Two hours after Tony had been arrested, Teresa showed up at the police station accompanied by one of her neighbors. She was hysterical before she walked through the door.

"Where's my boy?" she called out. "Tony Bruno. He didn't do nothin'. Ya don't have a right to keep 'im here."

Officer Malloy rushed forward and pulled Teresa into a private room. He sat with her until they brought Tony in.

"Oooh, Tony," Teresa cried.

Tony buried his face in his mother's chest. "Please get me outta here, Ma. I wanna come home. I didn't do nothin', I swear. I was trying to help the kid."

Teresa looked up at Officer Malloy. "See, he didn't do nothin'—he just tried to help."

"Mrs. Bruno, I understand that you're upset. There was a witness who said he saw Tony stab the boy." The officer paused.

"What happened to Rex? Is he OK?" Tony asked.

"He's dead," Officer Malloy stated.

Teresa ran her hand nervously over Tony's head. "It's gonna be all right, Tony. I don't know how, but it's gonna be all right."

"Mrs. Bruno," Officer Malloy began, "we will be moving Tony to a juvenile detention center. The van arrived right before you got here. I'm sorry. I can give you five minutes, but then Tony must go with the other officers."

Teresa clung to Tony with all of her might. "Where are they takin' him?"

"He'll be taken to a detention center in Lehigh County. Because of the seriousness of the crime, Tony will be held there until a formal hearing is scheduled."

"But that's far from here. How am I supposed to see him? How can they hold him in prison wit'out even knowing for sure that he did somethin' wrong?" Teresa screamed.

"I'm very sorry, Mrs. Bruno. Like I said, there is a witness who alleges he saw your son stab the other boy. We have to hold him. I'm going to give the two of you five minutes; then I'll be back in to take Tony out to the van."

When Officer Malloy left the room, Tony collapsed onto the floor and cried. The hopelessness of his situation was crushing in on him. *Should I tell my mother that Salvatore killed Rex?* But the thought of exposing Salvatore was horrifying. He could never turn on a friend. And what would Mr. Morano do? Tony quickly decided to keep silent. His fear of Johnny Morano outweighed his fear of the unknown. *Maybe they won't send me to prison. They'll see it wasn't me, and I'll go home tomorrow,* Tony thought in an attempt to gain control over himself.

Teresa sat on the floor next to Tony, and he mushed his body into hers. She stroked his hair for a while. "I want ya to listen to me real good, Tony. If the police ask ya any questions, ya tell them ya ain't gonna say nothin' wit'out a lawyer. Every person's got a right to a lawyer, and I'm gonna get ya one of those public lawyers. Prison ain't a nice place, not even a kid's prison. Ya mind your own business and stay away from anyone who is trouble. If other kids pick on ya, then I want ya to tell the guards. Understand?"

Tony was crying loudly; heavy distress from deep within him came out in sharp gasps. "I'm scared. I'm real scared. What are they gonna do to me there? Are ya gonna visit me?"

"I don't know, baby. I don't have none of the answers. Ya need to be strong...until we figure all this out."

Officer Malloy unlocked the door and pulled it open. "Tony, it's time to go."

Teresa helped her son to his feet and took him into her arms. "Don't let nobody see ya as weak. Ya can't let 'em see ya cryin'. That'll bring trouble to ya," she whispered.

The boy kissed his mother's cheek as Officer Malloy put his hand on Tony's forearm to lead him outside.

"I love ya, Tony," Teresa muttered.

"Love ya too, Ma," Tony said sadly.

As Tony left the police station, his eyes darted around, and his jaw ground from side to side. His feet dragged along the tile floor. He was hoping for an escape from the inevitable. He walked out of the police station and gimped into the waiting van to begin his new life. He was petrified. Tony did not understand what was to come, but every inch of his body told him it would not be good.

Chapter Twenty-Three

Tony could smell the rot of lost, stagnant lives when he entered the juvenile detention center. He was immediately taken to a room with showers and told to undress and get washed. After being searched for drugs, he was taken deep within his steel and cement home. The other juveniles watched him as he passed, the way snakes watch their prey, preparing to strike.

"Hey, pretty boy," a heavy kid with a shaved head yelled, "how about you come over here and suck my dick." The group of boys sitting with him burst into laughter.

Tony shrank away. He tried to block it all out, but his years of torment as a child pushed in on him. That same helpless feeling reclaimed his body, and he suddenly felt more vulnerable than ever in his life. He looked up at the guard escorting him to his new home. Tony searched for a glimmer of humanity in the man's eyes, anything to give him a reason to believe he would be safe, but the guard wouldn't make eye contact.

They walked for a minute longer, and the guard, his face void of all emotion, spoke to him. "Don't look at me, you little maggot. You got yourself into this mess, and now you have to pay for what you've done. Those boys will be the least of your worries."

Tony wanted to die. Right then. Right there. In the fluorescent lighting of the cold, hard prison. From that moment forward, Tony would never fear death. Instead, he considered death his friend, a friend he prayed would visit him.

The guard stopped at cell forty-four and turned to Tony. "Welcome home, asshole. This is where you will live and shit."

Tony peered inside the cell. "I'm by myself?"

"Yep. You're all alone to think about what a disgusting menace to society you are."

Tony didn't care what the guard said. He was at least a little happy that he wouldn't have to share a cell with the other boys. He'd noticed the majority of the boys were older than he was. Tony was only thirteen, younger than the other prisoners by three to four years—an age gap that left him at a disadvantage.

Although Tony was big for thirteen, he was small compared to the others he'd seen on his way in.

Tony walked into the small cell, and the guard slid the barred door closed behind him. He stood on the other side and looked in at Tony, who stood awkwardly, not knowing what he was supposed to do. The guard gave him a creepy smile; one side of his lip lifted, but the other didn't move, as though he'd had a stroke. Tony shuddered and inched back toward the bed that hung from the wall.

"Yeah, you're going to be a favorite here. I can see it already. That dark hair and skin and those pretty green eyes of yours. Yep, the others are going to like you."

When the guard left, Tony sat down on the metal frame of the bed. He put his face in his hands. I have to get out of here. I don't belong here. What's going to happen to me? Tony thought.

The cement walls surrounding Tony closed in on him, and he curled up in the corner of the metal bed frame in a tight ball. He must have been that way for hours because when the guard came to bring him to dinner, his legs were bloodless and filled with pins and needles. The guard standing before him was different from the one who'd brought him in.

"Inmate Bruno, I'm Officer Geltz. I'm here to take you down to chow. A couple things you need to know. I expect obedience from my inmates. That means no fighting, stealing, or drugs. Have I made myself clear?"

"Yes."

"Yes, what?"

"Yes, you've made yourself clear."

"No, it's yes, sir, Officer Geltz. You got it?"

"Yes, sir, Officer Geltz," Tony said.

Tony's eyes roved around the small cell. There was a lump the size of a Ping-Pong ball stuck in his throat.

Officer Geltz unlocked the door to Tony's cell. "Let's go! Get moving. You need a personal invitation?"

Tony hurriedly followed Officer Geltz out of his cell and down the open walkway. He peered into the other cells as they passed, noticing that he had the only single-person cell. Tony wondered if having a roommate would have been better; at least he'd have someone to sit with when he ate.

Tony entered the line at the cafeteria to wait for his food. As he looked around, the other boys glared at him. He wanted to run back to his cell and lock himself in. He was surrounded by large, angry young boys. Tony knew those angry stares were meant to intimidate him, and it worked.

All eyes were on Tony, the new guy, as he made his way through the food line. Most of the food looked like vomit. Other juvenile prisoners plopped it onto his tray. When he got through the line, he paused and looked for a place to sit. Tables of young boys ran in a line down either side of the room. Tony moved forward slowly. He tried to sit at a table just a few feet from the food line.

One of the seventeen-year-old boys looked at him sharply. "Keep moving, you fucking asshole. You can't sit here. We don't need any of the shit you're gonna bring with you."

Tony quickly moved on, feeling desperate to find a place to settle down. A table in the back of the cafeteria was almost empty. As he approached, Tony took a quick look at the four teens sitting at the far end of the table. He placed his tray down and quickly sat. Tony waited. The teens said nothing; they barely seemed to notice he was there. Tony took a couple of bites of the food in front of him and gagged it down. He rested his fork on his tray and glanced at the teens on the other end of the table. The four boys were frowning at Tony. He quickly picked up his tray and headed toward the entrance.

"Where do you think you're going, boy?"

"To my cell, sir, Officer Geltz," Tony said, not making eye contact.

"That's funny, Bruno. You haven't caught on yet. You don't have any freedom here. You never get to decide where you'll be or not be. This is chow time, and that means you sit at the table until it's time to leave. Now, get your murdering ass back to the table and sit down."

"I'm pretty sure those boys don't want me to sit wit' 'em," Tony said.

"Hmmm. Is that so? Well, let's go see then."

"No! We ain't gotta do that. I'll just go back and sit down."

Officer Geltz rubbed his chin. "No, I think I need to go check it out for myself. I mean, after all, you did just make a formal complaint about those boys at your table."

"Wait. No, I didn't. I'm not complainin' 'bout nobody," Tony said in a panic.

Officer Geltz grabbed the tray from Tony's hand and laid it on top of the trash can. Then he grabbed Tony under the arm and marched him to the table where he had been sitting. As they approached, the four teenage boys fell silent.

"I understand that you boys don't want Bruno to sit with you. Is that true?"

The teens stared at Tony with dead eyes.

"We didn't say nothing to him, sir," Dooley, the leader of the pack said.

"That's not what Bruno just told me."

"I guess Bruno's a liar then, sir," Dooley stated through clenched teeth.

"Then you don't mind if he sits with you. That's what you're saying, right?"

"'Course not, sir. This isn't our table. It doesn't belong to us. Nothing belongs to us because we're all criminals, and this is your house," Dooley recited, exactly as he'd been taught.

"Good," Officer Geltz said and turned to Tony. "You need to be careful about telling lies about other inmates. It could get them in trouble. I'm going to cut you a break since it's your first day, but if you ever lie to me again, you'll find yourself in more trouble than you can imagine."

Officer Geltz turned and walked off with a smile. Tony stood next to the teen boys. He didn't know what to do.

"You just made a big mistake, asshole," Dooley threatened.

"I...I didn't say all that stuff," Tony stammered.

"If you didn't say it, then go tell Geltz the Goon that he's a liar," Dooley challenged.

Tony shook his head. "I can't. He'll punish me."

Dooley looked at his friends. "You're right. What would be the fun of that when we can punish you ourselves?"

Tony slowly moved to the other end of the table and sat down in a heap. He didn't dare look over at Dooley and his friends. Tony already knew he would see more of them than he ever wanted.

Chapter Twenty-Four

The next morning Tony was let out of his cell, and he followed yet another guard, Officer Nash, to the showers. Inside the open shower stalls, he quickly undressed and allowed the warm water to wash over him. He was thinking about having to go back into the cafeteria and wished he could stay in his cell. I'd rather stay in my cell and starve to death, Tony thought.

Tony closed his eyes and put his face under the water. The first blow hit him in the shoulder, and he slammed against the tile wall. The second blow struck him on his lower back. He lost his footing on the wet tile floor and fell. His hip and shoulder slammed down awkwardly. A burning pain tore through his injured muscles. Shocked by the ambush, he raised his elbows up to his ears and covered his head.

Dooley lifted the pillowcase filled with bars of soap and walloped it down on Tony. Dooley repeated this several times, making certain the whacks were hard and painful, pummeling Tony as if he was trying to break bones. When he finished, Tony lay on the wet floor of the shower, naked and frightened. After a few minutes, he slowly got to his feet. His legs were sore. He stepped forward, and searing pain erupted from his ribs. Tony stopped and leaned against the old, cracked tiled wall and took several deep breaths. He wanted to get his clothes on and get out of the showers. He was worried that Dooley would come back and give him another beating.

Tony left the shower room and made his way back to his cell, just as the officer had instructed him to do. He sat on his bed. His body was throbbing. His arms, legs, and back had deep-purple bruises. He was grateful that he could hide the discolorations under his orange jumpsuit.

"Inmate Bruno!" Officer Nash yelled.

Tony jumped. "Yes, sir."

"Get your stupid ass down to the chow hall and eat. Your special escort is over. Once you're here twenty-four hours, you're on your own. That means you get up, shower, eat, work, eat, work some more, eat, take a shit, and then it's lights out."

"I didn't know. Ya told me to come back to my cell. I got it now...sir."

"Well then, get a move on. Why are you sitting there if you got it?"

Tony squeezed past Officer Nash, who took up most of the door space. He turned and hurried to the cafeteria. Once inside, Tony got his food then looked around, hoping to find another table where he could sit. He started toward the opposite side of the room from where Dooley and his gang were sitting, but Officer Nash tapped him on the shoulder.

"Your table is over there." Officer Nash pointed. "You sit with Dooley. Now, you run along, and if he or his rotten friends treat you bad, I want you to run back here and tell me like the little pussy that you are. Officer Geltz told me they gave you some trouble yesterday."

"I'll be fine. Those boys don't bother me," Tony lied, not wanting to add any fuel to the fire.

Tony made his way slowly toward the table. He tried his best not to limp. His adrenaline was coursing through his body, masking some of his pain. Tony laid his tray of food on the table at the opposite end from where Dooley and his friends sat. He looked at the slop in front of him.

"What's wrong, Bruno? This food ain't good enough for you?" Officer Nash said.

"No, sir. The food is fine. I'm just not that hungry."

Officer Nash gripped Tony's shoulder, digging his fingers into his already sore muscles. "If the food is fine, then let me see you eat it. See, it doesn't matter if you're hungry. This is your time to eat. You gave up your right to make choices when you killed that boy. Now, you start eating, or I can feed you in front of these boys like you're a baby."

Tony picked up his fork and shoved eggs into his mouth. The powdered eggs tasted like glue, and Tony had to stop himself from gagging.

"More, Bruno!"

Tony shoved another forkful of the yellow, rubbery substance into his mouth. This time he grabbed the glass of apple juice and took a swig to wash the food down. Before being told again, Tony lifted a piece of dry toast from the tray and took a bite; it was like eating cardboard. Officer Nash stood over him until Tony had finished all the food on his tray. All the while the other boys in the cafeteria watched, waiting and hoping that Tony would stop eating and Officer Nash would force-feed him.

Tony put his plastic fork down and looked up at the officer, feeling victorious that he'd finished the garbage that had been his breakfast.

"You left crumbs on your tray," Officer Nash said.

"I finished my breakfast just like ya said."

"Are you questioning me? You eat those crumbs on your tray, boy."

Before Tony could react, Officer Nash grabbed the back of his head and pushed it into the tray. "Lick 'em up. You lick up those crumbs right now, or you'll be sorry."

With Officer Nash's hand on the back of his head, Tony licked at the tray. The boys in the cafeteria snickered and laughed. When Tony had licked off every last crumb, the officer released him. Tony looked around the room at the boys and could see he had become their morning entertainment. Then he turned his head and looked to the opposite end of the table just as Dooley and his friend Hack gave each other a high five.

Tony lowered his head, feeling as though he were drowning in mud. Finally the boys were dismissed to go to work. Tony hadn't received a work assignment, and following orders, he went back to his cell. He thought about the night that Rex had died. It wasn't his fault, yet he was paying the price. He wondered what Salvatore and Vincent had done after they arrested him. His friends knew the truth of what happened to Rex. He thought about telling the guards who really killed Rex. His loyalty to Salvatore clashed with his need to escape his new hell. Before Tony fell asleep that night, he chose loyalty.

Chapter Twenty-Five

"**B**runo! Get your ass moving—your attorney is here to see you," Officer Nash yelled.

Tony followed the officer out of the cellblock and into a private room. The room was barren except for a table and two chairs. There was a man in his late fifties sitting at the table. He looked up over his glasses as Tony entered.

"Tony, my name is Roger Taft. I'm a public defender and have been assigned to represent you in court."

Tony sat in the open chair, and Roger looked at Officer Nash. "I'll take it from here," he said dismissively. Officer Nash gave Roger a hard glare and left the room.

"Are ya here to take me home now?" Tony asked.

"No, Tony. I'm a lawyer. I'm here to try and help you get back home. I've already spoken to your mother, and she knows I've come here to talk with you today. I'm going to ask you some questions, and I need you to be honest with me. It's the only way I can help you."

"How do I know I can trust ya?"

"There something called attorney-client privilege. That means you can tell me anything, and by law I can't tell anyone else. Do you understand?"

Tony nodded.

"Tony, did you stab that boy?"

"No, I didn't hurt no one. I tried to help Rex after he got stabbed."

"Do you know who did stab him?"

Tony hesitated, wondering whether to tell the truth. When he saw the lawyer gazing at him as if he could read his mind, he quickly blurted out a lie.

"No, I don't know who stabbed him. All I know is I didn't."

"There is a man who claims he saw you stab the boy."

"He's lyin'. He didn't see nothin'. That man didn't come outta the store until I was already tryin' to help Rex. He didn't see me stab 'im 'cause I didn't do it," Tony said with conviction.

Roger studied Tony, who held eye contact with his lawyer.

"Was anyone with you the night that Rex was stabbed?"

Tony hesitated again. "Nope, I was alone. I was walking by and saw Rex on the ground. I went over to try to help, and a man came out of the store. He saw me next to Rex and said I stabbed him."

"I see. Well, you have a detention hearing scheduled for tomorrow. Since you didn't stab the boy and you don't know who did, we will tell the judge that you didn't do it."

"Then what happens?"

"The judge will decide if he believes that you are innocent or if there is a chance that you stabbed the boy."

"What if they don't believe me?"

"If the judge doesn't believe you, there is a possibility that you will go to an adult court and a different judge will make a decision after hearing all the facts. Is there any more information you need to tell me?"

Tony shook his head. "I told ya everything I know."

"OK. Is there anything that you need?"

"Yeah, I need to get outta here. This place ain't good."

Tony shifted in his seat and winced when a stab of pain ran through his core.

"Did something happen to you, Tony? Has someone hurt you?"

"That don't matter. All that matters is that I get outta here."

Tony's eyes burned with sizzling tears. He tried to hold them back, but they spilled down his cheeks.

Roger leaned forward and put his hand on Tony's wrist. "If someone has hurt you, then I need to know."

Tony thought about telling Roger everything that had happened to him in the last twenty-four hours, but he was afraid of what the guards and other boys would do to him for being a snitch.

"I just wanna go home. I didn't do nothin' wrong, and there ain't no reason for me to be here."

Tony and Roger talked for a while longer. Roger was trying to build a level of trust. His instincts told him that Tony hadn't stabbed the other boy, but he also knew that Tony was lying about something, maybe protecting someone. Roger looked down at his pad of notes. There wasn't much to go with in court, and he was nervous that Tony's story wouldn't pass muster with the judge. He took in a long breath.

"I have to leave now. If you remember any other details of that night, anyone who may have seen you at the scene, then you tell one of the guards that you need to talk to me tomorrow before the hearing starts. OK?"

"Sure," Tony muttered. "Do ya think I'm gonna go home tomorra?"

"I don't know, Tony. I'll try my best. You hang in there and be careful."

Back in his cell, Tony thought about his meeting with Roger. He would not tell on Salvatore—not because Johnny had threatened him, but because Salvatore was his friend. Johnny had treated him terribly when he got to the house...he had made Tony feel like he was nothing.

Tony's only regret was that he hadn't run from the crime like Salvatore and Vincent.

Chapter Twenty-Six

L ater that afternoon, while Tony was eating dinner, Officer Geltz approached. Tony didn't make eye contact with him. He wanted to get through one meal without being bullied.

"I hear you met with your lawyer today. Word on the street is that he said you're a liar, Bruno. Everyone knows you're lying. Look around you—this room is filled with liars. I'll bet that you'll lose tomorrow. The judge is going to see that you are a conniving little bastard. What do you have to say for yourself, Bruno?"

"Nothin', sir."

"That's right. You don't have anything to say because you know that you're lying. You know that you killed that boy and are right where you belong. See these boys in here? These other boys have done stupid things, but you're the only one here for murder. That means you're the worst person in this room. I bet you'll get the electric chair," Officer Geltz taunted.

Tony's gut felt like it was filled with hot tar.

"I understand you didn't want to eat your breakfast this morning. I want to see your tray before you drop it off, and it better be squeaky clean. You understand me?"

"Yes, sir."

Tony sat and ate the foul-tasting food on his tray. He even scraped his finger against the plastic to make sure there was not a morsel of food left on it. When it was time to return to his cell, Tony walked his tray up to Officer Geltz and showed it to him.

Officer Geltz gave Tony a grave look. "I suppose tomorrow night you're going to need more food since it seems that you ate every last drop. You must be really hungry."

Tony left his tray on the rack and walked quickly back to his cell. He had been sitting on his bed when Dooley appeared in the doorway.

"You better hope that the judge lets you outta here. No tellin' what'll happen to ya if ya gotta stay in this place. We don't like snitches, and that's what you are, nothing but a snitch. You better watch yourself."

"I never snitched on anyone," Tony said, thinking of Salvatore. "I don't snitch."

"I don't believe you. Like I said, ya better hope the judge lets you outta here tomorrow."

When Tony was alone in his cell again, he thought about his mother. Out on the streets, he had felt like he was grown, but now in the dreariness of the prison, he wanted to curl up into his mother's lap so she could tell him that everything would be all right. Tony fell asleep with a small glimmer of hope that the next day he would be set free.

***

The next morning, Tony was handcuffed and then loaded into a van and driven to the county courthouse. There were three rows of chairs on either side of the aisle. Tony noticed his mother sitting in the first row. She was looking at him with worried eyes. She stood and tried to go to him, but a guard stopped her. Roger Taft shook Tony's cuffed hands, and they sat down together.

When the judge addressed Tony and asked him directly if he had committed the crime, Tony shook his head.

"I didn't do nothin' to Rex," he responded.

The judge responded with an emotionless response. "Did you see who killed the boy?"

"No. I was just tryin' to help Rex and this man came outta the store and said I killed 'im. He's lyin' 'cause he didn't see nothin'," Tony explained.

The judge leaned forward and propped his elbows on the table in front of him. His brow was taut and lips tightly pressed together. "Well, how do you know what the man saw? You claim you showed up after the boy was stabbed. Seems to me that you're lying."

Tony turned and looked at his mother. "I swear I ain't lyin'," he cried.

Before the judge made his decision, Roger argued that Tony did not commit the crime and that he was not a threat to the community. While Roger had delivered a compelling argument, the judge made a ruling to detain Tony because he didn't believe him and, the prosecutor had an eyewitness to the murder. Because Tony was so young and had no prior record, the judge decided not to transfer him to an adult court. Roger had convinced the judge that Tony deserved a chance to prove himself in the juvenile system and that sending the young boy to adult court without more supporting evidence would be unfair and unjust to a child who never had a record of violence.

After the hearing, a court officer brought Tony into another room inside the courthouse.

"Am I going home?" Tony asked.

"Your attorney is coming in to talk to you. He will explain everything."

A few minutes later, Roger Taft and Teresa entered the room. Still handcuffed, Tony jumped to his feet and threw himself into his mother's arms. After several moments, Roger instructed them to sit.

"What's gonna happen to Tony?" Teresa said, bawling.

"Well, there's good news and bad news. The good news is that the judge decided not to send the case to adult court. The bad news is that the judge has a reasonable basis to believe that Tony may have committed the crime. Tony's probation officer will have to file a delinquency petition within the next twenty-four hours. After that there will be an adjudication hearing."

"What's that?" Tony said.

"It's like a trial. The judge will let the witness come into court and testify against you."

"So when do I gotta come back here?"

"If the prosecutor needs more time to collect evidence, which I suspect he will, it could be ten days before we go back to court."

Tony turned to his mother. "You're gonna bring me back, right? I don't wanna come by myself."

Roger cleared his throat. "Tony, you won't be able to go home with your mother. You'll be taken back to the juvenile detention center to wait for the hearing."

Tony's mouth hung open, and he leaned in closer. "Mr. Taft, I can't go back there. You gotta tell the judge that I don't wanna go. All the kids are older than me. I...I can't stay there no more."

"I understand that you're scared, Tony. Now, if the older boys give you a hard time, all you have to do is tell one of the officers. OK? They have an obligation to keep you safe."

Tony shook his head. A sob caught in his chest, and he broke down.

"What is it, baby?" Teresa asked, moving her chair closer to Tony.

"Nothin'. I just wanna go home. I wanna be back in my own room," Tony wailed. "I'm scared."

"I know you're scared. I'm scared too. But right now ya gotta be strong. Ya gotta think good thoughts. Think 'bout gettin' outta that godforsaken place. Ya hear me?" Teresa said.

Tony looked at Roger. "Do ya think I'm gonna win?"

"I don't know. I wish I could give you some comfort, but I just don't know what's going to happen. I'll make sure that I'm prepared to ask all the right questions of the man who claims he saw you commit the crime. I promise both of you that I'll do my very best. That's all I can say," Roger said, his heart breaking for the mother and son.

Later that day, back in the detention center, Officer Nash paid Tony a visit.

"I hear the judge saw right through your bullshit."

"I'm not lyin'," Tony said.

"Ha! Keep telling yourself that. Let's get going. You're getting moved to another cell, one with a roommate," Officer Nash said with a twisted smile.

Tony gathered his few belongings and followed the officer down several corridors. They stopped at cell number twenty-two. Tony looked inside and drew in a breath. His cellmate stood with his hands on his hips and chest puffed out. His face was contorted with a hideous scowl, and Tony took a step backward.

Officer Nash pushed Tony into the cell. "Enjoy your new home."

Officer Nash walked away, and Tony stood, unable to move, his feet betraying him as he stared into the lifeless eyes of Dooley.

Chapter Twenty–Seven

W hen Tony tried to get on the upper bunk that night, Dooley grabbed his ankles and pulled him onto the floor. Tony belly flopped onto the cement ground. Dooley stood over his body.

"Your bed is on the floor. Consider yourself my pet. That means you'll do what I say, when I say to do it. If you don't, then I'll keep beating the shit outta of ya until ya eventually learn your lesson," Dooley growled.

Tony slept on the cold floor of the cell that night. He dozed in and out, his sleep disrupted by the acid that burned at his insides. He reminded himself that he had ten days...only ten days before he would find out what would happen to him.

In the morning Dooley shoved his sneaker into Tony's side.

"Get up. I don't want no shit from Nash 'cause your filthy ass is still sleeping."

Tony quickly rose and stared at Dooley, building up his courage, which was being fueled by his lack of sleep. "Why don't cha just leave me alone? I didn't do nothin' to ya. I ain't gonna be here that long, and then you'll never see me again."

Dooley curled his hand into a fist, pulled back his arm, and clocked Tony in the face. Tony flew backward against the wall of the cell. Half-conscious, he slid onto the floor.

"Who the fuck do you think you're talking to? Huh? You don't speak to me like that—got it?" Dooley screamed.

Hearing the commotion—standing where they couldn't see him —Officer Nash stepped in front of the cell door.

"Well, what do we have here? Is there a problem, Bruno?"

Tony shook his head, but his eye that had taken the punch was already closing from the swelling surface.

"Oh yeah? What happened to your eye then?"

"I fell off the top bunk, sir."

"I see." Officer Nash looked at Dooley. "Is that true? Did Bruno fall off of his bunk?"

Dooley shrugged his shoulders, and Officer Nash turned back to Tony.

"Are you lying to me, Bruno?"

"No, sir. I fell off of my bunk, just like I said."

"Well, if that's true, then why didn't Dooley see you fall? You've been here the whole time, right?" he asked Dooley.

"Yes, sir. I was here."

Officer Nash turned back to Tony. "So you must be lying."

"I'm not lyin'," Tony insisted.

"Well, then are you saying that Dooley is lying?"

Tony started to sweat. He didn't know which was worse, Nash or Dooley going after him. He quickly decided on Nash since Dooley would have access to him every night for the next ten days.

"No, Dooley ain't lying neither," Tony whispered.

"Get up, you little bastard," Officer Nash demanded.

Tony walked behind Nash as he was led into the shower. Officer Nash made all the other boys cease their showers while they watched Tony get undressed and take his own shower. The other boys were forced to stand away from the warm water. They shivered from being cold, and their anger toward Tony grew as they had to watch him shower. Their agitation made the air heavy with resentment toward Tony.

"Look, boys—Bruno's got a pencil dick," Officer Nash tormented.

The other boys laughed, but their anger towards Tony was mounting as they waited to get back under the warm water. When Tony finished dressing, he followed Officer Nash to the cafeteria. Nash stood side by side with Tony as he received his breakfast.

"Bruno wants more of that oatmeal. Give him more."

A second lump of gruel hit the tray. Tony could feel the bile creeping into his throat in reaction to the smell.

"You look real hungry, Bruno. I think you need some more prunes. Give him more," he said to the boy in charge of serving the cooked prunes.

By the time Tony got through the line, his tray felt like it weighed ten pounds. He made his way to the table where he was assigned and sat down. Tony stared at what appeared to be an insurmountable amount of food.

"Eat, Bruno!"

Officer Nash stood over him as he took one mouthful after another. Finally, unable to eat any more, Tony leaned to the side and threw up on the floor next to Nash. Officer Nash aggressively lifted the tray and threw it onto the floor.

"Get down there and eat every last bit of it!"

The cafeteria went silent. Even some boys who resented Tony felt sorry for what was about to happen.

Tony looked at Officer Nash with disbelief.

"Did you hear me? Get down on your hands and knees and eat every bit of that food and puke," Nash ordered. "You might waste food at home with your whore mother, but you don't get to waste food here."

Tony felt glued to his seat. Officer Nash grabbed him by the collar of his prison uniform and threw him onto the floor. He leaned over and pushed Tony's face into the food and vomit. Tony's nose hit the floor so hard it bled.

"I said eat!" Officer Nash screamed again.

Tony ate the mixture of food, vomit, and blood, licking and slurping it up like an animal.

"Faster!" Officer Nash yelled.

He pushed Tony's face deep into the foul contents. Tony resisted; he was having a difficult time breathing. Food was up his nose and lodged in his throat. Tony tried to flip onto his back, but Officer Nash was too strong. Suddenly, as Tony flailed his body to take in a breath of air, he felt Officer Nash become weightless. When Tony wiped the food from his eyes, another officer stared down at him. The officer looked at him with sympathetic eyes. He gave Tony a look of genuine concern. That moment was the first time Tony had felt any kindness since he'd arrived.

The officer extended a large hand to Tony. "I'm Officer Zody. My friend over here, Officer Nash, he gets a little carried away sometimes. Let me help you up."

Tony grabbed Zody's hand, and he was pulled to his feet by the kind man. Officer Zody motioned to a boy who was serving bread to come over.

"Bradley, you go ahead and clean up this mess for me," Officer Zody said in a calm manner.

Zody turned back to Tony. "I run the kitchen. See all the boys serving food and cleaning up your trays?"

"Yes, sir."

"They all work for me. I've been watching you since you arrived. It seems to me like you've been having a real hard time."

Tony nodded, feeling a deep bond with the man.

"You're a lot younger than the other boys here. That must be hard."

"Yes, sir," Tony mumbled, looking down at the floor.

Officer Zody patted Tony on the back. "Come on. Follow me."

Tony followed as all the other boys watched him. Tony thought he saw envy in their eyes, and for a moment, a trickle of power pulsed through his veins. He followed the officer into his office and sat in the chair across the desk from him.

"Have you been assigned a job yet?"

"No, sir."

"OK. First off, I want you to call me Zody, like all the other boys that work for me."

Tony smiled. "Thanks, Zody."

"How would you like to work here in the kitchen? The boys that work in the kitchen eat privately under my supervision. That way you don't have to put up with Officer Nash or Geltz. I've seen how they've been treating you. What do you say?"

"Wow. That'd be great. And I get to spend most of the day in the kitchen?"

"You sure do. Now, I heard that you are waiting for a trial that will be scheduled in the next ten days. Do your parents come to see you here?"

"Nah. We live too far away. My father, well, he don't like me too much, so he wouldn't come anyway. My mother would come more, but our car ain't that good, and she's afraid it'll break down if she drives it too far. She only comes when I gotta go to court. My ma's friend drives her 'cause she has a better car than we do."

Officer Zody reached over and touched Tony's arm. "That's a shame. You seem like a nice boy. I'm sorry that you can't see your mother more often. And what kind of father rejects his own child?"

"The kinda father that drinks too much and hits me and my mom."

"Is that so? I'm sorry to hear you've lived with such a horrible role model. I think that you're going to learn a lot working for me."

Tony sat up straight in his chair. "I'd really like that, Zody. I like to learn new stuff. When I'm learnin' new things I ain't so bored."

"Good. Then that's what we'll do. You can start now by helping with lunch."

Tony leaned back against the chair and relief washed over him. He'd finally had a stroke of good luck.

Chapter Twenty-Eight

That night, after serving dinner and helping put the dishes away, Tony walked back to his cell. He paused at the door and looked at Dooley.

"You're working for Zody now, huh?"

"Yeah." The tone of respect in Dooley's voice confused Tony.

"Ya can sleep up top tonight if you want," Dooley said, pointing to the upper bunk.

"That would be good. How come you're bein' nice to me?"

"I don't know. Just 'cause. Besides, you're gettin' your ass kicked by all the guards, so I figured I'd cut you a break. I can be mean again if you want me to," Dooley threatened.

"Nah. I'll take nice."

Tony watched Dooley for moment. "How come you're in here?"

Dooley casually glanced at him. "A few years back, I was arrested for stealing a couple of times. The court placed me with a family. They were supposed to be my guardians, but we didn't get along too good, so my probation officer had me sent back here. They're looking for another family that can take me. Thing is that I don't do the family stuff too good. My father raised me after my mother left him for his brother. I was raised with all kinds of fucked up. My father is in prison now, and I have no idea where that bitch mother of mine is. So I really raised myself. What about you?"

"The police think I killed somebody, but I didn't."

"I know why you're here. I was askin' about your family."

"Oh. My mother is a good lady, but my father is an asshole. He drinks a lot and gets mad. Ya know."

"Yeah. Parents can really suck. Anyway, like I said, you can sleep up top."

Tony gave Dooley a broad smile.

Dooley gave him a dirty look. "Look, man—just 'cause we talked don't mean that we're friends. You got some heavy shit goin' down, and I don't want nothin' to do with it. Understand?"

"Yeah, sure," Tony responded, confused.

The next morning Tony reported to the kitchen instead of going for a shower, as Officer Zody had instructed. Tony was partnered with a Latino boy named Diego who was in charge of teaching him the ropes. Once Zody made the introductions, he left the two boys alone to start cooking.

"How long you gonna be here?" Diego asked.

"Don't know. My trial will be in the next ten days," Tony said.

"What did ya do?"

Tony shot Diego a confused look. "I didn't do nothin'. They said I killed a kid, but I didn't. How 'bout you? How long you here for?"

Diego poured salt into a measuring cup and added it to the powdered eggs. "Not sure. I beat up this kid real bad in my school. Spent some time here and then got placed with a foster family. Then the fuckers moved outta state, and I got sent back here." Diego glanced at Tony. "They didn't wanna take me along. Ya know?"

Tony gave Diego a head nod. "Yeah, I know what cha mean."

"What do ya know about Zody?" Diego asked.

Tony looked at Zody through the window that separated the kitchen area from Zody's office. "I don't know. He's a nice guy. He helped me out yesterday when that prick Nash was fuckin' wit' me."

"Yeah, that's Zody," Diego agreed.

Tony worked throughout the morning and well into the afternoon before he and Diego stopped to take a break. Zody went out into the cafeteria and approached all the boys who worked in the kitchen. As he got closer, the boys went silent. Zody sat down next to Tony.

"So I see you all met the new guy. He's something special, isn't he?" Zody said, patting Tony on the back.

"Yeah, he's a quick learner too," Diego added.

"That's real good to hear," Zody said, looking at Tony. "It's important to be able to learn things quickly. It makes life much easier."

Zody stood and looked around at the group. "You boys take a little break and then get back in there so we have the food ready on time for dinner."

It was the end of the second day and almost nine o'clock. Tony had been responsible for making the instant mashed potatoes, and his hair and clothes were covered with white clumps. Zody walked into the kitchen just as Tony and two other boys finished cleaning up.

"All right. I think it's time to go back to your cells and get some rest." Zody stepped closer to Tony. "I think you're wearing more mashed potatoes than you served tonight." The officer pulled a clump of potatoes out of Tony's hair. "How about if I take you down to the showers? You have to be back here early tomorrow, and you won't have time to shower in the morning."

Tony grinned as he ran his hand through the sticky substance in his hair. "Yeah, thanks Zody," he said with a chuckle.

Zody turned to the other two boys. "You two go back to your cells. I'll see you in the morning."

Tony and Zody walked through the prison toward the shower. They chatted easily about the day.

"I'm real grateful that ya let me work in the kitchen. I mean, it's been a lifesaver."

Zody patted the boy on the back. "Well, you know, I saw something in you that told me you're a good kid. I'm happy I could help you. Just do what you're told, and you'll stay out of trouble. It's that simple."

When they got to the shower room, Tony undressed while Zody sat in a chair off to the side. Tony scurried under the warm water, washing the potatoes out of his hair first. He leaned his face up into the showerhead, and the long day of cooking and cleaning melted away. Then Tony felt an arm wrap around his waist.

"You're a nice kid, Tony. I want you to be very quiet," Zody whispered.

When Zody pulled Tony to him, the feel of the man's flesh sent him into a panic. Tony spun on Zody and pushed him away.

"Resistance is futile. It'll be easier for you if you just go with it."

Tony looked down at Zody's erect penis. His blood felt like boiling water coursing through his veins. His heart was beating so fast he thought his chest would explode. Zody grabbed Tony by the arm and forced him face first into the wall.

"Bend over."

Tony shook his head and tried to wiggle and squirm from Zody's tight grip.

"I said bend over," Zody commanded through clenched teeth.

Tony continued to resist him, moving and trying to break his body free.

Zody, ready for the fight, grabbed Tony and cuffed his wrist. Then he forced Tony onto the floor of the shower, slid the other cuff under a thin pipe that ran along the wall and fastened Tony's other wrist. Tony was now on his knees, bent over. His upper body leaned into the base of the floor where he was secured to the pipe.

Zody pulled Tony hips upward and entered him one hard thrust at a time. Tony screamed as his body and mind were violated. He moaned and begged Zody to stop until his voice was gone and no sound could escape his lips and he slid into shock. When it was over, Zody unlocked the handcuffs, and Tony crouched in the corner of the shower stall. Zody dried off and dressed. He walked over and threw a towel at Tony.

"Let's go. Dry yourself off and get dressed. You have to get some sleep."

Tony's mind was racing, yet he couldn't hold on to a single thought. His brain felt like it was floating in toxic waste, and if it wasn't for the pain of being sodomized, he might have convinced himself that he'd imagined the whole thing. It was too much for the thirteen-year-old to comprehend.

Tony walked back to his cell, focusing on taking one step after another. Dooley was lying on his bunk and looked up at Tony. He immediately recognized Tony's deadpan stare and knew that he was Zody's boy now. Tony had been initiated into Zody's sick circle. Dooley glanced at Zody, who gave him a vile grin, turned, and left. When Zody was gone, Dooley got off his bunk and leaned on the top bunk where Tony was lying, his eyes wide open with fear and confusion.

"You OK?"

Tony didn't answer.

"I know what he did to you. Everyone knows what Zody does to his kitchen boys. He made you his bitch tonight, didn't he?"

Tears slid out of the corners of Tony's eyes. "What am I gonna do?"

Dooley chuckled nervously. "You're gonna do exactly what he wants, or he'll make your life a living hell. That's the way it works. He made ya think he was a nice guy, huh?"

"Yeah. I thought he cared about me."

"He does care about ya, Bruno. He cares about getting his rocks off by puttin' his prick up your ass."

"Stop. Please stop. I wanna go home," Tony cried.

Dooley stood for a while, remembering the first time that Zody had done it to him. The shame of it disguised most of the physical pain.

"It'll get easier," Dooley offered.

"Ain't ever happenin' to me again. I swear I'll kill myself," Tony breathed.

"He already knows that you're thinking that. We all think that the first time. But you won't kill yourself because someday, someone, maybe you, will get back at him. You remember that—you remember that someday he will get his."

As Tony and Dooley lay in their own bunks, both boys thought about the nightmare of becoming Zody's bitch for the first time.

Chapter Twenty-Nine

D ooley was sitting at breakfast with his friend Hack the next morning.

"Zody broke Bruno last night."

Hack looked at him. "How do ya know?"

"I was up when he came back. We talked about it. There ain't no turnin' back for Bruno now. He's got at least eight more days to deal with Zody. I don't know if this kid is gonna come out of this OK. I kinda feel sorry for him."

"Zody's a fucking asshole, and so are the rest of these motherfucking pricks that run this place."

Dooley stopped chewing. "What are ya gettin' so worked up about? It wasn't you that just took a snake up the ass."

Hack cleared his throat. "I ain't worked up; I just think it's sick."

"Yeah, well, just feel lucky that it ain't never happened to you. Somehow ya never had to put up with that shit. Why is that?" Dooley reflected.

"'I don't fucking know why. Lay off, Dooley. I'm warning you."

The boys ate the rest of their breakfast in silence. When it was over, Hack asked permission to make a telephone call.

***

"Hey, it's Hack," he said to the man on the other end of the phone.

"What do ya know?"

"The Bruno kid got broke last night by the guy who runs the kitchen," he said.

"For fuck's sake. Bruno ain't even done shittin' yellow yet. I'll let the boss know. Call if anything else happens."

The phone line went dead. Hack walked to his job in the library, and while he worked the rest of the afternoon, he couldn't get Tony out of his mind. He had hoped the kid would be moved out of the facility before this happened. Hack wished he had the power to make it stop.

Big Paulie went over to Johnny Morano's house. He walked into the office and found Johnny sitting behind his desk.

"The kid's in trouble, Johnny. He got raped last night."

Johnny looked up, and standing in the doorway behind Big Paulie was Salvatore. He rushed forward. "Pop, you have to help Tony. You know he didn't kill Rex. I swear if you don't help him, I'll go to the police and tell them I did it."

Salvatore was shaking. The thought of Tony being raped in prison was hard for him to grasp. He didn't know exactly what that meant, but he knew that another man had done something sexual to his friend.

"You will do no such thing. You will do exactly as I say. Do you want to be the one in prison having grown men stick their dicks up your ass?" Johnny screamed.

Salvatore felt as though he had been punched in the gut. The reality of what was happening to Tony became crystal clear in his mind, and his stomach heaved.

Minutes later, when Salvatore had calmed down, Johnny approached him.

"Bad shit happens sometimes," Johnny began. "This is an unfortunate situation. You will not do anything stupid."

"How did Big Paulie find out what's happening to Tony?"

"One of our men has a son that's there. We had him on alert so he could report back. He gives Big Paulie updates."

"What are we going to do? We can't just do nothing," Salvatore shrieked.

"Yes, we can. We can do nothing," Johnny said definitively.

Chapter Thirty

Over the next two days, Tony was taken to the shower by Zody after all the work in the kitchen was completed. On the third night, when Zody had finished with him, Officer Geltz stepped up from behind Zody. Tony looked at him with horror.

"You're not finished yet, Bruno. You have me to take care of tonight," Geltz taunted. The man dropped his pants and stood in front of Tony. "Put it in your mouth, Bruno, and suck on it. When I come, I want you to swallow every last drop. If you let one fucking drop out, I'll beat the hell out of you and make you do it all over again until you get it right."

Unable to think, incapable of protecting himself, he gave in to Geltz. Tony gagged down the salty, snotty substance.

That night, back in his cell, Tony's resentment toward the guards set the stage for the remainder of his life.

"Ya all right?" Dooley asked.

"Like you fuckin' care? Why don't cha just leave me alone?"

"Calm down. I was just asking if you were OK."

Tony jumped off of the top bunk and crouched down close to Dooley. "How the fuck can I be OK? Ya know what's happening to me." Tony lowered his head, overwhelmed with shame. "Geltz came in after Zody tonight."

"I know."

"How?"

"I was in your shoes my first time through this place," Dooley admitted.

"This happened to ya?"

"Yeah, sure. It happens to a lot of us. Thing to remember is that when new boys come in, the perverted bastards will drop you and move on to the fresh meat. Once in a while they come back and get a piece of ass from us, but they stick with the new kids for the most part," Dooley said casually.

"Why doesn't anyone tell?"

Dooley sat up on his bunk. "Who the fuck are ya gonna tell? Come on. They're all in it together. Do you really think anyone in this place gives a fuck about you or me? They don't!"

"How do I make it stop?"

"Ya don't. All ya can do is hope that the judge lets ya go, and ya get the fuck outta this place. I'm telling ya, being out in the group homes and shit like that, it ain't any better. They might not fuck ya, but they do it in other ways. Sometimes it's the other boys treatin' ya like shit, and sometimes it's the people who run the place. See this tattoo?" Dooley said. He pushed his right wrist in front of Tony: tattooed letters running from his wrist to his elbow spelled out "SLAYER." "This is a gang I belong to in North Philly. This tattoo is what kept me alive in the places they've sent me. Nobody wants to come up against the Slayers. We always stick together and take care of business. If you get outta here, you need to find yourself a group of people that protect each other."

Tony thought about what Dooley had just said and realized that being a part of something bigger was something that he needed. "I don't know that I can feel any badder than I do now. I ain't never realized how messed up your brain can get, not till now. When I was a kid, I got picked on a lot, and puttin' up wit' those assholes in my school ain't nothin' compared to this," Tony confided.

Dooley felt the effects of his own unfortunate life. He had made bad choices and had paid the price for those decisions. Dooley closed his eyes. "Hang in there, man. There ain't nothin' that lasts forever. I learnt that a long time ago. I'm seventeen years old, and it don't matter if its good shit or bad shit—none of it lasts forever," Dooley said. "I just look forward to the day I can get back to my gang, back to the Slayers where loyalty and trust is everything."

The next several nights Tony was raped by Zody and Geltz. On the third night, Zody pulled a straitjacket out from a locker. "Let's go, we need to put this on you tonight. It's a special occasion, and I want to be certain that you behave."

With the straitjacket securely fastened, Tony thought he would stop breathing. He focused on inhaling and exhaling as he waited in one of the shower stalls for Zody to come back. He was standing up against the shower wall when Zody, Officer Nash, and Officer Geltz stood in the opening of the shower stall. Tony thrashed around, trying to escape the straitjacket.

"See, I told you we'd need that straitjacket tonight, Bruno. Good thing I was thinking ahead, huh?" Zody laughed.

That night, the night before his hearing in court, the three officers sodomized him repeatedly. The pain and shame felt like an endless dark pit. When the men were finished with him, Zody slapped the boy on the ass.

"Tomorrow is your hearing, tiger. I don't expect that you'll be getting away with murder, so I'm sure we'll see you back here until the judge decides where to send you. When you come back, I'm going to teach you some tricks. Little things, you know, that will make you be able to give us a better time. The crying and moaning is good, but we haven't even gotten to all the little pleasures that really make us feel good."

Tony stood, naked, restrained in the straitjacket, his life no longer his own, his soul stolen and kept in a dark box that felt like hell. The little hope he had that the judge would set him free had been extinguished. Now his fear of staying in the detention center escalated. Tony finally opened that door in his mind and looked into the doomed life that waited for him.

***

When Roger saw Tony the next morning, he noticed something about his client had dramatically changed. Tony entered the courtroom; his legs were spread at a distance and he didn't bend his knees as he walked. Tony's eyes darted around as if he was expecting something to jump out at him.

Tony approached the table where he was to sit. "Where's my ma?"

Roger was tense. He dreaded telling the boy, knowing what his mother meant to him. "She called last night. Something happened at home, and she can't make it."

"Oh." Tony lowered his head, but the tears that Roger expected didn't follow.

Roger looked into Tony's eyes. "Are you OK, Tony? You seem jumpy."

Tony lowered his eyes to the table. "I'm fine. Just get me outta here."

The judge walked into the courtroom, and Roger looked over at the prosecutor's table, which was still empty.

"Mr. Taft," the judge began, "I just received a call from the prosecutor's office. The prosecutor's only witness to this horrible crime was found dead in his home early this morning. Given this information, I am dismissing the charges against your client."

"Thank you, your honor."

Roger turned to Tony, who was in a trance. "That's it, Tony."

"What?"

"You're free to go."

Tony made eye contact with Roger. "Great," he said blankly.

"Is everything all right, Tony?"

"Do I have to go back to the detention center?"

"We'll go back to go through some paperwork," Roger explained.

"How long will I be there?"

"Not long. I'll be with you the whole time we're there." Roger touched Tony's shoulder, and the boy jerked away from him. "Come on, Tony. We need to leave. I'll drive you back home after we are finished at the center. How do you feel?"

"Like I ain't never gonna be the same again."

"Is there anything you want to talk about?"

"No. I don't wanna talk about nothin'. I just wanna go home."

Tony had changed in every way possible. The damage was done. The boy was broken. As he walked out of the courtroom, Tony wondered if all the people sitting in the chairs could see all the horrible acts he had been subjected to by the guards. Tony thought he saw disgust in people's eyes as they looked at him. Tony knew then that his time in juvenile detention would haunt him for the rest of his life.

Chapter Thirty-One

T rue to his word, Roger Taft stayed with Tony while he was processed out of the juvenile detention center. Roger worried about Tony's sullen state even after hearing the good news. Tony's eyes roamed around as if he was waiting for something bad to happen. As they left and were walking to Roger's car, Tony noticed Officer Geltz coming in for his shift. Tony stopped dead in his tracks, fear gripping him at his core.

"Is there something you need to tell me?" Roger asked, looking at the officer.

Tony shook his head. "Just take me home."

Roger drove toward Philadelphia. In his heart he knew something bad had happened to Tony, something that was beyond repair.

"Your family is going to be really happy to have you home," Roger said, trying to get Tony to talk.

"Yeah, sure. My mother will be happy."

"Tony, you haven't been gone that long. I want you to go to school and learn everything you can. You stay out of trouble and choose your friends wisely. You're a good kid. You have your whole life ahead of you, and this is your chance to show the world what you're made of."

Tony leaned his head against the passenger-side window. "I ain't never did nothin' wrong. I always been a regular kid. I ain't never gonna forget how bad it was to be locked up."

"That's good, Tony. That should keep you on the straight and narrow so that you never put yourself in a situation where you'd have to go back to prison. You have a lot to offer the world."

As Roger drove through South Philadelphia, Tony looked around him. Nothing had changed in the short time he'd been gone other than him, he was a different person. The familiar places that had once given him joy seemed foreign to him.

Roger parked his car in front of Tony's house. He looked up at the neglected home, sandwiched between two well maintained row homes. On the window frames, the once-red paint was peeled away, revealing the dry, rotting wood beneath. The small porch was cluttered with broken chairs, and the roof was dangerously sagging in the middle. Roger stood at the front door with Tony and knocked softly on the door.

Teresa appeared a few seconds later. "Oh, Tony. Thank God."

Roger stood in the doorway unable to inhale. Teresa's split and swollen lip paled in comparison to her blackened eye.

"Is everything OK, Mrs. Bruno?" Roger asked, staring at her mangled face.

Teresa put her hand up to her face. "Oh, this? Yeah, I'm fine. I came down to get a drink of water in the middle of the night. I slipped on the stairs and smashed my face into the railing. It's not as bad as it looks." She giggled nervously.

Roger didn't believe one word. He turned to Tony. "Well, this is it. You're home now."

"Does Tony gotta do anythin'?" Teresa asked.

"No, Mrs. Bruno. The charges have been dropped. All Tony has to do now is go on with his life and make us proud," Roger said, patting Tony on the back.

"Thanks, Mr. Taft," Tony mumbled.

Teresa gave Roger a hug. "Thank you for takin' care of my boy."

"Sure thing, Mrs. Bruno. I'm happy I could help."

After Roger left the Brunos' home, Teresa took her son into the small living room. She sat on the sofa next to him and took his hand in her own.

"Tony, I gotta tell ya somethin'."

"What?"

"Your father said he don't want cha livin' here no more. He said what cha done to that Rex boy is unforgivable. I argued wit' him the best I could. That's how this happened," she said, gesturing to her face.

"What am I supposed to do, Ma? Where am I gonna go?" Tony practically choked on the words as they fell from his mouth.

"I talked to Vincent's mother. She said ya can sleep on her sofa for a while till we figure out where ya can stay for good. I told her I'll give her a little money to help wit' the food and all, but you'll have to get a job, something ya can do after school so ya can help earn your keep," Teresa explained.

Tony started to cry.

"What is it, baby?" Teresa asked.

"I ain't got nobody in this world. There ain't no place I belong and no one who wants me around. I ain't done nothin' to make this happen. Why, Ma? Why does bad shit always happen to me?"

"Ya can't look at things that way, Tony. Sometimes bad shit happens to good people. Ain't no tellin' what the future will bring. Maybe you're gonna need to be stronger for somethin' else in your life and this is God's way of toughenin' ya up. I don't have the answers, but I want ya to know that I love ya. If I didn't have Macie to worry about, I would fight your father harder."

"Ain't ya afraid he's gonna hurt Macie too? What if he tells ya Macie can't live here?"

"I don't know. I just gotta take it one day at a time." Teresa took a deep breath and put on her most fearless face. "Look, ya ain't a baby. You're thirteen; you can figure this out. I'll help ya. We just gotta be careful your father doesn't find out. I'm afraid he'll kill me next time."

"Did he say he'd kill ya?"

Teresa nodded. "He said if he comes home tonight and finds ya here that he'll kill both of us."

"And you believe him?"

"I wouldn't put anything past your father. I think his heart is black, made of stone. I done all that I could to change his mind about ya, but he won't listen. Ya understand, don't cha, Tony?"

"All I understand is that I was born to a father who hates me, a father who beats my mother just 'cause he can get away wit' it. I understand that I can't live here no more and that I ain't got a family no more. I understand all of it," Tony growled.

"You'll always have me and Macie. I swear. I love you, Tony."

In pure desperation, Tony fell to his knees and put his head in his mother's lap. "Please Ma. Please, don't make me leave. I'm scared. I don't wanna be by myself. I wanna stay here wit' you."

Tony sobbed. His chest went in and out in rapid succession. He cried for all that he'd lost, not just on this day, but for the piece of him he'd lost in prison as well. Teresa put her hand on Tony's head. "Ya need to be brave. It'll all work out, but right now ya need to be strong, like a man. You're gonna be fine."

Tony's mother helped him to his feet and embraced him. He quivered in her arms, and she wished that she had the courage she told Tony he needed. She was putting her son out of her home—or Carmen's home, as her husband put it.

Tony composed himself and wiped his tears with the back of his hand. He stood and walked to the garbage bags on the other side of the room. "Is this my stuff?"

Teresa nodded. "I'm so sorry."

Tony went to his mother and held her tightly. "I know ya don't want this, Ma. I know what it's like to want to have control of somethin' that ya just can't. I learnt it in prison."

Tony left his mother and headed to Vincent's house. On his walk, the chilly night air bit at his face and crept under his clothing. The pain from his broken heart threatened to burst out of him in vicious anguish. He thought about how much his life had changed in the past two weeks. The memories of the guards raping him and forcing him to perform sexual acts on them ran like a horror film in his head. He couldn't feel real physical pain anymore. His manhood had been ripped from his body by three men paid to take care of him. As Tony walked up the porch steps of Vincent's home, he wiped the tears from his cheeks and opened the door.

Chapter Thirty-Two

V incent pulled the front door open and practically jumped into Tony's arms. Feeling ashamed, Tony pulled away and lightly patted Vincent on the back.

"Tony! I'm so glad you're here. Your ma called my ma, and you're gonna stay here for a while. A lot a shit has happened over the past couple a weeks."

"Oh yeah? What kinda shit?" Tony asked, trying to show interest.

"All kinds a shit. Salvatore's gonna meet us at Jim's Steaks tonight. He's been real worried about ya, just like me. Anyway, bring your stuff in, and we'll get going."

Tony dumped his plastic bags in Vincent's bedroom, and they left the house to meet Salvatore. The cold of the night air chilled Tony to his bones. Vincent had been chatting at Tony since he'd arrived and kept on going as they walked to South Street.

"So what was it like in prison?" Vincent asked.

"It was like shit. It was the worst place I've ever been in my life. Bad stuff happens in prison."

Vincent cocked his head to the side. "What do ya mean? What happened that was so bad?"

"I don't wanna talk about it."

"Well, if ya can't tell me, who are ya gonna tell? I'm your best fuckin' friend."

"I know ya are, Vincent. This ain't got nothin' to do wit' bein' friends."

Tony's resentment toward the guards who had abused him bubbled in his belly. In juvie he'd had Dooley to talk to about the sexual abuse. But now, back on the streets of South Philadelphia, he would have no one.

"Let's just say that people ain't so nice. Most of the kids there were a lot older than me. I got my ass kicked by one of 'em. A guy called Dooley who ended up being my cellmate. We sorta became friends before I left. The people who run the place, though, are worse than the nastiest people that roam the streets. They're fuckin' sick whacks that don't even deserve to live," Tony said.

The two boys had walked another block when they spotted Salvatore standing outside of Jim's Steaks. Salvatore extended his hand, and when Tony took it,

Salvatore pulled Tony to him and hugged him, just the way he sometimes saw his father do with his top men.

"I'm sorry about everything, Tony. I'll never forget that you kept your mouth shut about what really happened that night. You're a good friend. I know you've been through a lot."

The sadness in Salvatore's eyes made Tony's insides twist, and a low-grade nausea took root. The boys walked into Jim's Steaks and stared at the line that snaked through the ropes.

Salvatore handed Vincent a twenty-dollar bill. "Tony and I are going upstairs to get a table. Get us three cheesesteaks. OK?"

"Yeah, sure, whatever. I'll be up when I get 'em."

Tony and Salvatore sat at a table that overlooked South Street.

"We don't have much time before Vincent comes up with our food. I know what happened to you in prison. I mean, I don't know everything, but I know what that guard did to you."

Tony flushed. His ears felt like they were on fire. His shame was so profound that he thought he'd implode. Salvatore's words hung heavy in the silence between them. Tony watched Salvatore, waiting to see the repulsion and judgment he was sure would come.

Salvatore shifted in his seat. "I'm sorry that happened to you. When I found out, I told my father if he didn't do something to help you, I would go to the police." He lowered his voice to the slightest whisper and said, "And tell them that I killed Rex."

Tony nodded. He forced back the burning tears. "It was pretty fuckin' bad, man. I mean, it wasn't just one guard—there were three of them."

Salvatore gasped. He locked eyes with Tony. "I don't know how and I don't know when, but we'll get even with those pricks. We might only be teenagers now, but we aren't ever going to forget what they did to you. Do you hear me?"

"Yeah, I hear ya. I lost a piece of myself in that prison. I don't feel like I can be a real man no more. They did shit to me that was really fucked up. They made me do shit to them too. I don't even know who I am anymore, Salvatore. I got jacked up by a bunch of perverted assholes, my father won't let me live at home, and I ain't got nothin' but my mixed-up brains. I can't think right no more. You know, since I was a little kid, it seems like everything that I ain't makes me who I am. That's pretty fucked up."

"I don't get what you mean."

"I ain't loved. I ain't wanted. I ain't needed. I ain't good enough. I ain't normal no more. I ain't got a place to call my own. It's all about what I ain't. See what I'm sayin'?"

Salvatore reflected on Tony's words and then spoke with the wisdom of a fifty-year-old man. "You are a good friend. You are loyal. You are the bravest dude I know. You paid the price for something that I did. You got two great friends.

You got a mother and sister that love you and a father that is an ass fuck. Come on, Tony, you have a lot going for you. Can you see that?"

Tony hands fidgeted with the napkin on the table. "Yeah, sure, I see it."

But, even though Tony understood all the good things that Salvatore had said to him, he felt as though any good had been ripped from him. Tony was lost, and his need to belong somewhere, to something bigger than just himself, became ravenous.

"My father would like you to stop by and see him tomorrow."

Tony's fear antenna went up. "Why's he wanna see me?"

"I don't know. Maybe he wants to thank you. But he wants you to be at our house at noon. You'll be there, right?"

"Yeah, sure, I'll be there."

When Vincent joined them, they ate their steak sandwiches and filled Tony in on a new hot girl in their grade who'd just moved to Philadelphia from Chicago. Tony listened to his friends. He was happy to be with them again, but knowing he had to go see Johnny the next day gnawed at him. What now? Tony thought.

Chapter Thirty-Three

When Tony arrived at the Morano house just before noon the next day, his hands were sweating. He told himself that Johnny would thank him for taking the heat for Salvatore. When Alessandra opened the door, she smiled at Tony. Her sympathetic eyes made him relax slightly.

"It's good to see you again. Johnny is waiting for you in his office," Alessandra said.

"Nice to see you too. Is Salvatore in the office?"

"No, Salvatore had to run an errand for his father. Follow me."

Alessandra tapped lightly on Johnny's office door and opened it so Tony could enter, and then she pulled the door closed behind him.

As Tony waited for Johnny to acknowledge him, he shoved his hands into the pockets of his jeans to keep them from trembling.

Johnny looked up from the paper he seemed to be studying. "Hello, Tony. Come in and sit down." He gestured toward the leather sofa.

Tony sat gingerly on the edge of the seat. "Salvatore said ya wanted to see me."

Johnny took a seat on a leather chair across from Tony.

"Yes. First, I want to let you know that you did the right thing by keeping your mouth shut about my son. The consequences would have been grave if you had said anything."

"I would never rat out Salvatore...or Vincent neither."

"Good. Now, you may have been wondering why the judge set you free."

Tony shrugged his shoulders. "I dunno. My lawyer said the guy who lied about seein' me killing Rex died."

"That's right. The man died so that you didn't have to stay in prison. Do you understand what that means?"

Tony reflected for a moment. His eyes grew wider. "That you got me out?"

"Yes. I personally didn't get you out, but some people I know did. I want you to realize that you are now in debt to me for saving your life by giving you back your freedom. That means that when I need you to do something for me, you will do it without question," Johnny stated firmly.

"Like what kinda stuff will I need to do?" Tony said, squirming.

"We don't need to talk about that right now. When the time comes, you'll know it." Johnny lit a cigarette and placed it in an ashtray. "I understand you had a difficult time when you were in prison. There were some men who bothered you. Is that true?"

Tony wished he could disappear, vanish into the smoky air. He did not want to talk to Johnny Morano about what the guards did to him.

Johnny leaned forward in his chair, his eyes boring into Tony's. "I asked you a question."

Tony nodded and lowered his head. "Yeah, it's true."

Johnny sat back again. "You will need to be strong. You are useless to me in the state you're in right now. So let me set things straight for you. You will dig deep within yourself and get the fuck over it. I don't believe in feeling sorry for yourself. Let what happened to you fuel a spark of anger inside of you. Because here's the thing..." Johnny took another drag on his cigarette. "If you don't, then you will live your life like a sniveling, weak person."

Tony felt a surge of anger and hatred for the men who had violated him and now for Johnny, who was telling him how to be. He wiped his sweating hands on his jeans for a few seconds. His shoulders were tight and neck erect. He slowly turned his head and looked directly at Johnny. "I'll get over it. Ain't nothin' gonna stop me from gettin' what I want."

Johnny smiled. Tony's green eyes were backlit by the fire now burning in his soul.

Chapter Thirty-Four

For the five months that followed Tony's release from prison, he lived at Vincent's house. He only saw his mother and Macie once a week. They arranged to meet in the park or other locations because Teresa feared that her husband would come home and find Tony in the house. Tony continued to go to school, but his grades went from mediocre to bad. He had a hard time concentrating and often fixated on his memories of the abuse.

One night, Tony was hanging out with Salvatore, Vincent and a few girls from their school on the corner of Porter and Opal Streets. Julia, one of the girls, had a crush on Tony for months and was flirting with him. After the two talked for a while, Julia took Tony by the hand, and pulled him to the side of a building. She had leaned in to kiss Tony, when they heard Salvatore yelling.

"Back the fuck off! I'm warning you," Salvatore shouted.

Tony left Julia and raced around the corner.

"What's goin' on?" Tony said, his muscles tense.

"These assholes think they can tell us what to do," Vincent said, gesturing toward five teen boys who were a year ahead of them in high school.

"Oh yeah?" Tony walked up to the boys. "We got a problem?"

"Yeah, we do," Arnie said. "That girl over there wit' your faggot friend," he said pointing to Salvatore, "that's my girlfriend. Now, it looks like I'm gonna have to kick his smelly ass 'cause it ain't right to take another guy's girl out."

Tony's blood boiled, and he walked over to Beth, who was clinging to Salvatore. "Beth, is this little cocksucker over here your boyfriend?"

Beth's eyeballs were bulging out of their sockets. She watched Arnie and his friends, unblinking. She kept slinking behind Salvatore, as though he were a full-body shield. She shook her head. "He won't accept it's over between us," she whispered, keeping her eyes glued to her ex-boyfriend.

Tony didn't like seeing the fear in Beth's face. He knew what that fear felt like. He turned back to Arnie and his friends. "Looks like Beth wants to stay here wit' us. Why don't ya assholes go back into the hole ya crawled outta?"

Arnie grunted. "Ya think you're bad enough to take us, huh?"

Tony moved closer to Arnie. His chest flexed outward, and he edged up to Arnie so close he could smell his rotten breath.

Arnie pulled out a gun and stuck it under Tony's chin. "OK. That's good. Let's do this then." Arnie put his nose against Tony's.

Tony put his hands up above his head. "OK, you win this time. When you wanna come back wit'out that piece of metal in your hands, ya just let me know."

Tony turned and walked back over to Salvatore and Beth. "Let's go, Beth. We're gonna walk ya home."

Arnie and his friends followed at a distance as the six teens walked to Beth's house. Salvatore looked at Beth and gave her a sweet smile. "I'll see you soon, Beth."

Beth looked over her shoulder and nervously back at Salvatore, who was moving in for a good night kiss. However, Beth backed away from Salvatore and ran up the steps and into her house. Satisfied, Arnie and the other boys turned and walked away.

After Tony and his friends walked the last girl to her house, they went back to Salvatore's house for something to eat.

As they walked back to Salvatore's house, Tony was quiet until they were a block away. "What happened tonight wasn't cool," he began. "We was really at a disadvantage. Fucking Arnie, where the hell did he get a gun? We ain't takin' no shit from those douchebags. We need to get our hands on some metal."

"Whata ya mean, Tony?" Vincent asked.

"What I mean is those boys go around school bullying other people. They are even pushin' Beth around—we saw that wit' our own eyes tonight. I think we need guns for protection."

"How are we supposed to do that, Tony? I mean, how are we going to get guns?" Salvatore said.

"I don't know. All I know is I ain't gettin' pushed around ever again," Tony said.

Tony looked at Salvatore and then Vincent. "So what do ya say?"

Salvatore chuckled. "I say you're fucking crazy."

That night, as Tony lay on the sofa in Vincent's living room trying to sleep, his mind raced. He never wanted to be afraid again and was determined to take back his life. He hoped that Vincent and Salvatore would stand with him.

Chapter Thirty-Five

A few days later, Tony stopped at a fast-food restaurant for a cheap meal. He was eyeing up the boy in line directly in front of him. Tony couldn't help but notice the boy's tattoo, and his eyes focused in on it. The tattoo said Slayer.

"What the fuck are ya lookin' at?" the boy growled.

Tony started to perspire under his shirt. "Nothin'. It's just that I was in juvie with a kid that had the same tattoo as you."

"You know Dooley?"

Tony smiled at the connection. "Yeah, I was his cellmate for a while."

"You know what the tattoo means?"

Tony's voice cracked. "Sure, Dooley told me all about it."

"Oh yeah? Dooley don't tell hardly no one. So why all of sudden would he be tellin' you?"

"Some bad shit happened while I was there. Dooley said I needed to belong to something bigger...so that I can protect myself."

"What's your name?"

"Tony. What's yours?"

"Blast. What were ya in juvie for?"

"Cops thought I killed somebody?"

"Did ya?"

Tony shook his head. "Nah, I was just there when it all happened."

"Could ya?"

"Could I what?"

"Could ya kill somebody?"

"I don't know. I could kill those pricks that ran the prison," Tony admitted.

"Yeah, Dooley told us some stories about those guys," Blast said thoughtfully. "You live with your parents or you in a group home?"

"Nah. I'm livin' at my friend's house now. My father don't want me around."

"How's that goin'?"

"It's OK. Vincent, my friend, he's a real good guy, but I don't feel like I got nowhere that's mine."

"Ya wanna come hang out with me at our place?"

"Where do ya live?"

"North Philly. The Slayers run the fuckin' streets there. We don't take no shit from nobody. Since ya know Dooley, I can let ya come and check it out for yourself."

Tony shrugged. "I guess so."

Tony followed Blast onto a bus that took them into North Philadelphia. When they were seated, Tony asked, "How old are ya?"

"Sixteen. What about you?"

"I'll be fourteen in a month."

"The Slayers don't care how old ya are. All we worry about is takin' care of each other 'cause we ain't got families that care. Dooley's been in and out of juvie and group homes for a couple of years. He always finds a way to stay in touch, though. Someday when he gets out, Dooley will take back his position with the Slayers."

"What's his position?"

"Dooley was our leader. Still is in a way. Every once in a while, his mother gets a letter from him to give to us. He gives us ideas on how to make money and shit."

Tony was surprised. "Other than kickin' my ass once, Dooley was a pretty cool dude."

Blast laughed. "You don't know Dooley at all. That motherfucker will kill ya and not think twice about it. On the outside, everybody's afraid of him. Dooley has a black heart and is proud of it."

Tony watched out the bus window. The neighborhoods deteriorated the farther away they drove from South Philadelphia. A few blocks outside of North Philadelphia, he realized he might have made a terrible mistake by going with Blast. Tony sat up straight on the plastic seat.

"Relax, man. You wanna get in a fight or somethin'?" Blast whispered.

Outside the windows of the bus, people staggered, some screaming at each other. The homes were mostly boarded up. It looked like a war-torn country that Tony had seen on the news. There was trash and broken-down cars everywhere. He couldn't believe that people actually lived there. A few minutes later, when they were deep in the heart of North Philadelphia, Blast jumped to his feet.

"This is our stop."

Tony sat motionless for a few seconds, gripping the seat in front of him.

"Look, man, are you comin' or what?" Blast snapped.

Tony hoisted himself to his feet and followed Blast off of the bus. As his sneakers hit the edge of the road, Tony turned around and looked at the bus driver. The driver gave Tony a grave look, shook his head, shut the doors, and zoomed away.

Tony and Blast got off at Somerset Street and walked two blocks before they turned right onto North Water Street. He followed Blast to a brick row home painted dark brown. The paint had chipped away, exposing the brick in random places. Next to the house was a lot filled with large rejected household items, trash, wood, and broken tables and chairs. The house was two stories high. The black-shingled awning across the front of the home was detaching from the brick. Tony looked up. Some windows were boarded up with plywood, and others were gone, leaving large gaping holes in the building. A porch ran the length of the house. Tony stepped over the missing floorboards of the porch. The house to the left was covered in graffiti. Tony's stomach danced, and his instincts told him to run, but he didn't even know where he would run to.

Blast paused at the front door. "Listen, just be cool. My brothers don't take to new people lightly. Ya ready?"

"I guess so. I ain't lookin' for trouble."

"Ha! In this neighborhood trouble finds its way to ya."

Blast opened the front door and walked into a room where teenage boys and girls were sitting. The once-white walls were streaked with stains from leaks on the upper floors. The long wall to the right was covered in graffiti. In the middle was the word SLAYERS, and the artwork design around it included blood, knives, guns, and faces with pointed teeth, and other objects that represented the gang. The room fell silent as they all stared at Tony.

"Who the fuck is this?" Tony looked over at the tall boy with long, curly black hair. He had large brown eyes and full lips. The boy's mouth hung open slightly to reveal his silver front teeth. He was muscular, and his shoulders were set wide.

"Razor, this is Tony. I met him in the city. He knows Dooley. He shared a cell wit' him," Blast explained.

Razor pushed his girlfriend off of him and stood face to face with Tony.

"What do ya want?" Razor said.

"I don't want nothin'. I met Blast, and he asked if I wanted to come here," Tony said, trying unsuccessfully to keep the fear from his voice.

"So it's true ya were wit' Dooley?"

"Yeah. We shared a cell in juvie. He told me about the Slayers."

"If ya met Dooley, then tell me what he's got on his neck," Razor demanded.

"He's got a scar from where someone hit 'im wit' a knife. Told me the guy tried to slit his throat, but one of his boys shot the guy in the head. The scar is from his ear to the bottom of his jaw," Tony explained, running his finger in the spot where Dooley's scar was.

Razor nodded. "Motherfucker almost took our boy out wit' that move. Where ya from?"

"South Philly."

"Oh, look, fellas—we got us a South Philly sissy," Razor taunted.

"What's your problem, man?" Tony snapped. He immediately thought that Dooley had told the gang that he'd been raped in juvie and that they were mocking him.

Razor grabbed Tony around the neck with one hand and guided him across the floor, slamming him up against the wall. "My problem is that I don't like people that I don't know. If ya ain't from North Philly, then ya ain't worth shit."

Blast walked over and put his hand on Razor's forearm. "Come on, Razor. The kid ain't got nobody. He lives at his friend's house 'cause his father won't let him live at home. He's like us—ain't got nobody that cares about him. Besides, he knows Dooley."

Razor released his grip on Tony. "I don't give a fuck about your pathetic life. Ya ain't stayin' here; that's all I'm sayin'. Ya can hang for a while, then get your ass back on the bus and go back to your rotten life. Ya get me?"

Tony rubbed his neck; it was throbbing from Razor's death grip. He looked around the room, and, as if nothing had happened, the teenagers went back to partying and laughing.

"Come on, little man. Let's get a beer," Blast whispered.

Tony had talked with some of the boys, but he was uncomfortable until the second beer kicked in. The alcohol helped relax him, and he talked with them as he had talked to Dooley...cautiously. Hours had passed by the time Tony realized it was dark outside and he needed to get back to Vincent's house.

Tony walked up behind Blast. "Hey, I need to get back to South Philly. Where do I pick up the bus?"

Blast laughed. "I'll tell ya what. A couple of us will walk ya to the bus stop and wait wit' ya. Otherwise ya won't make it outta this place alive. Hell, ya wouldn't be able to walk these streets wit'out one of us in daylight. Someone will definitely kill your ass at night."

Tony felt both embarrassed and relieved. He wanted to protect himself, but he heeded Blast's warning and took him up on the offer for company. Once Tony was seated on the bus, he thought about how lucky the Slayers were to have each other. They were a group of brothers from different mothers, but it didn't matter to any of them. They were each other's family, and Tony wished he could have a feeling of family.

Chapter Thirty-Six

When Tony got off the bus in South Philadelphia, he walked to Vincent's house. As he stepped through the front door, he heard Vincent and his mother, Maria, arguing in the kitchen.

"I can't worry 'bout everyone, Vincent. I told Teresa that Tony could live here as long as she paid me some money to take care of food and stuff. Teresa hasn't given me a dime in the past month," Maria yelled.

"But Ma, he ain't got nowhere else to go. He's my best friend. Tony can give ya some money, and I'll get a job and help out too," Vincent pleaded.

"Oh please, Vincent. Ya boys are barely fourteen. Where ya gonna find a job? Huh? And what about school? Ya wanna grow up to be a dummy?" Maria pressed.

"I don't know where I'll get a job, but I will, and so will Tony. Come on, Ma, please. Where's he gonna go?"

"I don't know. That ain't my problem. You and your brother, Richie, are my problem. I've been working my ass off since your father died. I gotta work three jobs to keep food on this table and a roof over our heads. I can't lose everything because Teresa Bruno don't know what to do wit' her own kid. I like Tony and all, but I can't keep up wit' the cost of havin' 'im here."

"Maybe if Richie got a job instead of hangin' around here all day, he could help pay some of the bills," Vincent said, his temper boiling over.

"Richie ain't none of your business. He ain't as smart as you are, and he ain't got no ambition. Don't worry about Richie; he'll find his way. Besides, it ain't Richie's responsibility to pay for Tony neither. Get it through your head: Tony's gonna have to find another place to live. I'll call Teresa and let her know so that she can make some other arrangements for him. He can stay here for two more weeks, and then he's gotta go," Maria argued.

Tony slumped onto the sofa as Vincent stormed out of the kitchen. He stopped short when he spotted Tony and sat next to his friend.

"We'll figure somethin' out. I'm still gonna try to talk to my mom some more," Vincent said.

"Your ma is right. I ain't her problem. I'm gonna have to figure out a place to go. I can't live at my house. I'll end up in some kinda group home or orphanage or somethin'. I can't go to one of those places. I heard a lot of bad things about what happens to kids there."

Tony paused and sat back against the sofa.

"Maybe Salvatore will have some ideas. Ya know he's always good wit' coming up wit' shit that we don't even think about. Maybe ya can live at his house for a while," Vincent offered.

"Sure, we'll see if he's got any ideas. But there ain't no fuckin' way that I'll be able to stay at his house. Johnny Morano don't like me too much. I can tell."

"Whata ya talkin' about, Tony? Johnny likes ya." Vincent lowered his voice to barely a whisper. "Ya saved Salvatore from going to jail. How can't he like ya?"

"It doesn't matter to him what I did. Your ma said I got two weeks, so I gotta find a place to go. Maybe my father will let me live back in my old house again."

"Yeah! Maybe. That's a good point. We should go over and see your ma in the morning after your father goes to work," Vincent said, excited about a possible solution.

"Nah, you go to school. I'm gonna go over there by myself. I gotta do this on my own."

Tony and Vincent went up the stairs and into the bedroom. Tony walked over to Vincent's bed and dropped back on it, and Vincent plopped down next to him.

"I heard everything ya said to your ma. You're a good friend, Vincent."

"We're best friends, Tony. I ain't never gonna forget that. We'll always be best friends," Vincent said with conviction.

Chapter Thirty-Seven

The next morning, shortly after his father left for work, Tony knocked on the front door of his house. Teresa opened it slowly. Her swollen lip quivered when she saw her son. The sadness and defeat in her eyes gave Tony his answers.

"Hi, Ma. Vincent's ma called ya last night, right?"

Teresa pulled Tony just inside the front door and drew him into her arms. "Yeah, she called. I tried to talk to your father about you comin' back home." Teresa lowered her head, and shame hung over her like a storm cloud waiting to erupt. "He got real upset wit' me."

"Yeah, I can see that," he said, looking at her bruises. "It don't matter anyway; I found a place to live."

"Ya did?"

"Yeah, Ma. I called one of the guys I met in juvie, and his parents said I can stay wit' 'em for a while. Ya ain't gotta worry about me. I'll be fine," he lied.

Teresa hugged Tony tighter. "I'm sorry I can't be a better mother to ya. And I'm sorry that your father is so hardheaded."

"Yeah, I know, he's a big asshole."

"Tony Bruno, ya watch your language. Ya never let that good-for-nothing bast...I mean your father, get under your skin."

Tony smirked. "I gotta go, but I need ya to do me a favor. The kid I'm gonna stay wit' don't live too close to here, so I gotta go to the school near him. Can ya call my school and let 'em know I won't be comin' back? Just tell 'em I moved in with an uncle or somethin'."

"Yeah, I'll do that. Now where exactly are ya stayin'?"

"I don't know the address, but I talked to my friend on the phone. I'll still meet ya at the park every week, though, so we can see each other. Don't worry 'bout me, Ma; I'm gonna be fine."

"OK. I feel better about it knowing that I'll see ya at the park." Teresa leaned over and grabbed her purse from a table near the front door. "Here, ya take this money. Ya gotta have somethin' in your pocket. It's all the money I got right now."

Tony grabbed the small bundle of one-dollar bills, eight in total. "Thanks, Ma. I'll see ya later in the week at our spot. Try and stay out of Dad's way. I swear, I wanna beat the hell outta him for hittin' ya like he does."

"How your father treats me ain't your problem. Ya just focus on gettin' yourself to your new friend's house and get settled. You're a good boy, Tony. Someday you're gonna be a great man—ya remember I told ya that."

With a final hug, mother and son parted. Tony walked down the front steps, and as he walked down his block, he wondered, where will I go now?

Chapter Thirty-Eight

Two weeks later, Tony grabbed his plastic trash bags filled with his clothes and left Vincent's house. He stood at the front door with Vincent and his mother, Maria.

"I'm sorry, Tony. I just can't afford another mouth to feed."

"It's OK. Ya know we talked about all this, and I'll be fine," Tony said. "I appreciate ya lettin' me stay here for all this time."

Vincent moved forward and gave Tony a hug. "When am I gonna see ya? Ya ain't goin' to our school no more, and ya won't be livin' in the neighborhood. It makes me feel like shit."

"What are ya talkin' 'bout? I'll see ya. I'll be around. Somebody gotta keep you and Salvatore in line," Tony joked.

"Yeah, but it ain't gonna be the same wit'out ya here." Vincent lowered his head; he didn't want Tony to see his eyes welled with tears.

Tony put his arm around Vincent's shoulder and squeezed. "I gotta go. I'll see ya soon. I promise."

Tony left quickly. He walked to the empty lot where he'd been hanged from a tree by his now-best friend, Vincent. As he entered the lot, he remembered his mother's stories about the googamongers. When he was young, he'd been so scared of the unknown creatures that ate children. Now, knowing that the googamongers never existed, his heart felt damaged thinking about how cruel real people can be.

Tony schlepped his bags into the first floor of the abandoned building. He looked around him. The downstairs rooms were empty. The old wallpaper hung in shreds, and the hardwood floor was coated in a thick layer of dirt. He found stairs in the back of the building and followed them up to the second floor. Six doors were on either side of the narrow hallway, old entries to apartments. The only remnants of the people who had once lived here were random stoves and toilets.

In some apartments, there were blankets and stained pillows—Tony's confirmation that some of the people he'd followed slept there. He continued to the third floor. There were six more apartments. Tony crept through the building to an apartment in the far back corner. He pushed the creaky door open. There were openings in the walls where glass had once shielded the inside from the outside. Years of tree debris was scattered over the floor, thanks to the wind that carried unwanted limbs and leaves inside the building. Tony laid his plastic bags on the floor and sat next to them. He pulled his knees to his chin.

"I am the googamonger. I guess my ma was right—the googamonger did eat me, and now I am one," he said aloud.

Tony left his belongings and headed down to the Italian Market. He still had the eight dollars his mother had given him, and he needed to make the most of it. He bought half-rotted fruit from a vendor. Then he made his way over to a bakery. A bell over the door chimed as he entered the store. The short Italian woman behind the counter looked toward the door, and her eyes washed over him.

"How can I help ya?"

"I need to buy some bread or something. I need, um, do you have any that's a couple days old for cheaper?"

The woman put her hands on her hips. "I've seen ya in the market before. Your ma send ya here?"

Tony shook his head. "No. I'm livin' wit' my uncle now, and we need some food."

"OK," the woman said. "Come over here and pick somethin' out."

As Tony was looking at all the breads and pastries, a younger girl limped out from the back of the store. As she got closer, Tony noticed the sneaker on the end of her fake leg peeking out of the bottom of her skirt. He tried not to stare, but he couldn't help himself. He was fascinated. The girl, who looked to be about nine, smiled at Tony as she gimped over to her grandmother.

"This is my granddaughter, Ruth."

"Hi, Ruth."

"What's your name?"

"Tony."

"Nice to meet cha, Tony. This is my grandma; her name is Donata," Ruth said with a smile that warmed his heart. "How come ya look so sad?" she asked innocently.

"I ain't sad. I just gotta buy some stuff and get home," Tony responded.

"Well, ya look sad to me," Ruth said as she limped past him and went back behind the counter.

Tony turned to the woman. "Is this all old stuff? I don't have a lot of money."

"Just go ahead and pick somethin' out. I ain't got all day."

"How much for that big loaf of pepperoni bread?"

Donata removed it from the counter and wrapped it in brown paper. She handed the loaf to Tony.

"How much do I owe ya?" he asked.

"This one is on the house. If ya need more, ya come back and see me, and we'll figure out a price that works," she said, giving Tony a sympathetic smile.

"Thanks. I appreciate it." Tony started to walk out of the store but stopped short before leaving. "Hey, Donata?"

"Yeah, what is it?"

"Thanks for the bread. I won't forget how nice ya been." He looked at the little girl. "I'll see ya around, Ruth."

The old woman gave Tony a sorrowful look. "Yeah, sure, that's what they all say. Now go on home to your uncle's. Ya be safe—ya hear me?"

Ruth waved and called out, "Bye Tony. See ya again real soon."

Tony thought about Ruth and her grandmother as he walked back to the abandoned building, just a few blocks from where his family lived. Something horrible had happened to the little girl, Ruth, something that made her less than perfect. She had a physical defect, yet she had so much more than he did. Ruth had the love of her grandmother, a place to live, and food to eat. Ruth was happy, and in a small way her vibrant spirit had touched Tony dramatically, and that made him feel a little better about himself. It was his first day on his own, and he'd found a place to live temporarily and had already made two new friends. He hoped that Ruth and her grandmother were a sign that his life was about to get better.

Chapter Thirty-Nine

When Tony got back to his place in the abandoned building, he opened the brown paper and pulled off a piece of the pepperoni bread. He gobbled it down and then ate one apple from his bag of fruit. He sat alone with only the sound of the almost-bare trees rustling outside.

Tony was thinking about the night that Officer Zody had raped him in the shower. His stomach tightened, and it felt as though the food he had eaten was spinning in his belly.

"Who the fuck are you?" a man yelled.

Tony stood quickly and faced a man with long, greasy, black-and-gray hair. The man was as tall as Tony, and his clothes hung from his body, making him appear even thinner than he was. The man glared at him with authority.

"Ya own the place?" Tony said.

"No, but this is where a bunch of us live sometimes. We don't need no more freeloaders. Ya get me?" the angry man said.

"Look, Mister. I need a place to stay. I ain't got nowhere else to go. Besides, if ya don't own the place, then ya don't get to make the rules," Tony said with cautious bravery.

The man looked at Tony's belongings, and his eyes stopped on the bag of fruit. Tony saw the look of hunger, and he suddenly had a stroke of guilt.

"Ya hungry?" Tony said.

"Yeah. I ain't eaten nothin' since yesterday mornin'."

Tony unwrapped the brown paper and ripped off a hunk of pepperoni bread. He handed it to the man, who snatched it from Tony's hand and bit off a large piece.

"Don't think 'cause ya gave me a piece of bread it's gonna change anythin'. Ya can't be stayin' up in here. Lots of grown people squat in this buildin', and there ain't no room for little boys."

"Listen, Mister—I ain't no little boy. I'll be fourteen in a couple of weeks. I've been through a lot of bad shit in my life, and I don't want no shit from you," he growled.

The man chuckled until he was in a full belly laugh.

"What the fuck are ya laughin' at?" Tony yelled.

"Ya ain't old enough to even know what bad shit life can bring your way. You remember what I just said—lots of grownups squattin' here, and ain't none of 'em gonna want a kid around." The man turned to leave. "What's your name, kid?"

"Tony," he said solemnly.

"Well, Tony, I'm Erikson. If ya wanna stay safe tonight, I suggest ya sleep wit' your back to the door. That way ya know if someone is coming in on ya."

Erikson noticed that Tony's demeanor didn't change throughout their exchange. Tony wasn't some kid who had just ran away from home, and his instincts told him there was truth behind his comments about having a troubled life. That night, without Tony knowing, Erikson slept in the hall just outside of the door where Tony was staying, to watch over him.

In the morning, Tony shoved his bags and food into the corner of a doorless closet in the bedroom. As he walked through the hallway, he could see there were other people lying on the floor. He wondered how he'd been lucky enough to make it through the night without someone trying to share the space he was staying in. He brushed off the thought and started down the stairs. When he was on the second floor, there were people in the hall.

"Hey, no fuckin' kids allowed here!" an angry woman grumbled.

"Yeah," her husband chimed in. "There are other places for kids to go. Don't be takin' up our space."

"But I need somewhere to stay too. Ya ain't the boss here. So just leave me alone," Tony said.

"I'm the boss if I say I'm the boss," the woman retorted.

The woman stomped down the hall toward Tony, and he backed up against the wall. Even though she was a woman, he was prepared to defend himself if he had to. Then, Tony saw a man quickly follow her. Tony's limbs tingled as he eyed the large white man rushing at him.

"Whoa!" Erikson shouted and ran to stand next to Tony. "Leave the boy alone. He ain't doin' nobody no harm."

"Shut up, Erikson, ya fuckin' dopehead. Ya high again?" Sadie accused.

"Fuck you, Sadie. Ya ain't the boss of nobody here, and ya know it. Right, fellas?"

Some of the other homeless men who had gathered in the hallway to watch, nodded. Others shook their heads and went back into their rooms, not wanting any trouble.

"We all agreed when we started comin' here that we ain't gonna have no kids in this place. Kids invite trouble, and trouble invites cops," Sadie argued.

"I know what we all decided, Sadie. Ya ain't gotta remind me. Just remember that I was the one who brought you and Kevin here in the first place. If it wasn't for me, ya woulda froze to death last winter. I say this kid is different. We need to give 'im a chance," Erikson said.

Sadie cocked her hip to one side and pointed in Erikson's face. "If he stays, then he's your problem. If the cops come here, I'll make sure that nobody lets you back in. Don't give a flyin' fuck if ya brought me and Kevin here or not. It's already gettin' cold outside, and the rest of us need to be able to stay here to get through the winter."

"That's fine. I'll take care of the kid. He'll stay wit' me," Erikson said defiantly.

"That's fine wit' us, but if ya want 'im to stay, then ya can stay upstairs in that apartment. There ain't no room for 'im down here," Sadie said.

"Ya know, Sadie, ya can be a real bitch when ya wanna be. That's fine. I'll stay up in 3F wit' 'im. I ain't scared. I don't believe none of that shit anyway," Erikson said loudly to make sure that everyone heard him. He turned to Tony. "Come on, kid. Let's go get some fresh air."

When Tony and Erikson were outside, they walked a few blocks in silence.

"What's wrong wit' the apartment I'm stayin' in?"

As the two kept walking, Erikson gazed over at Tony with his large, piercing blue eyes.

"People think that apartment is haunted. There was a couple and their two kids that got murdered in that apartment 'bout fifteen years ago. After the crazy fucker killed 'em, he cut their heads off and hung 'em from the shower curtain bar." Erikson looked up into the sky. "The kids' heads too. They never caught who killed 'em, never understood why he did it neither. The sick bastard left a note, though. It said, 'All children who live here will die here.'"

Tony stopped and gave Erikson a baffled look. "That's pretty fucked up."

"There's more," Erikson said. "The reason why all the tenants moved out in a hurry is 'cause after that family was killed, a woman and her eight-year-old son moved in. They didn't know nothin' 'bout the murders that happened. The news people don't tell ya 'bout the murders where the poor people live. Anyway, that woman and her son disappeared a couple of days after they moved in."

"Maybe they just left," Tony offered.

"They found all their fingers shoved in a plastic bag hangin' over the kitchen sink. Twenty fingers in all, ten big ones and ten tiny ones. After that the owner had to close the building—landlord couldn't rent an apartment. All the tenants moved out real fast. None of the homeless people will sleep in 3F." Erikson paused, letting the gruesome details sink in.

"It ain't so cold right now, but in the next month it's gonna get freezin'. You and me are gonna need to board up those windows. We gotta get some paint so we can make the boards black; otherwise someone will notice that we put wood in 'em."

"Are ya afraid to stay in that apartment?" Tony said.

"Nah. I ain't afraid of much. I've been wandering these streets for the past ten years. "This here..." Erikson said, gesturing around him, "this is my playground. It's my home. This is where I belong. I've been sleeping in that apartment building for the past six winters. I call it my winter getaway."

"Your winter getaway just got moved to apartment 3F wit' me. Sorry 'bout that, Erikson. I didn't wanna cause ya any trouble. I just needed a place to stay for a while is all."

"How long is a while, kid?"

"I don't know. I hope only a few weeks, maybe a month. I ain't exactly thrilled about livin' in some old building that ain't got no heat or runnin' water—I can tell ya that much."

Erikson grabbed Tony's shoulder. "We need to get somethin' to eat. Ya might be just the thing I needed. A young buck like yourself will make a lot more beggin' than I ever can."

"Beggin'? Nah, I don't wanna do that."

Erikson's eyebrows crinkled as he stared into Tony's eyes. "Oh yeah? Ya got a better idea?"

Tony thought about it for a moment. "Nah, I guess not."

"Are ya hungry?"

"Yeah," Tony said with a heavy sigh.

"If ya wanna eat, then we gotta make money. Remember, I'm the fella that's gotta sleep wit' cha in the apartment of death."

"I know. Thanks again for doin' that."

"Sure. Ain't no big deal, kid. But from here on out, you gotta take care of me just like I took care of you. It's only fair. Don't cha agree?"

Tony appreciated Erikson's offer, but he couldn't stop thinking about how easily Officer Zody had lured him into his sick sex trap. His muscles tightened, and his jawline was prominent. Erikson noticed the visible change in Tony. He suspected there was more to the kid than he let on. He also knew that Tony was much stronger than the boy gave himself credit for.

Erikson cleared his throat. "I don't know what cha think I'm talkin' about, but I'm talkin' about sharing our stuff. Ya know, like our money, food, blankets, and shit like that."

Tony relaxed and nodded. "I can do that. I mean, we can do that. All right, teach me how to beg."

Chapter Forty

When they got to Center City, Tony sat on the sidewalk with his hands cupped. He looked up at people with puppy dog eyes just the way Erikson had taught him.

"Excuse me, Miss, I'm real hungry," Tony recited.

He recited the words, alternating Miss and Mister. Most people sped up their pace or moved closer to the street as they approached just to avoid him. It seemed as though thousands of people walked by him that morning, but only six people threw change into his cupped hands. After a couple of hours, Tony walked down the block to where Erikson was waiting for him.

"How did ya do?"

"I made three dollars and fifteen cents," Tony said miserably. "Beggin' is bullshit work, and I ain't doin' that no more. People make ya feel like dog shit, pretendin' they can't hear ya and actin' like I got cooties or somethin'."

Erikson patted Tony on the back. "Yeah, I hear ya. But hey, ya made us a little money. Let's go get somethin' to eat."

When Tony and Erikson walked into a small donut shop, the owner looked up at them. "Can I help you?" he asked quickly.

"We're lookin' to buy some donuts. Which are your cheapest ones?" Erikson said.

"They're all the same price. A buck and a quarter a donut or three for three dollars."

"Can ya give us a better deal?" Tony asked.

"What? Do you think you're at a flea market where you can bargain?"

Tony's shame washed over him. "Come on, Erikson—let's just leave."

The store owner zeroed in on Tony. The boy was dirty and disheveled. He'd seen kids like Tony many times before, but the kid's warm green eyes gave him a stab of sympathy.

"Here's what I can do. I'll give you three donuts at half price, a buck fifty."

"See! Now that's what I'm talkin' 'bout," Erikson exclaimed. "God bless you, sir, and thank you."

As Tony and Erikson walked toward the park, they ate their donuts as the older man explained life on the streets.

"Erikson, like I said before, I ain't gonna be livin' like this for a long time. I'm gonna find a place to work and get my own place."

"Oh yeah? Who the hell ya think is gonna rent a place to an almost-fourteen-year-old?"

"I don't know, but somebody will. I ain't got it all figured out yet," Tony said adamantly.

"Whatever you say, kid. So where ya gonna get a job?"

"Why ya always askin' me so many questions? It ain't like ya got your life all figured out, or ya wouldn't be livin' in an abandoned building," Tony snapped.

Erikson smoothed down the hair on his overgrown beard. "You're right. I ain't nobody to judge. I think it's good that ya want somethin' better for yourself. There ain't nothin' wrong wit' havin' dreams."

Erikson stopped walking and grabbed Tony by the arm.

"What?" Tony said.

"If you're gonna dream big, then I gotta give ya one piece of good advice. Don't cha ever take any drugs, 'cause once ya start, ya won't be able to stop. Ya see what I'm sayin'?"

"Is that what Sadie was sayin' this mornin' when she asked if ya were high again?"

Erikson nodded. "Started smokin' crack 'bout seven years ago. I was able to keep my job, hidin' it for a while, but after a year, I couldn't keep it together no more. Nothin' is more important than gettin' high. Ya need to remember that, 'cause once that monster gets ya, there ain't no gettin' away from it."

"How do ya buy drugs if ya ain't got no money?"

"I do stuff for people. Before I got hooked, I was a carpenter, a really good one. Even now, I work for people and make a little money sometimes. When shit breaks at my dealer's house, I fix it, and he gives me drugs in exchange for my work. Sometimes I gotta steal dope or steal from stores, like a sweater or some jewelry or somethin', and one of my dealers will exchange for dope. It all depends, but trust me, when ya gotta get high, there's always a way. So promise ya won't do drugs, not even if someone tries to give 'em to ya for free. That's how they get ya hooked, see? So promise me."

"Ya ain't gotta worry about me doin' drugs, Erikson. I've spent my whole life feelin' like I ain't never had control of nothin'. I don't wanna take anythin' that's gonna make me feel like I lost the little control I got."

"Promise!"

"Yeah, sure, I promise. You ain't gotta be so pushy all the time, old man," Tony said and poked Erikson in his chest. "How old are ya, anyway?"

"Thirty-three," he said sadly. "Ya have a good head on your shoulders. You're right in thinkin' 'bout gettin' a job—maybe ya can make somethin' of yourself. When ya do, just don't forget your friend Erikson."

"Nah, I don't forget nobody that helps me. I don't forget nobody that hurts me neither."

When the two arrived at the park, Erikson sat on a small plot of grass, and Tony sat next to him. It wasn't long before some of Erikson's dealer friends approached. Several tried to give Tony a free hit of crack, but he turned them down flat. Meanwhile, Erikson had negotiated two bags of crack in exchange for repairing a door in the home of a dealer.

Erikson went over to where Tony was sitting on a bench and sat down next to him. "I gotta go. I have some work to do at a dealer's house. Let's go."

"Wait. I don't wanna go to no dealer's house."

"Ya ain't goin' there, ya dipshit. We're goin' back to the apartment where I stash my tools."

"Oh. Are ya gonna get drugs?"

Erikson nodded guiltily. "Don't worry. I'll try and get us some money to buy a little food."

When they arrived back at their apartment, it was almost dinnertime. Tony helped Erikson move his tools and meager belongings up to 3F.

"Ya still got some food left, right?"

Tony looked in the bag of rotting fruit. "Yeah, I got enough for now."

"All right, then I'll see ya later."

"When will ya be back?" Tony asked.

"Later, kid. I don't know what time, but I'll be back."

When Erikson left, Tony sat on the floor of what was once the small living room. He rifled through his bags of clothes and layered on shirts to keep him warm from the cold October evening. Then he arranged his two plastic bags so he could sleep on top of them. As he laid his head down, the rustling of the bags alerted his senses. He stared above the kitchen sink and imagined the fingers hanging in a bag. He cringed as warm, intense tingling prickly heat covered his arms and chest. Fearful again, he rolled over on his side to face the wall, hoping that Erikson would come back soon.

Chapter Forty-One

The next morning when Tony woke up, Erikson was snuggled up next to him. Tony pushed Erikson away from him with a fury.

"Get the fuck off me," Tony screamed.

Erikson sat up slowly. "What's your problem?"

"I don't want ya layin' all over me," Tony stated.

"Ya know, Tony, not everybody wants to hurt cha. I was sleepin' close so we could make body heat to keep us warm. I ain't like that. Ya musta had some real asshole do some fucked-up shit to ya. Am I right?"

Tony stood and walked over to the other side of the room. He sat back down, leaning against the wall. "Yeah, I had...I had some guys do things to me."

"Your dad?"

"No, he's just a violent prick. I was sent to juvie for a while for somethin' I didn't do."

"The older boys do somethin' to ya there?"

"No." Tony paused, not sure if telling Erikson would make him more vulnerable. "Some of the guards did things."

Erikson got up and sat next to Tony. "They touch ya where they shouldn't have?"

Tony nodded. Tears fell from his eyes, and his chest heaved. Erikson put his arm over his shoulder.

"It's all right, Tony. Ya wanna talk about it?"

Tony shook his head but told Erikson the whole story anyway. When he was finished, the older man slumped against the wall. Living on the streets for so many years, Erikson had seen a lot of things, mostly girls being taken advantage of, but he wasn't prepared for the extent of abuse that Tony had described. He took a moment to collect his thoughts as Tony sat there regretting he'd told the story.

"Here's the deal, Tony. In life we gotta go through bad stuff. Ya can't let those bad things make ya who ya are. When ya get into trouble, the kinda trouble you've been in, then ya gotta learn somethin' from it. I ain't known ya for too long, but I already know that you're gonna be somethin' special when ya grow up. Now, wit' all that ya been through, ya gotta take that pain and turn it into somethin' bigger than ya. Someday, ya might find that someone else needs your help, and you're gonna help 'im 'cause ya know what it's like to be in pain."

"I hope you're right. 'Cause I don't feel like I can do nothin' right. When I was a kid, I was picked on all the time by kids in school and my father at home. I always thought I was bein' hurt real bad, but those guards taught me what pain is really about. I ain't talkin' 'bout the kinda pain that makes your skin hurt; I'm talkin' 'bout the kinda pain that sinks way down into your bones and becomes a part of ya. No matter how much ya try to get better, it stays inside ya and tears ya up. It makes your heart hurt, and sometimes I just wanna die."

"Die? No, kid. That ain't somethin' ya die over. Gettin' abused like ya did gives ya courage to move forward. We're all afraid of movin' forward 'cause we don't know what the future will bring. It ain't about layin' down and dyin', though. If ya did that, then those rotten pricks who assaulted ya would win. You're a winner, and ain't nobody, nowhere that can tell ya different. I feel like a weak boy next to ya. I had bad things happen to me, but I brought them on myself when I got hooked on dope. You, on the other hand, ya never asked for any of it, but ya never let it stop ya. I got high hopes for ya, Tony. I know you're gonna find your way to everything ya want in life, no matter what it is."

Tony rested his head on Erikson's shoulder. "Thanks, man. I appreciate ya listenin'."

Erikson rested his head on Tony's. "So, what's your plan for today?"

"I'm gonna go out and find a way to make money."

"If ya say so, then I believe ya will," Erikson said, rubbing his hand over Tony's greasy hair. "Ya might wanna see if ya can find a shower. You're a dirtball."

Tony laughed. "Yeah, I get it from you."

Erikson looked at his own hands. His fingernails were packed with filth, and the backs of his hands were covered with days of dirt.

Tony got to his feet. "I'll catch ya later."

"Sure. Be safe kid."

As Tony left the building, he felt a renewed sense of hope. It was the first time he'd talked to an adult that cared about what had happened to him in the juvenile detention center. Erikson's reaction had replaced his feeling of weakness with a feeling of strength.

Chapter Forty-Two

Tony walked toward the Italian Market. His right hand was in his pocket, and he wrapped his fingers around the money that his mother had given to him. He hadn't told Erikson about the six dollars he still had left, and a pang of guilt struck him.

Tony made his way to the bakery, and when he stepped inside, the warmth of the heat soothed his skin.

Donata looked up from behind the counter. "Well, look who it is."

"Hi, Donata," Tony said, excited that she was happy to see him again.

Ruth, who had been bent over filling the bottom of the display case, stood and peeked over the counter. "Tony! Hi, Tony. Me and my grandma tried a new cookie recipe this morning. You wanna taste one?"

"Sure I do, Ruth." Tony took the cookie and bit into its sweet substance, which dissolved over his tongue, making his taste buds dance. "Ummmm, this is delicious. Best cookie I ever had."

Ruth giggled. "Yeah, I said the same thing. Right, Grandma?"

Donata gave the young girl a loving smile.

"Anyway," Ruth said, "Are you here to buy something?"

"You bet. What cha got?"

Ruth pointed to the display case. The pastries all seemed too rich for Tony's pocket, but he listened intently as she described what things were and what they were made of.

"How come ya ain't in school, Ruth?"

"After the accident, when I moved in with my grandma, she decided to homeschool me."

Tony looked over at Donata.

"Kids can be cruel," Donata said.

"Yeah, don't I know it."

Donata moved closer to Tony. "Why aren't you in school?"

Tony smiled. "I get homeschooled too."

"I bet ya do," Donata said. "Let's see what we can get for ya."

Donata took two cupcakes and three cookies from the display case. Then she came out from behind the counter and grabbed a loaf of olive bread. "These should hold ya...and your uncle for a couple of days."

"How much?"

Donata pretended to add the items up in her head. "A dollar."

"Wow. That's a great deal." A second later Tony realized that all those things couldn't cost just one dollar, and his embarrassment silenced him for a moment.

"Ya know, I could do work for ya, if ya want. I can stand out here and sell stuff for ya."

Donata gave Tony an intense stare.

Tony gulped. "Never mind. I was just asking; ain't no big deal."

"No, no, I was thinkin'. Ya can't be out here 'cause ya don't know how things work. But I could use help in the kitchen, cleanin' up. Two hours a day. I can pay ya a dollar an hour," Donata offered.

The old woman was making enough money to take care of her granddaughter. She decided that ten dollars a week wouldn't bankrupt her. Besides, Donata suspected that Tony had nowhere to live and that he was lying about his uncle. She liked that the boy was humble and willing to work.

Tony hadn't answered Donata. He was still stunned that she'd offered him a job.

Donata put her hands on her hips. She took Tony's silence as negotiation. "OK, fine. I'll pay you, and give ya some pastries or bread."

"Wow, Donata. Thank you. That'd be great. When can I start?"

"How about now? I have a ton of dirty pans back there."

Ruth took Tony into the back of the bakery and showed him around. She gave him an apron and filled the deep sink with warm, soapy water. "Make sure the water is always real warm. If Grandma catches you washing with cold water, she'll get real mad."

"I got it, Ruth."

Alone in the kitchen, Tony got busy washing the pans. When he was finished two hours later, he went to the front of the store.

"All done, Donata. I'll see ya tomorra."

"Wait. Don't ya wanna get paid?"

Tony laughed. "Oh yeah. I guess I'm so happy to have a job that I forgot."

Donata handed Tony two dollars and a bag of baked goods. Tony turned to leave, but stopped short. "I owe ya a dollar for all this."

"Nope. We're even for today. I'll see ya tomorra."

Chapter Forty-Three

When Tony walked into the apartment, he found Erikson still sleeping, but the squeaky floorboards woke him. Erikson sat up, still in a slumber. He rubbed his eyes, hacked up phlegm, and spat it onto the floor.

"Ya look like shit," Tony said.

"Ya smell like shit," Erikson said and lay back down.

"Come on. Get up. I got us some food."

Tony opened the bag of baked goods and waved them under Erikson's nose.

"Goddamn, that shit smells good."

"It is good—in fact, it's great. Get up. Let's eat."

Erikson struggled into a sitting position, and Tony handed him a cupcake. He took a big bite.

"Druggies love sugar. Did ya know that?"

"Everybody loves sugar," Tony said with a mouthful of cupcake.

"Yeah, but we crave it like we crave dope."

"Why do ya keep doin' drugs?"

"Gives me great internal pleasure," Erikson stated.

"Whatever that means."

"You're right. I don't know why I said that; it was stupid. I do drugs because they're addicting. Once ya get high smokin' crack, ya can't get enough of it. You're always chasing that very first high. The first time is the best, but ya can't ever get it back again. It's like havin' sex wit' a woman for the first time."

Erikson regretted saying the words the minute they had left his mouth, but Tony looked at him confused.

"What's that like?"

"Havin' sex wit' a woman?"

"Yeah."

"Like the greatest thing you'll ever feel—that is, if ya love her. Man, when ya make love to a woman ya love, it's like...it's like swimming in a pond filled with silk. It ain't easy to describe, but someday when ya find a woman ya love, you'll understand."

"Do ya think that what happened to me in juvie changed me?"

"Changed ya how?"

"Maybe I won't be able to be in love wit' a woman."

"That's bullshit. I watched ya eyeing up those two girls in the park yesterday. They were cute, and you were watching them. How did that make ya feel?"

Tony blushed. "They were hot. I don't know—it made me feel like I wanted to talk to them." Tony blushed deeper. "I thought about what it would be like to kiss the one wit' the dark hair."

"Well, there ya have it. That proves that you're into women. But ya know, even if ya were into men, it wouldn't mean anythin' is wrong wit' cha. Those assholes in juvie are freaks; that's all about bein' into kids."

In his head, Tony agreed. "Ya want some olive bread?"

"Hell yeah!"

"So guess what else? I got a job today too. I'm workin' at one of the bakeries in the market. Donata is gonna pay me a dollar an hour for two hours a day, and she's gonna give me some of the shit she bakes."

"Little dude! You're awesome. Look at ya, one day out on your own and ya got a job and a steady stream of food. I told ya that you'll be somethin' great someday. Ever think 'bout what cha wanna be when ya grow up?"

"I know I wanna go after bad guys," Tony said with confidence.

"Maybe you'll be a cop."

"Nah. I wanna go after bad guys and teach 'em a lesson. Cops can't teach ya a lesson; they can only send ya to prison."

"Maybe you'll be a spy and give information to the government 'bout where the assholes live."

"I don't wanna do that either."

"Well, then what?"

"I wanna hurt bad people. I wanna make them suffer for making other people suffer."

"That sounds dangerous. Ya wanna be a vigilante."

"What's a vig-a-an-tee?"

Erikson laughed. "A vigilante. A person who takes the law into their own hands. Punishes people the way they decide they should be punished."

"Yeah, I wanna be somethin' like that. I don't know exactly what yet, but I wanna be able to do things my way. I'm already makin' a list of people, and if you're not nice to me, I'll add your name to it," Tony joked.

Erikson put his hands up, palms facing Tony. "Hey, I don't wanna be on nobody's bad list. Especially not yours. That sizzle behind your eyes tells me that you're gonna do what cha wanna do. I'll stay on your good side, thank ya."

Erikson stood and brushed off his dirty clothes. "I'm headin' out."

"Where ya goin'?"

"I'm goin' to find..." Erikson cut off his words.

"You're gonna go out and get high, right?"

Erikson nodded, but he diverted his gaze, ashamed of his addiction.

"Why don't cha try and stop doin' that stuff?"

"I told ya—once ya start, it's impossible to stop. That's why ya never, ever, and I mean never, try drugs."

Tony put his hands over his ears and hummed as Erikson stared at him.

"I heard ya the first time. I ain't never gonna do drugs, OK?" Tony asserted.

That night, as Tony lay on his bags of clothes, he thought about the people who had been murdered in apartment 3F and tried to imagine what they looked like. He realized it could have happened in the very spot where he was lying. His anger began as a slow simmer, and he wanted to find and kill the person who'd slaughtered those people who once lived in his only real home.

Chapter Forty-Four

The next morning at the bakery, Donata brought Tony back into the kitchen. She led him over to a small table in the corner. Tony looked down and saw towels, soap, and shampoo.

"Go through that door." Donata pointed. "There's a laundry basin back there where ya can get cleaned up. It'll give ya some privacy. After you're done washing up, then ya can get started on the dirty dishes." She started to walk away, "Make sure ya leave the basin the way ya found it...clean."

Donata quickly went to the front of the store, and Tony moved toward the door carrying the supplies and towels. Tony shut and locked the door behind him and quickly took off his clothes. He washed his hair first, leaning over the tub like he had seen his mother do in the kitchen sink when she dyed her own hair. Lathering up the washcloth, he rubbed the soft fabric over his body. When he was finished, he felt as if twenty pounds of grime had been lifted from him. The only thing he regretted was he hadn't brought his toothbrush with him, but when he opened the door, Ruth was standing outside. She looked up at him.

"Grandma said you need these."

Tony took the toothbrush and toothpaste from Ruth and went back inside the small room. The toothpaste stung his gums, but it was a good burn, a burn of clean.

Tony did his work with a joy he hadn't felt in a long time. He felt cleaner, he had a place to live, and he had met some strangers who had a positive impact on him. When he was finished for the day, he headed back to the abandoned apartment building.

"Tony!"

Tony turned to see his mother on the sidewalk behind him and went to her.

"Hi, Ma."

"Where are ya comin' from?"

Lifting the bag of pastries he said, "A bakery."

Teresa hugged Tony, and she could smell the sweet scent of the shampoo he had used. It gave her reassurance that her son was doing OK at his friend's house.

"That family you're livin' wit' treatin' ya good?"

"Sure they are. They're real nice. The dad talks to me a lot."

"That's good. When am I gonna see ya?"

"I'll meet ya at the park next week like we always do."

"I worry about cha, Tony."

"Ya ain't gotta worry. I'm doin' fine. Better than fine."

"Your birthday is next week. I can't believe you're gonna be fourteen already. I'll bring your present to the park wit' me."

"That'll be great," Tony said, happy that his mother remembered his birthday.

"I gotta go. I have to get dinner started before your father comes home," Teresa said.

"Maybe you can crush up some glass and stick it in his food," Tony remarked.

"Tony Bruno, don't go talkin' like that. Hurtin' people ain't the answer to nothin'. Your father will have to answer to God for all the things he does. So ya make sure that ya treat people good, 'cause someday you'll have to answer to God too."

"When I get to heaven, I'm gonna have a lot of questions that I want God to answer," he said defiantly.

"God don't need to answer to nobody. Ya gotta keep him in your heart and know that he makes everything happen for a reason. Things might not be the way ya want 'em right now, but God has a bigger plan for ya...for all of us."

Tony gave his mother a hug and said good-bye. There was no use in arguing with Teresa over her beliefs. It was her strong conviction she was living God's plan by staying with Carmen. Tony thought the whole idea was ridiculous. Tony had decided in juvie that if there was a God, he didn't keep watch over every single thing that happened to every person. Otherwise, why would he let those guards do those terrible things to him?

It was later than normal when Tony arrived back at the apartment building. He had only been in apartment 3F for a few minutes when Erikson came in.

"Hey, Tony, ya got any sweets?"

Tony handed him the bag from the bakery.

"There's a party tonight at a friend's house. Ya wanna come?"

"Dunno. Is it all old people?"

Erikson laughed. "You callin' me old?"

"Kinda," Tony stated with a smirk.

"It'll be a mix. The guy who owns the place has a fifteen-year-old daughter. She parties, so he lets her and her friends hang out."

"Yeah, sure, I guess so."

Tony wasn't in a partying mood. He was content sitting inside the dirty, cold walls of 3F. He had found comfort in the apartment where all the murders happened many years before. He pretended he was protecting the people who died there.

"Good," Erikson said. "I'm gonna take a little nap. When I wake up, we'll head out."

It was almost eleven at night when Erikson and Tony left for the party. They arrived at a small row home. Tony took in everything around him as they walked into the living area. The furniture was old and worn. A long sofa was filled with people holding beer cans and smoking cigarettes. The table in front of them had a smattering of white powder and bags of pot.

Erikson introduced Tony to some people, and within an hour of arriving, a drug dealer named Head approached him. Erikson had warned Tony that Head was trouble and that whenever the dealer met a new kid, either on the streets or at a party, he considered him or her new meat. Erikson had stressed that Head tried his best to hook the clean kids. Head always preached that hooked kids were future business.

Head pushed a crack pipe toward Tony. "Here, take a hit. You'll love this."

Tony shook his head. "No thanks, man. I don't do that."

"How do ya know ya don't do it? Have ya ever tried it?" Head said, pushing a small pipe closer to him.

Tony put his hand up. "I said, I don't do that."

"Just give it a try. It ain't gonna cost ya nothin'," Head insisted more aggressively.

Tony stepped backward. "What the fuck is your problem, man? I don't wanna smoke none of that shit. Why don't cha just leave me alone?"

Tony's angry words drew the attention of the people around them. His face was colored by a rush of blood. Erikson was close by and saw what was happening. He rushed over to Tony's side.

"What the fuck is wit' ya? Leave 'im alone, Head, or I swear I'll..."

"You'll what, motherfucker? What are ya gonna do? Try to take me; I will fuckin' crush you like an empty beer can."

Erikson grabbed Tony's arm and turned to leave.

Head curled up his hand, spun Erikson around, and, with high velocity, threw a punch into his stomach, just below the ribs. Erikson went to his knees; the pain was sharp.

Tony's anger boiled over and he threw a quick but powerful swing, connecting with Head's jaw. Head flew backward onto the coffee table, smashing on top of beer bottles and dope. Then he lay motionless. At first, Tony was scared that he'd killed the asshole, but one guy on the sofa, who was so high his eyelids were barely opened, poured his open beer into Head's face. When Tony saw Head start to move, he helped Erikson up off the floor and dragged him from the house. With Erikson's arm slung over Tony's shoulder, they walked two blocks in a hurried, awkward manner. Finally, Tony sat Erikson against the side of a building and let him rest.

Erikson was focused on breathing. Between smoking crack and the punch to his stomach, he was having trouble getting his breath.

"Shit, dude," he finally said, "ya throw one helluva punch."

Tony stared down at his fist. "Yeah, I actually surprised myself." He laughed.

Tony had been so intimidated in juvenile detention he had been too scared to fight back. But when he watched Erikson—a man he'd come to care for over the past week—getting hit, Tony's instincts overrode his raw fear.

That night, back in apartment 3F, Tony lay on the floor next to Erikson. The weather had turned much colder; it would be Halloween in less than a week.

"Hey, Erikson, I think we oughta get those boards up on the windows tomorra. It's gettin' cold, and the wind comin' through the windows is makin' it worse."

"You're right, Tony. That's what we'll do tomorra, first thing."

"I gotta go to the bakery in the mornin'. How 'bout when I'm workin' ya get the wood and black paint ya said we needed."

"I ain't got no money to buy that shit," Erikson rebutted.

"How much will it cost?"

"Well, I can use the closet doors for the wood. I guess it'll cost about four bucks for a can of paint."

"I'll give ya four bucks then."

Erikson curled up to fit his body under the short blanket that lay on top of him. "Yeah, it's a good thing ya got that job. We're gonna need some money come winter."

Tony propped himself up on his elbow. "Ya gotta get some work and earn some dough too. Ya can't be thinkin' we're gonna make it all winter on the money I make."

Erikson nodded. "Sure, kid. I'll get a job as soon as hell freezes over."

Tony lay flat on his back and stared into the darkness. He liked Erikson—the guy had helped him out—but he didn't like that Erikson wasn't willing to work. But that wasn't Erikson's thing. He glanced over at the man, who was already snoring.

How am I going to make it out of here? Tony asked himself.

Chapter Forty-Five

On Tony's fourteenth birthday, he met his mother in the park. She gave him a winter jacket she'd bought from the Salvation Army store. Tony knew the coat was secondhand because of the stain down the front, but that didn't bother him. He was happy to have a warmer jacket that fit him with winter approaching fast.

On his walk back to the abandoned building, Tony felt like the luckiest kid alive, with his new used winter coat. He realized then that people with nothing are grateful for everything, especially the small things in life, like satisfying basic human needs.

In the late afternoon, when Tony got back to 3F, Erikson was waiting for him.

"Hey. Happy birthday," he said, pushing an object toward him that was wrapped in newspaper.

"Ya got me a present?" Tony asked, touched by the gesture.

"Sure, I did. Go on and open it."

Tony sat on the floor and unwrapped the newspaper. Inside was an eight-inch hunting knife nestled into a leather pouch. Tony unsnapped the leather strap and pulled out the knife.

"Wow. This is really cool. Where did ya get it?"

"Got it when I was in the marines. Let me show ya."

Erikson lifted the leg of Tony's jeans and strapped the leather around his shin and calf.

Tony waited until he was finished. "Ya were in the marines?"

"Yeah. I was in for four years. Went in when I was twenty."

"Why are ya givin' this to me? Don't cha wanna keep it? It seems like somethin' pretty special."

"It is special to me; that's why I want ya to have it. Someday, ya might need it to protect yourself. If ya do, then you'll have a good knife to help ya out."

"What about you? Don't cha need to protect yourself too?"

"Ah, it's more likely that someone will give you shit 'cause you're young. I mean, once in a while, some snot-nosed thugs bust my balls, but they see me as an old man. You, on the other hand, you're a force to reckon wit', so ya need to make sure ya can take care of yourself."

Tony leaned over and gave Erikson a quick hug. "Thanks, man. This means a lot to me. I ain't never had nobody give me somethin' that was special to them. I'll always keep it wit' me."

Erikson turned away before Tony noticed the tears welling in his eyes. He'd never had children of his own, and Tony had quickly become the kid he never had. "Yeah, sure, kid. Happy birthday."

Tony pulled the knife from its leather holder. He had a flashback of Salvatore plunging his own knife into Rex. That night had changed Tony's life, and he wondered what his life was about and the reason he'd lost his innocence to the twisted, perverted guards in juvie.

"Why do ya look so serious?" Erikson said, interrupting his thoughts.

"I was just thinkin' 'bout some shit."

"Ya don't think about stupid shit on your birthday. Here," he said, pushing a bottle of cheap whiskey at him. "Take a swig."

Tony filled his mouth with the awful-smelling liquid. It felt as though he'd swallowed a fireball as it inched its way down his throat.

"Ew, what the hell is that?"

"Whiskey. Every fourteen-year-old boy should take a shot on their birthday." Erikson offered Tony the bottle again, but he turned it down.

"What are ya doin' tonight for your birthday?"

"Nothin'."

"Aw, come on. Ya gotta do somethin'. It's your birthday. How much money ya got?"

"Thirteen dollars."

"That's plenty. Let's go get dinner at that local rat trap on Eighth Street, and then we can go buy some beer."

"I gotta save my money."

"For what?"

"So I can get my own place someday. Where there are lights and water and heat."

"Kid, I hope someday ya do get outta here. Get a house and a car or whatever kinda shit ya want. But thirteen dollars ain't gonna make that happen. Ya need to make a lot of money to free yourself from the kinda life we're livin'."

"I don't care what I gotta do; I'm not livin' like this forever."

"Careful what cha wish for. People do really dumb things for money, Tony."

"Too late; I already wished for it, and ya know what? My wish is gonna come true 'cause I want it so bad."

"If ya say so, kid. Just remember, sometimes when we go after things that we want, the stuff that really matters disappears wit'out ya noticin'. Then one day ya stop and look around ya, and all ya want are those things ya used to have. Hang on to who ya are as ya go after what ya want and never forget about the shit ya love now. That's all I'm sayin'."

"What is there to love now? My life sucks," Tony grunted.

"Ya got your freedom. There ain't nothin' more important than that."

Tony scratched the top of his head. "Yeah, that's true. I guess you're right. Up until now I never really had freedom. I like being free."

Tony stood and walked to the door of Apartment 3F. "Let's go celebrate. It's my birthday."

Chapter Forty-Six

On Thanksgiving, Erikson and Tony walked through the freezing rain to a soup kitchen on Broad Street for dinner. As they entered the building, the scent of a cooked meal greeted Tony. His senses went haywire. His mouth watered, and his stomach gurgled. Tony picked up the pace as they headed toward the line of homeless people waiting for a hot meal.

Tony placed his paper plate on the table and sat across from Erikson. He dug his plastic fork into the mashed potatoes and shoved them into his mouth. Tony's eyes closed as the potatoes covered his tongue. It had been months since he'd had a hot meal, and his taste buds were going crazy. Tony wished the plate of food would last forever.

"Slow down, kid. We wanna take our time eatin'. After we're done this, we can get a piece of pumpkin pie from the table over there," Erikson said.

"But it's so good I can't help it. We ain't eaten nothin' this good in a while. How come ya never brought me here before?"

"I only come here on holidays. That's when people who gotta eat here are nicer. Every other day there are some mean assholes crawlin' around this place, looking to steal stuff and start trouble."

"Well, I don't know 'bout you, but I'm sure comin' back here. I ain't waitin' for a holiday no more," Tony said, eyes glued to his plate.

When they were finished eating, they sat and chatted with some people Erikson knew. They were waiting, just like the others, until the last minute to leave the warm, lit building. On their walk back to 3F, Erikson took a detour on his own, in search of his drug buddies. Tony was walking by himself, and in the distance, he saw Salvatore coming toward him.

"Tony! Where have you been?" Salvatore said, a smile lighting up his already handsome face.

"I've been around. I ain't seen ya in a while."

"You haven't seen Vincent either. I'm going to meet him now. Do you want to come?"

"Sure. I'll go wit' cha. So how is everything?" Tony asked as they walked.

"Things are good. Remember that hot new girl in our school we told you about?"

Tony nodded.

"Well, I went to the winter dance, and she was there. I asked her to dance, and she stayed with me the whole time. Afterward, Vincent and I took her and her friend to the Penrose Diner. When we got done eating, we took the girls out into the parking lot, and this chick let me feel her up. She's got a set of great tits on her. It was awesome. Vincent didn't get so lucky. He got to kiss the girl he was with, but she wouldn't give him any tongue. Vincent said she's a fucking prude and doesn't want anything to do with her."

Salvatore stopped talking and looked closely at Tony. He was noticeably thinner and he looked unkempt. His eyes glided over Tony's dirty, wrinkled clothing.

"How are you, Tony? You look skinny."

"Yeah, I lost a couple of pounds. Um, ya know, I'm running now and so when ya run, it makes ya thinner."

"Really?"

Tony paused before answering Salvatore's question.

"Nah, not really. I just ain't been eatin' too much."

"Why?"

"Well, the people I live wit' ain't got much to go around."

"How about if we go get something to eat after we meet up with Vincent?"

"I ain't got any money," Tony said, blushing with shame.

"Who gives a fuck about money? I have money. You know my Pop gives me money all the time."

"Then, yeah, sure, let's get somethin' to eat."

"You aren't really living with another family, are you?"

"Nope."

"Where are you living then?"

Tony told Salvatore, who already knew the buildings well. All the kids in the neighborhood had heard about the googamongers that lived there.

"Holy shit, Tony. You can't live there. I mean, you can't even take a shower."

"I ain't got a choice right now."

"Isn't there any place that can take you in? There has to be somewhere that kids without parents can go."

"Hell, no! I ain't livin' in no orphanage or nothin' like that. I heard about those places in juvie. They ain't no better than bein' in prison. Kids get beat up on by the other kids and sometimes by the grownups that run the house. No, thank you. I don't need any more shit in my life. Right now, I'm good where I'm at. There's this older dude, Erikson, that shares my space wit' me. He's a good guy—well, he uses drugs a lot—but other than that, he's a cool dude. He's been helpin' me out."

Salvatore hung his head. "I'm sorry. This is all my fault. If you hadn't gone to juvie because of Rex, you would still be living with your family."

"Ah, that don't matter. My father is a miserable prick, so it ain't like I was livin' some kinda great life when I was there," Tony said, but he still regretted not running away from the scene of the crime when Rex was killed.

Salvatore shoved his hand into his pocket and pulled out a small wad of money. He had three twenty-dollar bills. He pulled two off and handed forty dollars to Tony.

"Here, take this."

"I can't, Salvatore. I appreciate it and all, but I can't take your money."

"Look, dude, it's only forty dollars. My Pop will give me more money. Just take it. We don't have to tell anybody."

Reluctantly, Tony took the money.

"Thanks, man."

"You don't need to thank me. You're the one who did the time. Don't worry, Tony. I'll always look out for you. So will Vincent. Someday we'll be just like my pop and Big Paulie."

Tony chuckled. "As long as you're the one who gets fat like Big Paulie, 'cause it ain't gonna be me," he said, and punched Salvatore lightly in the arm. Tony ran, and Salvatore chased after him. They didn't stop until they arrived on Market Street, where they were meeting up with Vincent.

Vincent was happy to see Tony. The three teens walked to the diner, where they sat and ate pie with ice cream. They were enjoying each other's company, and hours passed before they decided to leave. When it was time to go, none of them wanted to go their separate ways.

"So we'll see you soon, right?" Salvatore asked.

"Sure, you'll see me," Tony said, shoving Vincent in the shoulder.

"Good, 'cause hangin' out wit' this pretty boy here," Vincent said pointing to Salvatore, "ain't easy. I need your ugly face around so I can look better to the chicks. Salvatore ain't gotta worry 'bout that. The broads at school are throwin' themselves at 'im."

Tony's eyes washed over Salvatore, and he smiled.

"Maybe Salvatore can throw ya some of his leftovers," Tony mocked.

"Yeah, that's exactly what I told him, but he doesn't want anything to do with it. Some bullshit about how he can catch his own women," Salvatore said.

"That's right," Vincent said. "Tell 'em, Tony—real Italian men don't need sloppy leftovers. We get our broads on our own."

Tony smiled wistfully at his two friends. He wished that hooking up with a girl was his sole focus, but he had bigger problems. He wanted to be back in the fold with Vincent and Salvatore, by their sides, living a normal teenage life.

The boys stood on the sidewalk and joked for a while longer. When Tony was alone again, on his walk back to his dingy place, he wished his life was more like

Salvatore's. He had money and clothes, and now he even had girls. His own life was like a shell with no substance, and he promised himself that he'd have all the things he wanted...someday.

Chapter Forty-Seven

T he city of Philadelphia was on steroids between Thanksgiving and Christmas. People scurried on the sidewalks. Friends were laughing and enjoying holiday festivities. Tony moved each day to different streets to beg for money after his two-hour shift at the bakery. People were a little more generous, and he'd even been given several one-dollar bills, instead of the usual pocket change. By Christmas Eve, between the forty dollars that Salvatore had given him, the money from the bakery, and the money he'd begged for, Tony had well over sixty dollars. He was determined to keep this a secret from Erikson, who would, without a doubt, try to talk Tony into spending it on beer.

On Christmas Eve, as Tony made his way back to apartment 3F, he stopped at the Goodwill store on Front Street and bought Erikson a scarf and hat. The lady who rang up the purchase looked at Tony closely.

"You doin' OK, son?"

"Yeah, sure I am. I'm just buying this stuff for...for my father. It's a Christmas present."

"Oh, I see. Well then, let me wrap it for ya."

Tony watched the woman cut a bag open and fold the sides in just perfectly. It made him think of his mother, and a stab of sadness pierced his heart. The woman used masking tape to secure the brown paper bag. When she finished wrapping the gift, she pushed the package toward Tony and handed him red and green markers.

"Go on. Take the markers and write your message on the masking tape. Ya can even draw a Christmas tree on the paper if ya want to."

Tony used the markers to write his greeting and handed them back to the lady.

"Oh, one more thing," she said, rummaging through the drawer below the cash register.

From somewhere deep inside the drawer, she pulled out a long piece of thick red yarn. She weaved it around the package and tied a bow on the top.

"There, now it's ready to give to your father."

Tony looked the woman in the eyes. "Thanks, lady. Means a whole lot to me."

"No problem. Ya have a Merry Christmas and a blessed New Year."

"Sure. Ya do the same."

The woman at the Goodwill store watched as Tony walked out of sight. She'd seen him over the past several months, on the streets, begging for money. He was no older than her own son, and she wondered how it was that such a young boy could be on the streets begging for money to survive instead of in school learning things that would help him survive in the adult world. It was a situation that broke her heart. She saw it every day. The lost children of the city falling victim to the cruel reality of nothingness. At these times she questioned God's will and asked for his mercy on the lonesome souls of the streets.

As Tony walked back to apartment 3F, it began to snow. The sun was setting and fewer people were on the streets as they rushed home for their Christmas Eve parties. By the time he reached the abandoned apartment building, the homeless squatters were in full party mode. People were in the hallways drinking and smoking. Someone had even trash-picked old Christmas garland and hung it on one of the railings. The usually somber people had been transformed into a group where joyfulness was contagious.

Tony found Erikson in the second-floor hallway. He could tell by the way the man swayed that he was well on his way to the stoned state he preferred over the sober reality of his life.

"Hey, Erikson."

"Tony! How ya doin'?"

"Fine. I didn't expect people to be celebratin' like this."

"Of course we celebrate. Just 'cause we ain't got 'things,'" Erikson gestured in air quotes, "don't mean we ain't got each other. Christmas Eve and New Year's Eve are the best two days of the year around this joint. We're luckier than the younger people. We got this old building, and that keeps us together, even though we get on each other's nerves a lot."

Tony patted his friend on the shoulder. "I'm gonna go upstairs and eat some of the donuts I got from the bakery today. I'll be back down when I'm finished."

"OK. I'm gonna stay here," Erikson said, leaning in close to Tony's ear, "and smoke this asshole's weed. He's so fucked up, he don't even know that he's been sharing it wit' anybody who stands near him." He nodded toward a thirtyish man with long, tangled hair that covered most of his face.

Tony laughed to humor Erikson, but he didn't think that it was funny. He wished his friend wasn't a drug addict. Sometimes, Erikson's addiction made Tony feel very alone. In those times, when memories of the prison rapes got jammed in Tony's mind, he felt isolated from the entire world and anything that was remotely normal.

Chapter Forty-Eight

It was almost eight o'clock at night on Christmas Eve when Tony left apartment 3F and walked to his family home. Tony slunk up the front porch steps to avoid all the creaky boards. He ducked below the front window and popped his head up. There, through the yellowed lace curtains, he saw his father sitting in his recliner, beer in hand, watching television. Macie was on the floor in front of him wrapping a present. And when Tony looked into the back of the house, he saw Teresa bustling around the kitchen. She was preparing the seven fishes for their traditional Christmas Eve meal. His mouth watered as he thought about the feast that his family would soon enjoy.

Tony squatted in that spot for the better part of an hour. He longed to be with his mother and sister. He thought about Christmas when he was a young boy. He and Macie had never received anything great from Santa, but there was a false sense of peace every Christmas Eve. His belief that a magical man existed had given him hope that someday Santa would use that magic to make his father love them all and transform them into a happy family. But Santa had let him down when he was kid, year after year. Now, as Tony reflected on the past, he remembered when he'd figured out that the magical Santa he'd believed in had never existed. It was his mother, stripped of all power, who had put the meager presents under the tree each year.

Tony's stomach clamped down hard as he realized that as bad as he thought his life had been before going to juvenile detention, nothing could be worse than his current pitiful existence. He was just a boy, not yet a man, and he wanted his teenage years back. He longed for his dignity, which he believed could only be returned when his rapists were held accountable for their crimes against him. But Tony knew that no one in law enforcement would believe him even if he came forward and told the truth. So now the truth was smothered in silence, and his existence was a balance of embarrassment and rage.

Tony bowed his head and asked God to keep his mother and sister safe. He quietly whispered, "Merry Christmas, Ma. Merry Christmas, Macie."

He wanted to knock on the front door and sit at the kitchen table with his mother and sister. He knew, however, that was only a fantasy and the very sight of him would send his father into a violent rant. With tears sliding down his cheeks, he sneaked back down the porch steps as quietly as he had crawled up them.

***

When Tony woke up on Christmas morning, he sat up and looked around the dreary room. He spotted a present sitting next to the tree that Erikson had made with empty beer cans by placing them into the shape of a triangle. He could hear the soft snore from Erikson and crept over to put the gift he had bought him next to the tree.

Tony got back into his sleep spot. He lay on his back, hands locked behind his head. How did you let this happen to me, God? Tony thought. What have I done that was so horrible to deserve all this bullshit in my life? You've been punishing me since I was born, and I want to know why.

Erikson stirred under his wool blanket, disrupting Tony's morbid thoughts, and Tony looked over with a smile covering his face. The older man's eyes fluttered open.

"Merry Christmas, old man!"

"Who the fuck ya callin' old?" he said, cracking a smile. "Merry Christmas, kid." Erikson sat up slowly. "I bought ya a present."

Tony sprang up, excited that they had presents to exchange. It was a reminder it was still Christmas day. Tony brought the two presents over and sat on the floor next to Erikson.

"Open yours first," Erikson said, rubbing the sleep out of his eyes.

Tony opened the used paper bag with grease stains from the slice of pizza that was once inside. Reaching his hand in, he pulled out a yellow-and-orange Koosh ball—a rubber ball with long rubber fringe on the surface. He held it in his hand and looked it over. The rubber fringe felt good against his fingers.

Erikson got up and walked to the other side of the empty apartment.

"Throw it to me."

Tony stood and threw the ball. A koosh sound filled the empty room, and Erikson grabbed the ball in midair.

"See, it's easy to catch and throw. It's real fun to use, addicting too."

Erikson threw the ball back to Tony, and he caught it by the stringy rubber fibers.

"Wow. I really like this. Thanks, Erikson."

"I bought it new too. Had to beg for two days straight to buy that thing."

"I appreciate it," Tony said, squeezing the ball in his hand. Tony lowered his gaze to the floor, feeling guilty that he'd bought Erikson a secondhand gift.

"What's wrong?"

"Nuttin'. Here's your gift," Tony said, handing him the wrapped present.

Erikson turned the package over in his hands. "Been a long time since I got a Christmas present." He read the messages Tony had written on the masking tape. Merry Christmas. Thanks for being my friend. Get a job.

"Ya lost me at 'get a job.'" Erikson chuckled.

"Well, open it."

Erikson slowly untied the bow of thick red yarn and unfolded the paper. He admired the black hat and scarf before lifting them off of the paper and trying them on.

"This is a real good gift, kid."

"I couldn't afford to buy new ones," Tony said.

"What are ya talkin' about? These are as good as new."

Truth was that Tony could've wrapped up dried turds and Erikson would have been grateful. He couldn't remember the last time he'd received a gift and was touched that the kid liked him enough to buy him a present.

"So let's go down to the soup kitchen and get us some breakfast," Erikson said, getting to his feet.

As Tony walked with Erikson in the bitter cold, he could hear his own heart beating in his ears. The streets were ghostly silent. It was the sound of people home with their families—people somewhere being loved. Tony listened hard to the noiseless city that seemed to have died around him, and he felt alone in the vastness of the tall buildings and overcast sky.

Chapter Forty-Nine

For New Year's Eve, Tony stayed in apartment 3F. Erikson had tried to convince him to go out and celebrate, but Tony wasn't interested in hanging around with a bunch of stoners. He liked to drink a beer or two, but all the pot smoking and drugs got under his skin. People changed into evil creatures when they were high. Tony didn't consider drug-induced fun any fun at all.

Tony lit a candle and grabbed the book Donata had given to him at the bakery that afternoon. Tony held the book in his hand, recalling her comments.

"Tony, ya gotta read, boy. I know ya ain't in school 'cause you're gettin' 'homeschooled,' as ya call it. That's fine wit' me, but cha gotta educate yourself along the way. Workin' here, cleaning pans in the bakery will give ya work ethic, but cha gotta expand your mind too. Women don't like stupid men."

"I ain't stupid, Donata. When I was in school, I got all As and Bs."

"I didn't say ya was stupid. What I'm sayin' is that ya gotta keep up on things. Make sure you're reading whatever books they're reading in your grade. Reading books is a different kinda education. Ya learn how to talk, how to act, and how not to act. Readin' teaches ya all kinds of things about life."

"Yeah, I guess that it's a good idea now that ya put it that way. Fine. I'll read it, but if it's boring, I ain't gonna finish it," Tony said.

"Keep that up, and I'll clip ya. Ya just follow my lead; I ain't gonna steer ya wrong," Donata answered and waved her fist at him. She disappeared upstairs. When she came back, Tony was elbow deep in soapsuds, scrubbing pans.

"Dry your hands," Donata insisted.

Tony obeyed.

"Here, I want ya to read this over the New Year's holiday. Then, I wanna discuss it when ya come back to work," Donata stated.

Tony took the book from her. "Lord of the Flies," he read aloud. "How do ya know I'm gonna like it?"

"'Cause I just know. All boys your age like this book," she said with confidence.

"OK, Donata. I'll try it. Thanks."

Tony stared at the book as he sat on the floor in 3F. He and Erikson now referred to their new home as the Apartment of Death. Tony pulled some of his summer clothes out of the trash bag and layered them on top of him to stifle the cold air that crept through every crevice in the old building. He leaned into the candle, opened to the first page of the book, and was immediately pulled into the story.

Tony read the story like a hungry baby waiting for its mama's milk. He was inspired by the boys living on their own, isolated from the rest of the world, with no adults to fuck things up. But Tony also knew firsthand that kids can make life hard too. Adults are too preoccupied with their lives and earning money, and some have kids for all the wrong reasons. They worry about acquiring "things" and proving to other people how happy they are, when many aren't happy at all. Kids, on the other hand, spend their time trying to find a social balance. Their predominant goal is to fit in, to be the kid whom the other kids like, to be popular. Isn't that what Ralph and Jack from the Lord of the Flies wanted? They battled with each other for popularity and acceptance...to be the boss.

Tony read the book right into the early-morning hours until his lids fluttered, and, try as he might to keep them open, they finally closed as he drifted into a sleep filled with dreams. His dreams brought him to the island with the boys from his book. At fourteen, Tony was the oldest one there with them. That instantly gave him power over the other kids. He was running through the jungle, and the crash of the waves against the shoreline was music to his ears. Then his dreams faded, replaced by darkness. The vibrant colors of the jungle disappeared, and now all he could see was black around him. He sensed something was wrong. He wasn't alone. Then two angry eyes opened in front of him; all he could see were thin white circles engulfed by dilated black pupils. Suddenly, ripped from his sleep state, Tony jerked upright. He felt like he was bound in a web of sinister hatred, and his fear paralyzed him because he knew the eyes belonged to Officer Zody.

Chapter Fifty

When Tony woke up again, it was almost noon on New Year's Day. He rubbed his eyes and looked down at the book that lay next to him. He couldn't wait to eat and get back to reading. He'd almost finished the entire book the night before, and he already had a feeling of sadness knowing that he'd be finished with the book before the day was over. Tony looked over at Erikson's sleep spot on the floor. He hadn't come home. That was rare for Erikson; he almost always staggered in, even if it was five in the morning.

Tony went to the second floor of the abandoned building to look for Erikson. A few months ago, he'd found his older friend sleeping on the steps, so high he couldn't make it to 3F.

"Happy New Year's, Tony," Stan, the bipolar man, said.

"Yeah, same to you, Stan. Hey, have ya seen Erikson?"

"Nah, he probably got too fucked up last night and didn't come home. Besides, it's been snowing for hours. We got a fuckin' blizzard goin' on out there."

Tony followed Stan into his apartment. Stan scratched the top of his dirty, bald head. Tony couldn't look away from Stan's straggly beard that lay over his collarbone. Stan gave Tony a nervous smile, showing his teeth stained a yellow-brown to match his index and middle fingers on his right hand, which were discolored from his constant chain smoking. It wasn't easy to clean yourself when you lived inside four walls with nothing in the middle. But there were public bathrooms and other ways to at least take care of the essentials.

Tony looked out the window. Stan was right—there had to be two feet of snow on the ground, and the flakes were falling from the sky, making it look like a dense fog.

"Damn, I didn't know it was gonna snow," Tony said, turning to Stan.

"That's 'cause we ain't got no TVs or radios. But Julia, that noisy bitch down the hall, came to tell me she heard it on the news. She was at the train station yesterday; that's where she heard it. Anyway, she came swooshing in here like she was fuckin' AccuWeather herself. I can't stand her. She's always telling me I need to get on medicine, like she's a fuckin' doctor or something."

Tony chuckled. "Well, I think that Julia was tryin' to share information about the weather, is all. Ya shouldn't get mad at her for that."

"Now you're takin' her side?" Stan asked, stepping closer to Tony.

"Nah, come on, Stan. Ya know I don't take sides."

"I don't know jack shit about cha, kid. Get the hell outta my apartment."

Tony shook his head and walked back into the hallway. He clomped down to the first floor, thinking about how nice it would be to live in a place of his own. With no sign of Erikson on the floor, Tony trudged back up to the apartment and sat on the floor. He picked up Lord of the Flies and started to read again. He had an uneasy feeling that fluttered in his belly, and he attributed it to the book.

At two o'clock that afternoon, with the snow falling even harder, Tony heard someone approaching 3F. He looked up, ready to give Erikson a load of shit for being out all night and day. Tony's gaze was met by Julia's.

"Tony, ya need to get the hell outta here. The cops are swarming the place. Left their sirens off so we couldn't hear 'em. They'll throw all of us out, but they'll take ya in 'cause you're just a kid."

"Shit!" Tony said, jumping to his feet. "Thanks, Julia."

Instead of running out of 3F, Tony followed the steps he and Erikson had agreed upon. He pulled the wood off of the back bedroom window and slid onto the rusted fire escape. The metal steps were covered in snow. Tony inched his way down the back of the building until he was on the ground. He walked through the narrow alley on the side of the house and out onto the street in front of the house. Tony looked into the empty lot; the grass was now buried by the snow, and police and paramedics were gathered around doing something.

Tony walked into the center of the commotion, and there he saw the top of the hat he'd given to Erikson for Christmas. He pushed his way to the front of the officials and knelt down in the snow next to his friend.

"Hey, kid, you know this guy?" an officer asked.

Tony focused his attention on his friend. "Erikson. Erikson! Wake up!"

The female paramedic put her hand on Tony's shoulder. "He's gone."

"Gone? What do you mean 'gone'? Do somethin'. Help him," Tony screamed.

"There's nothing we can do. It looks like he froze to death."

One policeman helped Tony to his feet. "You go on home now."

Tony slouched back into the blanket of snow. He clung on to Erikson. His body felt like a board, but he didn't care. Tony cried for the man who had taken him in. Even though they had only known each other three and a half months, Erikson was the closest thing to a father he'd ever had.

Tony sobbed as he nuzzled his face into Erikson's chest. He could smell the crack cocaine underneath his jacket. He knew the glass pipe was in the pocket inside his coat. Tony wanted to remove the pipe to maintain Erikson's dignity, but he couldn't risk taking it out in front of the police for fear of going to jail again.

"How do you know this man?" a police officer said, eyeing Tony suspiciously.

Tony looked up at the officer, tears freezing on his face. "I know him from the neighborhood. He was a real nice man. He helped me out once. Gave me advice when my ma pissed me off and I was gonna run away from home," he lied.

"All right, it's time for you to go. We have to get this man into the ambulance to take him downtown," the officer responded.

Tony took one last look at Erikson before he got up from the ground. He leaned into Erikson's ear. "I love you, old man. Watch over me, will ya?"

Tony stood, not knowing where to go next. The police were inside the abandoned house, making everyone leave. He watched them carry boards inside to barricade the main entrance to the building.

Tony walked, stumbling along wherever his feet took him. His thoughts and feelings were whirling around chaotically, like the blizzard he was walking through. Twenty minutes later, covered in snow and frozen to the bone, he was pounding on the door to the bakery, but no one answered. He sat in the deep snow on the step, giving up and waiting to freeze to death just like Erikson. The door to the bakery opened, and Tony looked up at Donata and Ruth staring down at him.

"What in God's name are ya doin' out here, boy?"

"I had nowhere else to go," Tony said and began to cry.

Chapter Fifty-One

"Tony, what happened to you? Where's your uncle?" Ruth asked with a child's innocence.

Tony looked at Donata before answering. "My uncle, well, he, um…something bad happened to him today."

"Is he gonna be OK?" Ruth said, wide eyed.

"I don't know, Ruth. Right now, I just need some time to figure stuff out."

"All right, 'nough talkin'. Let's get you upstairs into a warm bath. You're half frozen," Donata demanded.

While Donata filled the tub for Tony, Ruth chatted with him.

"Is your uncle sick?"

Tony averted his eyes from the child's gaze. "Yeah, somethin' like that."

"Will he get better?"

Tony shook his head.

Ruth's hand covered her mouth. "Where will you go if he doesn't get better?"

"I don't know yet, Ruth. I ain't had no time to figure things out." Tony looked at Ruth, her eyes revealed the panic that tumbled around in his belly. He didn't want Ruth to worry; she was just a little girl and had enough of her own problems. "You know what, though?"

"What?" Ruth said with hopeful anticipation.

"I always figure stuff out. I know a couple of places that I can live."

Ruth cocked her head to the side. "Then why did you come here and not go to one of those places?"

Damn, Tony thought, I can't get anything over on this kid. "Well, that's because they are all out of town for New Year's. They'll get home in a couple of days, though, and then I'll be fine."

"Uh-huh. So, what about your uncle, though? Are you gonna be able to look in on him? Is he in the hospital? Maybe Grandma and me can visit him and bring him some flowers. I can ask her," Ruth gushed, clearly wanting to help Tony.

"Ruth Caroline!" The sharpness of Donata's voice made the child freeze.

Ruth's back went erect as she swiftly turned to look at her grandmother, who was annoyed, judging by the fact that she'd used her middle name.

"Gram, I wasn't doing anything. I was just talking to Tony about his uncle. I wasn't bothering him. Was I?" Ruth said, her beautiful, innocent eyes searching Tony's face.

"Nah, ya can never bother me, Ruth. She was just askin' some questions, Donata. She didn't do nothin' wrong."

"All right then. Let's go, Tony. Your bath is ready. When you're finished there, I made some soup that I'll heat up for ya. Now get a move on. Throw me your clothes so I can put 'em in the washer while you're takin' a bath. They need a good cleanin'," Donata said, scrunching up her nose.

Ruth giggled, and Tony shot her a look. "You do kinda stink," the child teased.

Tony felt the blood rush to his face. At first he was embarrassed, but then as he focused on Ruth's sweet smile, he realized that Donata and Ruth meant him no harm. They had been very good to him over the past months—always with a friendly smile and a kind word.

Finally, Tony's frown turned into a smile. "Yeah, well, we all can't smell like cookies and cinnamon buns all the time," he said, reaching down and tickling Ruth. She giggled and squirmed away from Tony, until she lost her balance on the prosthetic leg and landed on her ass. Tony stopped and looked at Donata, waiting to be thrown out, but the older woman only laughed and walked into the tiny kitchen.

Tony undressed and wrapped the clean towel around his waist. He opened the bathroom door and handed Ruth his dirty clothes. She grabbed the clothes in one hand and pinched her nose shut with the other. This time Tony smiled and gently shut the bathroom door in her face.

Tony looked at the tub filled with clean water and eased himself in. The steamy bath felt foreign against his dirty, dry skin, but he liked it. He laid his head back on the edge of the tub, savoring every precious moment. He thought about where he would go next. He couldn't go back to apartment 3F; the cops had emptied the building and boarded up the entrance. His good feeling slid from his body, and Tony grabbed at his stomach as a seed of fear, a fear of the unknown, planted itself in the pit of his belly. He no longer had a place to sleep, and Erikson was gone too. The comfort of his bath now forgotten, Tony worried about where he would go next.

Chapter Fifty-Two

Tony emerged from the bathroom wearing a towel. He inched his way toward the living room, where he could hear the white noise of the television. Ruth was lying on the floor, giggling at a cartoon she was watching. Tony took a few steps into the room and caught Ruth's attention.

"Where's Donata?" he asked.

"Gram?" Ruth yelled.

Donata poked her head around the corner, and Tony waved at her. She marched out from the kitchen and led Tony into the bedroom, where she opened the closet and pulled out a dark-gray robe.

"Here, put this on. It belonged to my husband, God rest his soul. Anyway, your clothes are still in the washer. When you're finished puttin' that on, ya can come on out to the kitchen. I heated up the soup for ya."

Tony met Donata's eyes. "Thank you. I appreciate everything you're doin' for me."

Donata nodded, but before she left the bedroom, she turned back to Tony. "I really like ya, Tony. In my heart, I know you're a good kid. You have kind eyes, but there's also fire in there. Not too often ya see those two things together. There's somethin' real special 'bout cha. Get done so we can talk some more."

When Tony was dressed, he sat at the kitchen table and looked outside at the snow. It was still falling heavily.

Donata went to the stove and brought a bowl of hot soup back to the table. "Looks like ya might have to stay here wit' us for a couple of days. They ain't even gonna be able to get the plows down the streets. Biggest snowstorm we had in twenty years."

Tony's guts relaxed...he had a few days.

"Is there anybody ya gotta call to let 'em know you're here...that you're safe?"

"No, like I said, my uncle is sick. He won't be able to talk wit' me anyway."

"Oh yeah? Where is he?"

Tony laid his spoon in the bowl. "He, um, he's in the hospital."

"Yeah? What hospital?"

"I can't remember the name of it," he murmured.

"I see. What's your uncle's name?"

"Erikson…" Tony's words fell short. He sucked in a deep breath and rested his hands in his lap.

"Erikson isn't really my uncle. He's a guy that I met on the streets. He took me in. He kinda took care of me for a while. He's had a minor setback," he said, lying, "but he'll be back home soon."

Donata eyed him suspiciously. She didn't believe him, but at least he'd admitted that he wasn't with his real uncle.

"What happened to your father? Why ain't he takin' care of ya, instead of some stranger?"

"My father is a prick."

"Shh," she hissed, putting her finger to her lips. "I don't need Ruth talkin' trash."

"Sorry. My real father don't want me."

"What about your mother?"

"She can't do nothin' 'bout it. I have a little sister that she's gotta worry about."

Donata's face turned ashen. "That's a load of crap," she said, seething. "Your mother needs to step up and be a real woman. Tell that husband of hers how things are gonna work."

"She can't, Donata. My father, well, he whacks my ma around. He ain't a nice guy and gets drunk a lot too."

Donata was seeing the whole picture now. "So how did ya end up with Erikson?"

Tony told Donata the story about what had happened, leaving out the part about the guards in juvie.

"Somethin' happened to ya in that kid prison?"

Tony stared at the women. It was as though she had a window into his brain.

"Why ya askin' that?"

"'Cause ya got untamed fire in those eyes of yours—the kinda fire that tells me that ya ain't had it easy. What did they do to ya?"

Tony stared at the woman. She gently put her hand over his, silently urging him to talk, letting him know that it was safe.

"The guards did bad things to me. They did sex stuff to me."

Donata didn't budge. Her expression remained unchanged. She had suspected something bad but wouldn't have thought that the boy had been raped. She pushed herself to carry on the conversation even though her guts felt like someone was flushing them with drain cleaner.

"Can ya tell me about it? Have ya ever told anyone?"

Tony shook his head. "I have a friend that knows it happened, but I ain't never told nobody the things they did to me."

"Do you wanna tell me about it?"

"I don't know. Maybe."

"Ya know, Tony, here's the thing. Real bad stuff happens to people. What cha gotta remember is that if ya ain't done nothin', and someone hurts ya, it's because they're screwed up in their head, not you. What cha gotta understand is that ya didn't do nothin' to provoke what happened to ya. It's sorta like your ma—does she do things to make your father hit her?"

"No. She does everything he wants, but he still likes to punch her around."

"See what I mean? So these guards, they did things to ya that they shouldn't. Do ya understand what I'm tryin' to tell ya?"

Tony lowered his head. "I guess. See, I don't know how a girl is ever gonna like me if they know what I did."

"First off," Donata snapped, "you're too young to be thinkin' 'bout girls. Second, when ya find the right girl, she'll understand what happened to ya. If she don't, then she ain't the right girl for ya. Besides, just 'cause ya meet a girl don't mean ya gotta tell her your whole life story. Ya only tell the girl you wanna be wit' for the rest of your life."

"How will I know I wanna be wit' someone the rest of my life? That's a real long time."

"You'll know. When ya meet that person, it'll make ya feel whole. You'll feel like ya found your home, the place where you're free to be yourself."

Tony smiled at the woman's passion, but then the corners of his mouth bent into a frown.

"Those guards...they put their things up my butt."

Donata hoped that Tony didn't see her cringe. She nodded at him, but it was more to distract herself from losing her lunch. It took several moments before she could speak.

"Those bastards are gonna burn in the fiery depths of hell, Tony," she stated with certainty.

"They made me do stuff to them too," Tony paused, looking for the repulsion in Donata's face, but all he could see there was compassion and understanding. "They made me, ya know, blow them."

Donata sucked in a silent breath. She wanted to drive to the juvenile detention center and rip the guards to shreds.

"How many times did this happen to ya?"

"Every day that I was there."

"Holy Mary, Mother of God. What has this world come to?"

Donata put her face in her hands and wept. She cried for the loss of Tony's innocence. She cried at the thought of Ruth having horrible things happen to her. Pulling herself together, she straightened up on her chair and looked at the boy. She dabbed at her eyes with a napkin that was lying on the table.

"I'm sorry that I upset you," Tony said.

"No, ya ain't ever gotta be sorry 'bout tellin' the truth. I'm the one who's sorry that ya got violated in a place that's supposed to protect ya from the bad guys. I need ya to draw on that strength ya had in prison. Ya have great perseverance, the most I've ever seen in a person. Ya know what that means?"

"No."

"It means that ya can manage your way through the worst things that life throws at ya. Tony, ya got real stayin' power. Ain't nothin' gonna throw ya off of what cha want outta life. Ya find your purpose and see it through to the end. In a nutshell, ya got some big balls."

Donata gave Tony a smile that let him feel like he would be OK—that no matter what life tested him with, it would all work out because he had that perseverance gene.

Donata shook her head wildly, as if she was clearing cobwebs from her brain.

"Let's go see what Ruth is up to. I can let ya stay here for a couple of days, until Erikson is better. I wish I could let ya stay longer, but money is tight, and I gotta make sure that Ruth has everything she needs."

Donata was plagued with guilt, but she wanted to be honest with Tony. The last thing he needed was another person betraying his trust.

Tony beamed at her. "You're a real nice lady. Thanks for everything you've done for me."

Tony followed Donata into the living room and sat on the sofa. Ruth got up from the floor and moved onto the sofa next to him. She leaned against Tony, and the two of them laughed at the sitcom playing on the television.

Donata grabbed her knitting and relaxed in the chair next to the sofa. Then she glanced over at Tony and watched him laugh, easing the pain. Knowing him better now, and all that the boy had been through, Donata had a better appreciation for Tony's ability to adapt and overcome. Even if he didn't see himself as strong or a survivor, she knew better.

Chapter Fifty-Three

F our days later, after the streets had been plowed and the temperature had risen above freezing, Tony looked out the window of the bakery and knew it was time for him to leave. He wanted nothing more than to stay, but he knew that Donata couldn't afford another mouth to feed.

"I'm gonna head out after I'm done working," he stated casually.

"Where are ya gonna go?" Donata asked, conflicted by worry and relief.

"Oh, ya don't gotta worry. I can go to my friend's house till me and Erikson find a better place to live. It ain't no big deal."

Ruth was pouting. "But I want you to stay here," she whined.

Tony bent down and pulled Ruth into a hug. "I know, but I gotta go. I'll be back, though, I still gotta do my job—right, Donata?"

"That's right, Tony."

Now that the holidays were over, and business had slowed down, it would be harder for Donata to keep Tony on the payroll, even if it was only ten hours a week.

At the end of Tony's workday, he announced that he was leaving.

"Hold on; I got some things for ya," Donata said.

She handed Tony a warm winter jacket, scarf, hat, and gloves.

"Where did ya get these?"

"They belonged to my husband. They might be a little big on ya now, but you'll grow into 'em. Besides, they'll keep ya warmer than that coat ya came in wit'. I also put some boxers and socks in this bag, so ya can change. It's important to keep your feet and privates clean."

Tony had lost the small amount of clothes he owned when the cops raided the abandoned building. He was thankful that he kept the knife that Erikson had given him strapped to his leg; otherwise, he would have lost that too. He set out that day with the clothes he was wearing and the few extras that Donata had provided to him.

Tony didn't know where he was going. The sun was still up, and the temperature was a balmy forty-two degrees, but he knew as night fell upon him it would be cold again, and he needed to find shelter. Tony walked toward Center City, hoping to get a bed in one of the homeless shelters where Erikson had taken him for holiday meals.

That first night Tony was lucky. He ran into one of Erikson's old friends whom he knew, and, feeling sorry for Tony, the guy brought him into the shelter that night, pretending Tony was his son. That's when Tony realized that he couldn't go into the shelters on his own. If he did, the people running the place would question his age, and he'd end up in a youth facility. The next morning he had an idea about where to go. Tony walked to the fast-food restaurant where he'd first met Blast, one of the members of the Slayers gang.

Tony stood on the sidewalk all day, waiting, searching for Blast, but he never came. That night, Tony found two Dumpsters outside of a restaurant. He sat between them and placed newspaper overtop of himself. He spent the night between exhaustion, light sleep, and shivering. In the morning, he knew he needed to spend the nights inside, or he'd freeze to death.

On the second day, Tony once again stood on the sidewalk of the fast-food restaurant, hoping that Blast would come back. Again, Blast never showed up, and not knowing where else he could go, Tony got onto a bus headed to North Philadelphia.

Tony watched out of the window. He was keeping an eye on the landmarks, looking for familiar places and things he'd seen when he'd gone into North Philadelphia with Blast months prior. Dusks eerie glow blanketed the city and the streets looked older and more threatening. The aged, unattended row homes appeared as though they were all haunted. Tony stared out the window as the bus passed the small structures. The few homes dimly lit on the inside seemed depressed and forgotten, as if the buildings yearned to escape from the neighborhood.

Tony knew that wasn't true, though. Looks were deceiving. He remembered again that the worst humans were inside the walls of juvenile detention, where children were supposed to repent for their sins under the watchful, but helpful eye of the law. The contrast untwisted Tony's guts, and he felt a strong surge of fearlessness pump through his bloodstream. He noted the familiar looking place where he believed that Blast had gotten off of the bus. He didn't get off at the stop. That night he rode the bus back into Center City, sleeping as much as he could. When he got off of the bus just before two o'clock in the morning, he wandered the streets. Tony walked block after block so he wouldn't freeze to death, stopping only to rest for short periods of time. He had a plan, and the next day he would follow through with it.

Chapter Fifty-Four

Tony stood outside the fast-food restaurant the next day, but there was no sign of Blast. In the late afternoon, while the sun was still up, Tony got onto a bus to North Philadelphia. In the daylight, Tony recognized areas of the neighborhood as the bus drove deeper into the dregs of North Philly. Then, on the corner, he saw the burned, gutted car with the ripped American flag coming out of the center of the car hood. Even in the roughest of neighborhoods, people were proud of their country. In this neighborhood people lived in squalor and destroyed each other, and a host of elderly people were stuck in their homes as the neighborhood fell apart around them. There was an epidemic of drugs, gangs, and death. The good people who wanted to live normal lives were the casualties among the riffraff that had claimed the streets and turned them into what was known as the Badlands of Philadelphia.

Tony got off of the bus on Somerset and traced the route he'd taken months ago. Ten minutes later he was standing outside of the row home used by the Slayers. Suddenly, he wondered what he was doing there. These kids could kill him. Tony took several deep breaths and knocked on the door.

A tall man opened the door. His broad shoulders filled the doorway, and his thick arms and biceps were crossed over his chest. Tony looked into the man's closely set black eyes. Tony swallowed hard as he read the tattoo across his forehead: Snake Eyes.

"Ya fuckin' lost, asshole, or ya lookin' to get killed?"

Tony held his head high. He knew the only way to be respected was to demand it. "Nah, man. I'm lookin' for Blast. He here?"

Snake Eyes turned into the house. "Blast? Your girlfriend is here to see ya."

Tony's blood pressure skyrocketed; he didn't like being demeaned by a low-life, scum-sucking pig. Before Tony could let Snake Eyes's comment boil in his belly, Blast was standing at the door.

"Hey, Tony, man, what are you doin' here? You lookin' to get killed?"

Tony stood tall. "No, I'm lookin' for a place to stay. With people I can call my own. I've been on the streets for a couple of days."

Blast looked behind him. All the gang members were listening, and he didn't want them to see the empathy he had for Tony. That would be considered a sign of weakness. Gang members didn't show weak emotions; they were programmed to feel loyalty, anger, and ruthlessness.

"Yeah, so what cha want wit' me?"

"I thought maybe ya could help me out. Give me a place to stay for a while. It's fuckin' freezin' out here."

Blast stepped aside and nodded for Tony to enter.

Razor was standing in the doorway to the kitchen. "What the fuck, Blast? Ya think we're in the business of takin' in stray cats now?"

Blast turned and gave Razor a hard glare. "Nah, I don't think that. But don't forget he knows Dooley. I think we should let 'im in, ask 'im some questions. We are always lookin' for new recruits."

"New recruits from the hood, not from South Philly, ya fuckin' moron," Razor snapped.

Blast looked to his other brothers. "Come on. Razor's in charge while Dooley's in lock-down, but ya all know we have the right to vote."

"You fuckin' defying me, boy?" Razor yelled and stepped closer to Blast.

Blast stood his ground. All the gang members knew that Blast was the most deadly of them all. The only reason Dooley had left Razor in charge was because they were cousins. But it was Blast that led the fights. It was Blast they all leaned on to come up with a plan of action for dealing drugs and protecting their territory. Without Blast, they would flail around violently with no prospect for obtaining wealth and power.

Snake Eyes glared at Tony. "I'm wit' ya, Blast. We gotta have a vote that he can stay temporarily. Then, if we like 'im enough, we'll see if he can make it through our initiation to stay for good."

Tony's eyes were glued to Razor, who was glaring at Blast with his hands rolled into fists. Tony suspected that Razor didn't like being challenged.

A boy who looked about Blast's age stood up from the chair in the corner. "I'm wit' Blast and Snake Eyes. We give the kid a chance. Ain't none of us would be here if we didn't get a chance to prove ourselves."

Tony took a better look at the teen. He was strikingly handsome with a chin that had a prominent cleft, making it look a little like an ass. However, it didn't take away from his good looks; it actually made him better looking.

The room of people had gone silent to listen to the handsome kid. Then the male and female gang members talked among themselves.

Tony leaned into Blast. "Who's that?"

"That's Chin Ass. He's been my best friend since we were four years old."

"Oh yeah? I have a couple of good friends back in South Philly who I've been close wit' since I was a kid. Ain't nothin' better than good friends," Tony said, trying to make a deeper connection with Blast.

The ten main Slayer members convened in one of the upstairs bedrooms. After a lot of heated debate and arguing, the members voted eight to two that Tony could stay on. Razor was pissed, and his younger brother, Boner, who had voted against Tony staying with them, was equally annoyed that Razor was overruled.

The gang members thudded down the worn wooden steps and into the living room. Tony stood from the folding chair he had been sitting on and faced them.

Blast went up to Tony. "We voted that ya can stay for now. That means we see how ya do, and if ya live up to what we expect, then we vote again to initiate ya."

A small smile formed on Tony's face until Blast hauled off and punched him in the arm. Tony withstood the punch—it hurt, but he barely lost any ground. Then each of the other nine main members waited their turn to punch Tony in the same arm. Razor and Boner waited until last. Boner drew back his body, like a baseball pitcher, and put all of his weight behind the powerful punch. Tony's arm was already throbbing, and now he wondered if he'd be able to lift it. The pain was intense, and he still had Razor left.

Tony looked into Razor's eyes. The gangster smiled at him wickedly and looked down at his own hand. Tony followed his gaze to a hand with large, bulky rings on every finger. Tony braced himself as Razor's face crunched up, like an angry toad whose face was covered in warts. Nothing could have prepared Tony, though, for the pain that shot through him when Razor made contact. He thought that his shoulder broke on impact, but Tony would have died on the spot before he gave Razor the pleasure of seeing the agony he was in.

When the members had finished, Blast stood beside Tony and handed him a shot of cheap tequila. Tony threw it back, hoping to ease the pain.

"You'll be fine in a day or two," Blast whispered. "Don't rub it in front of everyone. Wait a little while; then go upstairs into the bathroom. Lock the door, and do what cha gotta do to get the feeling back in your arm."

A little later, when the members were back to partying, Tony went up to the second floor and stripped off his shirt. Above the sink was a cracked mirror. Tony studied his reflection, feeling as though the broken little boy was staring back at him. His arm and shoulder were throbbing when he tried to lift his arm away from his body. A fiery pain sliced through his shoulder; he couldn't move his arm more than an inch or two from his waist. He turned sideways in front of the mirror to get a good look at the damage. His entire shoulder was covered with deep-red, irate blotches from the blood trapped just beneath the skin's surface.

Tony knew from his childhood experiences that over the next couple of days, the bruises would turn blue and dark purple. He rubbed his arm gently, but even that gave him severe pain, so he went back downstairs and waited patiently for others to talk to him. He might have been new to the gang, but he would not kiss anyone's ass—all he was looking for was a place to stay and people to keep him company. He couldn't know the price he'd pay for those two basic human needs.

Chapter Fifty-Five

Tony's first night, he slept in the Slayers' house on the second floor, in a barren room with three single mattresses on the floor. The mattresses were stained, and there were no sheets or blankets, but it was a step up from what he had in apartment 3F. Tony was sharing the room with Blast and Chin Ass, so he felt he had at least two allies in the group.

Tony woke before the other two and wandered downstairs. Razor was already up. He was sitting on the sofa cleaning his gun.

Razor looked up and gave Tony a sneer. "Blast and some of the others might think it's OK that you're here, but not me. I see ya for the sniveling asshole that ya are. Let me be real clear: stay outta my business, and don't try to be friends wit' me. If ya survive here the next month, I promise you that you'll never make it through the initiation. Ya ain't got the grit or the balls. I see right through ya. You're afraid of your own fuckin' shadow."

Tony held eye contact with Razor. On the inside, his guts were having a dance party, but Tony followed his instincts and established his ground, even if it was in a small way. After a minute, Tony relaxed his shoulders and smirked. "Guess what, Razor? I ain't here to cause ya no trouble, but I ain't afraid of you or no one else either."

Tony went into the kitchen and looked in the old refrigerator for something to drink. Finding nothing there, he turned the spigot on and let the cold water run. Cupping his hands, he drank from the tap, and when he turned around Razor was standing behind him.

"Ya know, just 'cause you're staying here for a while don't mean that shit is free. You're gonna need to pitch in…to help pay for stuff, like that water you was slurping up."

"Sure, man. I'll pitch in—ya ain't gotta worry."

"Oh, I ain't worried. I just don't like ya."

"Why is that? Ya don't even know me."

"'Cause I hate all you cheesesteak-eatin', South Philly–Italian motherfuckers."

Tony walked past Razor and into the living room. By then, Blast and Chin Ass were sitting on the sofa smoking cigarettes.

"Wassup, man?" Blast said, nodding at Tony.

"Nuttin'."

Tony sat on the chair next to the sofa. "So what do you guys do all day?"

Blast blew out a cloud of smoke. "What cha talkin' 'bout? We do what we're doin' now. Hang out. Smoke some dope. Get laid. Today we're gonna try to get our hands on some meth so that we can sell it. Gives us the money we need to buy more guns and ammo. We're plannin' on gettin' some next week, but this week we're just chillin'."

Tony looked around the depressing room. He was already getting antsy just thinking about spending the day in the gloomy living room.

Tony stood from his chair. "All right. I'm gonna head into the city. I need to earn some cash."

"Yeah? How ya gonna do that?" Chin Ass said.

"I got a job at a bakery in South Philly," Tony said and threw Razor a dirty look. "Lady lets me work there a couple of hours a week."

"I told you fools that he's a little faggot," Razor snapped. "What fuckin' gang member do you know works at a goddamn bakery? Ya gotta be fuckin' kidding with this shit."

Tony spun on Razor. "There ain't nothin' wrong wit' what I do. I ain't no faggot either, so don't call me that again."

Razor took a couple steps forward and punched Tony on the side of the face. Tony stumbled backward from the hit, got his balance, and, with his anger fueled by the last six months of his life, lunged at Razor. He grabbed him around the throat, and while Razor was on the floor, he began punching him in the face, using the arm that wasn't bruised. Blast and Chin Ass sat for a prolonged moment, watching Tony, fascinated by his strength and fighting capabilities. Then they got up from the sofa and pulled Tony off of Razor.

"Whoa, Tony. Come on, calm down," Blast coaxed. "He might be an asshole, but he's still our leader until Dooley comes back."

Razor got up off of the floor in a flash. He flexed his hands, and he was bouncing from one foot to the other, like a boxer getting ready to start a new round. However, his face was flushed, and if the boys had looked close enough, they'd have seen the fear in his eyes—his fear of Tony.

Blast took Tony upstairs to the bedroom. "Listen, Tony. Ya can't go around beatin' other members' asses. That'll just get ya in all kinds of trouble wit' the club. Sometimes you're gonna have to defend yourself against someone here, but not just 'cause they call ya a name. That'll make everyone think that ya can't handle your shit. There's a balance here, and ya gotta find it. If that was Dooley that ya just pounded on, you'd be dead. Razor's a fill-in, but don't underestimate him—he's a vindictive prick. I know ya don't want anyone to think you're a pussy, but that's something you can prove on the streets. Ya got it?"

Tony nodded. "So I'm just supposed to let that dickhead say whatever he wants to me? He already told me this mornin' if I make it a month here that he'll make sure I don't pass the initiation. What the hell does that mean? What do I gotta do to be initiated?"

"Guys get beat in. All the gang members stand in two lines. You gotta make it from the beginning to the end of the line gettin' your ass kicked wit'out screaming. It ain't pretty, and, I ain't gonna lie, it hurts like hell, but if ya wanna stay here and be a part of us, that's not the worst thing ya gotta do."

Tony gasped. "What's worst thing? Is there something else?"

"Yep, after ya get beat in and survive that, ya gotta get a Slayer tattoo."

Blast put his arm in front of Tony, and he saw the same tattoo that Dooley had. Just the word SLAYER, in multiple colors running from his wrist to his elbow. "Now, this shit here..." Blast said, pushing his arm closer to Tony, "this shit hurts. All these letters gotta be filled in, and that's a lot of skin to cover. They gotta use lots of needles. The Slayers don't let ya take months to do it. So you're back in that chair before the first shit gets to heal, and then they are puttin' more ink in your arm. These other tattoos," Blast said, showing Tony a green one on his other arm and a couple of black ones on his legs, "they didn't hurt as much 'cause I picked tattoos that don't need a lot of fillin' in."

Tony looked over the tattoos. He always thought they were cool, although his mother hated them and had threatened bodily harm if he ever got one.

"The tattoo seems like nuttin' compared to gettin' beat in. That just sounds dumb."

Blast winced. "Look, man, that's what we do, and ya ain't helpin' yourself by sayin' the shit we believe in is dumb. Maybe Razor is right, and ya are scared. If you're meant to be a Slayer, you'll have to get through gettin' beatin' in just like the rest of us did. Remember, after a month, we take another vote to see if we even want ya to be a permanent member. So don't say shit that's gonna piss people off," he said, with an icy edge in his voice.

"I'm sorry, Blast. I didn't mean to hurt your feelings, but if Razor's got anything to do with me bein' a Slayer, then I won't make it a month. The guy hates me, and I don't even know why."

"Fuck, Tony. Get a grip. People hate other people for all kinds of reasons. It don't mean just 'cause someone hates ya that it changes anything in your life. If ya haven't figured it out already, most people are self-centered, and they don't care to see what's good about ya. If they think you're a threat, don't matter if it's real or not, then assholes like Razor will do whatever they can to make sure that no one likes ya. Do ya think for one minute if Razor wasn't related to Dooley that he would be in charge right now? Ain't no fuckin' way that would happen. What I think is that Razor sees the same thing in you that I see, and that scares

187

the piss outta him. So stop whining like a pussy—just knock that shit off right now—'cause that ain't what this gang is about."

"Yeah, fine, I got it." Tony hesitated for moment but had to know. "What do ya think ya see in me? Ya said Razor was scared of it."

Blast gave Tony a tight smile. "Ya look and smell like a killer."

Tony laughed. "You're kiddin' me, right?"

Blast inched his face closer to Tony. "Do I look like I'm fuckin' kiddin'? We're all animals, man. We smell each other, and we don't even know it. Those smells tell ya how other people feel. Ya knew that Razor didn't like ya, right?"

Tony nodded.

"That's what I mean."

Tony put his hand on his forehead. "I hate to break it to ya, but Razor made it clear he hates me as soon as he saw me. "

"And before he ever talked to ya? Did ya know he didn't like ya?"

"Yeah, I did. I knew he was an asshole with a big fuckin' attitude that don't know shit about shit."

"That's because ya smelled the scent he gave off," Blast said.

Tony cocked his head and gave Blast a confused look. "How the fuck can ya know ya don't like someone if ya ain't never met 'im?" Tony growled.

"Right there," Blast said, pointing at Tony's clenched teeth. "That's what I'm talkin' about. The anger that's right under the surface, all pent up in your guts. That's why I know you're a killer or will be one day."

"Whatever, man," Tony said, but in his heart, he knew there was some truth to what Blast told him. Not that he wanted to be a killer, because he didn't, but he wanted respect, and more than anything, he didn't want to be afraid anymore.

Later that night, as Tony lay on his mattress listening to the steady sound of Blast's snoring breaths, he wondered if he was doing the right thing, trying to join the gang. But he had nowhere else to go, and, other than Razor and his brother, Boner, all the other guys had been nice to him. Tony thought about his two options, the gang or being alone on the streets until something came along. Tony wanted to be a part of something; anything was better than trying to survive alone.

That night, Tony decided he would do whatever was necessary to be a Slayer.

Chapter Fifty-Six

Tony learned quickly that the bad things he'd done with Salvatore and Vincent were nothing—were nice, even—compared to the kind of things the Slayers did. In the two weeks since he'd arrived in North Philadelphia, they had stolen two cars, fought with a rival gang so viciously that one of the rival gang members had both legs broken, and burglarized the house of a drug dealer where they stole bags of cocaine. Tony had gone with the gang, designated as the lookout, but Blast told him that his time was coming to prove himself.

Tony had taken the bus back and forth to South Philadelphia several times a week to work at the bakery. Now, it was more about seeing Donata and Ruth; they made him feel human.

Tony was leaving the bakery one day, heading back to North Philadelphia. He'd had a particularly good day at the bakery. Donata and Ruth had made him a special cake to celebrate his moving into the new "foster home" that Tony had lied about. He left feeling good about himself. As he walked down Ninth Street, he heard his name being called and turned around.

"Tony, where the fuck ya been?" Vincent said, running toward him with Salvatore following.

Tony was beaming. "Hey, you guys. It's good to see ya. How ya been?"

Salvatore shoved his hands into his pockets. He still carried the guilt of Tony being raped in juvenile detention and the shabby life he was living as a result. Salvatore had talked to Big Paulie about Tony's experiences to get more information and then he'd gone to the public library to research things that happen in prison. Salvatore clearly understood that because of him, his friend Tony had lost his innocence and maybe even his manhood. Salvatore had vowed to himself that he would pay Tony back for the price he'd paid for him.

Tony noticed that Salvatore seemed to feel uncomfortable; he was quiet and wouldn't make eye contact.

"How about a cheesesteak at Jim's?"

"Um, well, I ain't got that kinda money to spend," Tony said.

"I'll pay; let's go," Salvatore offered.

After the boys finished eating, they walked to Front Street.

"Where ya been livin'?" Vincent asked.

"I'm livin' wit' some guys I met in North Philly."

Salvatore's eyes got wide. "North Philly. What the fuck are you doing there? My pop and Big Paulie have told me some gruesome stories about the shit that goes on in that place. You have to be careful that somebody doesn't kill you."

Tony smirked. "Yeah, it ain't the nicest place to live, but I met some guys, and now I'm livin' wit' 'em."

"What guys?" Vincent said, true concern in his voice.

"Guys, just some guys. What's the problem?"

"How old are these guys?" Vincent shot back.

"What's the difference?"

Vincent stopped walking and grabbed Tony by the arm. "How can ya be livin' wit' some guys that ya don't even know? How old are they?"

Tony pulled his arm away gently. "Some of them are older, and some are around my age."

"Then who pays for all of ya to live?"

"We all do. We chip in. Look, I wasn't goin' to no foster home. I lost enough of myself in juvie. I met some guy who brought me to meet his friends. They said I could stay for a while, and that's all there is to it."

Salvatore listened intently, but he knew Tony wasn't telling them everything. "You need to be careful with the people you pick for friends. My pop tells me that all the time. Your friends are the people who can make you or break you."

"That's real nice to hear, Salvatore, but ya got a nice house to live in wit' parents that buy ya everything."

"Yeah, pretty boy," Vincent added, "ya don't know your ass from a hole in the ground when it comes to bein' poor." Then Vincent turned to Tony, with his eyebrows taut. He stared at his friend for an extended moment. "Ya just remember, if ya need us, we'll always be there for ya. Ya gotta be careful, ya know—people ain't always as nice as they seem."

Tony considered Vincent's words. In the short time he had lived with the Slayers, he'd found that Vincent was right.

Chapter Fifty-Seven

Tony had been living with the Slayers for three weeks when Blast approached him in the living room.

"We got a job tonight. You're the point man."

"What's that mean?" Tony asked, but he already knew.

"It means that you gotta do the dirty work."

Tony hesitated. He'd known this day was fast approaching, but now that it had arrived, he felt trapped. His hands were sweating, and his heart felt like rolls of thunder in his chest.

"What do I gotta do?"

Blast's face was void of emotion, which sent a trickle of dread through Tony.

"There's an old couple about a mile from here. We know they stash their money in the house 'cause the old guy tells everybody that he doesn't believe in banks; he says nobody can trust a banker."

"Has he done somethin' to the Slayers?"

"No, he ain't done nothin'. It's about taking his money."

Tony stood up from the sofa. "That don't sound right. I mean, we don't even know these old people, and they ain't done nothin'."

"Are ya sayin' ya ain't gonna do it?" Blast asked, his voice laced with annoyance.

The other gang members looked at Tony, waiting for an answer. Tony looked around the room; the growing pressure from the other boys pressed in on him. His glance stopped at Razor, who was smirking, as if he could read Tony's thoughts.

Razor took a few steps toward Tony. "I fuckin' told ya, Blast. I told ya this idiot was a pussy. Ya didn't want to listen—now look, Tony looks like he wants to cry. He's too scared. He's a weak, sniveling weasel that needs to take his ass back to South Philly where he belongs."

"Kiss my ass, Razor," Tony snarled. "I ain't afraid. I just don't think it's right to steal from people who ain't got nothin'. I ain't sayin' I'm not gonna do it; I'm just sayin' it's dumb."

"Good; it's settled then," Blast said, interrupting him, before Razor could respond. "Tonight ya get to prove to us what you're made of."

Tony nodded, but inside he was twisted. He realized that he already knew too much about the gang to walk away. They would never let him leave; he was a threat to their criminal life.

That night, Tony snuck into the house of the elderly couple. One of the Slayers had eavesdropped weeks prior while the old man had mentioned to a friend that the safest place to keep money was in a freezer.

"Ya see," the eighty-year-old had said, "nobody ever suspects the freezer, and if there's a fire, it'll be the last place to burn.'

Tony prowled around the first floor. He entered a small living room, and to his right, he could hear the hum of the refrigerator. He stepped cautiously into the kitchen in the dark and listened intently for sounds of movement. Nothing. Tony moved toward the hum of the motor. He opened the freezer and reached his hand inside. In the back, underneath the food, his fingers found two bags with small boxes inside. Tony slid one out quietly and put it into his coat. His hand reached back into the freezer and grasped the second one. He paused a moment, released the bag and pulled his hand out. He quickly left the house the way he'd entered. He would tell no one that he hadn't taken both bags of money.

"Let's see what ya got," Blast said, when they were down the block from the house.

Tony pulled the plastic bag from his coat and pushed it at Blast, who opened the bag and pulled out stacks of twenty-dollar bills.

Blast looked at Tony. "Was this all that was there?"

"Yeah, that's it. I guess the old guy was a big talker."

Back at the Slayers' house, Blast threw the bag of money on the beat-up coffee table. "Count it," he directed another member.

Tony had stolen five thousand dollars. He was plagued with guilt. He didn't like hurting people who hadn't hurt him.

"Good job," Blast said.

That night as Tony lay on the mattress in the upstairs bedroom, he thought about what he'd done. It made him feel insignificant. He felt like a bully, a piece of shit who just stole from defenseless people. It was the last thing he wanted to become.

Chapter Fifty-Eight

In the final week of Tony's probation in the gang, he and Blast were walking to a nearby convenience store. They passed a house where the door was wide open, and they stopped walking and turned toward the screaming. Inside, a man had his young girlfriend by the hair as he delivered punches to her face and back. Tony charged into the house and grabbed the man around the neck. Anger and frustration coursed through Tony's veins, and he punched the man until he fell to the floor then kicked him in the ribs. Blast grabbed Tony's arms, which released him from his fury trance.

"What the fuck, man?" Blast growled. "This ain't none of our business."

"I don't care. Ya understand?" Tony screamed back. He walked over to the teenage girl lying on the floor trembling.

"You OK?"

The Asian teen nodded. "When he wakes up, he's gonna kill me," she said, her voice quivering.

Tony looked at Blast. "She can stay wit' us, right?"

"No, man, it don't work like that. The girls who stay at the house are Slayers."

Blast bent down and looked closely at the girl. She was pretty, with long black hair and light-brown eyes. He noticed a tattoo of a dragon on the inner part of her wrist.

"What's that tattoo mean?" he asked.

The girl looked at him bewildered. "Nothing. I got it 'cause I like all the colors."

"Ya belong to a gang?"

She shook her head.

Blast looked at her lustfully. "This your father?"

"No. He's my...my boyfriend."

"Ya mean your pimp?"

A tear splashed onto her cheek. "Yeah."

Blast's heart sped up; his hormones cranked high. "What's your name?"

"Reena."

Blast reconsidered his initial stance, knowing that the girl could make money for the Slayers. "All right, Reena. Ya wanna come wit' us?" Blast said, extending his hand to her.

Reena nodded, put her hand in his, and Blast pulled her up.

Tony watched. He was no longer sure that it was a good idea for Reena to go with them. Blast's demeanor had changed, and if there was one thing Tony had learned over the past month, it was that all the gang members exploited everything and everyone that didn't belong to their circle.

Back at the Slayers' house, Blast walked in and pulled Reena inside.

"This is Reena. She wants to stay wit' us for a while. Maybe even be a part of our family," he said in a flat voice.

The other male gang members lustfully looked at Reena while the female gang members gave her scowling looks.

"If that bitch wants to stay here, she's gotta earn it," Goldie said.

Tony watched intently. Goldie was the head of the girls and Razor's girlfriend. She was tall with thin legs, big boobs, and a thick, flabby middle. She wore her clothes too tight and her dark brown hair down to her waist. Tony found out later that they called her Goldie because of her obsession with beating up other girls and stealing their gold jewelry.

Goldie was hovering over Reena, and Reena shrank away.

"Take your shirt and bra off, bitch," Goldie ordered.

Reena removed her clothing. Having been a prostitute for the prior two years, it didn't bother her to show her body. Reena stood in the middle of the room. Her firm body made Goldie more irate.

"Ya think you're good enough to be here wit' us, huh? Let me tell ya right now—you'll be my bitch. That means you'll be out on the street making money; you got that?"

"It ain't no different than what I've been doin'," Reena responded.

"Yeah, well, it is different 'cause I'll be your motherfucking boss and master. That means you'll do what I say when I say it."

Goldie took Reena's nipples between her fingers and squeezed. Reena stood facing her until she couldn't take it anymore and went down to her knees.

"Yeah, I thought we'd have to toughen ya up a bit," Goldie mocked. She turned to the other female members of the gang. "Bitch looks like she needs an ass whooping."

With that, five other girls converged on Reena. They punched, slapped, and pinched the teen until she was lying on the floor curled up into a tight ball.

"Get your filthy ass off my floor," Goldie yelled.

Reena uncurled her body and slowly got up on her hands and knees. Goldie pulled her foot back and kicked the girl in the stomach. On instinct, Tony shot forward. Razor positioned himself in front of Goldie before Tony got there.

"What the fuck is your problem?" Razor snarled, chin jutting out and eyes fixed like stone.

"She's had enough. Ya can't just keep beatin' her," Tony said, matching Razor's intensity.

"You don't make the calls here. Understand? Not even if you do get initiated."

Tony looked down at Reena, who was staring up at him. Blood dripped from her mouth onto her chin. When her eyes met Tony's, she quickly looked back at the floor.

"That might be true, but I ain't standin' here watchin' this shit happen."

Tony turned and walked into the kitchen and grabbed a warm beer. He guzzled it down and went back into the living room. Reena was sitting on the floor, leaning against the far wall. The girls were standing around her telling Reena how ugly, worthless, and fat she was. Tony shook his head and walked outside. Blast followed him.

"She'll have a better life wit' us then she did wit' that asshole if Goldie decides to give her a chance."

"How? She gets the shit kicked outta her for nothin' and gotta go sell herself on the streets 'cause Goldie said so?"

Blast nodded. "That's how it works here. That's what our life is about. Ya gotta grow your balls bigger if ya wanna survive this shit. Thing is, in the end, this will be the safest place you'll ever live. There'll be a lot of men that will cover your ass and help ya outta bad shit. It's all about not bein' alone anymore. If Reena stays, she'll eventually have a family, or at least a place where people will know her name. Besides, Goldie is real protective of her whores on the street. She's got seven of 'em now, and she don't let nobody fuck wit' 'em. As long as they are bringing money into the club, she keeps 'em safe."

"Oh yeah? How does Goldie do that?"

"Bitch ain't got no heart, just a big empty hole inside her chest. Ya don't wanna cross her 'cause she always gets even. Has three brothers a lot older than us that watch out for her too. They're wit' another gang, an older one, a motorcycle gang...one that we get along wit' mainly 'cause of Goldie. She's got lots of power, so be careful," Blast explained.

"Oh, so that's what's wrong wit' her—there ain't nothing inside pumping real blood through her veins. She ain't gotta be so fuckin' mean all the time. Goldie talks to everyone like they're nothin'. I stay away from her 'cause I could feel she's no good," Tony admitted.

Tony looked down the block and back at Blast. "I guess we're all no good. All we do is hurt other people so we can live."

Blast lit a cigarette and blew the smoke in Tony's direction. "You're missing the point. We ain't just about hurting people and stealin' shit. We're all about having a place to belong. This," Blast said, waving his hand at the rundown house, "is where we thrive. It's where we know we go to lay our heads. Yeah, we ain't the nicest people, but we ain't the worst people either. Our own families have let us down, but unless you cross the Slayers, they'll always have your back. That's what counts."

"I guess so," Tony said, unconvincingly.

Blast gave him a soft punch on the shoulder. "You ain't seen nothin' till ya lived through a girl getting initiated. It'll make your initiation seem like a fuckin' party."

Tony hated to ask, but he had to know. "When is my initiation?"

"Next week. On Wednesday night."

Tony squeezed his hands into fists. He was dreading everything he had coming to him, but more than that, he wasn't sure about signing up for life with the Slayers. He was so young. He wanted more out of his life than just being in a gang.

Blast put his arm over Tony's shoulder. "Let's go inside. The fun is about to start."

Chapter Fifty-Nine

I nside the house, Reena was still sitting against the wall, looking around the room with wide eyes. She had been ordered by Goldie to sit where she was and not move a muscle. Tony plopped down on a wooden chair next to the sofa. Tony didn't think this was 'fun', he felt sorry for Reena and wanted to help her, but the odds were against him.

The next night, as Tony sat on the sofa drinking a beer, Goldie came down the steps with her hand twisted into Reena's hair, dragging her behind. The two girls stood in the middle of the living room.

"Do what I just told ya, bitch," Goldie barked.

Reena obeyed and took off all of her clothes and lay in the middle of the floor.

Goldie gave Razor a jagged look. "You go first. I don't want to catch no diseases from any of these pricks," she said, gesturing to the other gang members.

Razor stood over Reena and unzipped his pants. He stepped out of them and sat on top of Reena in his boxers.

Tony leaned over to Chin Ass. "What the fuck's happenin'?"

Chin Ass kept his eyes glued to the scene. "Bitch is gettin' raped in."

"Wait. What?"

Chin Ass turned to Tony with a shut-the-fuck-up look on his face. "Ya heard me. That's what we do. We rape the bitches in."

Tony watched Razor grab Reena around the throat and choke her. Tony stood up from his place on the sofa, but Chin Ass pulled him back down. Razor let go of Reena's throat, and as she gasped for air, he jammed himself inside of her. Reena's eyes darted around the room.

When Razor was done, Goldie stood over top of Reena and kicked the girl in the hip. Then Goldie hacked up phlegm and spat on her. "Ya ever go near my man again, I'll skin your skank ass alive," she threatened.

One by one, the gang members had sex with Reena. By the fifth gang member, her pain was so unbearable that Reena made sharp squealing noises.

Goldie walked up to the twenty-seven-year-old riding Reena and put her hand on his head. He stopped moving. He looked up at Goldie. "What the fuck?"

"What the fuck? This whore needs to shut the fuck up and stop squealing like a pig."

Goldie bent low and put her face into Reena's. "Ya wanna stay here and be my bitch, then I better not hear one more fuckin' sound come outta your mouth. If I do, I'll bring ya back to your old pimp and give 'im a baseball bat to bash your brains in wit'. Then I'll help him hide your body."

A stream of tears rolled out the sides of Reena's eyes as she lay on the floor, hosting ten gang members, one after another. By the seventh member, her pain had turned to a fiery torture. She'd slept with a lot of guys on the streets, but never more than four in a night. On the streets, it wasn't always intercourse either.

Some of the gang members were rough with Reena. Several of them slapped her in the face. Some pinched her in sensitive places. But one, the nastiest of the members, hog-tied Reena and sodomized her. Tony almost threw up watching, seeing for the first time what he had looked like in that same compromising position.

Tony looked away from the horrific scene. His own ghosts lingered over him like a shroud—the haunting memories of the past with the three guards at juvie. He could still feel the shame he wore on the outside, a result of his wounds that marked him forever on the inside. He wanted to help Reena, but he knew he couldn't fight the whole gang and that she had "willingly" agreed to the barbaric ritual so she could become Goldie's bitch. Tony intimately knew the isolated, dark feeling of loneliness from Reena's dead stare. Loneliness was his worst enemy; not having the love of another human was a fate worse than death. Reena's face was now void of emotion. The mask of solitude made her look older than her eighteen years, and Tony understood that for Reena to escape her desolate world, she was pledging herself to an eternity in hell surrounded by demons.

"What about Tony?" Blast asked, when the last member had finished.

Tony's heart seized in his chest. He wanted nothing to do with the twisted ritual being done to the girl.

"No. He ain't a member, so he don't get to participate," Razor snapped.

Blast threw his hands up in disgust and walked out of the room. Finally, Tony was happy to be left out of something. He remembered what the bus driver had told him when he was a kid: "Sometimes bein' left out is better than bein' let in. Remember that." He didn't believe he could have gone through with it even if they'd tried to force him. As damaged as he was, Tony hadn't had intercourse, hadn't lost his virginity to a girl. He clung to this pure thought; it made Tony feel like he had a small sliver of humanity left in him.

The "rape-in" of Reena churned over in Tony's mind for the days that followed. He was finding it less appealing to be a Slayer. He didn't like how they treated women, and he wasn't a fan of being expected to do things against his core values. He thought about going back to South Philadelphia, even a foster home, but

Tony convinced himself that the Slayers would find him, and he'd be punished, probably killed, so he resolved himself to stay.

***

On Wednesday night of that week, the gang members stood on either side of the living room, and the girls watched from the kitchen, egging on the violence. Tony had to make it through the entire line of the ten main members without running, screaming, or fighting back.

Tony stood before the group of members in a pair of jeans and a T-shirt.

Razor spoke in a booming voice. "On the count of three, ya start walkin' through. One. Two. Three."

Tony stepped in front of the first two members, who punched him in the head and back. The members beat him through the line as he was passed to the next members. Their thumps were relentless, and Tony wondered if he'd make it through the next eight members alive. As each twosome beat him and then pushed him to the next two, the intensity of the beating grew. He felt as though he was about to die when he got pushed to the last two members, Razor and Boner. While Boner was slamming Tony with his fists, Razor pulled his belt from his pant loops and whipped him with it. Tony was on the floor by then, and Razor jumped into the air and brought his booted foot down on Tony's back. After almost thirty seconds of Razor's out-of-control rage, Blast and a few of the older members stepped in.

"He's had enough, Razor. You're gonna fuckin' kill 'im," one of the members yelled.

"That's right! I'm gonna kill 'im 'cause he don't belong here. He never should've come up for membership," Razor grunted through heavy breaths.

Blast grabbed Razor by the shoulders. "We voted. It was a majority. He got in and made it through his initiation. Now you gotta accept him like any other member in this room."

Razor looked down at Tony's still body on the floor and slammed one more kick into his spine. Then, he and Boner walked out of the room and left the rest of the members to deal with the pile of flesh they'd left on the floor.

Blast and Chin Ass got Tony up to the bedroom, and some of the girl members bandaged his wounds and held ice on his swollen, bulging face. It would be several days before Tony could make it out of the bedroom. For the first three days, the skin around his eyes was so engorged that he couldn't see.

A week later, Tony sat in the living room with his brothers. He was happy that the initiation was over and that he finally belonged somewhere.

Chapter Sixty

Two years had passed since Tony was initiated into the Slayers. In that time, Dooley, his cellmate from juvie had been sent to adult prison, because he killed another inmate for selling drugs to his regular customers. The details that the judge heard were sketchy. Other inmates that were eyewitnesses said Dooley killed the man in self-defense, but the judge didn't buy the whole story, and Dooley was sentenced to another fourteen years. This meant that Razor retained his position as head of the Slayers until Dooley served out his sentence. The gang was disappointed to hear the news. Some of the gang liked Razor and others not so much, but they all knew that Dooley was a much better leader and had been hopeful he would be back in North Philadelphia soon.

Tony tried to keep himself busy, and he didn't love the gang the way the others did. The gang helped him to survive, but he didn't agree with a lot of their beliefs. Tony would be turning sixteen and he was no further along in figuring out what to do with his life than when he had joined. He was bored of the same old routine, which included robbery, selling drugs, and violent battles with rival gangs. With each criminal act, there was no greater outcome or positive impact on his life. Tony was lonely, and the only normalcy he had in his life was the time he spent at the bakery with Donata and Ruth. Even that had become a source of ridicule by the other gang members. But for Tony, it wasn't a matter of working a job anymore; it was a safe place for him to go and be loved by Donata and Ruth. They were his secret family, the two people that could never be taken from him.

Tony was on his way to the bakery one morning when he heard a group of young people screaming. He walked into the alley, where he could see a fight in progress. Tony approached cautiously, and he spotted a girl being beaten by three other teen girls. A small group of teens had gathered around and were cheering on the out-of-control beating.

"Whoa! She's had enough," Tony said, in a commanding voice.

Tony squeezed his way between the three girls and the victim and took a few stray punches to his body. They felt like love taps compared to the violent fistfights he had since joining the Slayers. The most rabid of the teen girls sneered at him.

Her face filled with fury, and he knew it was in his, and the victim's, best interest to get them both out of there.

"We're gonna leave. Whatever point ya were tryin' to make has been made," Tony said, lifting the beaten girl to her feet.

The teens watched Tony. They had seen him around. He was a very big kid, and word on the street was that he belonged to a gang, so they retreated, claiming victory.

Tony walked the girl out of the alley and sat her down on the curb. "Stay here; I'll be right back."

A few minutes later, Tony returned with two bottles of water. He opened the first one and gingerly took her chin in his hand, tilting her head to the sky. The girl was semi-coherent, her face bruised and bloodied. Tony slowly poured the bottle of water over her face, not only to revive her, but also to clean off the blood so he could assess the damage. In his time with the Slayers, he'd learned several tricks about cleaning up war scars.

The girl looked at him, and her eyelids fluttered.

Tony gazed into her eyes. They were a vibrant blue, and they looked electrified as the sun bounced off them and gave him a small glimpse into her innocent soul. Her eyes glistened with tears as she held his stare.

"What's your name?"

"Kate," she croaked.

Tony lifted the water bottle to her lips, and she took a sip. The water slid down her dry throat and felt as though it extinguished a fire that had confiscated her airway.

"Nice to meet ya, Kate. I'm Tony."

"Thank you for helping me," she said in a small, frightened voice.

"Why were those girls kickin' your ass?"

"One of them thought I was trying to get with her boyfriend."

"Were ya?"

Kate shook her head slowly. "I don't even know who her boyfriend is. Before she hit me, she said her boyfriend keeps watching me. She said if I even look at him, she'll kill me."

"But ya don't know who he is?"

"No."

"Well, that girl sounds like a real psycho."

Kate smiled at him.

"How 'bout if I walk ya home?"

Tony helped Kate to her feet and slowly walked her into Southwest Philly. It was a sketchy neighborhood, and he was on high alert.

"Those girls live around here?"

Kate shrugged. "I don't know them. They've been following me around the past couple of days. I think maybe they saw me in the park earlier in the week.

I went there to read, ya know, find a place where I can be quiet with my own thoughts."

Tony looked around him. People were on their porches, drinking and listening to loud music. He understood exactly what Kate was saying, about being alone with her thoughts. He too tried to escape the noise that rang in his own head, to fight off the outside world that was covered in sound pollution.

"That's my house there," she said, pointing.

Tony looked up. There were ten row homes connected, each one in disrepair. Boarded-up windows and old room air conditioners hung dangerously from the rotted wooden windows. The red brick of the houses was so neglected that the exterior looked covered in black paint. Tony helped Kate up the steps to the porch, which was filled with green trash bags, piled as high as his waist.

"You live here wit' someone?"

"Yeah, it's me and my mom. She works a lot, so we don't have time to clean the place up," she said, gesturing to the trash bags overtaking the porch.

"She home now?"

"No, she doesn't get home till ten most nights. You...you, wanna come in?"

"Sure."

Tony followed Kate into the house. It was dark inside. Kate turned on the lamp next to the sofa. The bulb cast a dreary yellow glow over the room. He looked around him; it wasn't much better than where he was living in North Philadelphia, but the silence of the home made it feel creepier, more depressing than his own living conditions.

Kate went into the kitchen and threw on the light switch. Tony watched as cockroaches scurried back under the refrigerator to the warmth of the motor that hummed out a grotesque tune. Kate pulled the door open and grabbed the only can of soda on the shelf.

"So you don't mind the roaches?" Tony asked.

"What do you mean?"

"Ya didn't even jump or scream when ya saw them running on the floor."

Kate's shoulders slumped. "No, I'm used to them. When I'm here by myself sometimes they make me feel like someone else is in the house." She took a sip of the soda and handed it to Tony. "That's pretty sick, huh?"

"No, it ain't sick. I get it. There's all these people in the world, and ya can be standing in the middle of 'em, but it's still the loneliest place to be. Just like you, I didn't grow up in the best place."

"Where are you from?"

"South Philly," Tony said proudly.

A prolonged silence was cast over them. Tony looked Kate over, noticing her ripped high-top sneakers and worn clothing. Not that he looked much better, but at least in the gang, there was some money he could spend on clothes now and again. Kate caught Tony looking her over and pulled her overworn sweatshirt over her chest and crossed her arms. The move wasn't lost on him.

"Hey, look, I ain't no kinda freak or nothin'. I just wanted to help ya out. I better get goin'."

Tony turned and walked toward the front door. Kate rushed up behind him.

"Will you come back?"

Tony gave her a confused look. "If ya want me to, I will."

"I do want you to," she said, looking down at her feet. Kate took in a long breath. "I'm not used to people being nice to me. I keep to myself...I don't really have many friends...or any even."

"How old are ya?" he asked.

"Sixteen. You?"

"The same. Well, in a couple more months, I will be. Anyway, ya better put some ice on your lip. It's pretty swelled up."

"So then I'll see ya again?" Kate asked, her voice dripping with desperation.

"Yeah, you'll see me again."

Kate leaned into Tony and kissed him softly on his cheek. As she did, he could smell the sweet aroma of the cola on her breath, and it reminded him of hot summer nights on the streets in South Philadelphia. "Thanks for helping me today. I'll see ya soon."

Tony flushed, not from embarrassment, but from a stirring in his heart. He'd never been attracted to a girl before, not like Kate. She was different, yet so much like he was.

Tony opened the front door and turned to her, "How 'bout I come by tomorra, and we can go get a slice of pizza?"

Kate smiled, cracking her lip open further. When she tasted the blood, Kate dabbed at her lip with the sleeve of her sweatshirt. "That would be fun. Can you come around four tomorrow afternoon?"

"Yeah, I can do that. See you tomorra then."

As Tony walked back to South Philadelphia, all he could think about was Kate's soft lips pressed against his cheek. For a moment, he felt like a wimp thinking that way, but then he let the harsh, loveless rules of the gang slip into the background, and Kate's sweet face came into the foreground of his mind. Tony needed to know more, much more, about the girl behind the blazing blue eyes.

Chapter Sixty-One

At four o'clock the next afternoon, Tony knocked on Kate's front door. He had thought about her since they were last together. Tony felt a connection to Kate he couldn't explain. Kate seemed pure—as though she were new to the world—yet she carried a sadness that made him want to help her.

When Kate opened the door, Tony drew in a silent breath. She was dressed in jeans and a V-neck shirt. Her breasts slightly bulged above the V, tastefully revealing the mounds of smooth flesh. He took every bit of her in. Kate was tall and slender. With her hair out of the sloppy ponytail from the day before, her silky, blond ringlets hung just below her shoulders. Her blue eyes were backlit by the hot embers glowing in her heart as she stared at him. They gazed at each other for a prolonged moment; then Kate's plump pink lips parted to reveal a dazzling smile.

"Do you want to come in for a minute?" she asked.

"Sure."

Tony followed her inside. He thought, She's beautiful; I didn't see that yesterday. How did I miss her beauty? They stopped in the living room, and Kate turned to face him.

"You're gorgeous," he blurted.

Kate blushed a deep velvety red. "Thanks."

"You looked different yesterday. Other than that scab on your lip from that stupid bitch, I wouldn't have recognized ya."

"Well, I had on a sweatshirt with my hood up. I like to hide myself from the people in this neighborhood. My mom taught me that it's better to look like shit so people leave ya alone. You know what I mean?"

"Your ma is smart. Do ya always do what she tells ya to do?"

Kate chuckled. "If I don't want my butt kicked. My mom has pretty good advice, though. She ain't much for beating around the bush. She tells it like it is."

Tony took a step toward the door. "Should we get goin'?"

As they walked, Tony told Kate about his job at the bakery. He wanted to appear normal to her, afraid he'd scare her off. They had just gotten to the end of Kate's block and stopped to look for cars before crossing over to the other sidewalk.

"Hey, baby, ya clean up real fuckin' good," a male voice called out. "Why don't cha come over and give me some of that candy ya got goin' on?"

Tony looked in the direction of the man's voice. A Hispanic man smiled back at him. The guy looked to be in his mid-twenties. He was leaning over the decrepit wooden railing of his porch. Tony left Kate on the sidewalk and stomped up to where the guy was standing.

"You got a fuckin' problem?" Tony barked.

"Nah, I ain't got no problem. Just enjoyin' the view," he said, licking his lips and smiling at Kate.

Tony grabbed the man by his shirt and pulled him off of the porch, bringing the railing with him. The guy tried to fight, but Tony had two years of experience learning the art of street brawls. He'd practically killed a man who'd slashed Blast in the leg with a knife.

Tony straddled the guy. He punched him in the face only twice before he went unconscious. He stood and dusted off his pants and then walked back to Kate. She stared at him with horror in her eyes.

"Why did you do that?" she whined.

"What? Kick his ass? 'Cause he ain't got a right to say shit to ya."

"I get that. But I live here. What am I supposed to do when you aren't with me? Are ya trying to make me a target? I told ya, I do my best to keep a low profile. Look at all the people staring at us."

Tony looked around him. On either side of the street, people were watching. He hadn't even known they were there. Now, his impact crushed into his gut.

Tony lowered his head and took Kate's hand. "I'm sorry. You're right. I could bring trouble to ya. It was real stupid. I swear I'll think next time."

Kate shrugged, but fearful thoughts of what people in the neighborhood would do to her when she was alone crowded into the corners of her brain.

Tony lifted her chin. "I'll just have to come and get ya every day to make sure you're safe."

Kate gave him a lame smile. "Yeah, like that's realistic."

"Come on," Tony said, taking her hand. "Let's go get some pizza. We can talk more 'bout how we'll need to spend more time together." He gave her a comforting smile.

Kate was quiet during the remainder of their walk, and Tony was sorry he had lost his temper. He didn't want her to think that he was some kind of asshole that would hit her, as he'd seen so many of the Slayers do to their girlfriends.

At the pizzeria, Tony pulled Kate's chair out for her, and she sat down. He sat across from her and took her hand into his own.

"I'm real sorry, Kate. I know that ya don't know me, but I ain't an asshole. I can't help but get mad at people who ain't got no right making people nervous."

"I know, Tony, but I have to live with those people. And you're right, I don't know ya. So ya come along and help me. Then the next day, ya beat up some guy from my own neighborhood. Then I never see ya again, and ya left me with a bad situation on my hands. My mother will kick the living shit outta me. You don't have a right to do that. It ain't fair."

"How 'bout if I tell the guy I'm sorry. Would that make ya feel better?"

Kate gave him a small smile. "That would probably help. So that he doesn't take it out on me."

"Done. When I walk ya home, I'll talk to 'im. Now, what kinda pizza ya want?"

Chapter Sixty-Two

Tony and Kate had just finished eating their pizza when Vincent's voice echoed through the small restaurant.

"How are ya? What's goin' on?" Vincent said, plopping down in the open seat. Vincent looked Kate over, admiring her and wondering where she came from.

"I'm doin' good since I saw ya yesterday," Tony joked. "This is Kate."

"Hi, nice to meet ya, Kate. I'm Vincent. I'm sure Tony told ya all about me already."

Kate giggled and shook her head. "Nice to meet you too."

Vincent turned to Tony. "Oh, ya didn't tell her 'bout me? What's wrong wit' cha?"

"We just met yesterday. I didn't want to scare her off," Tony chided.

"Where's Salvatore?" Tony asked.

"He's meetin' me here. We got some dates lined up for tonight," Vincent said.

"What kinda dates?"

"The kinda date where a man takes out a girl. What the fuck kinda date do ya think I'm talkin' 'bout?" Vincent looked from Tony over to Kate. "You two wanna join us?"

"Maybe another time. When we finish here, I gotta walk Kate back home and tell some guy that I beat the shit outta that I'm sorry."

"Oh yeah? Ya need any help?"

Tony shook his head. "Nah, I shouldn't have done what I did. Put Kate here," he said, nodding toward her, "in a bad space."

Vincent laughed. "That's Tony. He ain't got no tolerance for ignorance." After a moment's pause, he added, "Ain't none of us got tolerance for assholes."

Salvatore joined the group, and after a few minutes, he too extended the invitation for Tony and Kate to join them. He laughed when Vincent told the story about Tony having to tell some scumbag that he was sorry for kicking his filthy ass.

Kate sat with the three handsome teens. She felt very comfortable and safe with them. She'd wished for the kind of friends Tony had her whole life. They told

Kate stories about when they were kids, trying to make her laugh. After a couple of hours, Tony stood and put his hand out to Kate.

"I better get ya home," he said. Tony gave his friends a head nod. "I'll see you two around. I'll be at the bakery tomorra."

"Is that an invitation to come over and get some free shit from that old lady?" Vincent said.

"No, it ain't. You oughta come over and buy somethin', ya cheap bastard."

Vincent and Salvatore promised to stop by the next day. As Tony walked Kate back to her house, he felt excited about the prospect of being with Kate. He barely knew her, but that didn't matter; he felt a sense of belonging when he was with her. He hadn't felt so good about anything in a long time, and it was a welcome change in a life that had fallen short for him.

"Your friends are great. Are they the guys you live with?" Kate asked.

"Nah, they're my friends since I was a kid. The guys I live wit', some are all right, and some are the biggest pricks you'll ever meet."

"Why do you live there if they're pricks?"

"'Cause when I didn't have any place to go, they let me stay there. They let me be a part of their family."

"Are there any adults?"

"There's older guys, but it ain't like they're parents or nothin'."

Kate was thoughtful for a moment. "Is that tattoo on your arm part of living with those guys?"

Tony looked down at the Slayers' tattoo. "Yeah."

"Aren't the Slayers a gang? I heard about them back around Christmastime. They were on the news 'cause one of the members killed some cashier he was trying to rob."

Tony lowered his head. Kate's description only verified, once again, that he had become a lowlife just like his fellow members. "Yeah, that's us. The dude who killed the cashier was always outta control, though. He never shoulda done that."

"He never shoulda robbed the store or killed the cashier?"

"Killed the guy." Tony paused. "Look, Kate," he said, feeling judged, "I ain't never claimed to be some saint. I can't help that the only people I got do bad shit. I do bad shit too so I can live."

"Have ya ever killed anyone?"

"Nah. Never had to. I'm more about gettin' even wit' the other gangs. My members like me to be in front of the fighting, which is fine by me 'cause I'm fighting scumbags the same as us."

"I don't think you're a scumbag. I never said that. I was just curious. What's it like to be in a gang? Are people afraid of you?"

"I guess some people are," Tony admitted.

"Do you like that people are afraid of you?"

Tony shrugged. "Not really—only when it means somethin', I guess."

"What does that mean?"

"It means that when someone is fuckin' wit' one of the members, don't matter if it's one of the boys or girls, people back down when they find out who we are."

"There are girls in your gang?"

"Sure there are. But it ain't like we go out wit' 'em or nothin'. I mean, some of the guys and girls are together, but I ain't wit' no one, if that's what you're thinkin'."

"Good. That's good to hear."

Kate stopped walking, and Tony looked at her. "What's wrong?"

She nodded toward the Hispanic man's house.

"Yeah, yeah, wait here. I'll be right back."

Tony left Kate on the sidewalk and went up to the door. He knocked, and a moment later, the Hispanic man with a helluva black eye opened the door.

"What do ya want?" he said.

Tony took his hands out of his pockets just in case he needed to use them.

"See that girl that you were sayin' nasty shit to?"

The Hispanic man looked over Tony's shoulder and spotted Kate. "Yeah."

"You so much as look in her direction, and I'll come back here and break every rotten bone in your body. She better never tell me that you or any of these other dicks around here said somethin' to her. Don't look at her. Don't tell her she's pretty. Don't say a foul fuckin' word to her. Don't smile at her. Pretend she's fuckin' invisible. An invisible grenade will explode in your ugly face if ya so much as fantasize about her when you're lying in your bed alone at night. You got me?"

Tony opened his hands and extended them palms up toward the man, as if in a plea for peace. The Hispanic man saw the Slayers' tattoo, which was exactly what Tony wanted. "Yeah, man, yeah, I hear ya. Ya ain't gotta worry 'bout me."

"Good. Now, I want cha to wave to my girl."

The Hispanic man looked over Tony's shoulder and gave Kate a quick wave of his hand.

"Ya have a good night." Tony turned and walked back to Kate.

"What did you say to him?"

"I told 'im I was sorry and didn't mean to hurt 'im or cause ya any trouble."

"What did he say?"

"He said he understood that he never shoulda called out to ya. Said to tell ya he was sorry and he won't do it again. He said he knew it was ignorant."

"See? Don't ya feel better that you apologized?"

"Sure. Come on, Kate. Let's get cha home."

Tony and Kate sat on her front steps and talked for over an hour; then he stood to leave. Kate stood in front of Tony, and he put his arm around her waist.

"Can I kiss ya?" he asked.

Kate smiled and nodded enthusiastically.

Their mouths slowly came together and Tony pulled her closer to him. He gently separated her lips with his tongue, and a sensation of pure joy ran through him. He could've stood in that spot and kissed Kate until he died. When they parted, their eyes met.

"You're the first boy I ever kissed."

"Oh, yeah? How was it?"

Kate blushed. "It was good, but I mean, I don't really have anything to compare it to."

"Here, compare it to this," he said, leaning in and sharing another kiss.

"You better go. My mom will be home soon."

Tony held Kate tightly. "I'll see ya tomorra," he whispered.

"I can't wait," she rasped.

As Tony caught the bus back to North Philadelphia that night, he felt as though he had left something behind—as if he'd forgotten something important, something that he would need. All he could think about was Kate. He wanted to be with her more than anything else in the world. He was still thinking of Kate when he walked into the Slayers' house and was met with the unexpected.

Chapter Sixty-Three

When Tony stepped through the door of the Slayers' house, an acidy smell filled his sinuses. The living room was cloudy, and heavy white smoke hung in the air. The smell was overbearing, and he quickly tried to identify what had happened. The girls were screaming at each other, and most of the male gang members were standing around, whispering.

Tony found Blast in the kitchen. "What the hell happened?"

"That brainless bitch Tanya brought some neighborhood thugs in the house to party. They smoked up most of the crack we had in the back. She cost us a lot of money. Whatever they didn't smoke they stole. We're putting together a group to go out and find them."

"Where's Tanya?"

"She's upstairs. Razor and a couple others took her up there a while ago. They're beating the hell outta her."

"Why does it smell so bad in here?"

"Because the assholes smoked a shit-ton of it in here and then burned all the plastic bags that we use to sell it."

Tony eased his way up to the second floor. He could hear Tanya screaming and begging for her life. By the time he reached the bedroom where they had her, a bunch of the members were gathered in front of the open doorway. Tony, being taller than most of them, had a view inside the room. Tanya was lying on the floor while Razor and Boner took turns kicking her. Between their kicks, Goldie would scurry in and punch her.

Tony looked at the member next to him. "They're gonna kill 'er."

"Maybe. She deserves whatever she gets. Tanya knows the rules. She knew better than to steal from us, and now she's gotta pay the piper."

However, Tony didn't agree. He believed in some rules of the house, and he thought Tanya had done a stupid thing. But he also knew that Razor, Boner, and Goldie thrived on violence and power. After a few more seconds, Tanya was nonresponsive. She no longer flinched or buckled at the blows they were giving her.

"Hey," Tony yelled. "Think she's had enough?"

Razor looked up at him. His eyes were glazed over by fury, and his hair was disheveled. He was breathing hard and slightly bent at the waist. "She's had enough when I say she's had enough. Mind your own fuckin' business."

In that short moment, one of the other girls dropped to her knees next to Tanya. She shook her, while the rest of them looked on. "Tanya," she yelled over and again. Then she placed her fingers on Tanya's neck.

"She's dead! You fuckin' killed her!" the girl screamed.

Razor faced everyone. "Let me be crystal clear. Anybody who touches our dope, steals our dope, or gives our dope away is dead. Anyone that lets people come into our house and fuck wit' our stuff will be dead too, just like this fuckin' tramp."

Razor roughly pushed his way through the gang, followed by Boner and Goldie. He stopped next to Tony. "Get rid of her body," he commanded.

Tony knew the other members were watching him. He nodded, went into the bedroom, and hoisted Tanya over his shoulder. He took her into his bedroom and wrapped her in a blanket and then carried her down the steps, heading toward the front door.

"Whoa, dude," Blast said, going after him. "You can't just take her outside like that."

"No? Then what the hell am I supposed to do wit' her?"

"Come on," Blast said. Tony followed Blast into the basement, where there was an assortment of moldy junk. They walked over to an oval-shaped metal tub.

"Put her in there," Blast said and walked to the other side of the basement. When he came back, he was carrying two hand saws.

"You're kiddin' me, right?"

"No, it ain't no joke. We gotta break her down into smaller pieces and burn them, and then we throw whatever is left into the river. It'll make it practically impossible for anyone to figure out who the hell she was."

Blast took the saw and removed Tanya's leg just below the knee. He paused and looked at Tony. "Come on, man. I'm helping ya here. Get moving."

Tony had seen and been a part of the violence since joining the Slayers. He had shot a guy in the leg once when the guy had pointed a gun in his face. He'd even saw the carnage of drive-bys that his gang had done. Initially, the blood and dead bodies had haunted his vision, made him see the coldhearted predator in man. After a time, he'd come to view the killing no differently than a coroner regards his or her job; it was just part of what they did; it came with gang life. This was the first time, though, that Tony had to dismember anyone, let alone someone he knew. He picked up the saw, drew in a deep breath, and hacked through Tanya's arm.

It wasn't long before Tanya became unrecognizable as the metal tub filled with all the parts and pieces of what had been a human less than thirty minutes prior.

Tony now realized how precious life could be, and his thoughts dwelled on Kate, as he desperately wanted to feel love in his heart especially while performing a despicable act with his hands.

Chapter Sixty-Four

Cutting Tanya into pieces weighed heavily on Tony's mind. It made him wonder what kind of a man he was turning out to be. To offset the grungy feeling it gave him, he thought about Kate, and the warm feeling thawed his blood. It was late in the afternoon when he knocked on Kate's door. When she answered it, her red, bloodshot eyes stood out against her pale face.

"What's wrong?"

Kate sniffled, and Tony brushed away the tears clinging to her cheeks with his fingers.

"My mom is sick."

"She'll be OK. Don't worry so much," Tony said.

"No, she won't. The doctor said she has cancer."

"What kinda cancer?" Tony asked, not knowing what else to say.

"Pancreatic cancer. She told me this morning."

Tony did not understand what having pancreatic cancer meant. He stood quietly for a moment. "Can they cut it out?"

Kate shook her head. "Her doctor said it's too far gone. Cancer is already in her other organs."

Tony hesitated for a moment. He didn't want to upset Kate more than she already was, but he needed to ask. "Is she gonna die?"

"Yeahhhhhhh," she screeched in a long, drawn-out wail of despair.

Tony pulled her to him, and she sobbed against his chest. After a while, Tony looked down into her face.

"What's your mother gonna do?"

"Nothing. She said she wants to die in peace. The doctors offered her to try new things, to see if they can make her live longer, but she said she ain't gonna be a lab rat for nobody."

"Oh," he said sadly, "is she home?"

"Yeah, you wanna meet her?"

"Sure, I guess so. Is she up for meetin' me?"

Kate smiled softly, her expression mixed with sadness and love. "I told her all about ya. She knew you were coming today. She would really like it if you came in."

Tony followed Kate inside. Her mother was sitting on the sofa, covered with a blanket, a box of tissues next to her.

"Mom, this is Tony."

Tony stepped closer, and Kate's mother looked up at him.

"Nice to meet cha, Tony. I'm Darren. I heard a lot about ya. Kate's been tellin' me about cha all day."

"How...how do you feel, Darren?"

"Like a piece of shit stuck in the treads of a work boot."

Tony laughed. "Sorry, I didn't mean to laugh."

"Well, me and Kate have been cryin' all day. Ever since the doctor called this morning. So hearing someone laugh ain't so bad right about now."

Tony crossed his arms over his chest. He felt awkward and intrusive.

Darren held his gaze. "Listen, Tony, relax. Ya don't know me or Kate too well, but I'm happy that my baby has someone that she likes. So I don't want cha to feel uncomfortable. It's my own fault, really. I work all the time and never go to the doctor like I ought to. All I care about now is making sure that Kate is gonna be OK when I'm gone."

Kate threw herself next to her mother. "Please don't say that," she wailed. "And it's not your fault...I read today that pancreatic cancer is real hard to find because there aren't any symptoms. It doesn't mean you can't beat this, Mom!"

Darren put her arm around Kate. "I told ya what the doctor said. I might not have too much longer. We gotta be thinkin' about what's gonna happen to ya. Maybe Tony can help."

Kate's mouth dropped open, and she stared at her mother. "Tony and me don't even know each other that well. This ain't his problem. We're only sixteen years old."

"I never said it was Tony's problem. But if ya like 'im the way ya said and he likes you, then maybe we can figure somethin' out. We ain't got no family. I'm gonna call tomorra to see if there's a place the city can put ya after I'm gone. All I'm sayin' is that maybe Tony can check on ya. So that ya have someone that ya can trust."

Darren's statement hit a nerve with Tony. He knelt down in front of the mother and daughter. "I know kids who lived in those kinds of places. That ain't gonna be no good for Kate. There's gotta be somewhere else."

"Where? She can't stay here," Darren explained. "She's underage, and our landlord won't have it. Besides, she ain't gonna have the money to pay no rent. He'll kick her out as soon as I die. He's a real jerk-off, that one."

"We can figure it out," Kate whimpered. "I need ya to stay here with me."

Darren took in a deep breath. "I wish I could, baby. But ya know I've always been real wit' cha and told ya the truth. It's the only way to live. Otherwise, ya just spend your life bein' disappointed or waitin' for shit that never happens."

Darren hoisted her small frame from the sofa. She'd gone to the doctor in the first place because she'd been vomiting for weeks. At first, she'd thought it was the flu, but when it didn't stop, she knew something worse was going on inside of her.

After they heard the bathroom door close and lock, Tony sat on the sofa next to Kate and put his arms around her.

"Don't worry, Kate. I'll figure somethin' out. I just need some time to think."

"What are ya gonna figure out?" Kate ranted. "I need an answer right now! I want my mom to be here with me, forever."

Tony inched closer to Kate. "I got an idea."

Kate nodded. "What kinda idea?"

"I want ya to meet somebody. Maybe they can help ya...ya know, when your mother is gone."

Kate's head hung. She knew her mother was going to die, but it was still too soon for her to accept it. Tony saw the vacant look in her eyes, and his heart bled, his chest heavy with sorrow for Kate. Tony kissed Kate softly on her neck and moved up until his mouth found hers. They shared a bittersweet kiss mixed with tenderness and sadness. Tony stood, pulled Kate to her feet, and wrapped her in a tight embrace. In that moment, Kate felt safe and she wanted to cling to Tony for the rest of her life.

"Your mom can stay here by herself for a little bit, right?"

"I guess so."

"Can ya tell her we're goin' out for a while?"

Kate walked to the bathroom door. She gently placed her ear on the door and heard Darren retching. "Mom? Are you all right?"

"Yeah, I'd be fine if it wasn't for this fuckin' cancer," she growled.

"Is it OK if Tony and I go out for a while?"

"Sure, Kate. Just make sure that he walks ya home. And will ya bring me some ginger ale when ya come home?"

"Yeah. Are you sure you'll be OK by yourself?"

"I'm dying, Kate. It don't mean that I can't be alone for a few hours. Ya can't be here wit' me all the time."

Kate placed her palm flat against the weathered bathroom door. "I love you."

"I love you too, baby. Have fun. Be careful."

Thirty minutes after leaving Kate's house, they were in the Italian Market. Tony and Kate were walking hand in hand when they reached the bakery. Tony pulled the door open, and the bell over top jingled. Donata looked up from a cake she was decorating, and her face lit up.

"So you're the young lady that Tony keeps talkin' about. He hasn't shut up about ya for two days," she said, rushing forward, wiping her hands on her apron.

"Well, I guess I know ya can't keep any secrets," Tony said mockingly.

"Oh, hush up. You're Kate, right?"

Kate smiled. "Yeah, nice to meet ya."

"I'm Donata. Come in, honey. Tell me about yourself," she said.

As Kate and Donata chatted, Tony went behind the counter where Ruth was placing cookies on a tray in a perfect line for the display case.

"Hey, Ruth," Tony said, bending and giving her a hug.

"Hi," Ruth said nonchalantly.

"What's wrong wit' cha?"

Ruth flashed a look in Kate's direction. Her lips were pressed together, and she stared at Kate through squinted eyelids. Tony watched the young girl in fascination. He knew that Ruth liked being special to him and that she probably felt threatened by Kate. Tony put his mouth close to Ruth's ear.

"Kate don't change how I feel 'bout ya, Ruth. You'll always be my favorite girl," he whispered.

Ruth spun on him. "Really? Because you're the only friend I have. And if she takes you away from me and Gram, then we won't see you anymore. I thought you loved us."

"Of course I love you guys." Tony said, chuckling. "Really. There ain't a girl on this planet that can take your place. Ya see, the difference between you and Kate is that she's my girlfriend, but you, you're my family already. Ya ain't got nothin' to worry about. You understand me?"

Ruth crossed her arms and pouted. She thought about what Tony had said for a moment. "So are you saying that if you had to pick between me and her, you'd pick me?"

Tony gave Ruth a hug. "I'm saying there's plenty of me to go around and that I can take care of both of ya, Donata too."

Ruth hesitated a moment; then she slipped her arms around Tony's neck, and he lifted her off of the ground.

"Hey, Kate," he yelled, "this is Ruth. She's my best girl, so ya gotta make room for her," he said, winking from across the room.

Kate moved forward. "Hi, Ruth. I can see why you're Tony's best girl. Don't worry—I know where I stand."

"Put me down," Ruth said to Tony. Ruth hobbled over to Kate and gave her a hug. "I guess you're OK. But you know, Tony has been a part of our family for a lot of years. I'm just warning you that if you fall in love with him, he'll still love me more."

"Got it," Kate said. "Can I help you put those cookies on the tray?"

"That would be great," Ruth said. She took Kate by the hand and led her behind the counter.

Tony sauntered over to Donata, who had been watching them all intently. "You're a good boy, Tony. I like that girl."

"Good, I'm glad you like Kate. Let's go in the back. I need to ask ya for a favor."

When Tony and Donata were alone, he told her the situation.

"Tony, look, I wanna help, but I don't even know this girl. I mean, you barely know her. I can't bring a stranger into this house. What about Ruth? What kinda grandmother would I be, lettin' a stranger stay here?"

"I know, Donata, but ya gotta trust me on this. I feel it in my gut. She's a good girl, but she's gonna need someone there for her when her mother dies."

Donata rubbed her temples with her index fingers. "Let's see how it goes. Her mother is still alive. Why can't she live with you when the time comes?"

Tony had already thought about that. The Slayers let no one outside of the gang visit the house, let alone live in the house. The only possible way for Kate to live there was if she was eligible for a rape-in. Gang members were restricted to dating only the Slayer women. Their motto was that outsiders couldn't be trusted with the secrets of the gang. There was no way Tony would entertain Kate being a part of a gang, so he had placed all his hopes on Donata stepping in to help.

"She can't, Donata. It's all guys. It ain't no place for her."

"Tony, you know I can't afford another mouth to feed."

"I'll help out. I'll find a way to pay ya money for her to live wit' cha."

Donata put her hands on her hips and shook her head. "I can't make no promises right now, Tony. I wanna help, I really do, but let's see what happens. Let's wait until the time comes. OK?" she said, placing her hand lovingly on Tony's cheek.

"So ya ain't sayin' no," Tony said, giving her a brilliant smile he hoped would melt her heart.

"Right, but I ain't sayin' yes either. Get it straight, and stop hearing what cha wanna hear. That's your problem—ya don't listen all the time," she said lightheartedly. Donata grew serious, "Tony, ya got a big heart, but cha gotta realize that ya just met this girl. She's nice and all, but remember that ya don't know her yet."

Tony took Donata's face in his hands and put his nose gently to hers. "You're right. I don't know her that good, but I swear when I met her, it was like I knew her my whole life. I feel like shit when I ain't wit' her."

"First off, watch your language. I don't want Ruth pickin' up any of your bad habits." Donata placed her hands over Tony's. "They call that love at first sight. That's what it sounds like ya got. Just go slow and make sure it ain't your little head thinkin' for your big head."

"Oh, you can say that, but I can't say the word shit?"

Donata patted his shoulder. "Just be careful. That's all I'm sayin'. Take it slow. You're still young."

Tony nodded to appease Donata. He glanced over at Kate and Ruth. They were both innocent. They were both full of love. They both wanted to be loved. He admitted to himself that it was awfully quick that he'd fallen for Kate; it had only been a couple of days. But he'd spent time with some of the girls in the Slayers gang. They were always selfish and clingy. They had nothing interesting to talk about. They didn't read books or like to spend time alone with their thoughts. Kate was the girl that made Tony want to be a better person. She demanded nothing from Tony, and that made him feel appreciated and valued. Tony's biggest dilemma now was how he could be with Kate and still be a part of the Slayers.

As Tony walked Kate back to her house, she talked excitedly about Ruth.

"She's a great kid. I hope someday, when I have a little girl, she's just like Ruth." Then she lowered her voice to just above a whisper, even though they were far from the bakery. "What happened to her leg?"

"Car accident. Her parents died. Ruth almost died too."

"Wow," she breathed, "I can't imagine losing both of your parents..."

Kate stopped in the middle of the street and fell to her knees. She covered her face with her hands and bawled.

Tony lifted her into his arms and sat her gently on the curb. He took a seat beside her.

"I'm just like Ruth," she wailed. "Soon I won't have any parents either. Oh, Tony, what am I gonna do? I'm scared. I've never been without my mom."

"I know you're scared. Look," he said, lifting her chin with his fingers so he could gaze into her eyes, "I ain't got no one, and things worked out for me. I'm not gonna leave ya alone to figure it out on your own; I'm gonna be right here next to ya. I swear to ya, Kate, I'm gonna do everything I can to help ya. I know it ain't the same as havin' your mother, but ya gotta know that you'll have somebody who cares about cha."

Kate grasped Tony in a tight embrace. "You promise that you'll be here?"

"Yeah, I promise." Tony looked down at her and wiped a tear from her cheek. He gave her a mischievous smile. "If you're nice, I'll even let ya kiss me once in a while."

Kate giggled, not because what Tony had said was overly funny, but because the stress of the day had played on her emotions. She was in the early stage of mourning her mother and starting a new relationship with Tony. Her emotions played at odds: happiness against sadness, new love against loss of love.

When Tony kissed her good-night on her porch, she shut her eyes tight before she opened her front door and stepped inside to face her greatest fear, losing her mother.

Chapter Sixty-Five

O ver the months that followed, Tony visited Kate and Darren every day. Darren had worked her way into Tony's heart. She was brassy, and he admired her for facing death with unrelenting courage. Still, it broke his heart to watch her deteriorate as time passed.

"Oh, look who's here," Darren said one Saturday afternoon.

"Yeah, ya know I'd never miss a chance of being wit' you two."

Kate watched as her mother and her boyfriend spoke.

"I wanna talk to you two about somethin'," Darren said solemnly.

"What cha got?" Tony asked casually.

"Well, it's been a while since we talked about what's gonna happen to Kate. Seems to me like you two are in love. Am I right?"

Tony and Kate hadn't said "I love you" to each other yet, but Darren was right—they both felt it.

"Mom, come on. Please stop. It's not right."

"OK, fine. Well, it seems to me that you like bein' together."

"Sure we do," Tony said.

"I was wonderin' how you two could be together for good, after I'm gone."

An awkward silence fell over them all. Tony wished he could be the knight in shining armor, and he hadn't given up hope on Kate staying with Donata. In fact, Tony had brought Kate to the bakery several times a week since she'd first been there hoping Donata would get to know her well enough to let her live with them for a while.

"Ya know, Darren, I've been doin' a lot of thinkin' about what's gonna happen to Kate. I ain't got all the answers right now, but here's what I know. My family kicked me out when I was thirteen, and I had no idea what I was gonna do. I didn't have a person in the world who could take care of me. My mother and little sister cared about me, but they weren't no help. I know from experience that we ain't got all the answers all the time, but if ya wanna make somethin' better and ya keep lookin' for it, then you'll find it. I ain't worried about what's gonna happen to Kate, and you shouldn't either. All ya need to know is that I ain't gonna leave her to figure it out on her own."

"Thank you, Tony. I wish there was a sure answer, but ya told me what I needed to hear."

A few hours later, Tony and Kate took a walk into South Philadelphia to meet up with Salvatore and Vincent. The two teens were very fond of Kate, and she had become a natural addition to their close circle of friendship.

Tony reminded himself that he couldn't stay too long. He had to get back to North Philadelphia because the Slayers were planning an attack on a neighboring gang that had harassed one of the girls in the house.

"What are ya scumbags doin'?" Tony said, walking up to the bench where his friends were sitting.

"Waitin' for some dumb motherfucker to ask us what we're doin' so we can kick his ass," Vincent replied. He leapt to his feet and went over to Kate and gave her a hug. "So you're still hangin' wit' this shit stain, huh?"

Kate smiled. "Yeah, I love hanging with Tony."

"How's your mom doing?" Salvatore asked.

Kate's eyes clouded over. "She's getting worse by the day."

Salvatore grabbed Kate's hand and pulled her down next to him on the bench. "I don't know anything about losing a parent. I'm not sure I could handle it if something happened to my mom or dad. I want you to know that Vincent and I will be around if you need us."

Kate laid her head on Salvatore's shoulder, and he squeezed her into him. Tony watched, with a swell of appreciation, as his childhood friend comforted Kate.

"Thanks, Salvatore. That means a lot to me." Kate turned and looked at Tony. "You have good friends."

"Yeah, they're all right," he said, pushing Vincent.

"Hey," Salvatore began. "Vincent and I are going to Atlantic City in two weeks with my mom. We have our own room. Why don't you two come with us?"

Kate shook her head slowly. "I can't leave my mom right now...I don't know how much longer..."

"Right," Salvatore said. "Next time, then."

"How 'bout you, Tony? Ya wanna come wit' us?" Vincent asked.

Kate held her breath, waiting for Tony to answer.

"Nah, I'm gonna hang here wit' Kate. Ya know, keep an eye on things."

Kate exhaled. She didn't know what she'd do if Tony was gone and her mother died. Kate gave Tony a grateful smile.

Salvatore perked up, trying to break the somber mood. "How about if you and Kate come over to my house for dinner this Saturday? My father will be in New York, and my mom is going to make dinner for Vincent and me. I know she'd love to see you and to meet Kate."

"Yeah, that sounds real good. How 'bout it, Kate?"

Kate smiled bashfully. She still wasn't totally comfortable in her own skin. With Tony, she felt like she could be herself, and she had started to relax with Salvatore and Vincent. However, she could see that Tony really wanted to go, and she didn't want to let him down, not after he'd turned down a weekend in Atlantic City to stay with her.

"I think that would be a lot of fun," she finally said.

"Good. We'll see you around six o'clock."

An hour later, as Tony walked Kate back to her house, he could sense an uneasiness from her he hadn't felt earlier.

"Somethin' wrong, Kate?" he finally asked.

Kate turned to him. "Nothing is wrong—it's just that Salvatore seems to come from a rich family. I mean, I don't really have anything decent to wear to his house. I'm embarrassed to show up in an old T-shirt and jeans. Look at my sneakers—they're falling apart, and they're the only shoes I own besides old snow boots that are too small for me."

"You ain't gotta worry about all that. Mrs. Morano is a great lady. She don't care 'bout what we wear; she only cares 'bout how we act. Besides, I think ya look great all the time," he said, giving her a peck on the lips.

Kate appreciated Tony's kind words, but he was always trying to make her feel better. She decided to talk to her mother about it to see what Darren thought she should do. Then her mood saddened as she realized that her mother wouldn't be there much longer to give her advice.

Chapter Sixty-Six

Tony walked inside Kate's house behind her. The only light in the room was the illumination of the television, which cast a blue-gray shadow over Darren.

"Oh, good. You're home," Darren said, a weak smile playing on her lips.

"Tony and I got invited to his friend's house Saturday night," Kate blurted out.

"That's nice. Whose house ya goin' to?"

"Salvatore's. Mrs. Morano is cooking dinner for all of us," Kate said.

"Mrs. Morano?" Darren asked, sitting up straighter on the sofa.

"Yeah. Do you know her?" Kate asked.

"I don't know her, but I know of her." Darren shifted her gaze to Tony. "Ain't that Johnny Morano's wife?"

Tony nodded; the question was laced with accusations.

Darren stared at Kate. "Johnny Morano is the head of the mob here in Philadelphia. Ya know what kinda trouble that'll bring into your life?"

Kate looked stunned. She opened her mouth to speak, and before she knew it, the words came out like a flash flood. "You don't have to worry, Mom. Tony isn't part of the mob; he's in a gang."

"What?" Darren screamed. She shot off of the sofa and stood in front of Tony. "Why didn't I know this?"

Tony shifted his eyes to Kate. "There ain't much to know."

"Holy Mary, Mother of God, what the hell have I done to my little girl?"

Tony put his hand on Darren's shoulder, but she jerked away.

"What gang?" she demanded.

"The Slayers," he responded, feeling abnormal.

Darren focused intently on her daughter. "Kate, this has to stop. You're playin' wit' fire here. I've seen the aftermath of what those slugs do to people."

"No, Mom. You need to stop. All these months you've seen that Tony and I are doing fine. You encouraged us to be together. Now, just because you found out he's in a gang, you want us to stop. He's still the same person he was before you knew all of this."

"Do ya have any idea what you're gettin' yourself into? Gangs and Mafia...what else, Kate? Are ya sellin' drugs on street corners too?"

Kate stomped her foot and started to cry. "That's not fair. We haven't done anything wrong."

"Maybe you haven't, Kate, but how about you, Tony? Have ya done things that ya shouldn't have?"

"I've done things I ain't too proud of like anybody else. But I swear to ya, I don't go around pickin' on people for nuttin'. I don't get my rocks off on bein' mean. I only do what I gotta do when there ain't no other way. What cha see on the news don't ever show ya the whole story."

Tony's blood was simmering. He felt exposed and no longer good enough for Kate.

"Besides," Tony continued, "I ain't brought Kate around the Slayers, and I ain't goin' to either."

"Oh, but you'll bring her around the Mafia? To the house of a man who kills people for a livin'."

"The Moranos are good people. Especially Mrs. Morano. She ain't caught up in anything," Tony said defensively.

"Mrs. Morano enjoys her expensive lifestyle from the blood that her husband spills in the streets."

"It ain't like that, Darren."

"Stop," Kate yelled. "Mom, you're dying. Tony is the only person I have in my life besides you. If you chase him away, it won't only break my heart, but it will leave me to face my life without you all by myself. I don't care what gang he belongs to or that his friend's father is the boss of the Mafia. All I care about is being with Tony. Can't you understand that?"

Darren lowered her head and thought for a moment. She was exhausted, having expended all of her energy. She locked on Tony's eyes. "If ya ever put Kate in harm's way, I'll haunt cha from my grave."

"Ya ain't never gotta worry about that. I'll do whatever I gotta do to keep Kate safe...and happy."

Later that night, after Tony left, Kate approached her mother.

"I don't have anything to wear to dinner at the Moranos'."

Darren glared at her daughter for a minute. "Help me up."

Kate pulled her mother up from the sofa and followed her into the bedroom. As they walked through the cluttered row home, Darren let out a big sigh. "Kate, I don't like what's goin' on here. My daughter goin' to some dirty mobster's house ain't what I ever dreamed of for ya." Darren opened her closet. "Get that box down," she said, pointing to the shelf above their heads.

Kate slowly reached up, grabbed the box, and placed it on her mother's bed.

"Open it up," Darren said with determined resolve.

Kate gasped when she opened the box. She pulled out a black sweater with small pearls sewn around the neck. "Where did you get this?"

"I saved up some money. I bought it for you to wear...someday...when I'm gone. To my...funeral. But I think it's better ya wear it to dinner. That way, the sweater will remind ya of good times. I ain't crazy about cha goin' over to the Moranos'—don't think that's changed." Darren took in a deep breath. "But I trust ya. I want cha to be real careful. Tony is involved with bad groups of people...a gang and the mob."

"Tony isn't involved with the mob. We are going to the Moranos' because he's been friends with Salvatore since he was little," Kate pleaded, wanting to hear her mother's acceptance of Tony.

Darren understood her daughter's plea for acceptance. Darren knew she would die and didn't want to leave Kate with fear in her heart. "Tony's a nice boy, OK? I'm not questionin' his intentions for ya. But you're young, and ya need to understand that the people he associates wit' aren't good people. Their lives are all about money and murder. Ya gotta get that through your head, so if things ain't goin' right between you and Tony, ya run away as fast as ya can."

Kate hugged Darren. "I swear to you that I'll be careful. You still like Tony, right?"

"Please, Kate. Who couldn't like Tony? He's a good guy. I just don't like his choice of friends."

As Kate lay on her bed that night, she thought about all that had happened during that day. She worried that her mother was right but couldn't deny that she felt complete with Tony beside her. Kate promised herself that if things ever got bad, to where she was fearful being with Tony, she would run away as fast as she could, just like her mother had told her to do.

Chapter Sixty-Seven

On Saturday night, Tony drew in a breath when Kate opened the door. She was wearing the new sweater with jeans and her mother's only pair of good shoes, which were a little too big on Kate.

"You look great," Tony said.

Kate blushed. "Thanks. Ready?"

Tony brushed by Kate and went in to see Darren. "How are ya feelin'?"

Darren motioned for Tony to come closer. He put his ear next to her mouth, and she whispered, "It's gonna be soon. Ya make sure she ain't left alone. Ya keep checkin' on us every day."

Tony took her bony hand in his own. Darren had lost so much weight that her skin hung on her body like an oversized shirt. "I'll take care of her. Ya ain't gotta worry. When we're done at Salvatore's, we'll come back and sit wit' cha awhile."

Darren patted Tony's hand. "OK. Ya go and have fun. Just remember you're dealin' wit' bad people."

When Tony and Kate arrived at the Moranos' house, they were greeted with the scent of homemade Italian food. Kate took in a deep breath, savoring the aroma that danced in her nose and made her mouth water.

Salvatore was giving Kate a hug when his mother, Alessandra, floated up the hall behind them. "Tony Bruno, get over here and give me a hug," she said.

"Hi, Mrs. M. It's real good to see ya." He leaned in a little closer. "Even better to smell your cookin' again. Salvatore don't know how lucky he is."

"Well, I've been asking where you've been for forever. Finally," she said, shooting Salvatore a scathing look, "my son decided to indulge me and have you over."

"It ain't his fault, Mrs. M. I've been livin' in North Philly, and I ain't got a whole lot of time to hang out."

Tony turned toward Kate. "This is my girlfriend, Kate."

Alessandra took a few steps toward Kate and extended her delicate hand. Kate put her hand in Alessandra's. "It's very nice to meet you, Kate. My son tells me that you've captured Tony's heart. I'll tell you, that isn't easy with these boys. By the way, your sweater is precious."

Kate's heart leaped; she'd been right to make sure she wore something nice. "Great to meet you too, Mrs. Morano. Whatever you're cooking smells delicious."

Kate was nervous, and her hand was sweating in Alessandra's cool hand. She slowly inched it back to her side.

"Where's Vincent?" Tony asked.

Salvatore shrugged. "You know him—he's never on time," he said, as he led them into the kitchen.

Vincent arrived just before Alessandra served the salad.

"Mrs. M, was ya about to eat wit'out me?" Vincent said, faking a hurt look.

Alessandra glanced over her shoulder and gave him a warm smile.

The group sat and ate the courses that Alessandra put on the table. The boys talked about the neighborhood and excitedly discussed the new café that had opened in the Italian Market.

Alessandra put the main course of veal parmesan on the table. Tony speared a large piece with his fork and plopped it onto his plate, "So, what's your pop doin' in New York?" he asked.

"Business. He's working on a deal with a family that sells produce."

"The freshest fruits and vegetables you can find on the East Coast," Alessandra added.

"How's business been for him?"

Salvatore met Tony's gaze. "He's doing really well. Vincent and I have been helping with some of the vendors in South Philly."

"What kinda help are ya givin' 'im?"

"What's with all the questions?" Salvatore said. He clearly didn't want to discuss the mob business in front of Kate or his mother.

"Nothin'. I just...I'm gonna need to make some extra money soon and thought maybe there was some work I could pick up."

Tony had to figure out a way to make more money once Darren died. It was his only chance of getting Donata to let Kate live with them. The old woman couldn't afford to take on another person, not on the meager salary she earned from the bakery.

"Why don't you swing by tomorrow around noon? My pop will be home by then, and you can ask him if he has any work for you."

Tony shoved a stuffed shell into his mouth and nodded. "Yeah, good, tomorra," he garbled. "I'll come by tomorra."

When Tony announced that he and Kate were leaving, Salvatore got up from his chair slowly. "I'll drive you two back."

"Whata ya mean? Since when do you drive?"

"Since my pop bought me a car and gave it to me yesterday before he left."

"Are ya shittin' me?" Tony exclaimed.

"Tony Bruno," Alessandra said sternly.

"Sorry, Mrs. M. Are ya kiddin' me?"

"Nope. Come on. I'll give you a ride to Kate's."

The teens thanked Alessandra for dinner and headed out back to Salvatore's new car.

"Fuckin' A, Salvatore. I can't believe your dad bought this car for ya. This don't look like just any car neither. Your pop musta paid a fortune for it. Hell, it's nicer than anything I've ever seen," Tony said excitedly.

The four teenagers climbed into the new Bentley.

Salvatore beamed with pride. "Yeah, my pop said it's important that I drive a nice car. He said that if you want respect, you have to give people a reason to show you respect."

Vincent looked over the front seat at Tony and Kate in the back. "He also told Salvatore that this car is gonna get us laid every night."

Tony scowled at Vincent.

"Sorry, Kate. I meant that it was gonna get me and Salvatore laid every night," Vincent explained.

Kate giggled. "I knew what you meant. But I thought Salvatore wanted a real girlfriend."

Salvatore met her eyes in his rearview mirror. "Only if I can find a girl just like you, Kate."

"Hey, keep your eyes off my girl," Tony said mockingly.

At Kate's house, the couple stood and watched Salvatore and Vincent drive off. Kate turned to Tony. "So do you think about that too?"

"Think about what?"

"Getting laid?"

Tony nervously rubbed his chest. "I mean, sure I do. Look at you. You're gorgeous, Kate."

"When you said I was your girl, did you mean that?"

"Of course I did. Ain't we together almost every day?"

"Yeah, but we never talked about us being, you know, exclusive."

"What's that mean? Ya got some dude on the side I don't know about?" he said, nuzzling her neck.

"No. It's just that we've never...done anything more than kiss. I mean it's been over six months."

"Wait." Tony laughed. "So you're asking me why I ain't tryin' to get in your pants?"

Kate slapped Tony's chest. "No, you perv. I'm just trying to find out if you like me in that way."

"Course I do. I wanna take it slow, is all. Ya know, I got the gang, and I don't want cha to get hurt."

"What do the Slayers have to do with anything?"

"I just gotta be careful," he said evasively.

"Careful of what? What aren't you telling me? Do you have a gang girlfriend?" she said, sounding panicky.

"No. I don't want none of those broads. It's just that…the Slayers don't let anyone date outside the members."

"Oh. Are you saying they get to tell you everything to do?"

"No, I'm sayin' it's complicated. I don't want ya to get hurt." Tony's frustration was building, not with Kate but because he had the Slayers to answer to and because they dictated some aspects of his life. "Can we just drop it?" Tony looked deep into Kate's eyes. "I love ya, Kate."

She drew in a sharp breath. "Oh my god, I love you too, Tony. I was so afraid to say it to you, though."

"Well, now we've both said it, and we both mean it. Let's go inside and see how Darren's doin'."

As they walked hand in hand up the rickety front porch, Tony and Kate felt the love flow between them.

Chapter Sixty-Eight

"Where the hell have ya been, Bruno?" Razor snapped when Tony got home from Kate's house.

"What's it to ya, Razor? You my fuckin' mother now?"

"No, I ain't your whore-bitch mother, but I'm the leader of this gang. We've noticed the last six months you're here less and less. Makes some of us wonder if you're bein' a traitor. Maybe you're out there tellin' other gangs our secrets," Razor said, his voice dripping with poisonous venom.

"Ya ever call my mother a name like that again, and I'll snap your fuckin' neck," Tony said, rushing at Razor.

Some of the other members stood between the two teens.

"Stop changin' the subject, Bruno. Razor asked ya a question—where ya been hidin'?" Boner said, his bloated belly hanging a foot in front of the rest of his chest, making his stumpy body more of an eyesore.

The members in the room were intent, waiting for an answer. Tony felt small under the scrutiny of so many eyes watching him.

"I got some family issues...been spendin' some time in South Philly."

"What kinda family issues?" Boner asked.

"The cancer kind. OK? It ain't nobody's business but mine. I handle my shit here. There ain't nothin' that I was supposed to do that hasn't been taken care of," Tony said.

Several members nodded.

Razor puffed his chest out. "I thought the reason ya came here was 'cause ya didn't have family that wanted you. Now all of a sudden ya got family issues. Somethin' don't smell right."

"You all know my story," Tony said, turning and making eye contact with several of the other boys. "My father is a mother fuckin' prick, but my mother ain't. She might be weak and ain't able to stand up to him, but she ain't never done anythin' wrong to me."

"Your mother threw ya outta your own house, ya moron," Razor barked.

The verbal jab stabbed Tony in the heart. "I know what she did, but it ain't 'cause she didn't want me."

"Right, it's 'cause she cares more about herself than she does you. Open your eyes. I don't give a shit if she got cancer."

"I can't turn my back on her; I ain't made that way. Just like I can't turn my back on none of you, 'cause you're my brothers," Tony said in a mellow voice, trying to defuse the situation.

"Tony's right. I get what he's sayin'," Smoke said, one of the least verbal members, cut in. "Remember what happened wit' my mother? That fuckin' bitch let her boyfriend beat the shit outta me day in and day out. But when that prick turned on her, and Josie," he said, pointing to one of the girls in the room, "saw her sitting on a curb with her arm all busted up and face all broken, I went and found that no-good bastard and stabbed him till he swallowed his last breath with a mouthful of blood. Don't mean I see her now, but I did what I had to do. I get cha man," Smoke stated and slapped Tony on the back.

Tony noticed the tension of the other gang members visibly dissipate. He took that opportunity to change the subject. "How are we handlin' our shit tonight?"

Razor's lip curled in a snarl. "Like we always do. We're gonna go after those pricks who raped Charity. Nobody fucks with our bitches. She's all freaked out and scared and shit. We can't have it."

Tony turned and looked at Charity as Blondie gave her a hug. She had been severely traumatized when a rival gang pulled her into a van and gang raped her.

Razor turned to the room of gang members. "No knives tonight. What they did to Charity deserves bullets. I wanna kill as many of them as we can. This ain't no joke. Nobody fucks wit' our bitches. Got it?"

There was grumbling in the room, and Tony went upstairs to the bedroom to grab more bullets for the gun he kept tucked in the back of his pants, except when he was with Kate. Tony had bought a secondhand ankle holster so Kate wouldn't accidently stumble across it.

The Slayers set out that night into the darkness of the unsavory streets. When they came upon the house where the other gang members lived, they spread out. Razor and Boner were the first two through the front door, immediately followed by Tony and Blast. The bullets flew through the air as the Slayers killed as many gang members as they could. Tony fired his gun several times, but always aimed for arms and legs, all the places that weren't deadly. One member ran upstairs, and Blast yelled to Tony, "Get him."

Tony ascended the stairs, two at a time. He pounced on the teen in the hallway, flipped him over, and put the gun to his head. The teen had no fear; instead his whole persona was projecting hatred.

"I recognize ya. I didn't before, but I do now," the teen said to Tony.

"No, ya don't. Shut the fuck up," Tony growled.

"Yeah, I know ya real good. My aunt lives on the street where that little girlfriend of yours lives. Ya know the one wit' the blond, curly hair. I've seen ya there a lot. Do the Slayers know ya got yourself a bitch that ain't part of the gang?"

Tony could hear Razor's voice coming up the stairs as he sat on the teen with his gun to the boy's head.

"Hey," the rival gang member yelled, "your boy here has a little secret."

Tony's instincts to protect Kate took over, and before the teen could say another word, Tony pulled the trigger of his gun, splattering the boy's head across the walls and floor of the hallway.

"What was he talkin' 'bout, Bruno? What secret ya got?"

Tony hoisted his body from the floor and faced Razor. "I ain't got no secrets. The prick was lookin' for a way not to die. Don't cha know a scam when ya hear one? I thought ya was the expert on death, but cha don't seem to know the game too well."

Tony tried to look calm, as if nothing had happened, while jumping beans did a jig in his belly. He began to sweat, and regret for killing the boy settled in his bones, seeping into his soul. I just killed another person, but he didn't give me a choice. It was him or Kate, he thought. Tony had hurt many people during his time with the Slayers, and he may have even killed some without knowing it, as stray bullets were always a part of gang battles. But this was the first time he'd looked into someone's eyes and pulled the trigger with the intent to kill—the intent to silence the boy who was ready to reveal his secret life with Kate.

Tony stepped over the boy's dead body, and his eyes swept over the carnage he'd left on the ground. He walked down the stairs and out the front door, where some of the other Slayers were waiting.

As Tony stood with his gang, he hoped they couldn't see his pulse throbbing through his veins. He rubbed his forehead, trying to understand his own feelings, trying to convince himself that he had done the right thing, but the frosty layer of ice over his heart remained intact. Tony swiftly followed the other gang members as they left. By the time they reached the Slayers' house, a warm feeling ran through Tony's body. The regret he had felt earlier was erased. The boy he had killed had been about to put Kate's and his life in jeopardy. Tony cringed, thinking how awful it would have been had Razor found out the truth. He had no choice but to embrace the belief that he'd done the right thing. It gave him a sense of power and peace. He would kill or be killed if either was necessary to protect Kate.

Chapter Sixty-Nine

At noon the next day, Tony knocked on the Moranos' front door. Salvatore answered and led Tony into his father's office.

"Hello, Tony," Johnny Morano said and then took a long sip of his coffee.

"Hey, Mr. Morano. How ya doin'?"

"I'm doing just fine."

Tony turned to Big Paulie, who was slouched on the overstuffed leather sofa and nodded.

"Looks like ya grew a little since we seen ya last. Put a little meat on those bones," Big Paulie stated.

"Yeah, sure," Tony acknowledged, feeling flattered and insulted at the same time.

"I'm leaving, Pop," Salvatore said, walking toward the office door.

"No. Just close the door. You can stay."

Salvatore followed his father's instructions and sat on the sofa next to Big Paulie.

"What can I do for you, Tony?" Johnny asked.

"Well, I wanted to see if ya got any work for me. I got this girlfriend, Kate, and her mother's dying. Kate ain't got nowhere to go after she dies. I know a lady that I think she can stay wit', but I gotta make money to pay for her to stay there."

"What is it you want from me, Tony? I haven't seen you in quite some time. Trouble tends to follow you."

Tony bit back the words that clung to his tongue. He had an overwhelming desire to punch Johnny in the face.

Instead, Tony swallowed hard and cleared his throat. "Anyway, I really need a job so that I can help my girlfriend. If ya ain't got no work for me, that's fine—just say so," Tony said, feeling agitated.

"I see." Johnny turned to Big Paulie. "Do we have any work that Tony can do for us?"

"Sure, Boss. He can collect money from our business partners. I'm sure Salvatore and Vincent won't mind letting Tony in on some of their business," he said, turning to Salvatore, who shrugged and nodded in response.

"All right. Tony, you can work with Salvatore and Vincent. They'll teach you what needs to be done," Johnny said, standing and extending his hand.

Tony lurched his hand forward, and Johnny grabbed on and held it.

"Consider yourself very lucky to be working for us," Johnny stated, still gripping Tony's hand in his own.

"I do, Mr. Morano. I really appreciate the opportunity."

Johnny leered at Tony and looked down at their hands. Suddenly, Johnny jerked Tony forward, pulling his body overtop of the desk.

"What the fuck is that?"

Tony was confused. A trickle of fear ran through him. He followed Johnny's glare. "A tattoo. That's all."

Johnny's eyes burrowed into Tony's forearm. "Slayer? Am I to understand that you are a gang member? You belong to the Slayers?"

Salvatore shuffled to the edge of the sofa, suddenly fearful for Tony. His father's voice revealed a smoldering anger.

Tony tried to pull his arm back, but it was no use against Johnny's strong grip.

"Yeah, but that don't mean nothin'." Tony's voice quivered.

"You fucking idiot. It means everything. I don't let gang members work in my business. You're all a bunch of street trash. How dare you come into my home and ask me for a job." Johnny turned and glared at Salvatore. "Did you know that this piece of white trash is in a gang?"

Salvatore remained silent and shook his head. He took a few seconds to find his voice. "No, I didn't. But I do know that Tony helped me. I don't care what Tony does. He went to prison and never ratted me out. When he went away, you said that's what good friends do for each other, the kind of friends that you keep for life."

"You're right. I did say that. However, the fact that your 'friend' is a gang member changes everything."

"But, Mr. Morano, if that guy who lied and said he saw me kill Rex didn't die, I woulda been in prison for a long time. I was willing to do anythin' to help Salvatore."

Johnny came around his desk and stood toe-to-toe with Tony. Johnny's posture was rigid, his jaw taut, and his eyes fixed on Tony. "Yes, that's right. The so-called witness died suddenly, and you didn't spend years in prison. I'd say that you got off easy—that someone came along and saved you from paying for a crime that you didn't commit. You should be grateful for such good fortune."

Tony took a step backward. "OK, Mr. Morano. I understand. Ya ain't gonna give me a job. I'm just gonna leave."

"Yes, that's right. Leave. Crawl back into the bottomless shithole that you came out of and don't come back here again. Oh, and if I have any trouble from those Slayer pricks of yours, it will make your stay in juvenile detention seem like a dream vacation."

Tony turned and left Johnny's office silently. Alessandra called to him as he went to the front door, but Tony didn't look back. He rushed outside and walked at a fast pace to the next block until he was jogging, and then he burst into a sprint. He ran as fast and hard as he could until he felt as though his lungs would combust. He slipped down a small side street and leaned against the wall. His head was spinning, and he rested his hands on his knees as he tried to catch his breath. Finally, his heart beat normally, and Tony realized he was crying. He tried to stop the tears, but they were relentless. Gloom bubbled up from the depth of his very being; the hot, salty tears continued until his body was racked with sobs.

Tony slid down the brick wall, pulled his knees up, and rested his head. Once again, Tony felt as though he were a small child, rejected and judged by everyone around him. Tony had no love for the Slayers, but he needed to survive, and when he'd needed someone most, they'd been there for him. It was all he had. Seeing Johnny's reaction and remembering Darren's disapproval of him being a gang member made him feel as though he were nothing. What did I do to deserve this life? He wondered . . .

Chapter Seventy

O ver the next three months, when Tony wasn't with the Slayers, he spent his free time at Kate's house. Kate had sat vigil over her mother. By now, Darren was rarely alert, as the pain medication the doctor had given her made her high most of the time. When Darren was awake, she talked to Kate and tried to give her the advice she would need when she wasn't around.

Darren had been out of it for a little over a week, more so than usual. Tony was sitting on a lopsided recliner watching football when Darren woke and asked for Kate.

"She's in the kitchen. I'll get her," he said.

Kate rushed into the living room, took her mother's hand, and sat on the floor next to the sofa. "What's wrong? Is everything OK?"

Darren nodded and gestured for the glass of water on the folding table set up next to her. Kate held the glass while her mother sipped at the water. Darren coughed a few times, trying to move the phlegm that blocked her voice.

"It ain't long now, baby. I wanna tell ya some things so that cha know what I would be thinkin'. First, you make sure that when ya get married, ya think of me walkin' ya down the aisle. I'm gonna be right there wit' cha. And then when ya have a baby, I'm gonna be smilin' down from heaven on my precious angels. There's gonna be times when ya need advice from a woman. Ya like that lady Donata, the one that ya visit at the bakery, right?"

Kate was crying. "Yeah."

"Well, ya talk to Donata when ya need to. Women see things different than men. We got more feelings, and sometimes those feelings confuse the hell outta us. Makes us all mixed up in our heads."

"I don't want you to leave me," Kate said, beginning to bawl.

"I don't wanna leave ya either. But God is callin' me home. I don't know why. Seems pretty cruel, if ya ask me, but there must be some reason."

"I hate God! Stop talking about him. You act like there's some great reason that he is taking you and leaving me here alone. There is no great reason; he's taking you from me because he's mean and selfish. I want you right here with me. When I think about you not being here, I can barely breathe."

"You'll learn to live different, that's all. Ya gotta go on. I know ya don't like it, and neither do I. But it ain't gonna do ya no good wasting your life 'cause I died. I would feel like I killed both of us if ya did that. Ya understand me?"

"Yeah," Kate said with a heavy heart.

"Can ya get me some ginger ale?"

Kate rose to her feet and headed into the kitchen. As soon as she was out of the room, Darren waved Tony over to her.

"It ain't long. I'm tryin' to hold on for Kate, but my insides feel like they're liquid. Kate's gotta stay here the next few days. If I pass when she ain't here, it'll make it harder on her. When I go, she's gonna need ya to be strong...to help her carry on. She'll be eighteen in a year and a half. I was livin' on my own when I was that age. It's gonna be hard, but she can do it." Darren paused and took in a few shallow breaths. "With your help, she can make it through."

"I told ya a million times, I ain't gonna leave her. She's my life, Darren. I need her just as much as she needs me."

Two days later, lying in her bed next to Kate with Tony standing over them, Darren died. She was thirty-nine.

Over the next three days, Tony only left Kate to check in with the Slayers. He had told some members that his mother had died and he needed to help his sister get settled. Blast had made sure that Razor knew that Tony wouldn't be around, but Razor didn't care about Tony's home situation; he still didn't trust him.

A few days later, Salvatore picked Tony and Kate up at her house. Kate's sadness filled all the empty space in the car.

Tony had arranged for a small memorial service at Darren's church, and the priest, who barely remembered Darren, agreed to do the service for free. Tony, Kate, Salvatore, Vincent, Donata, and Ruth arrived at the church following Sunday Mass. Tony had made sure there were people there to honor Darren, but, more importantly, to support Kate.

Darren was cremated and her ashes placed in a thick cardboard box that Kate kept with her at all times.

"I'm sorry about your mom," Salvatore said as he drove toward the church.

"Me too," Vincent muttered.

At the church, Tony helped Kate out of the car. She clutched the box with her mother's ashes to her chest. When she got inside and saw Donata and Ruth sitting in the front pew waiting, she felt a sense of gratitude that overwhelmed her further.

Tony looked around the small, outdated space of the empty old church. He was ashamed to be there, after all the bad things he'd done. The gloominess of the church erased the little bit of hope that he'd once held in his heart. He felt like he was a kid again standing in the open lot where the googamongers lived. His grief had settled into his bones. He was very fond of Darren and had grown to love her, but the inescapable feeling of helplessness wedged its way into his body. Once the service was over, he'd have no way to help Kate like he'd promised. The feeling of inadequacy made his throat feel dry and raw.

Once the mourners were seated, the priest led them in a short prayer and asked God to take Darren into his loving arms and give her comfort and peace in his kingdom. Before any of them could get up to leave, Kate stood and faced the five people who had come to pay their respects.

"My mother was a good woman. She taught me that love is more precious and rare than anything money can buy. She was my guiding light. We never had much, but we always had each other." Kate's chest was jumping, and she lowered her head to let her sorrow flow. After a moment she collected herself again. "I want to thank all of you for coming here to be with me. My mom was so afraid I'd be alone after she died, and Tony and all of you alleviated her only fear of death. I will never forget that you were here for me. No matter what happens to me now, I'll always know that there are five people in this world who supported me when I needed it most."

Kate took a step forward and staggered, her grief crushing in on her. Tony jumped to his feet and grabbed her around the waist before she collapsed. He was a lost child again, not knowing how to comfort the person he loved most in the world. He couldn't take care of her as he had promised, and they had yet to discuss what would happen once they left the church that day.

The others rushed to Kate's side.

"Sit her in the pew," Donata instructed.

The older woman sat next to Kate and placed an arm over her shoulder.

"It'll be OK, Kate. I lost my mother when I was twenty-seven. I thought it was the saddest day of my life until I lost my daughter several years ago. But through all of my heartbreak, I focused all my love on Ruth," Donata said, trying to comfort her.

"But I don't have a Ruth," Kate wailed. "I don't have anything."

Tony wanted to tell her she had him. He believed that, but it wasn't enough, to survive, Kate needed...a place to sleep...a place to eat...a place to call home.

Donata cupped Kate's face in her hands. "You do have somethin'. Ya just said it. Look around ya; there are five people here that care about ya."

Kate looked at each of them. Her eyes were glazed over, and Tony wondered if she could see through her veil of sorrow.

Donata looked up at Tony; his young face looked older. The lines on his forehead and around his eyes spoke of the pain he felt for Kate.

"Here's what we're gonna do. For now, you're gonna come and stay wit' me and Ruth until ya can figure things out."

Kate lifted her face, and a smidgen of relief flashed through her body.

"Then what?" Kate asked.

"I don't know. But Tony..." Donata said, looking at him, "he's very clever at figurin' his way out of bad things. Aren't cha?"

Tony nodded. He understood the financial sacrifice Donata was making. He had asked the older lady to let Kate stay with her and Ruth, but he had also promised to help with money. It was a promise he couldn't live up to, and this embarrassed him, made him feel small. "Thanks, Donata," Tony said. "I'll find a way to fix this."

"OK, let's get goin'. You boys take Kate to her house and help her pack some things. Then ya bring her over to my place."

When Kate was in the backseat of Salvatore's car, Tony walked over to where Donata and Ruth stood watching.

"I know this ain't what cha wanted to do," Tony began, "but I promise I'll figure out somethin'. It might take me a little while, but thanks for doin' this. Ya didn't have to do nothin'."

"The girl is distraught. She don't need no more crap in her life right now. I'm helping ya out here, but this ain't a long-term fix. I need ya workin' on what comes next," Donata said gently.

Tony hugged Donata and then Ruth. "Thank you. I owe ya."

Donata walked to the curb and hailed a taxi, and Tony watched them drive off. He turned back to Salvatore's car, and daggers of worry slashed at his insides.

Chapter Seventy-One

Tony looked around Kate's sparse bedroom. There wasn't much to pack. She had barely any clothes worth taking with her. He followed Kate into Darren's room and stood behind her while she feverishly went through her mother's drawers, as if looking for hidden treasure.

Tony walked up behind Kate and put his arms around her. "Salvatore will be back in an hour or so to pick us up. Can I help you find something?"

She turned to him, a frantic expression on her face. "My mom had a ring. She only wore it on special occasions. I need to find it."

"What's it look like?"

"It's a gold ring with an aquamarine in the center and two little diamonds on either side."

"Aquamarine?"

"A light blue stone, Tony. Are you gonna help me find it?"

"Where'd she keep it?"

"In this drawer, Tony," she squealed.

Tony gingerly moved Kate off to the side. He went through the drawer. It was filled with old T-shirts and worn-out, weathered shorts. He went through the shirts one at a time. Then he pulled the shorts from the drawer and placed them on the bed.

"See?" Kate screeched. "It's gone."

Tony kissed Kate on the forehead. "Give me a minute, will ya?"

Tony turned his attention back to the five pairs of shorts. He lifted them and went through each pocket, wondering why Kate hadn't thought to do the same. When he put his hand into the front pocket of the last pair, his fingers fumbled upon a tissue. He pulled it from the pocket and unwrapped the tissue slowly. Inside was the ring, Tony held it between two fingers and showed it to Kate.

She threw her arms around his neck. "Thank you, Tony. This is the only piece of real jewelry my mother owned. It was very special to her...and to me."

"Who gave it to her?"

"Right before I was born, my father won it in a card game. Just so happens I was born in March, and the aquamarine is the birthstone for March. He gave it to her while she was still in the hospital. She called the ring her blue baby. My mom told me that other than me, it's the only nice thing my father ever gave her. She loved it because it always reminded her of me, not him."

"Hold out your hand," Tony said.

Kate extended her hand, and Tony slipped the ring onto her finger. "Looks beautiful on ya. I think ya should wear it all the time, not just on special occasions. That way you'll know your mom is always beside ya."

Kate sat on her mother's bed and pulled Tony down beside her. She kissed him on his neck, and he closed his eyes softly, reveling in the feel of her lips on his skin. Kate lay back on the bed and pulled Tony down with her. Her tongue trickled over his upper lip, and he opened his mouth and ran his tongue over hers. Tony put his hand under Kate's shirt and cupped her breast. Her back arched at his touch, and she leaned over and unbuttoned his jeans. She glided her hand effortlessly inside of his boxers. Tony lifted her shirt over her head and unsnapped her bra. Her breasts stood before him, begging for Tony to take them into his mouth. He smoothly removed her skirt, and she lay in his arms in only her panties.

"Tony, I'll love you till the end," she purred.

"Till the end, Kate."

Kate gripped Tony's penis, pressing her groin against his. Tony's jeans were still at his ankles, so he bent down, unsnapped the holster holding his gun, and placed it under the bed, putting his jeans on top. The two lay side by side. They kissed and held each other, flesh on flesh, heart to heart.

"Make love to me," Kate begged.

"Are ya sure? I mean, I know you're upset about your mother. Is this the right time?"

Kate leaned down and pulled Tony's boxers off. He knelt over her naked, his muscles flexing and his handsome carved body a temptation she couldn't resist. He pulled Kate's underwear off and threw them to the side. Still kneeling over her, Tony put his mouth over one of her breasts and wiggled his tongue back and forth across her nipple. His hand slowly slid down her sternum; it felt like a feather as his fingers wisped past her belly button and lower abdomen until he tenderly put his fingers inside of her. Kate moaned, a sweet sound of pleasure, and he continued to touch her, ever so gently.

Tony knew from the purring sounds she made and the warm wetness between her legs that Kate wanted him. Tony looked into Kate's face. "Please," she begged, "I wanna be one with you."

Tony eased himself inside of Kate. His lust was on the brink of explosion, but inside of Kate, making love to her, there was a mixture of lust and love. It was the most joyful feeling he'd experienced in his life. Kate pushed her pelvis forward and back, forward and back, as Tony rhythmically slipped up and down.

It was only a few minutes before a sound erupted from Kate, as she burst into an orgasm. Tony opened his eyes, breathing in the scent of the apricot shampoo she'd used that morning. The look of joy and satisfaction on her face turned him on further, and a few seconds later, Tony surged with his own orgasm. It exploded inside of him, and he felt weightless, as though his body and mind were made of magic stardust—an instantaneous moment of floating in a warm sea filled with fireworks, and his body and mind went to a place of bliss. He wanted to stay in that state forever.

When they finished, Tony lay beside Kate. For the whole time he and Kate had been together, the thought of making love to her had made him nervous. After all, he had never had sex with a girl, and that thought had always given him anxiety. He'd been worried that he wouldn't be able to perform—that he wouldn't be capable of allowing the images of the prison guards to leave his mind.

Now, after having sex with the girl he loved, he hoped he was free of the chains that kept his mind bound to his tragic past.

Chapter Seventy-Two

K ate moved into the cramped quarters above the bakery with Donata and Ruth. Tony helped move her few belongings into the small space. There were two bedrooms, and Kate slept on the floor next to Ruth's single bed.

"I know there ain't much room here for ya. But Donata and Ruth are good people. As soon as I can save some money, you and me can get our own apartment," Tony said, trying to lift her spirits.

"I'll be fine here. I'd be better if you were staying here with me." Kate looked around the tiny living room. "I know that's not realistic, and I'm real grateful to Donata, but I wanna be with you."

"I know ya do, and I wanna be wit' you too. But we gotta take one small step at a time. That's the way life is sometimes—we want things right now, and when we can't have 'em it makes us feel bad. But you'll see, in a couple of days this will feel like home. Then, one day, me and you will be together for real. When things ain't goin' the way ya want them to, that's when ya gotta fight harder and go after what cha really want. That's all I know how to do, Kate, so believe me, your life ain't gonna be like this forever."

Tony was giving Kate a passionate kiss when Ruth walked into the living room.

"Ewww," Ruth bellowed.

Tony chuckled. "Ya say ewww 'cause you're twelve. When you're sixteen, almost seventeen," he added, "ya ain't gonna think there's anything ewww about kissin' your boyfriend."

Ruth smirked at the couple. "When I'm almost seventeen, I won't have a boyfriend. I don't want one. Boys smell, and they act like idiots."

Tony creeped over to Ruth and lifted her off the ground. "Are ya callin' me smelly?"

Ruth giggled. "You're the smelliest."

Tony put her back down and kissed the top of her head. "Tell Donata I'll check in tomorra."

Ruth's face brightened; she loved being around Tony. "OK. We're making cinnamon buns in the morning. Maybe if you're nice to me, I'll save you one."

"Oh, ain't ya sweet. If ya don't save me one, I'm gonna roll around in your bed and make it smell bad."

Ruth put her arms around Tony's waist and squeezed. Then she turned and hobbled into her bedroom.

"Ya gonna be OK?" Tony whispered to Kate before he left.

"Yeah, I'll be fine."

***

As Tony rode the bus back to the Slayers' house that night, he fantasized about what it would be like to live with Kate. He had never felt needed until he met her. He'd never felt loved the way she loved him. He had never felt good enough until she made him realize he was a good person. Kate was becoming the center of his world.

Tony lay on the mattress in his room that night, remembering the love he'd shared with Kate that afternoon.

"Hey, Tony," someone called from downstairs.

Tony got up and walked down the stairs. In the middle of the living room was a girl no older than fourteen. "What's up?"

"Krista here," Blast said, nodding toward the girl, "needs our help. Her older sister, Arlene, got beat up today by some drunk assholes."

"From another gang?" Tony asked.

"No. Just some ass hats from around the neighborhood. A couple of us are gonna go teach 'em a lesson."

Tony cocked his head to the side. "Since when did we start fightin' battles that don't belong to the Slayers?"

"Tony makes a good point," Smoke said.

Blast gave Tony a disparaging look.

Tony watched him. Blast's mouth was twitching, and he was blinking rapidly. "What gives?" he asked Blast.

"I used to date Arlene when we was younger. Ya know, before I became a Slayer. Arlene's a real nice girl. That's why Krista came here. To see if I'd help them out. Rotten assholes threatened to kill her the next time they saw her."

Tony turned to the girl. "Your sister do anythin' to piss 'em off?"

Krista's face crunched up, and her head jerked backward. "No, my sister is real nice to everybody. She don't have no enemies. When she grows up, she's gonna be a teacher so she can help other kids that are poor like us."

Tony turned back to Blast. "Ya clear it wit' Razor?"

Blast's eyes grew wide, and he walked Tony outside to the curb. "I ain't askin' Razor's permission. We can take care of this, and as long as we don't bring any bad shit back to the Slayers, then he ain't gotta know. Besides, I don't care what Razor thinks. This is somethin' I gotta do. I was young when me and Arlene dated, but I still love her. Ya see, the thing is, when I joined the Slayers, I broke it off 'cause ya know what bitches gotta do to belong. I wasn't havin' her raped-in. She was a good girl, and I couldn't do that to her."

"I understand that. Count me in," Tony said, thinking about Kate.

Tony's respect for Blast skyrocketed. They had something more in common than being decent guys who were violent. They had a protective place for girls they loved.

Tony, Blast, and Smoke walked the mile with Krista back to her home. When they arrived, Arlene was at the door.

"What have you done, Krista?" Arlene said.

"It's all cool," Blast said. "She's just worried about ya."

"I don't need any more trouble than I already got, Blast. Just go home and leave us alone."

Blast moved closer to get a better look at Arlene. "From those bruises on your face, looks like you're making a bad decision tellin' us to go home."

Arlene pulled Krista inside, but before she shut the door, Tony put his foot in the doorjamb. He bent down to Krista. "What cha did by walkin' to our place by yourself was real stupid. Ya coulda got yourself hurt."

Krista's lower lip quivered.

Tony gave her a warm smile. "What I'm sayin' is don't do that again. I'm also tellin' ya that ya got some real balls doin' what ya did. It's good to protect your family. Next time ya got a problem, ya come find me in the Italian Market—I'm there all the time—but don't come walkin' to our place. Got it?"

Tears slid down Krista's cheeks and her head hung in shame.

"OK," Tony said, looking at Krista and up at Arlene, "we're gonna go take care of this. Ya know where to find me if ya need us to come back."

Tony watched the tension drain from Arlene's stiff limbs. He gave her a nod, and Arlene gently shut the front door. Once Tony heard the bolt on the door click, he turned back to his friends.

"Now you're prince fuckin' charming?" Blast mocked.

"Hey, I got a way wit' women," Tony said, shoving Blast from behind.

"Since when? Ya ain't been wit' any of our bitches since ya dumped Digger."

Digger was one of the girls in the gang. She had wanted Tony to kill her brother in-law, whom she hated with a passion, to show her he wanted to be her boyfriend. When Tony had refused, Digger had stopped showing interest in him, which was fine with him. They had only made out a few times, and she was a rough kisser with a tongue that felt like sandpaper.

"Digger wasn't worthy of my Italian greatness. Who cares about her anyway? Let's go take care of these assholes and make sure they never fuck wit' Arlene again."

Blast knew which boys had beat up Arlene. He explained to Tony and Smoke that the boys they were looking for were losers who hung in an alley next to a local pawnshop. They got their kicks off of smoking pot, drinking beer, and bullying people.

They found the boys where Blast had expected. Blast approached first, walking quickly toward the boys with his hands clenched into fists. He stood in front of the largest guy.

"I hear ya beat up on Arlene," Blast said.

The boy guzzled the rest of his beer and burped in Blast's face. "What's it to ya? She your little hoe?"

Blast pulled back his arm and clocked the boy in the face. He fell to the ground, momentarily stunned.

Tony and Smoke went after the other two teens, and within seconds there was a good old-fashioned street brawl in the alley.

The boy Tony was fighting suddenly pulled out a knife and waved it at him. "Come on, motherfucker, show me what cha got," he snarled.

Tony reached into the back of his pants and pulled out his gun. He pointed it at the boy's head and rushed him until the gun was touching his skull.

"This is what I got. Now what cha have to say?"

The teen dropped the knife and put his hands up over his head. Tony took the butt of his handgun and whacked the boy in the head. He collapsed to the ground, unconscious.

Tony then turned to the others, who were still punching away at each other. He waved his gun around. "Who wants to die?" he growled.

The boys halted; even Blast and Smoke stopped to look. Tony's face was red, and the muscles on his arms were rock hard. Tony walked over to the larger teen, the one Blast had been fighting. He placed the gun against the boy's head.

"Here's how it's gonna work. Ya ever fuck wit' Arlene or her sister, and we'll hunt ya down and kill all of ya. Tonight, ya got a break, just a beatin'; next time ya won't live to tell about it. Do you get me?"

The teen nodded; his right eye was swollen, and blood ran down his cheek.

Tony looked at Blast and then at Smoke. "Let's get outta here."

As the three of them walked back to the Slayers' house, they were quiet. Smoke left them and went to a bar to have a beer. Tony and Blast continued to walk back to the house.

"Ya love Arlene, so you oughta be wit' her," Tony said.

"I told ya; she's a good girl. I'd rather not have her then share her wit' all our gang at the house. She's too good to be a Slayers' bitch."

"I didn't say nothin' about her being a Slayer. Ya know, ya can see her, and nobody's gotta know about it," Tony hinted.

"You're outta your mind. You have any idea what they'd do to me and Arlene if Razor found out I was seeing someone who doesn't belong? When I first joined the gang, I was with Arlene, and they told me straight up, either lose her or she becomes one with the whole gang."

Tony stared into Blast's eyes. "Razor ain't gotta know it."

Blast laughed, hard. "Let me tell ya somethin', brother. There ain't nothin' that Razor don't find out about. He's got people all over the city who tell him shit. People will do anything for a bag of dope. Dooley, his cousin you shared a cell wit' in juvie, he set that up long before he went away."

Tony's belly flopped, and the veins in his temple hammered against his skull. He hadn't known about the informants. Tony's forehead tightened, his skin forming into lines of worry. Now he had a real reason to be concerned.

Chapter Seventy-Three

The next day, Tony kept looking over his shoulder as he made his way to the bakery. His paranoia of Razor having him watched was overbearing. Unlike Blast, giving up Arlene for the Slayers, Tony couldn't give up Kate for anything. He'd fight to the death before letting someone stand between him and the woman he loved. However, he was realistic too, and he fought an ongoing internal battle between loving Kate and protecting her.

When he walked into the bakery, Kate ran up to him and put her arms around his neck. "Tony, I'm happy you're here," she said.

Tony unwrapped her arms from his neck and took a step backward.

"What's wrong?" Kate said, shocked.

"People can see us through all these windows."

"So?" Kate's heart was racing. Short, choppy breaths took over. She felt faint. The last thing she could bear was losing Tony.

"Go into the back. I'll meet ya there," Tony ordered.

Kate's head hung as she shuffled across the floor and entered the back room where the ovens were located.

"What's goin' on?" Donata asked, having witnessed the encounter.

"Nothin'. I just need to talk to Kate in private."

Tony wouldn't dare tell Donata about the Slayers; she would surely want Kate to leave if she thought that Ruth was in danger.

When Tony entered the back room, Kate was leaning against the large stainless steel sink. Her head was dipped low, and she was wiping her tears away. Tony approached slowly and stood before her. She glanced up at him, her heavy eyelids appeared to melt into her downturned mouth. Tony wrapped his arm around her waist and pulled her to him.

"Listen. I found out the Slayers have a shit ton of druggies all over the city that will dime us out for a bag of dope. We just gotta be careful. This don't mean we ain't together, but we can't let anyone see us. Donata can't know nothin' about it; she'll put ya out if she knows I'm in a gang."

Kate lifted her head. "But we've been together all this time, and nothing ever happened."

"Yeah, well, we just got lucky. A while ago Razor was questioning where I was all the time. I told him my mother had cancer. Razor's the head of the Slayers, and the guy can't stand me. He'd like nothin' more than to hurt me. We just gotta lay low."

"Are you saying I'm not going to see you?"

"No, I ain't sayin' that. I'm sayin' we gotta be more careful now that I got this information. That means we can be together, but only when I know it's safe."

"Well, that sounds like never."

"It ain't gonna be never. In fact, I'm gonna go talk to Salvatore, see if maybe he can help us out."

"How is he gonna help us?"

"I'm gonna have 'im pick ya up, and I'll meet ya places. That way, it'll look like you're wit' him."

Kate rested her head on Tony's chest and let out a long sigh. Tony held Kate for a long time, gently rubbing the small of her back. When he released her, they kissed passionately.

"I'll see if Salvatore can pick ya up around eight tonight. Make sure you're ready."

Tony turned to leave, and Kate grabbed his hand. He turned back to her.

"Till the end, Tony," she said in a ragged voice.

"Till the end. Don't worry. It'll all be fine."

Tony left Kate in the kitchen, said good-bye to Ruth and Donata, and set off to find Salvatore. He found him at a luncheonette not too far from the Morano house. Salvatore was sitting alone, eating a burger.

"Hey," Tony said as he pulled back a chair and sat down. He reached over to Salvatore's plate and plucked off one of the French fries, doused it in ketchup, and shoved it into his mouth.

Salvatore lifted his hand for the waitress, and she rushed over to them. "Can you bring another burger and fries for my friend?"

After the waitress left to place the order, Salvatore turned his attention to Tony.

"My father doesn't want me hanging around with you. He said because you're part of a gang that you're off limits."

"Oh yeah, what did you say to that?"

"I told him that you're a good friend and I don't give a shit what gang you belong to."

Tony raised his eyebrows. "Kinda risky to disobey Johnny Morano."

"Yeah, well, he's my father. What's he going to do? Kill me? I don't think so. Anyway, I told him that I'm almost eighteen and can make my own decisions."

"Ha! How'd that go?"

"He slapped me in the face," Salvatore said, turning his face so Tony could see the light bruise on his cheek. "Anyway, I reminded him that the mob is all about brotherhood. I also reminded him of what happened to you in juvenile detention when you were protecting me. He knew I was right and gave me this death glare for a while; then he smashed a glass he was holding into the wall. That's when Big Paulie stood up and whispered something to my father. His shoulders relaxed, and he came back over to me. I thought he was going to kick my ass, but he just patted me on the shoulder and left his office. After he left, I looked at Big Paulie and asked him what he had told my father.

"Big Paulie said, 'I just reminded him that when we was young, me and him was in a gang. That's how we got started workin' wit' the Bonanni family. We was havin' a war wit' a rival gang. Now, your pop had his gun kicked outta his hand early in the fight, but that didn't stop 'im. Made 'im even more crazy. Anyway, this guy snuck up on me from behind; he was holdin' a gun to my head, and the asshole told me to say my prayers. The next thing I know, your father tackles the guy to the ground and beats 'im to death wit' a big rock. One of Bonannis' men saw 'im do it and took a liking to your father, thought he had balls for a young guy.'"

"I asked Big Paulie, 'Then why is my father judging Tony for being in a gang?'"

Salvatore took a bite of his burger before continuing. "Big Paulie smiled at me and explained, 'Because when we joined a gang in New York, we was badass teenagers. We ate, drank, and slept violence. That's the way it was in those days on the streets of New York. We were wild and got ourselves into a lotta trouble. He's afraid that Tony is gonna get ya into trouble like we did. Anyway, he got taken in by the mob when he was real young. The mob didn't like street gangs, but your pop, he was a real schmoozer, and once that mobster told the godfather 'bout how your father beat that guy in the middle of a gang war, they wanted him bad. Once he got accepted, your pop took me to see the captain of the New York crime family, and the guy liked me, said I had potential. After that, I left the gang and worked wit' your pop. I think he needed to be reminded of where he came from, no different than Tony.'"

Tony listened to Salvatore as the waitress placed his food in front of him. He was shocked and relieved to hear that Big Paulie and Mr. Morano had been gang members and had turned their lives around. It gave him hope that someday, he too, could leave the Slayers. There was nothing he wanted more in the world than to leave gang life behind and be free to love Kate.

Chapter Seventy-Four

S alvatore arrived at the bakery shortly after eight o'clock that evening. When Kate saw the Bentley from the bedroom window, she hurried down the steps and out the side door. She approached the car quickly, and Vincent stepped out of the passenger side and opened the back door for her. Kate smiled at Vincent, her nose wrinkled, and she slipped into the backseat. Once Vincent was in the car, he turned back to Kate.

"Tony said we gotta treat ya good. Ya know, act like we're gentlemen."

"Correction," Salvatore butted in. "He said you need to act like a gentleman; I already am one." Salvatore leaned over the front seat, and Kate leaned forward, and they pecked each other on the cheek. "How are you doing, Kate? Things working out for you here?" he said, pointing at the bakery.

"Yeah, things are fine. I mean, so far—it's only been a couple days. Donata and Ruth are great, but I feel like I'm taking up space that they barely have for themselves." The volume of Kate's voice lowered, and the boys strained to hear her. "I miss my mom," she murmured.

Salvatore put the car in drive and looked into the rearview mirror at Kate. "We're going to a party tonight. One of the girls that I'm dating is having a bunch of people over. Tony is meeting us there."

Kate shut her eyes and relaxed into the soft leather of the car seat for the remainder of the ride. When Kate walked into the party, Tony rushed over to her.

"See, I told ya that Salvatore would help us."

Vincent forced an aggressive cough. "Yeah, Vincent too," Tony added.

Vincent leaned in. "That's what friends do for each other. I'm just hopin' Johnny will let ya work wit' us one day."

"All I know is I gotta do somethin' different. The Slayers got me off the street when I was younger. I was just too stupid to know that once I was in, I can't just walk away. Ain't what I thought it was, and I gotta figure a way out," Tony replied.

That night, Tony and Kate found a quiet room to be alone. At first, the girl Salvatore was dating told them they couldn't be in her father's study, but Salvatore pulled her aside. Salvatore was over six feet tall, handsome and muscular. The glow of his honey-colored eyes easily made his dates confuse desire for love, and this made it easy for Salvatore to convince girls to do things they normally wouldn't.

Tony and Kate snuggled on the sofa. "Kate, I'm gonna get outta the gang. I don't know how, and I don't know when, but I'll make it happen. Ya just gotta trust me. Then you and me can be together."

"I hope so. I love Donata, but I can't live there forever. I feel like a burden to them. Besides, with you being a Slayer, we are putting them in danger. I feel guilty about not letting Donata know. What if someone from the gang does something to them? I wouldn't be able to live with myself. Could you?"

"No, I couldn't, but ain't nothin' gonna happen to them. The gang will come after me, not them," he assured her.

In his heart, Tony knew the Slayers didn't care who they hurt or even killed if it meant finding their own justice. Kate's words played over in his mind. He was so caught up in his own need to be with Kate that he hadn't thought about Donata or Ruth. Tony's guilt bubbled over, and his arms and legs got stiff as his muscles flexed. As he looked around the large study, his eyes saw objects, but his mind couldn't register them.

"Let's go out and find Salvatore. I gotta get movin'. I got some work wit' the Slayers tonight," Tony huffed.

Kate clung to his arm, trying to keep him on the sofa next to her. "No, Tony. Let's stay a little longer."

"Look, Kate. I got shit I gotta do."

Kate smacked back against the sofa, as though his words were striking her in the face.

"Fine," Kate said and stood. "Let's go then."

Kate walked toward the study door. Tony grabbed her arm and turned Kate to face him.

"I'm sorry, Kate. I didn't mean to hurt your feelings. I just got a lot of shit I'm worried about. Ya forgive me?"

Kate's scowl softened. "I guess so," she purred, "but I want to help you. You're not all alone."

Tony kissed her forehead. "I know. We'll figure somethin' out together."

Before Salvatore left with Kate that evening, Tony pulled him off to the side. "I need ya to do me a favor. Ya gotta keep an eye on Donata and Ruth. They're my family. I haven't seen my mother in years, and they opened up to me and helped me when I had nowhere else to go. Now, they're helping Kate too."

Salvatore raised his eyebrows. "You don't have to worry about them. They'll be protected. Vincent and I will take care of it. We'll keep watch over them."

"How ya gonna do that?" Tony asked. He wanted more than just words; he wanted specifics.

Salvatore rested his hand on Tony's shoulder. "I can't explain right now. However, I want you to remember who my father is. Vincent and I have been working for him, and with that comes a security that you can't find in other places."

This information gave Tony enough peace to put his worry to rest for now. Tony gave Salvatore a hug, and he felt the gun in the back of Salvatore's jeans. Tony patted it. "Is that what I think it is?"

"What? You think that you are the only one who carries a gun? Like I said, Vincent and I work for my father. That means we are potential targets. The only difference between your gang and the business my father runs is that we don't have fucked-up rules about who we can date, and we run a real business. Sure, there are people who get in the way, and, like the Slayers, we need to handle them, but it isn't our primary business."

Tony ran his fingers through his thick hair. "Maybe someday I can work wit' ya and Vincent. For now, I just gotta keep doin' what I'm doin' wit' the Slayers. Until I can get outta there wit'out gettin' myself killed."

As Tony headed back to North Philadelphia, his hands shook and his eyes darted around, taking in the people and activity of the city. He wanted to turn back time, to do things differently. He would have rather been homeless than held hostage by a group of guys he had never fully believed in. Tony wanted his freedom more than anything.

Chapter Seventy-Five

O ver the weeks that followed, Tony continued to live two lives: one where he fought other gangs over drugs and threats to the Slayers and another where he worked at the bakery as if he was the most normal person in the world. He and Kate stole moments in the back of the bakery, kissing and touching each other. Donata knew what was going on in the kitchen, but she left them to it, remembering how she and her husband would do anything to spend precious loving moments in private.

It was a warm, sunny day in April. Tony had overslept, and when he woke at noon, he rushed to dress and get into the city. Donata would be pissed that he was so late. When he arrived at the bakery just after two o'clock, he found the door locked.

Tony banged on the bakery door. "Donata," he yelled, "open up."

He saw Kate peek her head out from the back. She hurried toward the door, and without a word, she unlocked it and scurried into the kitchen. Tony followed; something was wrong. He leaned over, grabbed his gun from his ankle holster, and shoved it into the back of his jeans as he followed Kate.

"What the fuck is goin' on?"

"Oh, Tony," Kate cried. "Ruth was working up front this morning when two guys walked in and asked for a couple loaves of bread. When she turned around, they jumped over the counter and grabbed her from behind. Donata and I were still upstairs."

Kate put her face in her hands and wept.

Tony gently pulled her hands away. "What happened to Ruth?"

"Oh God, Tony, they pulled off her fake leg and beat her with it. They beat her until she blacked out. She's in the hospital. Donata called right before you got here; the doctors said those guys hurt her real bad."

"Who the fuck were they?" Tony asked, rage overflowing.

"I don't know. Donata told me to stay here and wait for you. She needs you to go to the hospital. Ruth woke up once and asked for you."

Tony took Kate by the shoulders. "You stay here. Keep the door locked. If anyone asks, I wasn't here. You got me?"

Kate nodded. "I'm scared, Tony. What if they come back?"

Tony scribbled a number on a piece of paper. "Call Salvatore. Tell him to come over and stay wit' cha. He and Vincent will keep ya safe."

When Tony got to Children's Hospital, he quickly found Ruth's room number and took the escalator steps two at a time. He burst through the door of Ruth's room and found Donata sitting in a chair with rosary beads laced between her fingers.

"Tony, where have ya been? Oh Tony, how could this happen to us?" she cried.

Tony held Donata for a few moments before he went over to the bed. Ruth's cheeks were colorless, a shade paler than the white sheet tucked under her chin. Her bruises stood out like a full moon in a starless, black sky. One eye was swollen to the size of an egg. She had bruises on the sides of her face. The doctors had shaved one side of her head to stitch the open gash on the side of her skull.

"Who did this, Donata?"

The older woman shook her head. "I don't know. I wasn't there," she wailed. "I let her open the bakery and then took my time getting downstairs. This is all my fault—I didn't protect her."

Tony watched Donata melt into a mound of flesh on the chair as she cried. His mind raced. He was worried that it was the Slayers. Had Razor found out about Kate?

Tony stood over Ruth for close to an hour. Finally, her good eye fluttered open. "Tony," she whispered in a soft voice.

"Yeah, Ruth, I'm here. Ain't nothin' bad gonna happen to ya ever again."

Ruth gave him a tiny smile. Tears dribbled from the sides of her eyes. "I'm scared," she managed.

"Don't be scared. You're safe. Do you know who did this?"

Ruth nodded, ever so slightly.

"Tell me." Tony leaned down to put his ear next to Ruth's busted lips.

"The Walsh brothers," she breathed.

Tony's nostrils flared. "Brian and Kenny?"

Ruth gave a small nod.

Tony's feet were spread out, his elbows pointed in opposite directions as though they were wings, and his chest was thrust forward.

Ruth groaned.

"What's wrong?" Donata shrieked, jumping from the chair.

"It hurts. My head hurts," Ruth muttered.

Tony strode out to the nurses' station. His body was rigid and commanding attention. "Ruth," he said pointing to her room. "She's in pain. She needs somethin'."

"In a moment," the nurse responded.

"No. Not in a moment. Right now," he growled, banging his fists against his thighs.

The nurse, startled, bolted out of her chair, shoved a bottle into her pocket, and headed into the room. Tony stayed with Ruth until she was sleeping soundly.

Tony turned to Donata. The skin around her eyes was bunched up, and her blank stare was a window into the pain she was feeling for her granddaughter. "I gotta go, Donata. I'll be back later. You stay here wit' Ruth."

Donata stood and hugged him. She clutched at his shirt, grabbing and releasing a handful of fabric.

"She's all right. Ruth's gonna be fine," he assured her.

Donata released Tony and sat back in the chair and prayed. Tony took one last look at the two people he loved. His anger was intense, and his desire for revenge burned inside of him.

Tony left the hospital and took a cab into North Philadelphia. He didn't have time to take the bus.

He opened the door of the Slayers' house. Smoke looked up as the door banged against the battered wall, and he lowered the bong from his mouth. Tony stood in the doorway, stiff as a board, his mouth down turned. Smoke turned to the girl sitting next to him.

"Get out," Smoke told her. The girl quickly scurried upstairs. Smoke stood and walked over to Tony. "What's got you all jacked up, man?"

Tony snorted. "That bakery where I work. The little girl, Ruth, got fucked up today."

Smoke took Tony by the arm. "Let's step outside."

The two walked for several blocks before Smoke stopped and turned to face Tony. "Tell me what happened."

Tony quickly repeated the events that had occurred at the bakery.

Smoke rubbed his forehead. "Goddamn, that's some fucked-up shit." He paused, looking at the ground and then back up at Tony. "So what cha wanna do?"

"I need someone to drive me. I have a plan, but I need a car."

Smoke looked up and down the street, trying to decide what to do. Helping another Slayer deal with something unrelated to gang business was deeply frowned upon. He knew there would be repercussions if the other members found out. But underneath Smoke's tattooed, bearded exterior was a man with a big heart. He'd lost his whole family when he was young, and after many failed attempts at living in foster care, he'd found the Slayers.

"All right, I'm in."

Tony's eyes widened. "You serious? Ya know what will happen if that asshole Razor finds out."

Smoke grunted. "That pussy ain't gonna find out shit."

"I'm gonna see if Blast will help," Tony said.

Smoke pursed his lips.

"What?" Tony said, his voice heavy. "He knows about protectin' people. Didn't we fuck up those maggots for screwin' around wit' his old love, Arlene?"

Smoke pulled on the waistband of his jeans. "Yeah, you're right. Let's go talk to him."

At first, Blast was hesitant, but Tony was convincing. "We helped you wit' Arlene. Smoke and me know ya still love her. Wouldn't ya kill somebody who ever hurt her again?"

"Yeah, I would."

"Well. These are people I love. Helped me when I didn't have nothin' to eat. Ya know I still work there 'cause they're like family to me."

"OK. I'm in. When?"

Tony cocked his head to the right. His eyes bulged from their sockets. With his teeth clenched, Tony said, "Tonight."

Chapter Seventy-Six

L ater that night, after waiting outside a neighborhood pub in South Philadelphia, where the Walsh brothers were drinking, Tony and Blast took the brothers at gunpoint. Smoke drove them to an abandoned factory on the outskirts of the city. They forced the brothers into an old, unused factory and tied their hands behind their backs. They were side by side, on their knees, watching the other boys intently.

Tony's gun was dangling from his hand as he circled them. "I remember when you two idiots tormented the shit outta me. Slappin' me in the head when ya walked by, kicking me in the ass when ya snuck up behind me. Tellin' me I was a loser and that I should kill myself." Tony scratched at his temple with his free hand. "Yeah, I was little then, an easy target. I see that ya still like to go after the easy targets; that's 'cause ya ain't nothin'. You're nothin' but two little bitches." Tony lifted his gun and waved it in front of their faces. "This time ya fucked wit' the wrong people."

"We don't know what you're talkin' 'bout, Bruno," Brian Walsh snapped.

"Oh, ya don't? OK, well, let me explain it to ya. Ya know that little girl, Ruth, the one who lives wit' her grandmother at the bakery? You two beat her so bad she's layin' in a fuckin' hospital bed as we speak. That's what I'm talkin' 'bout."

"Come on, now. We didn't mean nothin'. We just got carried away. We'll do whatever ya want. I swear," Kenny Walsh pleaded.

Tony glared at Brian. "You see, Brian, you fucked wit' my family, and I don't take that lightly. Ruth is in the hospital because of what you did to her. Lucky for her she doesn't have permanent brain damage. I bet you thought it was real funny when you yanked her fake leg off and beat her wit' it. Right?"

"Well, I wouldn't say funny, but ya gotta admit it's a little amusin'," Kenny Walsh, the younger brother said.

Tony couldn't believe what he'd just heard. "Sure, Kenny, I understand. Tell me, how funny do you think this is?"

Tony grabbed Kenny's ankle, forcing him to drop to his side. Tony pulled the knife that Erikson had given him years prior from under his pant leg. He held the blade right below Kenny's knee. Putting his weight behind the knife, Tony began to saw through Kenny's leg with the serrated blade.

A few minutes later, Kenny's screams stopped as he faded into unconsciousness. His brother, Brian, watched Tony with a panicked expression. Brian began to twitch. A valve seemed to have opened on his forehead, and his grim face was covered with sweat.

"See," Tony said, seething and looking at Brian. "Take a good look at your smartass brother. I bet he don't think it's so funny now, huh?"

"No, you're right. It ain't funny, Tony. Please just let us go. We ain't never gonna do stupid shit like that again," Brian begged, watching his brother bleed to death.

"You're right. You will never do anything like this again."

Tony stepped over Kenny's limp body and picked up his newly amputated leg. He raised the long stump high into the air and beat Brian over the head with it. Tony didn't stop pounding him with the leg until Brian was covered in blood and bruises.

Tony leered at Brian; his heartbeat filled his ears with a steady rhythm, so loud he could no longer hear anything else around him. Images of Tony's childhood raced through his mind. He remembered walking home from the bus stop and a group of boys surrounding him. Brian had grabbed him by the shirt and was punching and slapping him. He'd tried to escape Brian's hold, but he hadn't been strong enough. When Tony had fallen to the ground, the boys had taken turns kicking him. Then they ripped his jeans from his body and walked away with them. Tony had to walk the rest of the way home in his T-shirt and underwear. His mother was in shock when she saw him. Tony's father had heard about the incident at the bar and beat Tony with his belt that night for being such an embarrassment to him.

More childhood images of what the Walsh brothers had put him through flooded his thoughts. Tony was cranked tight, and his jaw was jutting out when he focused on Brian again. "Get ready to go to hell."

Tony lifted his gun and shot one deadly bullet into the side of Brian's head. As brain bits sprayed on the wall behind him, Brian's body slumped onto the floor. Blast and Smoke looked over at Kenny. Most of his blood had drained from his body, and he died quietly.

Tony finally turned to Blast and Smoke. "I appreciate ya helpin' me out here tonight. I owe ya one."

Blast and Smoke stared at Tony. Blast's mouth hung open, and Smoke reached into the pocket of his black leather jacket, pulled out a cigarette, and lit it.

"You're one brutal motherfucker," Smoke began. "I seen a lot of shit in my day, but nothin' like that."

"They fucked wit' my family."

Blast turned and walked out of the warehouse. "Let's get the fuck outta here."

As Tony walked to the car, his legs felt wobbly, and his fingers fidgeted on the seam of his shirt. "Smoke, can ya give me one of those cigarettes?"

Smoke threw the pack to Tony and then the lighter. He lit one and inhaled deeply, thinking about what he had just done. He knew the Walsh brothers deserved what they'd gotten, but in his blind rage, he'd performed a gruesome act, worse than anything he'd done before. The thing that worried him was that he had no remorse.

Chapter Seventy-Seven

Johnny Morano looked at his son with surprise. "Are you telling me that Tony killed the Walsh brothers?"

"Yes, that's what I'm telling you. Even though Donata buys all her baking supplies from us, and with that should have come protection, it was Tony who took care of those two assholes."

"How do you know this?"

"Tony told us about it." Salvatore turned to Vincent, who nodded in agreement.

"Why would he do this?"

"Because Donata and Ruth were like his family, Pop. They helped him out when everyone else turned their backs on him." Salvatore glared at his father. He knew they should have done more for Tony. He'd lost so much, taking the blame for Salvatore's crime.

Johnny turned to the two boys. "Listen to me, boys. Tony did the right thing to those Walsh maggots tonight. In our family, we believe in an eye for an eye."

"Yeah, well, Tony ain't in our family—remember, Mr. M.?" Vincent said.

Johnny shot Vincent a threatening look.

Salvatore spoke up quickly. "It's true. We need guys like Tony. He would die to protect the people that he loves. That's what you and Big Paulie are always preaching to us. You realize that the gang he is in will punish him if they find out he killed the Walsh brothers."

"That's not my problem, Salvatore. Tony's a big boy, and I'm sure he can take care of himself."

Salvatore's shoulders slumped forward, and he slowly shook his head. He gave his father a bitter smile and raised his hands in the air as if to plead on Tony's behalf.

Johnny waved a dismissive hand at his son. "Go. Go find your mother. Tell her to put on a pot of coffee. Some of the men are coming over tonight. We have real business to take care of."

When Salvatore and Vincent left the office, Johnny turned to Big Paulie.

"What do you think?"

"I think Tony has balls of steel. I told ya a while ago that boy would be someone to watch out for someday. Looks like that day has arrived, Boss. That kid is willin' to do shit that other people couldn't stomach. When it comes to protectin' his own, like he did wit' Salvatore and now Donata and Ruth, he'll do whatever it takes. Salvatore's right. That's the kinda man we need in this family. The kinda person who experienced the dark side of life, so when push comes to shove, he don't think about what he's got to lose 'cause he never felt like he had nothin' anyway. Tony's a lot like you, when ya was young and full of hate. Ya know as well as I do, Tony's a born mobster."

Johnny nodded. "That he is. Still, there's something about him that gets under my skin."

"I know what it is. Ya see a lot of yourself in 'im. He's full of hate and anger. Ya gotta look past that so ya can see his potential, just like the Bonanni family saw it in you."

"You're right, Big Paulie. As much as I hate to admit it, Tony's got that balance of good and evil—the two things that keep a man loyal and deadly. Let's keep Tony on our radar. If the time comes that I feel like he's good enough to join us, you'll be the first to know," Johnny stated.

Chapter Seventy-Eight

A month later, Tony and Kate had snuck away to a little restaurant off the beaten path. They had just finished eating a sandwich, and it was almost dusk. Tony grabbed Kate in the back of the restaurant and gave her a kiss.

"All right. You head back to Donata's. I'll be followin' ya."

"I wish we could be together like a normal couple. I hate hiding all the time."

"Yeah, it won't be forever. Razor has been up my ass, asking all kinds of questions. He thinks I should be in North Philly more. Accused me of selling information to other gangs. He's a dipshit, and we need to be careful. We been through all this before."

Kate didn't want to argue, so she gave Tony a quick hug and left. Tony waited a few seconds before following her. When he stepped outside, a man leaning against the building groaned. Tony looked at the man, and, noticing he was drunk, quickly followed after Kate. Had Tony looked closely, he might have known it was a Slayer recruit dressed in layers of men's clothing, holding a half-empty bottle of Southern Comfort.

Once Kate was inside the bakery and the door locked behind her, Tony walked toward the bus stop that would take him back to the Slayers' house. The night was dark; the cloudy sky blocked the light from the moon and stars. It was unusually quiet, and all Tony could hear were the distant taxi drivers honking their horns. A block away, Tony saw Salvatore's Bentley pull up to the curb in front of a well-known steak house. Tony lifted his arm to yell for Salvatore and Vincent when they got out of the car, but stopped short. Another driver pulled up the block behind the Bentley but remained behind the wheel with the engine running. Tony ducked out of sight. He kept low to the pavement, making his way down the block. Tony was acting on his instincts. There was an increase in pressure in his head, a sign that danger was looming.

Tony was lurking in the shadows of the buildings, only twenty feet from where Salvatore and Vincent stood finishing a cigarette before going into the restaurant. Two men were approaching from behind them, the car they came from still running with the lights off.

Tony reached for his gun in the back of his pants, but before he could pull the trigger one of the men shot Salvatore, hitting him in the right shoulder. Tony shot and killed the man in the next instant.

"Vincent!" Tony screamed.

Tony got his next shot off, killing the second man instantly. Then he ran toward the parked car. The driver put the car in drive and hit the gas. Tony ran into the middle of the street, firing three quick shots. The third shot hit the driver in the throat, and the car veered into a parked vehicle.

Tony ran over to the sidewalk. Salvatore was lying flat on his back.

"Help me get 'im to the car," Tony instructed Vincent.

Within seconds, Tony was in the backseat with Salvatore. Vincent jumped into the driver's seat and sped to the Moranos' house. Vincent ran from the car to get Johnny.

Vincent banged on the door, and when Alessandra answered, he pushed past her and barged into Johnny's office.

"What the fuck?" Johnny snapped, aiming his gun at Vincent.

"Somebody tried to kill Salvatore. He's been shot."

"Where is he?" Johnny demanded.

"He's in his car. Out front."

Johnny didn't have time to process the information. "Move it," he yelled to three of his top men. Within seconds everyone was in motion. "Call the doc," Johnny yelled as he ran to the front door.

Johnny flung open the back door of the Bentley. Inside, Tony was holding his wadded-up shirt tight on Salvatore's shoulder. Johnny gave Tony a grave look.

"How bad is it?"

"I don't know for sure. He's lost a lot of blood, but he's alive."

"Get Salvatore into the house," Johnny instructed Big Paulie. Another mobster helped Big Paulie, and less than a minute later, Tony was sitting in the back of the Bentley alone. He quickly got out of the car and ran. He knew Johnny Morano was volatile; his hairpin temper could trigger, and he'd go after Tony without knowing what happened. Tony didn't want to stick around.

***

Chaos ensued inside the Morano home. Salvatore was brought up to his room, and Johnny stayed with his son. When the doctor arrived Johnny left Salvatore and found Vincent.

"What the hell happened?" Johnny asked.

Vincent related the story to Johnny. Then he said, "If it wasn't for Tony bein' there when he was, me and Salvatore would be dead."

"I see," Johnny said. "Where is Tony now?" he said, looking around the room.

"He left right after we got Salvatore inside. He slipped outta the car durin' all the commotion."

"When you see Tony again, you tell him I said thank you."

Vincent beamed. "Does that mean Tony can work for ya now?"

Johnny leaned into Vincent. His eyes were blazing, and the boy shrank away. "It means tell him I said thank you," he repeated, his lower jaw protruding beyond his upper.

Vincent held his hands up in front of his body. "All right, Mr. M. I got it."

The next moment, Johnny's eyes flickered with a fiery passion. His expression was set hard and the muscles in his body tense, and his hands slowly clenched into fists. He glowered at Vincent, as though he were possessed by Satan himself. He studied Vincent as if he was waiting for him to say something to piss him off. Vincent squirmed under his scrutinizing stare. The air in the room had grown thick—it felt like it was a hundred degrees; it was stifling.

"What happened, Mr. M.? Did I say somethin' wrong?"

Johnny broke the uncomfortable silence. "It angers me to think that someone dared to try and kill my son."

Vincent subtly nodded and then cautiously spoke. "Yeah, I know. But like I told ya, Tony killed all three of the guys. He saved both of us. I think that's somethin' real good that came outta somethin' real bad."

"Shut it!" Johnny screamed.

Vincent slowly backed out of the room and crept up the stairs. He sat next to Salvatore's bed and watched his chest rise and fall. The doctor had given Salvatore morphine, and he slept quietly. "You're alive 'cause of Tony. Your pop don't wanna see it, but he will as soon as ya wake up. Ya gotta make this right for Tony," Vincent whispered.

Chapter Seventy-Nine

I t took Tony several hours to fall asleep. He wondered if Salvatore was still alive. When he finally fell into a deep sleep, his dreams were of Salvatore, bleeding and gasping for air. He had been asleep for three hours when he was awoken by beer being poured into his face. He shot up from his mattress. Two Slayers pulled Tony to his feet and restrained him.

"What's your problem?" Tony yelled, all his senses stinging.

Razor gave him an ugly smile, his silver front teeth making him look more demonic. "We know ya got a bitch. Dudley saw ya wit' her last night. Ya wanna tell me about her?"

"I don't know what you're talkin' 'bout." Tony looked from the guy on his right to the one on his left keeping him restrained. "I suggest ya get the fuck off me."

In response, they gripped Tony harder, pushing his arms upward behind his back.

"What the fuck?" Smoke blurted from behind the group of Slayers. "What's goin' on here?"

Razor whipped on Smoke. "Bruno's got a bitch that he's seein'. One that ain't a part of us."

Smoke looked at Tony intently. "Let 'im go. We don't know it's true. Besides, if he is seein' someone, maybe he was gonna bring her here to become a Slayer."

Tony shook his head. "If there was someone, I'd never bring her into this shithole."

Razor punched Tony in the mouth, and blood dribbled down his chin.

"Let 'im go," Smoke said again and moved in to grab Tony.

The two Slayers held tight to Tony's arms. Smoke turned and stood nose to nose with Razor. "You may be our fill-in leader, but ya don't make decisions about anything wit'out everyone agreeing." Smoke looked around the room, and heads nodded—Smoke rarely took a stand on anything, so when he did, the other members listened.

"Let 'im go," Smoke growled at Razor.

Razor looked around the room. Scrutinizing eyes were on him, waiting for his next move.

Razor met Tony's eyes. "You and me both know ya got a bitch on the outside. If we see ya wit' her ever again, I'll kill her myself. If she ain't one of us, that makes her a threat to all of us. Let 'im go," Razor said.

Tony moved his arms back and forth to get the blood flowing again. Slowly the gang members left the bedroom, except for Smoke.

"Ya got a bitch on the outside?" Smoke asked.

Tony held his gaze but didn't answer. He didn't want to lie to Smoke, but it was too risky to tell him about Kate. Silence filled the room as they watched each other.

"I gotta get goin'," Tony finally said.

"Where?"

"Goin' to the bakery. Ruth's comin' back today."

Smoke nodded and turned to leave. He stopped short of the doorway and looked back at Tony. "If ya do got a girl, ya better be careful. If Razor can prove it, he's gonna get the others to back him," Smoke warned.

"What about you?"

Smoke lit a cigarette. "What about me?"

"Can Razor get ya to back 'im?"

Smoke riveted his eyes to the floor. "Nobody gets me to do nothin' I don't wanna do. But ya gotta remember, we got rules for a reason. Just watch what you're doin'."

When Smoke left the room, Tony looked around him at the empty beer bottles and ashtrays. He was afraid for Kate. He felt trapped, and his stomach felt filled with acid. He didn't take the warning lightly and knew Razor would make good on his threat.

Tony dressed quickly and left the house. On the bus ride into South Philadelphia, he weighed his options. He stopped at Vincent's house before going to the bakery to make sure that Salvatore was OK. He was relieved to learn that, while serious, the gunshot had not been life threatening. By the time he arrived at the bakery, he'd made his decision.

When Tony walked into the bakery, he ignored Kate and went upstairs to find Ruth. He sat down on the bed next to her.

"How you feelin'?"

Ruth pushed her hair back from her face. The swelling was gone, but the yellow-purple bruises on her face reminded him of how he'd let her be hurt. He averted his eyes from the place on her skull where the hair had begun to grow back. The scar was long and ugly, a testament to the beating she'd endured.

"I'm OK," she said in a shallow voice.

"Good. I wanted to check on ya. I gotta go downstairs. I got work to do."

Tony touched the top of Ruth's small hand.

"I'm scared," Ruth whined.

"Ain't nothin' to be scared about. The Walsh brothers ain't never comin' back here again."

"Are you sure?" Ruth asked, her eyes bloodshot from crying.

"I'm positive. Ya trust me, don't cha?"

Ruth pouted and gave him a nod.

"Good. When I tell ya somethin', I mean it. I just want ya to rest so you can get better and make me some of those cinnamon buns that I love."

Ruth relaxed into the soft pillows stacked behind her. Tony kissed her gently on the cheek and walked down the steps into the bakery. He grabbed the rubber apron, marched over to the sink, and turned on the water to wash the dirty pans.

"What's with you?" Kate asked, as she entered the kitchen.

Tony glanced at her. "Nothin'. I just got things on my mind." He dried his hands and looked Kate in the eyes. "There are some things I gotta take care of. I ain't gonna be able to see ya for a while."

Kate crossed her arms over her stomach. "How long is a while?"

"I don't know yet. A while. Maybe a couple of months."

"I don't understand. Are you done with me? I mean, if you're breaking up with me, don't you think I deserve an explanation?"

"I ain't breakin' up wit' cha. I just got some business to take care of, and I'm lettin' ya know I won't be around. That's all."

Kate's mood went from sad to angry.

"Fine," she yelled. "Just go and take care of your business then. You're a fucking jerk. You could at least tell me the truth. You don't want to be with me, then go on and live your life, and I'll do the same."

Tony reached out to Kate, but she pulled away. His facial expression softened; he was disturbed that she was hurting so deeply.

"Kate, I love ya. It just ain't safe for me to see ya for a while."

Her eyes bulged. "Do the Slayers know about me?"

"Yeah. One of 'em saw us at the restaurant last night. Went back and told Razor. I won't be comin' back here for a while. It's the only way I can keep them away from you," Tony said.

"Oh, Tony," Kate cried, "what are we gonna do?"

"We ain't gonna do nothin'. This ain't your problem. I'll handle it myself. For right now, I'm gonna lay low and stick around the gang, make sure they trust me, till I can think of a way to leave them for good."

"How will I know you're OK?"

"You won't. Ya just have to stay strong."

"I can't."

"Sure ya can. You're the strongest person I know. All this bad shit happened to ya, and you're still movin' forward, workin' to get a better life."

"What if Donata wants me to leave?"

Tony had already figured out that problem on the bus ride into South Philadelphia.

"Then you call Salvatore. He and Vincent will help ya."

"Salvatore knows that the Slayers found out about us?" Kate asked.

"No, but Vincent does. I stopped at his house before I came here and told 'im. Salvatore and Vincent are good friends. They won't let me down."

"But what if Salvatore and Vincent say they can't help me?"

"They won't."

As Tony hugged Kate good-bye, his heart crushed inside his chest. Not knowing when they'd be together again, they clung to each other for a long time.

"I'll see ya again. I love ya till the end, Kate."

Kate kissed him. "Till the end."

Tony took a long look at the woman he loved and left the bakery with a purpose...to find his way back to Kate.

Chapter Eighty

The next three months, without seeing Kate, Tony fell into a deep depression. He hadn't gone back into South Philadelphia—in fact, he hadn't even left the run-down neighborhood where he lived. Tony wanted to put as much distance between Razor and Kate as possible. Tony spent a lot of time with Smoke but never confided in him about Kate.

One afternoon, Tony was sitting on the sofa in the living room staring at the television. He felt like a prisoner again. Even after three months of not leaving North Philadelphia, Razor still had members follow Tony when he went to the store or took a walk. Smoke had warned him that Razor was watching and waiting.

"Hey, man," Smoke said as he entered the room.

Tony gave a nod of his head.

"What cha doin' today?"

Tony scratched his crotch. "Nothin'. Blast told me that we gotta meet up wit' those douchebags we buy our weed from tonight. I fuckin' hate dealin' wit' the drugs."

"Yeah, we never know what we're gonna get when we do a big deal. Dangerous shit. Just part of livin' the life of a gangster," Smoke said lightheartedly.

"Whatever. This life sucks. The Slayers' motto should be 'Steal, cheat, and lie.'"

Smoke sat down next to Tony. "Gang life ain't for everybody."

Tony looked at his friend. "Is it for you?"

"I guess so. I mean, I got all the pot I wanna smoke and all the ass I wanna tap, and I get to use my gun enough to keep me happy."

"Yeah, sounds really fuckin' great," Tony commented.

Smoke ran his hand over the Slayers' tattoo on his forearm. "Ya know, sometimes I think about what it'll be like when I get older. I can't live here forever, right? I mean, where do old gang members go when they aren't useful anymore?"

This piqued Tony's interest; he'd never thought about getting old. "That's a good point. What happened to the members that used to be here?"

Smoke guzzled from his beer can. "They're either dead or rotting in prison."

"That ain't much to look forward to. I mean, I'm gonna be eighteen before I know it. You're one of the oldest dudes here, right?"

Smoke nodded. "Yep, I'll be twenty-eight this year."

Tony's throat closed. His legs felt like someone was sticking him with needles, and he fidgeted.

"What's wrong wit' you?" Smoke asked, watching the transformation.

"I can't stay here for ten more years. I don't wanna be doin' this when I'm old," Tony said, fingers of dread inching up his spine.

Smoke laughed. "Oh, so now I'm fuckin' old?"

"I didn't mean it like that."

"Yeah, I know what ya meant. Look Tony, ya don't just walk away from the Slayers—ya know that. Right now, ya gotta relax. There ain't no easy way outta this life. Ya know too much."

"Who am I gonna tell? I did shit to people. Why would I snitch on anyone here?"

"It ain't about snitching to cops or nothing. It's about giving information to the other gangs that wanna take us out. Ya been here long enough to know that."

Tony settled back against the worn sofa. "Yeah."

Smoke asked, "Why don't we take a ride into Center City? Ya know, a change of scenery."

"Yeah, that sounds good."

An hour later, Tony and Smoke were walking into the Reading Terminal Market. As they walked through, trying to decide what to eat, the smells made Tony's stomach rumble. They had decided on a slice of pizza, not only because it looked good, but also because it was inexpensive. They picked up their slices and sat at an empty table to eat.

"Tony!" Vincent said.

Tony stood up and gave Vincent a hug. "Salvatore," Tony said, "you're lookin' real good." The two gave each other a quick hug.

"It took a while to recover, but I'm doing great now. I almost have full motion in my arm," Salvatore said, moving his arm in a wide circle.

"What the fuck, man. Where the hell have ya been?" Vincent said, plopping into a seat and taking a bite of Tony's pizza. Then he looked at Smoke. "Who the hell are you?"

Smoke dropped his pizza and glared at Tony.

"It's cool," Tony said to Smoke. "These are my friends that I told ya about. The guys I grew up wit'."

Vincent extended his hand. "I'm Vincent."

Smoke shook his hand, and when he did, Vincent and Salvatore noticed the Slayer tattoo.

"Smoke."

"I'm Salvatore."

"Yeah, good to meet cha."

"Come on, Vincent, ya need to buy me another slice of pizza to replace the one ya just stuffed your face wit'," Tony said, looking down at his empty paper plate.

Vincent got up, and the three of them walked toward the pizza counter.

"How's Kate?" Tony whispered as soon as they were out of earshot.

Salvatore leaned in. "She's good. She called me when you first spoke to her. We check on her every couple of days. We saw her yesterday. Donata's really upset that you disappeared. She's worried something bad happened to you."

Tony pressed his thumb and index finger to the bridge of his nose. "Fuck. I never even thought about that."

"Well, you don't have to worry. I told Donata that you had to go out of town for a while, and I assured her that you're fine," Salvatore said.

Tony jutted his jaw toward Salvatore. "But..."

Salvatore took a deep breath. "But she can't keep the place going anymore. She doesn't have the money to support Kate. I've been giving her some money here and there, but the extra cost put her behind in her mortgage, so she had to take out a loan from my father."

"Your father? Why would he loan her money?"

"Part of the business. I talked him into letting her have a cheaper payment, but it's really hard on her."

Tony shoved his hands in his front pockets. "Did Kate say where she's goin'?"

"She doesn't know. She'll probably start at a homeless shelter. I'm doing everything I can to help," Salvatore said, embarrassed.

"I know ya are."

"Have you figured a way out of that gang?" Vincent asked.

Tony's head hung, and he shook it sadly.

Salvatore put his arm over Tony's shoulder. "I'm doing everything I can to help with that too."

Chapter Eighty-One

Salvatore sat down on the sofa in his father's office across from Big Paulie.

"Pop, we have to talk."

Johnny looked up from the newspaper he was reading. "What's on your mind?"

"Tony. You know he's a gang member. He's trying to find his way out. I want to help him."

Johnny's face flushed red with anger. "That's not our problem. How many times do we have to go over this?"

"Until I can convince you to help him. He went to prison for me, where he was repeatedly raped. Then, three months ago, he saved my life. How many times does he have to help me before we help him?"

Johnny shook his head. "You don't know what you're asking me to do."

"Then tell me."

"The mob and gangs don't interact. They have no order, no code of ethics. They kill each other for not living the way the gang dictates."

"Exactly. That's why Tony needs to get away from them. You know that girl Kate that lives with Donata?"

"What about her?"

Salvatore pushed up to the edge of the sofa. "She's Tony's girlfriend. They haven't seen each other in three months because the gang found out about her. Now Donata needs her to move out because of all the debt she's in. The girl is going to a homeless shelter, and Tony can't even help her."

"Again, Salvatore, not our problem. A lot of people are homeless. Get your head out of your ass. Tony should have never joined a gang. Did he think he could waltz in and out whenever he wanted? That shows me that he's stupid," Johnny said, banging his fist on the desk in front of him.

"He was thirteen with nowhere to go. Because of me!"

Johnny stood. "Don't you ever raise your voice to me again. Just because you're my son doesn't give you special privileges to be disrespectful. I am the boss of this family, and I have a lot of people under me that need to be taken care of. Now, you want me to get involved and save your pathetic friend. What's in it for me?"

Salvatore's mouth dropped open, and he paused for a moment. "Tony can work for you, just like Vincent and I do." Salvatore looked over to Big Paulie for help.

Big Paulie cleared his throat, and Johnny gave his attention to him.

"We talked about this, Johnny. Remember where we came from, and now all Salvatore's sayin' is that he wants to help his friend. Ain't nothin' wrong wit' that," Big Paulie stated.

"Right. Exactly. You were a gang member once in New York. Big Paulie told me all about it. Why was it OK for you but not for Tony?"

"It's none of your fucking business what I did when I was young!" Johnny screamed, shooting a deadly look at Big Paulie.

Johnny leaned back in his chair. "If Tony wants out, then I need a job done."

"What kind of job?" Salvatore asked, knowing Tony would do anything to be with Kate.

"There are men from New York who want to see me dead. They want to take over our business here in Philadelphia. This is no small job, and a lot is at stake. I don't know if I want to put this in Tony's hands."

Salvatore listened intently. He would do anything for Tony.

"Vincent and I can help him. What do we have to do?" Salvatore asked.

"Now wait a minute. I can't have you involved in this. These men are deadly. They know you're my son. They will kill you to get to me."

"None of those men from New York know me. They've never met me."

Johnny considered Salvatore's request. He didn't like sending his own blood in for a job this big. He knew the risk of being killed was high. He leaned forward on his elbows.

"You can't do this job. I'll allow Vincent to go with Tony."

Salvatore slumped over. "You're not willing to risk my life, but you're willing to risk theirs. That's what you're saying. Right?"

"Yes. That's right. If you want me to help your friend, this is the only way I'll agree to it."

Salvatore pressed his hands to his face. "And if they succeed, you'll do whatever it takes to help Tony. That's what you're saying?"

Johnny smirked, knowing the odds of either boy coming out alive were slim. "That's what I'm saying."

Salvatore stood and strode over to the office door. "It's a deal."

Chapter Eighty-Two

S alvatore and Vincent drove one of the old Cadillacs into North Philadelphia looking for Tony. It was a dangerous thing to do, and Johnny had them followed by some of his most ruthless men. They had a general idea of where Tony lived based on stories he'd shared with his friends about the neighborhood and the gang. They had been driving in North Philadelphia for a while and turned right on Dauphin Street. The sun was almost down.

Salvatore and Vincent glared out the window of the car. There were hookers, drunks, and drug addicts strewn on the sidewalks. The two white men stood out among the primarily black community. Salvatore pulled his car up to the curb, where several prostitutes were standing.

"If you're lookin' for dates, ya might wanna think about where ya are, white meat," a hooker yelled.

"We ain't lookin' for no dates. We're lookin' for the Slayers," Vincent said.

"You whities better turn that fuckin' car 'round and go home to your mommas. If Razor sees ya in his neighborhood, he'll kill your asses," the hooker said.

Vincent opened the car door and stepped onto the curb next to the hooker with the big mouth. "What's your name?"

The prostitute looked Vincent up and down. He was big, and his entire being screamed fearlessness. "Jizzie."

"Well, listen, Jizzie, we ain't fuckin' around. Tell us where we can find the Slayers, and we'll leave ya alone. Trust me—it's in your best interest."

"Don't know," she said, turning her back to Vincent, "but if I sees any of 'em, I'll be sure to let 'em know ya was lookin' for 'em. What's your name again?"

"Ya just tell 'em that death is lookin' for 'em. Can ya do that?" Vincent said.

Jizzie looked into Vincent's eyes. There was a heated glow behind his irises that gave her an icy sensation in her bones. "Yeah, if we sees 'em, we'll tell 'em."

Jizzie turned to the other hookers standing behind her. The group of scantily clad women took off in the opposite direction. Jizzie and the others wanted to find Razor and warn him about the pricks looking for the Slayers. That would score them a couple bags of free dope for sure. As they walked toward the row home that the Slayers called home, several of the soldiers and associates from the Morano family followed them in the shadows.

Salvatore's plan was already coming together.

Chapter Eighty-Three

"**S**low down, bitch!" Razor yelled at Jizzie. "How the hell ya expect me to understand what you're sayin' when you're huffin' and puffin' like a fat cow? Maybe if you stopped eatin' like a pig and lost some of that blubber, you'd be able to walk a few blocks wit'out needin' CPR."

Jizzie bent over and put her hands on her knees to steady her breathing. "Like I was tellin' ya. There are some assholes lookin' for the Slayers. They was askin' where they could find yas. I didn't tell 'em nothin', though. I came runnin' right here to warn ya," she said, waiting to be rewarded.

"Oh yeah? What did these assholes look like?"

Jizzie stood up straight and then cocked her hip to the right and scrunched her face at Razor. "They looked like assholes."

Razor backhanded Jizzie in the face. "Whore, who ya think you talkin' to like that? I will tear your ass up, then turn your babies out on the street to hook for me too."

Jizzie held the side of her face. "They was big. The one who did all the talkin' was real tall. Taller than you."

"That ain't tellin' me shit. Have ya ever see 'em before?"

Jizzie squirmed. "No, but they was drivin' a Cadillac. An old one."

"Ya did good by comin' here and tellin' me and my crew. Now, get your fat black ass back on the street and make me some money."

Jizzie held Razor's gaze.

"What cha waitin' for?"

"I was thinkin' ya might give me a couple of bags, seein' that I came here and told ya about those men that were lookin' for ya."

Razor looked over at Boner and gave him a nod. Boner reached into his pocket and threw three bags of white powder onto the floor in front of Jizzie, who pounced on them.

"Damn girl, you like a fuckin' dog gettin' a treat. Get your nasty ass outta my house," Razor said.

When Jizzie was gone, Razor turned to the other gang members. Tony was among them and had watched everything unfold.

"We got business to take care of tonight. I want us all out roaming the streets. We find those motherfuckers tonight!" Razor commanded.

***

Salvatore and Vincent had followed Jizzie to find out where the Slayers lived. Now, they could look for Tony over the next few days. The next evening, they drove back into North Philadelphia in a beat-up pickup truck that Johnny had given them to use. They watched the house for hours. Finally, shortly after nine o'clock, they saw Tony saunter down the wooden steps and head away from the house. He walked three blocks before entering a small corner store with bars on the windows and the door. Tony knocked on the window, and the man behind the counter buzzed him in. He came out a few minutes later carrying a bottle of soda.

"Yo," Vincent said from the truck window.

Tony turned toward the voice and looked at the truck he didn't recognize, but he couldn't see inside.

"Tony, come here," Vincent snapped.

Tony reached for his gun in the back of his jeans and slowly walked over to the truck. He was almost next to it when he realized it was Vincent.

"What the hell is wrong wit' ya? I was ready to blow your fuckin' head off," Tony stated.

"Get in," Salvatore said.

Vincent moved into the middle of the truck seat. Tony scanned the area on every side for anyone watching. When he felt it was safe, he climbed in beside Vincent.

"Drive straight," Tony said. "Make a right at the next street."

Salvatore followed the directions and within a few minutes, they were parked in a secluded church parking lot.

"I come here sometimes, when I wanna get away from the house," Tony admitted. "It's peaceful here. None of the gangs mess with churches—well, one or two might—but it's one of the safest places in this shithole town."

Tony was nervously talking. He had convinced himself that if Salvatore and Vincent had come into North Philadelphia to look for him, something horrible must have happened. He took a deep breath and put his back up against the passenger door.

"What happened?" Tony said, bracing himself.

"Nothing happened. Relax," Salvatore began. "I spoke to my father about helping you. He agreed," Salvatore said quickly, not wanting to prolong the suspense.

"Are...are you fuckin' jokin'? Don't mess wit' me about this. You'll break my heart," Tony warned.

Salvatore gave him a broad smile. "No, I'm not joking."

Chapter Eighty-Four

Tony let the news sink in. Was it possible for him to get away from the Slayers? Was he dreaming?

"What do I gotta do?" Tony barked.

"How ya know ya gotta do somethin'?" Vincent asked, intrigued.

"'Cause ain't nobody gonna help ya if ya ain't givin' somethin' in return. I learned that a long time ago. So what is it?"

Salvatore clutched at the steering wheel and straightened in his seat. "There is a New York family that wants to see my father dead. Four top hit men are having a meeting at Dante and Luigi's on Thursday night. Shortly after they arrive, you and Vincent will go to the restaurant. The man at the front will seat you to the right of their table. You'll act like eighteen-year-old boys on a dinner date with some girls...the girls will be provided and can be trusted not to talk. When the check is given to you, the restaurant will be empty except for you and the table of men who are your targets. The girls dining with you will go to the bathroom, and that's when you will take care of business. Once it's done, you will leave immediately; my father will be waiting for you at my house."

"Who are these men?" Tony asked.

"They are from one of the New York families. They want to take over our business in Philadelphia. My father had many fights with this family when we lived in New York. Now they want to bring their shit to our city. He can't stand for it. You have to kill these guys to show my father what you're willing to do in order to be with Kate...to get away from the Slayers," Salvatore said.

It felt as though the air had been sucked from the cabin of the truck. Tony slouched back against the door and let his head rest on the window. His thoughts went immediately to Kate.

"What happens if I ain't able to kill all of 'em?"

Salvatore looked down at his hands. "My father won't help you."

"Wait," Vincent yelped. "Ya didn't tell me that part. What the fuck is that?"

"It's the deal I was able to make with my father." Salvatore took in a deep breath. "Look at it this way: you both are good with a gun. It's easy. You take them out quickly, and it'll be over."

Tony cocked his head to the side. "I ain't never killed someone that hasn't hurt somebody I love. This feels a little, ya know, fucked up."

Salvatore met Tony's eyes. "You are killing for people you love. I want my father to live, and you want to be with Kate. She needs you, Tony."

Tony nudged Vincent. "Are you willin' to do this? I mean, ya ain't got no reason."

"I got two reasons, you and Salvatore. I don't need no more reason than that. I'm in it wit' cha. Someone's gotta be there to protect your sorry ass."

Tony nodded. "You're a good friend, Vincent."

"Tony, I asked my father if I could help you, but he refused. I just want you to know that I tried to be there too."

"I appreciate that. Don't worry; I know you're a good friend. Ya got me this one chance outta here, didn't ya?"

Salvatore gritted his teeth. "I did, but I'd feel better being by your side."

"Fine, we'll take care of it," Tony said.

"What about the girls?" Vincent asked.

"What about them? You do what needs to be done, and you leave. My father said the girls will find their way home."

***

On Thursday night, Tony and Vincent walked into the restaurant and were seated to the right of the New York mobsters. As the teens took their seats around the table, the mobsters eyed them suspiciously. The boys fell into easy teenage banter with each other and showered attention on their dates, a sure sign that the only thing on the boys' minds was getting laid. After several minutes of the mobsters watching the teens, they turned back to their own dinner and talked quietly among themselves.

Right after dessert was served, the waiter brought the check and laid it in front of Tony. The girls headed out of the dining room, and as soon as they were out of sight, Tony stood and shot the closest man in the back of the head. Vincent got off two shots in rapid succession, hitting both targets in the head, while Tony quickly turned his gun to the fourth man and shot him through the neck. The entire slaughter took less than four seconds.

Tony and Vincent swiftly left the restaurant and headed toward the Moranos'. Vincent smacked Tony on the back. "We were perfect. They didn't know what hit 'em."

"Yeah, I know. It just don't feel good when ya don't even know the people you're killin'. What if Johnny was lying? What if these guys were innocent and never gonna kill 'im?"

Vincent stopped walking. "Ya think he'd make us do that if it wasn't real?"

"I don't know, Vincent. I don't know Johnny Morano from shit. All I know is I just killed two men that he didn't like—that's what I know for sure."

Twenty minutes later the boys walked into the Moranos' house. Salvatore was waiting in Johnny's office with his father, Big Paulie, and a few other mobsters.

Big Paulie stood and went to Tony. He whispered, "Killing for revenge is necessary, but killin' to protect the godfather is the most respectable act you could've done."

Tony shook Big Paulie's hand, but Tony felt uneasy—as though he'd just done something that wasn't necessary.

"Tony," Johnny's voice cracked through the air, shaking him to his core. "You have proven to all of us that you will do whatever is required of you. You and Vincent killed four very powerful men. There have been many heads of families that wanted these men dead for a long time. You have succeeded where other men didn't dare." Johnny looked at his men, "We can't believe you came out of it alive. Those men suspect everyone. Now, as a reward, Tony, we will get you removed from your gang."

"What about me, Mr. M.?" Vincent blurted out.

"Vincent, you will be handsomely rewarded. I will forgive the money your mother borrowed from me to pay off her mortgage when she was in default of her loan."

"Wow, Mr. M.," Vincent breathed, "that's gonna make her real happy."

The room fell silent for a few seconds.

"When?" Tony's voice boomed aggressively.

Johnny Morano's face pinched. "Soon."

Tony felt as though his heart fell through his stomach, out of his ass, and hit the floor. He'd thought his reward would be immediate—that he'd never have to go back to the Slayers—but he was wrong. He couldn't contain his anxiety.

"How soon?"

Johnny's face contorted. "Whenever I decide. That's how soon."

Salvatore and Vincent drove Tony to the edge of North Philadelphia; he'd have to walk the rest of the way in. The boys were somber at first. Vincent, unable to take the solemn mood, slammed his hand on the dashboard of the pickup truck.

"What the fuck, Salvatore? Your father was supposed to help Tony. Ya heard what he said: we killed four powerful men tonight. It ain't right; it ain't right at all."

Salvatore jerked the truck over to the side of the road, the tires screeched against the blacktop as they came to an abrupt halt.

"He's my father, Vincent. You can't talk about him like he's a piece of shit. He gave me his word, and he'll make good on it," Salvatore yelled, just as frustrated as Tony and Vincent.

"Listen, Salvatore," Tony began in a calm tone. "Ya gotta talk to 'im. Let him know the urgency around gettin' me the fuck outta here so I can help myself and Kate. Can ya do that?"

"Yes. I will talk to him tonight, as soon as I get home."

"All right, good," Tony said.

"Let's meet in Center City on Saturday afternoon, at the coffee shop," Salvatore instructed.

"That's two days away," Tony said, calculating the time.

"I know. But at least by then I should have a better answer. My father is being a hard ass. He didn't like you questioning him about it. He expects to tell people what he's willing to do and when."

"Ya coulda fuckin' told me that," Tony snapped.

"Yeah, I'm sorry, Tony. Don't worry. I'll make this right."

By the time Tony got dropped off it had started to rain. He stood on the side of the street as Salvatore and Vincent drove away. As he watched the taillights of the truck disappear, he felt isolated from the world again. He felt hopeless. Tony stood on the street as the skies opened up and the rain beat down upon him. The only sound was the rain falling from the sky, hitting against the car roofs and rushing into street drains.

Tony stood perfectly still, his heart heavy with conflict between his love for Kate and his hate for Johnny Morano. He tilted his head back, and the pouring rain mixed in with the tears that had sprung from his soul. He tried to gather himself, to stop crying, but he was too broken. He allowed himself to cry and grieve for the life he'd never had, and finally, summoning the last bit of courage, he walked back to his purgatory, the place his gang called home.

That night Tony lay in his bed and worried. He worried that the Slayers would find out he'd killed mobsters, he worried that the New York family would come looking for him, and he worried about what would happen to Kate.

But what ate at his gut the most was the vulnerability that choked him. He was at the mercy of Johnny Morano to make good on his promise. He clung to the hope he hadn't been set up and he would soon be free.

Chapter Eighty-Five

T he next morning, Tony stomped down the steps from the second floor. When he got to the landing, he looked around the living room, where the core gang members were gathered. Tony rubbed the sleep from his eyes. They were all staring at him.

"What's goin' on?" Tony asked.

Razor sneered at him. "Seems that some big-ass mobsters were killed last night. Ya know anything 'bout that?"

"No, why would I?"

"Well, because when ya left, we had ya followed." Razor stepped closer to Tony, violating his personal space.

Instinctively, Tony took a step backward. "So what?"

"So we know that cha were at that restaurant last night. We also know that ya were wit' a guy we ain't seen before, another Guido like you. And ya went to a pretty nice house after. Ya wanna explain what that's all about?"

Tony's guts felt like they were filled with red ants and wasps. He told himself to remain calm. His fear was mounting in his chest, and he breathed deeply.

"What's it to ya where I was? I was out wit' an old friend. That against the rules all of a sudden?" Tony fired.

"Nah, it ain't against the rules. But killin' mobsters, now that's against the rules. If it ain't a kill the club agrees on, then ya can't do it. Ya know the fuckin' rules, Bruno. Don't act dumber than ya really are."

"Whatever, Razor. You're always lookin' for a way to make my life miserable. You're an asshole."

Tony walked away, toward the kitchen. His lungs felt like they were raging with fire, and he needed time alone to exhale. Razor didn't let him pass, though. He grabbed Tony's shoulder and squeezed his fingers down deep into the muscle. Tony shrugged him off with a heavy jerk. Razor stepped back. His eyes squinted, and his smile was toxic.

"Go ahead, Bruno. Walk in the other room. Just know that from now on, we'll be watchin' every move ya make. Ya either belong to the gang, or ya don't. I'm willing to bet ya don't...and once everyone here knows what you're about, you'll be dead."

Tony walked past Razor, and the gang members separated as he entered the ratty kitchen. He could feel someone behind him. He opened the refrigerator door and pulled out a soda. Tony put the can to his lips and turned to see who was behind him.

"I don't know what's goin' on wit' cha. But whatever it is, ya gotta stop what you're doin'. Razor ain't playin'," Smoke said.

Smoke's eyes were soft, nonthreatening, and Tony's muscles relaxed.

"He's makin' shit up," Tony stated.

Smoke shook his head slowly. "Get dressed. Let's go for a walk. I need to grab a case of beer."

Tony hesitated. Smoke turned to leave the kitchen. In a quiet but stern voice, he said, "Come on. Get movin'."

As Tony and Smoke walked to the beer distributor, they shared an uncomfortable silence. Unable to stand it anymore, Tony said, "Why did ya want me to come wit' cha?"

"I need to talk to ya about what you're doin'. I know ya got another life, wit' that little girl and her grandmother. But this shit about the mob, that's where ya gotta draw the line. Ya see, 'bout ten years ago, we had a run-in wit' some of the mobsters that run South Philly. Nobody wants to talk about it, so I'm gonna tell ya myself. One of the Slayers—his name was Koonce—he was hangin' around wit' one of those mobsters' daughters. Now, everybody in the gang knew it. In those days, ya could have a piece of ass wherever ya wanted, but it all changed real fast. The mob didn't like that Koonce was seeing one of their women. They threatened 'im. Told 'im if they caught the two of 'em together, they'd cut his fuckin' balls off."

Tony and Smoke had stopped walking and faced each other.

"So...Koonce and this chick decided they didn't care what the mobsters wanted. They kept seein' each other until one night, when they were leavin' a movie theater together, the mob threw Koonce into the back of a sedan. The next mornin' when Koonce wasn't around, some of us got worried. So, we put on our gear and were planning on goin' into South Philly to look for him."

Smoke paused and shook his head at the memory. "Ya see, Koonce was a real good guy. He was a gangster, but he had a big heart, really cared about the other members. I admired him. Looked up to him. Ya woulda liked 'im a lot too. Anyway, he taught me how to shoot a gun and pick up broads." Smoke was smiling, reminiscing about Koonce. Then his face got stiff, and he looked up at Tony.

"We were gettin' ready to leave and stepped out on the porch. In front of the door was a big cooler. I'm talkin' 'bout one of those real long ones that those fancy places use for parties. Anyway, I went over and opened the cooler. At first, it just looked like bloody water. It was real dark and creepy looking. We had one of the recruits reach in to find out what was in it. He pulled out a cinderblock, and that's when Koonce's body floated to the surface. His face was bloated, and his eyes were bulging out of his head. We figured they drowned him in the cooler after they fucked 'im up. When we got him outta the cooler, he wasn't wearing any pants, and his balls had been cut off. We found them stuffed in his mouth."

Smoke ran his fingers through his hair several times, as if trying to wipe the image from his memory.

"Our leader at the time, well, he went fuckin' ape shit. Wanted to go after the mob. Needed to get even. He was our leader, so we all followed him. But the mob was waitin' for us, ya know. We got ambushed before we even got outta North Philly. Five members died. Three of 'em burned alive inside a car when it exploded after bullets hit the gas tank. It was a real bad time for us. We were down six members, and I gotta say, it brought us to our knees. So we backed off and took our losses. After that, no member could date outside of the gang...that's when we started raping-in our bitches. So ya see, ya hangin' out wit' mobsters is a big deal for a lot of the guys."

Smoke put his hand on Tony's shoulder. "It's a big deal for me too. The mob took Koontz, who was like a father to me. The only father I ever had."

Tony kicked a stone lying on the sidewalk. "So you're tellin' me I gotta live my life based on somethin' that happened ten years ago? Look, I got friends in South Philly from when I was little."

"What I'm sayin' is, if the Slayers see ya wit' friends that are mob related, they're gonna kill 'em."

Tony's face flushed, and he raised his hands, balling them into fists. "No, that ain't gonna happen. Nobody fucks wit' people that I care about. Just like I wouldn't let nobody fuck wit' you."

Smoke patted Tony's arm, trying to calm him down. "You're a man. What cha decide to do is up to you. I'm just tellin' ya depending on which way ya go wit' this, there could be consequences. Ya need the information so ya can make a good decision."

Tony's anger was boiling over. "I ain't deciding between the Slayers and my friends from my old neighborhood. Ain't nobody got a right to tell me to do that either."

"Yeah, Tony, the Slayers got every right. Ya knew what you was gettin' into when ya decided to join us."

"What if I don't want to be part of the Slayers no more?" Tony screamed in a fit of rage.

"Then bad shit is gonna happen to ya. I'm givin' it to ya straight. That's all I can do to help ya."

Tony dropped to his knees on the pavement, head cradled in his arms. The life drained from his body. His limbs went limp. His skin felt like it was crawling with bugs as his blood rushed to his extremities. He stayed on the ground for several minutes until he decided.

He wouldn't be able to leave the Slayers. He wouldn't be able to live with himself if anything bad happened to Vincent or Salvatore. His heart hung heavy and thudded rapidly inside his chest as he thought about never seeing Kate again.

Two days later, Tony sat on the sofa with Blast. He was supposed to meet Salvatore and Vincent in Center City that day to find out when Johnny would help him out of the Slayers. Over the days that passed, Tony thought about the story that Smoke had shared with him. He knew if he tried to meet the boys in Center City, he would be followed by one of Razor's goons and that he would be putting his two childhood friends in harm's way. So he decided not to meet them, giving up his only hope to be with Kate again.

Chapter Eighty-Six

S alvatore glared at his father, who was sitting at his desk, stoking a thick cigar.

"You made a promise," Salvatore said accusingly. "Tony didn't show up today. We think that the Slayers did something to him."

Johnny laid the cigar in the ashtray. "I'm sure he realized that he isn't good enough for the mob. He's where he belongs, with that group of degenerates. What does he call them? The Sloths?" Johnny said and laughed.

Salvatore crossed his arms over his chest as Vincent watched, hoping that Johnny didn't turn on his own son.

"You know, Pop, I always thought you were a stand-up guy. You used Tony to get what you wanted with no intention of ever helping him."

"Oh, I always had intentions of getting him out of the slum. However, it's on my terms, Salvatore, not on Tony's and not on yours," his father growled.

Salvatore's face turned crimson, his eyes were narrowed and hard. "If you won't help him out, then I will."

Johnny banged his hand on the desk and stood up. "You will do no such thing. You will do nothing until I give you permission."

Salvatore leaned in. "What are you going to do? Kill me?"

Johnny walked around to the front of his desk and faced Salvatore. He held his gaze for a moment, and then he slapped Salvatore in the face, sending his son flying sideways into the desk. Vincent lurched forward to help steady Salvatore. From behind, Big Paulie put his hand on Vincent's shoulder. He put his mouth close to Vincent's ear. "Don't interfere with this. Ya stay outta of it."

Salvatore regained his ground. "Well?" he demanded. "What are you going to do then?"

Johnny was pissed at his son, but his bravery ignited a deep level of respect for the boy.

"We go in a week from today," Johnny said. "Let me be clear with you. Once Tony is out, he will be under your command. If he fucks up, so do you. Son or no son, you want this so much, then you got it."

Salvatore gave a terse nod and looked at Vincent. The two left Johnny's office together, and it wasn't until Salvatore was in the kitchen that he exhaled.

***

One week later, a rival gang paid off by the Mafia lured the Slayers in through a third-party offering, a drug deal they couldn't refuse.

The Slayers drove five cars to the location of the drug deal. Gun in hand, Razor got out of the car and looked to the others, who filed out behind him. Tony was in the back of the group standing next to Smoke. Razor walked over to the waiting pickup truck.

The man inside the truck put the window down. "Brought a lot of people wit' cha. A little overkill, don't cha think?"

Razor's silver teeth glistened as his lips turned up into a wicked smile. "Yeah, well, when we gotta deal through a dealer we don't know, we take extra measures to make sure nothin' goes wrong. Where's the stuff?"

The man opened his door and stepped onto the grassy surface. He walked to the back of the pickup truck, and Razor and four other gang members followed. The man released the tailgate and dropped to the ground, rolling under the truck. Confused, Razor turned and looked around him. In an instant, bullets were flying, and he watched gang members get shot and drop to the ground.

Razor raced to the other side of the truck for protection, but they were surrounded. The gang members were shooting at the cars that had descended upon them. Tony quickly fled inside of Smoke's truck to be shielded from the stray bullets. When the shooting slowed, Tony got out of the truck and stayed low to the ground. The darkness of the night made it hard to get a clear target, and the guns being fired sparked the black night with jagged, blinding light.

Tony heard Razor's voice. "Stop! Hold up!"

There was an angry fear in the shrieking words. The gang stopped firing their guns and followed Razor's voice. Razor was being held around the neck by a humongous man. His arms were thick and tattooed. Razor had his hands up by his sides. The gang members cautiously moved closer.

The headlights of a car turned on, and suddenly Razor looked like he was on stage about to give a performance. Tony took his aim on the monster that had Razor in a throat lock. A suited figure walked cavalierly over to Razor, and the headlights doused the man. Tony removed his finger from the trigger of his gun when he recognized Johnny Morano.

Johnny, much taller than Razor, leaned down and looked him in the face.

"So are you the leader of this..." Johnny waved his hand toward the gang standing in random places, their guns tossed off to the side and mobsters behind each of them, "disgusting pack of wild animals?"

"Fuck you," Razor said in a garbled voice.

The man holding Razor tightened his fist and swung it into Razor's mouth, knocking out two silver teeth. Blood gushed from the site of impact.

Johnny pulled a cigarette from a pocket inside his suit jacket. He lit the cigarette and blew the smoke into Razor's face.

"As I was trying to explain before this maggot spoke..." Johnny raised his voice to make sure everyone could hear him. "Where is Tony Bruno?"

Smoke gave Tony a quick glance; three mobsters now stood between them. Tony stepped forward. His heart was racing, and he thought it would combust in his chest.

"Oh, there's Tony. Come over here," Johnny commanded.

Tony swiftly walked to Johnny. His palms were sweating, and he staggered slightly as his legs went weak. It felt like hours to Tony, but was only seconds before he was standing next to Johnny.

Johnny roughly grabbed Tony's forearm. "What's this asshole's name?"

Tony looked out at the other gang members; they were seething with hatred for him.

"Razor," Tony mumbled.

"Razor...what a peculiar name." Johnny grabbed a handful of Razor's hair. "Tell me, why do they call you Razor?"

Razor remained silent; he was gripped tight with anger.

"Seems as though the cat got his tongue," Johnny said, turning back to Tony. "So you tell me, Tony—why do they call him Razor?"

"His sharp tongue," Tony stated, not understanding Johnny's intent.

"Oh, I see. That makes sense to me. Well, my name is Johnny. I'm sure you know who I am. Let me explain something to you, Razor. In my line of work, we make sure that our crimes are very personal. Now, if I didn't know your name, I wouldn't have been able to personalize my visit for you."

"What the fuck do ya want, ya goddamn douchebag?" Razor blurted.

"Well now, there it is. There's that razor-sharp tongue of yours. It would seem to me that you would refrain from opening your diseased mouth and letting shit fall out of it. I mean, in the predicament you're in right now, any smart man would keep his fucking mouth shut."

Johnny took a final drag from his cigarette, threw it to the ground, and smashed it under his expensive Italian-leather shoe.

"Razor, here's what we are going to do. Tony will be coming with us now. He has done some work for me, and I think that he's better off serving me, instead of you. Do you have a problem with that?"

Razor glowered at Tony and then looked back at Johnny. "Bruno is a useless piece of shit. Ya can take 'im and shove 'im up your stank dago ass. Ya don't scare me. You're just a piece of shit that don't know how to get your hands dirty, makin' your men do it."

Johnny looked at the ground. A strained smiled was on his lips. Then Johnny grabbed Razor by the neck and slammed him into the truck. The mobster holding Razor pulled his hair back and pressed his jaw down. Johnny pulled a handkerchief from his pocket and gripped Razor's tongue.

"That's where you're mistaken, Razor. I don't have a problem doing any of the dirty work, as you call it. I'm going to leave you with a parting gift, so you'll remember who you're dealing with."

Johnny pulled out a box cutter from his other pocket and slowly pushed the blade up. As he did, Razor's eyes grew wide, and he thrashed against the man holding him.

Johnny took his time putting the blade into Razor's mouth, and, holding his tongue tight with the handkerchief, he sliced off Razor's tongue with deliberate slow movements. Blood gushed and streaked down Razor's chin, and finally, Johnny drew back his hand with the muscular organ inside the handkerchief. He pulled on the waist of Razor's jeans and dropped the tongue down his pants.

Razor was screaming, the expression on his bloody face was a mixture of pain and loathing. Not able to remain calm, Johnny punched Razor in the face, and he flopped to his knees. Johnny punched and kicked him until he himself was exhausted. Then Johnny straightened up, brushed his hair back into place, and readjusted his suit jacket. He turned to the other gang members.

"Let this be a lesson for all of you. You all think you're big and bad, but you're not. You're nothing but a group of losers. Remember that, and don't let me find any of you within ten miles of my neighborhood."

Johnny walked back to his car and stopped. "One more thing," he announced. "I know every single person that belongs to the Slayers, even those whore bitches of yours. Be mindful of your actions because they can get you all slaughtered."

Tony threw a last glance at Smoke over his shoulder as he followed behind Johnny and slid into the backseat of the car next to him.

"What the fuck just happened?" Tony said, still reeling from the surprise attack.

"You just became indebted to me," Johnny said, with a coldness that sent a trickle of fear up Tony's spine.

Chapter Eighty-Seven

Tony followed Johnny into his office, and Johnny closed the door. Tony stood watching, not knowing what to do. Johnny went around his desk. He sat down in his chair and crossed his arms over his chest. He stared at Tony as if he were watching a movie. Johnny sat forward in his chair, his body stiff and his lips tightly pressed together.

"Now you are free of your scumbag friends," Johnny said.

"Yeah, thank you. I didn't know what was goin' on at first. And then…"

"Shut up! I'm not your friend, and I don't care about what you think. Let's get down to business. First, you will need a place to live. I'm going to let you live in one of my apartments on North Broad Street. Your rent will be deducted from your pay."

Tony shuffled. "How much is my rent?"

Johnny glared at him. "Does it really matter? Stop asking stupid questions, and try to pay attention. Do not interrupt me again."

Tony's muscles tightened under his clothing. He held his breath in to keep from exploding.

"You will work for me and do whatever you are told. If you are able to prove that you're worth keeping around, I will reevaluate your value to the family business. Your job is to do what I say, when I say it. You keep your mouth shut and your eyes open. If anyone asks if you work for me, you are to deny it. Understood?"

"Yeah."

"Good. Now, go out to the kitchen and join Salvatore and Vincent. They're waiting for you."

"I got a question," Tony said boldly.

"What?"

"Why do ya hate me? What did I ever do to ya?"

Johnny shot up from his seat and leaned over his desk. "Because you do not have control over your emotions and actions. You don't think things through. You don't consider how your decisions will impact you and others in the future. That makes you a loose cannon and a danger to the people with whom you associate.

So, what you need to do from now on is think about the things you do and say. Understand that if you bring any trouble to this family, I will fucking kill you with my bare hands. Now, get out of my office."

Tony averted his eyes to the ground. "I got another question."

"Jesus Christ, what?" Johnny snarled.

"When do I get to move into my apartment?"

"Salvatore will bring you over there tonight. The piece of shit who lived there before you, left some furniture that you can use."

Tony nodded. He looked Johnny in the eyes. "When do I get paid?"

Johnny huffed. "I see you have a lot to learn. You will be paid weekly."

Tony's head hung.

"Do you have a problem?"

Tony shoved his hands in the back pockets of his jeans. "Well...I...I only got ten bucks on me. I'm gonna need some money for food and stuff."

Johnny reached into his pocket and removed his wallet. He opened it up, and Tony saw a stack of hundred-dollar bills. Johnny pulled one out and handed it Tony. "Here, this should keep you until next week. Don't come back asking for more until pay day. You need to figure out how to make it last until then."

Tony reached forward and took the money. He turned and left the office, closing the door behind him. He took his time walking through the house so he could gather himself. When he entered the kitchen, Salvatore got to his feet and greeted him.

"Good to see you, man," Salvatore said as the two hugged.

When Tony saw Salvatore and Vincent, the evening's events faded away. He went to the kitchen table and shook Vincent's hand before he sat down.

"How'd it go?" Vincent asked.

"It was crazy. The mob rushed in, and before I even knew what was goin' on, I saw Johnny swoop over, grab Razor, and cut his fuckin' tongue out."

"What did my father say to you just now?"

Tony rested his elbows on the table. "I'm gonna work for him. He's gonna let me rent one of his apartments on North Broad. I don't know, Salvatore, he didn't give me much more info than that and wasn't too happy when I tried to ask 'im any questions. He told me that I don't think about how my decisions are gonna impact me later. He's right about that. I'm gonna try and do better wit' my decisions from now on. What do you know?"

Salvatore leaned in closer to Tony. "Pretty much the same as he told you. The good news is that we'll be working together."

"What pretty boy is tryin' to say," Vincent chimed in, "is that you'll be working for him. But don't worry 'bout it. I work for him too, or so he thinks."

"That's fine wit' me," Tony said. He breathed deeply. At least working for Salvatore he could be himself. Tony leaned back in the chair. "How's Kate doin'?"

Salvatore peeled an orange he'd plucked from a bowl on the table.

"Kate is fine. Vincent and I have been checking on her. I've been giving Donata some cash so that she could live there a little longer...at least until you got out of the Slayers. Kate really wants to see you. She doesn't know anything, and I expect you to keep your mouth shut about what went down tonight. Make up a believable story to satisfy her."

Tony reached his hand across the table, took a slice of orange, and shoved it into his mouth. The sweet juice danced over his tongue. He hung his head over the back of the chair and looked up at the ceiling. For a moment he was lost in the ornate woodwork that had been custom built for the Moranos.

"How long ya think it takes to learn how to do something like that?" Tony said, pointing to the circles of wood around the tiers of the beveled ceiling.

Salvatore and Vincent looked up.

"Don't know, don't care," Vincent said.

"I'm thinkin' it must feel real good to be that good at somethin'."

Tony looked at his friends.

"You're good at what you do too," Salvatore said.

Tony laughed. "Oh, yeah? What the hell am I good at?"

"You're a good friend who can use a gun better than some of those old geezers that have been shooting their entire lives. Speaking of that, who taught you how to shoot?"

"Nobody taught me. I just did it. Sort of like breathing. When I hold a gun, it feels like it's a part of my hand...ya know, like my fingers."

Salvatore pushed his chair back and stood. "Let's get you to your new place."

Tony stood. He grabbed an apple and orange from the bowl and waved the fruit at Salvatore. "Breakfast—I gotta have somethin' to eat when I wake up."

Chapter Eighty-Eight

O n the ride to Tony's apartment, Vincent jabbered about all the women he was sleeping with. It was white noise and music to Tony's ears. Finally, Salvatore pulled the car over, and Tony looked out the window at the twin home.

"This it?" Tony said, pointing to the brick house. It was an old, narrow building with two front doors. It seemed to Tony that the builder had thought about building row homes and stopped with the first building.

Salvatore opened the car door. "Yeah. There are eight apartments, two on the top and two on the bottom in each house."

The boys walked toward the back of the house, where there were two sets of metal stairs. Tony followed Salvatore to a door on the second floor—the door to his new home, a place he could finally call his own.

The entry door of Tony's new apartment led into the kitchen. Tony stepped inside and cringed, his nose filled with the sour, rancid smell of rotted food and urine. He scanned the room and shuffled through the trash strewn over the floor. The kitchen sink and small counter on either side of it were piled with dishes, pots, and small, broken appliances. There were five cabinets, two on the wall next to the sink and three below. Two cabinet doors were missing. A thick coating of dust clung to the greasy appliances and counters like gray peach fuzz.

"This place is a shithole," Vincent said, his hand covering his mouth and nose.

"Don't be a dick. It's a place for Tony to live," Salvatore said.

Tony lowered his eyes and waved his friends off. "I used to live in a house with no heat or running water—where the googamongers lived. So this ain't so bad. Just needs to be cleaned up a little is all."

The boys proceeded into the small living room, where there was a thin love seat next to an old TV table. A crib mattress sat lonely in the middle of the floor, stained with large brownish spots. A few random toys left behind by the previous tenant looked lost and spooky. Tony dragged his feet over the worn carpet, making his way into the only bedroom.

There was a single bed with a wooden headboard pushed up against a small window covered in yellowed lace. The floor was cluttered with discarded clothing, mostly children's. The mattress on the bed frame was partially covered by a soiled light-pink sheet. The once-beige carpet showed thick trails of black, the wear of many years of neglect.

Tony turned and walked to the bathroom. The toilet was filled to the brim with orange-brown water that threatened to push away the crooked toilet seat that hung over the edge. The sink across from the toilet was covered in rust and mold. The front of the white bathtub was streaked with grime, and inside the tub a single layer of cockroaches lay dead in their final resting place. Tony looked at the lifeless black bodies. My new home, Tony thought, where insects came to die.

"Aw, goddamn, that's disgusting," Vincent grunted, crunching his eyebrows and pursing his lips.

As Tony looked into the tub, he agreed.

"Will you be OK?" Salvatore asked.

"Sure. I'm gonna be fine. Tomorra I'm gonna go to the bakery and see Kate. Ya know, I'm just gonna take it a day at a time. Do we got any work tomorra?"

"Yes, Vincent and I will show you the ropes, get you familiar with collecting the money that the store owners pay to my father."

Tony gritted his teeth and turned away from Salvatore.

"Something wrong?" Salvatore asked.

Tony thought, Yeah, the mention of your no-good father makes me want to slice him up into tiny pieces. Instead he said, "Nah. Everything is fine. You guys can head out; I'll be OK."

"Look at it this way," Salvatore said, trying to be optimistic. "Maybe someday we will all be made men. You know, in the mob. This is the first step to getting closer to it."

Tony spun on Salvatore. "Made men? I don't know what you're talkin' 'bout. I ain't gonna be made into nothin'. I've been fightin' my whole life. Fightin' for everything. Fightin' just to stay alive. So the Mafia ain't gonna make me nothin' 'cause I'm gonna be the kinda man I was meant to be."

Salvatore chuckled. "Calm down, man. You don't have to be so jumpy."

Salvatore started jumping on one foot, and Vincent soon followed, mocking Tony. They didn't stop until Tony's scowl turned into a smile. Within seconds the three men were standing ankle deep in garbage, laughing. Tony was in a good mood by the time his friends left. He looked around him and welcomed himself home.

Chapter Eighty-Nine

After Salvatore and Vincent left, Tony stood in the middle of the filthy living room. He pushed empty soda and beer cans off of the love seat. He lay on his back, and before he drifted to sleep, he remembered the look on Razor's face when Johnny Morano cut his tongue out. Razor had deserved that and much more, not just because of how he'd treated Tony but because of the way he'd abused the others with his position in the gang. Tony only wished he could have cut Razor's tongue out himself. Cold and exhausted, he curled himself into a fetal position and fell asleep.

The next morning, Tony rose and looked around him. He was living in squalor—there wasn't a clean spot in the whole joint—but he smiled anyway, because it was his new home. There was running water and electricity, more than he'd ever had on his own before.

Tony left quickly and walked to the bakery. When the bell rang above the door, Donata, Ruth, and Kate looked toward the sound.

"Tony," Kate yelped and ran into his arms.

Tony grabbed on to Kate and breathed in her scent. A warm sensation rushed through him.

"I've missed you so much, Kate," he said quietly.

Tony unraveled his arms from Kate's waist and strode over to Donata. He put his arm around her shoulder and kissed her on the cheek. "How've ya been?"

Donata covered her mouth with a trembling hand. A tear slid down her cheek. "We're doin' the best we can. We sure did miss ya around here," she admitted.

"Thanks for takin' care of Kate," Tony said, glancing at Ruth, who was standing behind the counter with her hands on her hips. "I think somebody is waitin' to say hello to me."

Tony walked over slowly. "How's my best girl?"

Ruth studied him closely. "Where have you been? Why haven't you come to see us? I was in the hospital for a long time, and you only came once."

"What? You're mad at me?"

Ruth crossed her arms over her chest. She pressed her lips together and averted her eyes. Time seemed to slow as the young girl considered the question. "Yeah, I'm kinda mad at you. I mean, I was waiting for you to come back, but you didn't."

"Don't be mad at me, Ruth. I had to take care of some business. So I can take care of myself. Ya know, pay for my own food and have a place to live."

"You don't look like you're taking care of yourself," she said, eyeing his dirty clothing.

Tony grabbed his T-shirt and gave it a strong sniff. "Peeeee-uuuuu. I smell pretty bad, huh? But you know what? I'm doin' much better now."

"Are you going to be around from now on, or do you have to go away and 'do business' again?"

"Nope, I'm back for good. Now can I have a hug?"

Ruth burst into tears and threw her arms around Tony's neck. He lifted her into the air. Tony gently put her back down and addressed them all. He tilted his chin up and tucked his hands under his armpits. "I got an apartment over on North Broad Street and a job too."

"What? You have an apartment?" Kate said.

"Yep, it ain't much, but we can fix it up and make it a home," he confirmed.

Kate's eyes grew larger. She blinked slowly, her long lashes accentuating her amazing blue eyes. "We?"

"Yeah, we. You and me. Once we get it fixed, we can have Donata and Ruth over for dinner," he rambled.

Donata loudly forced the air out of her lungs.

Tony turned toward her. "I know this has been hard. But everything is gonna get better now. I promise."

Donata and Ruth joined Tony and Kate. "We're happy for ya, Tony," Donata said.

Donata gently slid her hand down Kate's arm. "Ya better go upstairs and get your things together. Your boyfriend here has come to take ya home."

As Kate packed, Ruth lay on the bed and chatted with her. By the time they came back downstairs, Donata had packed a large bag of breads and pastries for the couple. They all walked to the door together, promising to see each other later in the week.

Tony and Kate left the bakery and walked the first block in silence, both wondering what the future held and excited to leave the past behind.

"How did you get away from the Slayers?" Kate asked.

"Johnny Morano," he stated simply.

"Will you work for him now?"

"Yeah, that's the deal."

"Deal?"

"Yeah, the only way I could get him to help me was to make a deal. If he got me out, I'd work for 'im. Ain't no big thing. Salvatore and Vincent have been working for him a long time."

"Right. So are you sure you're ready to live with me?"

Tony glanced at Kate sideways. His eyes sparkled with freedom. "I never wanted anythin' more in my life."

Chapter Ninety

Tony unlocked the apartment door and followed Kate inside. Her fingers glided over her forehead and gripped the front of her hair; she lifted it away from her face and held it at the top of her head.

Tony put Kate's bags down and nervously walked deeper into the kitchen. "It ain't the best, but we can clean it up. Make it our own." He held his breath, waiting for her to turn around and run.

Kate walked across the kitchen. The trash crunched under her feet. "Wow. I wasn't expecting this. I mean, you're right—with some hard work we can make it better." She gave Tony a weak smile and rubbed her palms on her jeans.

They placed Kate's bags on the love seat and set out to shop for the essentials they needed. When they returned to the apartment, they started with the kitchen. They bagged up the trash, and kept the things they could use. It took most of the morning to clear out the garbage before they could clean.

Tony was on his hands and knees as he wiped down the cabinet doors. He stopped scrubbing and looked over at Kate, who was washing the few dishes they had salvaged from the previous tenants.

"I wish I coulda got us somethin' better. You know, a nicer place to live."

Kate walked over to him, bent, and kissed him. "It's not the nicest place on earth, but it's our place. We have to start somewhere. When we're done, it'll be perfect."

Tony took Kate by the hand and led her to the bedroom. He threw the sheet they had bought at the Goodwill overtop and sat. Kate stood over him, and he grabbed her hand, gently pulling her down to him. Their limbs were entangled as they passionately kissed.

Tony pulled away from Kate and looked into her blue eyes. "There's somethin' I gotta tell ya."

Tony's tone of voice made Kate sit up. Her back was straight, and she pulled her knees to her chest and held them there with her arms. "What? Is something wrong?"

Tony's shoulders slumped, and he lay back on the mattress, staring at the cracked ceiling above him. "No, well, yeah, somethin' is wrong. Some bad shit happened to me, and I think ya oughta know about it. I mean, we gotta be honest wit' each other, right?"

Kate put her hand on his chest. "It can't be that bad. Come on—tell me."

"It's about when I was in juvie. I was...I was...ya know, the guards did things to me."

"What kinds of things?"

"Sex things," he admitted.

Kate gasped and immediately put her hand over her mouth. "How? I mean, how could that happen?"

"Jail is a real nasty place. It's just like the streets. Really bad shit happens, and ya can't figure out what cha did."

"How many times?" Kate asked, wanting to hear that his horrific suffering was brief.

"Lots of times. Once it started, it was every day. I wanted ya to know 'cause you're the first girl I ever had sex wit'. I'm learning how to love, ya know, and to have sex. When we made love the first time, it was great. Made me feel normal."

Kate put her warm hand on his cool cheek. "You are normal. Those assholes who hurt you are the ones that aren't normal." She clutched his chin in her hand and pulled his face toward her. "Whatever happened to you was horrible. You didn't do anything to deserve it. My mother taught me that people do shitty things to other people because they know they can get away with it. That's why she was so worried about me in my neighborhood."

"Yeah, I guess that makes sense. I wanted ya to know 'cause sometimes I remember what they did to me when we're together. That makes me feel real weird 'bout it all. It scares me. Makes me feel like I don't know what I'm doin'."

Kate's chin tilted to her chest. "These men hurt you really bad?"

"You have no idea, Kate. They used me like a piece of meat. Took turns wit' me like I was a ride at an amusement park. They stole my spirit. I wanted to die. My life felt over until I met ya. You're the only good thing that's ever happened to me."

"That's not true. You have Salvatore and Vincent; they're good friends."

"You're right. But that's different. I love 'em and all, but it's different wit' you. When I was in juvie, I was afraid that I'd never be able to be wit' a girl. Made me real confused...and embarrassed. Even tellin' ya makes me feel weak, like I'm a little pussy."

Kate lay down next to Tony and put her head on his chest. "It doesn't make you weak. You were able to get through it. Getting through fucked-up shit just makes you stronger. Look at all that you've done for me. I would be alone right now if you hadn't come along and saw past the girl who was always hidden under the hood of her sweatshirt. You were going through your own stuff but stopped to help me when those bitches were kicking my ass." Kate let out a light giggle. "You know what it's like to be in agony, and that made you want to stop my agony. I think you're very brave."

Tony smirked. "Brave. That's not how I see myself. Seems like people are always havin' to save me. First the Slayers saved me; then Johnny Morano had to save me from them. Same shit when I was a kid. Ya know?"

"Don't be so hard on yourself. We all need saving. For me, that's the difference between good and evil. We all do bad things, have bad thoughts, but when the time comes when someone needs our help, we step up to it. Look at how much you've given to Donata and Ruth."

Tony pulled Kate closer to him. "I just wanted ya to know. Seein' that we're livin' together, I didn't think it was good to have secrets." After a long pause, he continued, "Seemed like the right thing to do. I've been pushin' it all down since it happened, but I was afraid that someday ya might think somethin' is wrong and wanted ya to know what I'm workin' out in my head."

"I don't know anything about what you went through, but I do know that I love you and that you can count on me to help you work through it. The fact that you shared this with me makes me love you even more."

Tony flinched. "I don't get that. Why would ya love me more? That don't make no sense."

"Because you shared your secret with me. You put yourself on the line and let me see what makes you the person that you are, which is wonderful."

"Yeah, well, there's more. I wouldn't be able to hide it from ya. I have nightmares. I wake up scared and sweaty," he admitted.

"How long have you been having nightmares?"

"Since I got outta juvie. Vincent used to wake me up from them when I lived at his house for a while."

"Did you have them when you lived with the Slayers?"

Tony nodded. "I got lucky. Had two pretty good friends there, Blast and Smoke. The first time I sat up yellin' in the middle of the night, they woke up and talked to me. From then on, when I had a nightmare, one of 'em would wake me up to stop it."

"Did you tell Smoke and Blast what happened to you?"

"Sorta. I told 'em that things happened in juvie, and they didn't ask me any more questions."

Tony and Kate lay silently, lost in their own thoughts. Then they heard a soft knock at their door.

Tony moved off of the bed. "You comin'?"

Kate lifted her hand up, and Tony pulled her to her feet. He wrapped an arm around her waist and pulled her forward, kissing her softly on the lips.

"I've never been so happy," he said.

"Me too. It's a new beginning for both of us. We're gonna be together forever," she said, squeezing him tightly.

The couple moseyed to the door, where Salvatore and Vincent were waiting. Tony pulled it open and greeted his friends.

"We brought shit," Vincent said, raising the bags he was holding in the air.

"Oh yeah? What kinda shit?" Tony mused.

The two boys had a couple bags of groceries from the Italian Market.

Salvatore put two more bags on the kitchen counter and pointed to them. "These are clothes for you to wear. Vincent and I went through our stuff so that you'd have something else to wear besides those filthy rags on your back."

Tony grabbed the bags from the counter and pulled out a shirt he knew had belonged to Vincent. "Did ya wash this stuff?" he joked.

"Hey, fuck you, Tony. My mother washes my clothes, so don't be questionin' her. She's a damn good clothes washer," Vincent quipped.

Salvatore looked around the kitchen. "Hey, you two did a great job. It looks much better."

"Yeah." Tony draped his arm over Kate's shoulder. "We make a good team."

"You know, I was thinking this morning that we have to go back to school soon," Salvatore stated.

Vincent grunted.

"Yeah, it'll be good to graduate high school. Start working full time, and, you know, move on with life," Salvatore said. "Are you going back to finish, Kate?"

She blushed and turned her eyes away from them all. "No. I decided to take my GED. I'm going to find a job; we need the money."

"Ya don't need to do that, Kate. Ya need to finish school," Tony said.

"Getting a GED is just like finishing high school. Besides, that's what I want to do."

Kate grabbed the grocery bags from the counter and put things away. She didn't want to talk about it with any of them. She had decided, and that was that. Besides, being underage made it impossible for her to return to school. Where would she tell them she lived? Who would be her guardian? Kate would do nothing to jeopardize her life with Tony.

Tony watched Kate as she unloaded the groceries, while his friends yammered about the things they wanted to do before summer officially ended. He couldn't concentrate on what they were saying because he was preoccupied by his own thoughts. I will do anything to make Kate happy. I love her so much it hurts.

Chapter Ninety-One

J ust as Johnny Morano had stated, Tony was tied to the mob and executed the demands placed upon him. On the day following Tony's freedom from the Slayers, Salvatore and Vincent brought him around South Philadelphia to introduce him to the store owners indebted to the mob. Tony was taught that store owners bought their goods at inflated prices in addition to paying the mob to protect them. This protection included being shielded from any problems from the police and politicians on Johnny's payroll.

Tony understood quickly the influence and power that Johnny Morano and his mob had on the city. Everyone who lived in South Philadelphia knew of the mob boss, even if they didn't know him personally. And Tony quickly found out that Johnny had store owners and businessmen at his mercy for goods. If Johnny found out that the goods he provided were being bought elsewhere, the owners turned up dead or their stores were destroyed.

Before lunch Salvatore and Tony entered a restaurant owned by Alberto, an Italian immigrant. Alberto was having a hard time making a profit, given how much he had to pay the Morano family, and he informed Tony and Salvatore he wasn't paying them anymore.

"I'm-a tired of-a Johnny thinkin' he can-a take-a my money. I don't-a get nothin' for payin' him this-a money. You can-a tell-a him to kiss-a my ass. I'm-a finished with all of this," Alberto argued.

"Alberto, you know very well that my father provides you with a service. He makes sure that all of your licenses are renewed with the city, and he supplies you with the produce and meat that you need to run this place. You don't want to do this, Alberto. So go and get us the money you owe, and we will never speak a word of this to him."

"What did I-a just tell-a you? I'm not-a gonna pay-a no more money to Johnny. I can buy all my-a meat and produce at half-a the price I pay-a Johnny. He's a thief. I can-a not even make-a any money from-a my business. I'm-a sick-a this shit, and I say-a no more."

Salvatore's eyes narrowed, and he gave Tony a slight nod of his head.

"Look, I just met cha. And here's the thing, ya gotta pay what ya owe," Tony warned. "Nobody wants to hear ya cryin' 'bout money. It ain't such a good idea not to pay for the stuff ya got. So why don't cha be smart and go get us Johnny's money?"

"I just tell-a you—I ain't gonna pay-a no more. Johnny Morano is a thug who-a rips off hard-a working people. So kiss-a my ass," Alberto said.

Tony turned as if to leave but quickly spun and grabbed Alberto by the arm. He forcefully bent it behind Alberto's back, and with a quick movement, an unnatural popping sound filled his ears as he dislocated Alberto's elbow and shoulder. Alberto's scream pierced through the peaceful music playing in the background of the empty restaurant. Tony pressed him against the wall and put his own body weight against the man.

"Maybe you-a go and-a get the money now, Alberto?" Tony said.

Alberto nodded in jerky movements.

Tony escorted Alberto to his office, where he used his left hand to fill an envelope with money. Tony took the envelope and headed for the front door. He turned to look at Alberto.

"I suggest ya don't do this again. I'm tryin' to help ya out here. If ya don't pay like you're supposed to, you're gonna end up dead. That much I know," Tony said.

Tony followed Salvatore out into the warm sun.

"Man, is that guy dense?" Tony said.

"Once in while these store owners forget who they are dealing with, that's the kind of shit we take care of real fast."

"Was that Alberto guy tellin' the truth? Does the mob make 'em pay more for stuff that they can buy cheaper on their own?"

Salvatore glanced at Tony. "There's a markup on things. Think of it this way. You just moved in with Kate and want nice things. Maybe someday get married and have a family, right?"

"'Course I do."

"The only way we can make money is if the family makes money. That means whatever we supply to people—food, weapons, drugs, women, you name it—we have to charge more than we are paying. That's how we make a profit." Salvatore chuckled. "A good fucking profit too. Anyway, that's how you make your money. If the mob didn't make a lot of money, then my father couldn't afford to pay you, right?"

"Yeah, I see that."

"Good. Consider the markup necessary to keep you and Kate able to live."

Tony shook his head. "I'll do whatever I gotta do to make Kate happy. Let me ask ya, though: do you ever feel bad for these people?"

"Nope. My father is a businessman. Just like any other business, he has to make sure the family earns a living. Do you see doctors and lawyers giving their services away for free? No, you don't, because it's a business. Think of it that way," Salvatore said, patting Tony's arm. "The Slayers did the same shit that we do: protect their assets and build their business."

Tony nodded quietly. He thought, Salvatore is right; the Slayers hurt innocent people to get what they needed to survive. It didn't make it right, but like the bus driver, Marge, told me as a kid, it's a matter of eat or be eaten.

Chapter Ninety-Two

Within a few weeks, Tony and Kate had a livable apartment. They had bought a few pieces of furniture at a thrift shop and retrieved other discarded items that people put out for trash. Nothing matched, and the apartment still had a dreary overtone, but Tony felt good about the home they had created.

On a warm, rainy Wednesday night, Salvatore and Vincent came over to Tony's apartment. Kate was making dinner for them all. The three young men sat at the table as Kate rushed around the kitchen, excited to be serving her first guests.

Kate put a pan of lasagna in the middle of the table, between the salad and garlic bread.

"Damn, that smells real good," Vincent said, reaching for the spatula.

Salvatore waited until Kate took her food before he filled his plate. "Thanks for having us over for dinner, Kate," he said, giving her a genuine smile.

Kate giggled nervously. "Don't thank me yet. I don't know how good this is going to be. Donata gave me the recipe, but she's a great cook. I hope it's OK."

Tony put a forkful of lasagna into his mouth. "Mmm, it's delicious," he mumbled through his food. He believed that everything Kate did was perfect. Tony didn't care what other people thought, not even his friends—Kate was the center of his life, and he felt lucky to have her.

Salvatore rested his fork on his plate. "I wanted to tell all of you that my mom rented a suite in Atlantic City next week. If you're up to it, we can all go for a week. It won't cost you anything but the food that you eat."

Tony looked at Kate, and she looked back at him. Her eyes glimmered with excitement. Tony took her hand. "What do ya think?"

Kate's smile lit up her face. "I think that would be great. I've never been to the ocean before." She turned her attention to Salvatore. "Are you sure your mom doesn't mind?"

Salvatore grabbed another piece of garlic bread. "Of course not. That's why she got a suite. She loves having all of us around."

"What about your dad?" Tony asked skeptically.

"What about him? He's not going," Salvatore said.

"I don't mean that; I mean, what about work?"

"It's fine. I'll have a couple of the other guys cover for us. My father doesn't care as long as shit still gets done."

Tony breathed a sigh of relief; he didn't want to disappoint Kate. "All right, then; that sounds great. We're in. Kate don't start workin' for a couple more weeks, so we ain't got nothin' holdin' us back."

"I didn't know ya got a job," Vincent said, giving Kate a smile.

"Yeah, I did. I'm working at Osteria. They're starting me as a dishwasher," Kate said, flushing with embarrassment as the words left her lips. "I start in two weeks. I...I...I'm just starting out as a dishwasher, but I hope that I can be a server. There's a lot more money, because of the tips."

"Good for you," Salvatore said, noticing her red face and nervous demeanor. "In fact, I know the owner, so after you work there for a month or so, I can talk to him for you."

"That would be great," Tony cut in. "Kate's real good at everything she does. Once she gets to know the place, she'll be runnin' it."

"I'm sure she will. I'll talk to him, Kate."

Kate brushed the top of Salvatore's hand with her own.

"Hey, don't be hittin' on my girl," Tony joked.

Salvatore rolled his eyes at Tony.

"So when do we leave for the shore?" Vincent cut in.

"Saturday."

Tony sat back in the wooden chair and rubbed his full belly, taking loud breaths. "Yeah, Saturday is good."

When Tony and Kate lay in their narrow bed that night, they talked about the things they would do in Atlantic City. Kate rolled onto her side and flung her arm around Tony's waist.

"We don't really have money to go away."

Tony kept his eyes closed, soaking up the softness of the pillow that cradled his head. "Well, we ain't gonna get many chances to go to the beach, so we gotta take what we can get. We got about two hundred bucks saved."

"But we need so many things."

"We'll get things later. Right now, we're goin' on vacation. I don't want cha to worry 'bout stupid shit like that, OK? I'm gonna make plenty of money, so much money that ya ain't gonna worry about workin' if ya don't wanna. Just like Mrs. Morano."

"That's great, Tony Bruno, but I want to make my own money. If my mom taught me anything, it was to be independent."

"Strong women turn me on," Tony murmured, running his hand up her shirt.

That night, just like other nights prior, Kate woke Tony from a nightmare. He had been yelling and thrashing in the small bed. When she woke him, he was soaking wet and breathing hard.

"It's all right; you're at home. It was only a nightmare," she cooed.

Tony looked at Kate with sad eyes. Then he put his arm around her, no longer feeling alone, and went back to sleep in a dreamless state.

Chapter Ninety-Three

On Saturday morning Salvatore pulled his car up to the apartment. Tony threw a small bag in the trunk and slid into the backseat next to Kate, nuzzling close to her. When they arrived at the hotel, Tony stood in the lobby and looked around. The hotel, also a casino, was filled with noise from the slot machines. He scanned the elaborate pictures and lighting throughout the lobby.

"This place is pretty fuckin' great," he whispered to Kate.

The four of them went to the front desk, and Salvatore gave the women his name. "Yes, Mr. Morano, welcome. Your mother said you'd be arriving soon. Here are your keys; take the elevator to your left up to the top floor. You'll need to swipe your key card in the elevator to get you up to the penthouse."

Tony took Kate's hand and followed Salvatore onto the elevator. When the doors opened to the penthouse, Tony's breath caught in his throat. "Wow, are ya kiddin' us?" he said aloud.

The elevator opened to a large living room. There were light-brown leather sofas and chairs in front of a large window and a solid mahogany coffee table that ran the length of the largest sofa. To the left were two doors, and in the corner, a large bar with granite counter tops and high-back barstools.

"My mom's and sister's room is over there," Salvatore said, pointing at the master bedroom to the right. Their double doors were left open, and Tony could see the king-size bed and some of the impeccable furnishings.

"Vincent and I are in this room," Salvatore said, continuing his tour. Tony looked inside at the two queen beds in the middle of the room. Off to the left was a sitting area with a television. "You and Kate are in here," Salvatore continued and stepped into the last bedroom.

Tony walked in behind Salvatore. "No shit, this is where me and Kate are sleepin'?"

The room had a king-size canopy bed. The sheer fabric around the bed was drawn closed, and through the fabric, the bed looked serene and inviting, a safe haven tucked away from a cruel world. The glass wall at the foot of the bed ran from floor to ceiling overlooking the ocean. In the opposite corner of the room was a huge gas fireplace made of stone. A cream-colored velvet love seat perched before it, inviting romance into the room. Kate grabbed Tony's hand and squeezed it softly.

"Unpack your stuff and meet us out in the living room," Salvatore said, closing the door behind him.

Tony turned to Kate. "I can't believe all of this," he said. "This is the nicest place I've ever been."

"Me too," Kate said with a giggle. "And we're here a whole week."

Kate followed Tony to the enormous window and stood next to him.

"Ya know, I ain't never did anythin' in my life that made me feel special. This place, this room, it makes me feel special. Look at all the people on the beach. All the families. I ain't ever had none of that. They all look so happy; now I get to be happy too," he said, pulling Kate into him.

Chapter Ninety-Four

Tony and Kate explored all the nooks and crannies of their hotel room. They found one delight after another. Expensive soaps, shampoo, and lotions. Thick fleece robes in the closet. They opened what they thought was a closet door and found a refrigerator filled with drinks, fruit, cheese, and candy.

"Do ya think we can eat this stuff?" Tony said, worried about making their money stretch.

Kate shook her head skeptically. "We better ask Salvatore first. We have to keep track of what we're spending."

A short time later, Tony joined his friends in the living room, and Kate sat next to him.

"There's a fridge in our room," Tony said.

"Yeah, there's one in all of the rooms," Salvatore said, seeing Tony's uneasiness. "Eat whatever you want. They fill them up every day. It's a part of being in the penthouse."

"Yeah? That's cool. I like this penthouse shit." Tony looked around. "Where's your mother?"

"She and Gianna went downstairs to make an appointment to get their nails done. They're making one for you too," Salvatore said to Kate.

"Oh, they don't need to do that. I mean, we're on a budget," Kate responded.

"My mom doesn't care about money. She doesn't need to. Listen, she likes to take care of people, so just go along with it. OK? It'll make her feel good," Salvatore said, trying to put Kate at ease.

Kate wrung her hands. "Well...sure, I'd love to have my nails done. I mean, I guess I would—I've never had them done by someone before. I've always done my own."

The elevator door opened, and Alessandra stepped out with Gianna.

"Oh good, you're all here," Alessandra began. "Kate, we made an appointment to get a manicure and pedicure at four o'clock this afternoon. I also ordered dinner in tonight. The chef will come up and cook it here."

"Where?" Tony said.

"Where what, Tony?"

"Where's the guy gonna cook?" he said, looking around the spacious room.

Alessandra laughed and walked over to yet another door that looked like a closet and pulled it open. "In here."

Tony walked over and peered inside the kitchen. His eyes scanned all the basics: stove, oven, refrigerator, and dishwasher. "This is livin'," Tony said, smiling at Alessandra.

"Yes, it is. Mr. Morano works hard so that we can enjoy the better things in life," she stated.

Alessandra relished that she could show off a lifestyle that Tony hadn't seen before. Only two months prior, Salvatore had confided in her that Tony had been raped in juvie only to be turned away by his own parents when he was released from detention. Alessandra couldn't fathom turning one of her children away, and her empathy flowed deeply for Tony. That's when she decided a week in Atlantic City would be a gift that she'd love to give to Tony. Alessandra, the polar opposite of Johnny, was drawn to the underdog. Giving to the poor and downtrodden eased her guilt about spending the dirty money her husband made at the hands of others.

Alessandra turned to the teens. "It's early, and I've asked the hotel to set up a cabana for us on the beach. Let's all get changed and go down."

Everyone agreed, and Gianna ran off to her bedroom to put on a bathing suit. Tony watched Kate, her face frozen as though she'd just seen a ghost. He walked over and sat down next to her.

"What's wrong?"

Kate's eyes filled with burning tears. "I don't have a bathing suit. I don't even own one. We were coming to the beach—what was I thinking?"

Overhearing the conversation, Alessandra asked, "What size do you wear?"

Kate nervously pushed herself to the edge of the sofa. "I'm a size four."

Alessandra picked up the telephone from the end table. "Yes, this is Mrs. Morano. Can you please send someone up with size-four swimsuits? I need them for a teen, so send up your trendiest. How quickly? Very good, we'll see you in ten minutes."

Alessandra put the receiver back on its cradle. "I'm going to change into my suit. By the time I'm finished, the women from the boutique downstairs should be here."

Kate collapsed back into the buttery soft leather of the sofa. "I can't believe this, Tony. I feel like I'm in a dream, a dream that I don't want to ever end."

"Yeah, me too." Tony got close to Kate's ear. "Working for Mr. Morano ain't so bad after all. Well, Mrs. Morano ain't so bad; Johnny's still a dick."

Kate turned to Tony, raised her eyebrows, and put her index finger over tight lips. "She'll hear you."

Tony shrugged and went into their room to change into shorts.

Ten minutes later, Kate was in the master suite with Alessandra and a woman from the boutique. The lady had brought a dozen different bathing suits. Several were a little too skimpy for Kate's liking, and in the end, Alessandra insisted that she keep four. "We're here for a whole week, Kate—you'll need more than just one," Alessandra said.

When Kate was alone in the bathroom changing, she looked at the price tags. The cheapest one was $140, a sum that Kate thought was too much, yet the experience of being taken care of and catered to was one she would never forget. It was addictive.

The group spent the rest of the day on the beach. There were hotel staff nearby that brought them everything that makes for a great beach day. The sun was high in the cloudless sky, and Tony was lying on a cushioned lounge chair letting the sun warm him, his muscles glistening from the lotion he'd applied. Tony leaned over to Kate's chair. "Wanna go for a walk?"

Tony and Kate walked along the water's edge, hand in hand. They were quiet at first, taking in the beauty of the endless body of water.

"Are ya happy?"

Kate smiled. "Yeah, I'm really happy. It's so peaceful here. There's something about the ocean that makes me calm. You know what I mean?"

They stopped walking and turned toward the sea. Tony focused on the water as it receded and then crashed against the shoreline. The mist of the salt water clung to their skin. The sight and sound gave him a sense of peace. "Yeah, it makes me feel like there ain't nothin' wrong in the world. Like my whole fucked-up existence, until now, was just a stupid nightmare. I wish I could keep this feeling inside me forever."

"We can try to keep this feeling inside of us. All we have to do is remember. Besides, with both of us working, we'll be able to come back again," Kate said with careless optimism.

Tony and Kate spent the rest of the days in Atlantic City lost in all the pleasures that Alessandra cast upon them. Tony knew it would be a hard adjustment to go back to their meager apartment and tried to put the end of the week out of his mind so he could enjoy every minute of the vacation.

"Are you having a good time?" Salvatore asked midweek when he and Tony were alone on the beach.

"I'm havin' the best time of my life. So is Kate. I really appreciate ya bringin' us here."

"Of course. You're kind of fun to hang out with. And my mother loves Kate. Look at them," Salvatore said, pointing down the beach.

Tony watched from his chair. His heart fluttered as he fixated on Kate and Alessandra laughing together. "Yeah, Kate is a good girl."

"She sure is if she's willing to put up with you," Salvatore joked.

"Yeah, well, fuck you too, ya momma's boy," Tony fired back.

Salvatore took a soda from one of the hotel staff. "What the hell is Vincent doing?"

Tony sat up and looked toward the water, where Vincent was trying to do handstands as the waves kept knocking him over. "I think his mother dropped 'im on his head when he was a baby."

Tony and Salvatore laughed and settled back into their chairs.

"Life only gets better from here," Salvatore stated.

Tony looked at his friend and then back at the ocean. "I don't know how much better it can get than this right here."

Chapter Ninety-Five

T he euphoric feeling from vacation still lingered as Tony helped Kate out of the car at their apartment. He grabbed their bag and leaned into the open car window.

"I'll see ya guys tomorra."

"Yeah, we'll be over to pick ya up 'round eight tomorra morning. We got a lot of work to get done," Vincent answered.

Tony patted his hand on the car as he turned away.

"Tony?" Salvatore said.

"Yeah?"

"We have a meeting tomorrow morning at one of the warehouses. A group of Russians want to buy guns from us. My father will run the whole deal. We stay quiet during these meetings."

"So now what? You're accusin' me of bein' a big mouth?"

Salvatore chuckled. "No, I'm just filling you in on the basics. Have a good night."

Inside the apartment, Tony looked around. It was a far cry from the lush hotel, but he was grateful to have a place to call home.

"Are ya ready to start your new job?" Tony asked Kate as they settled in.

"Yeah. I mean, I wish I wasn't a dishwasher, but once Salvatore talks to the owner, I hope I'll be able to wait tables."

"I'm sure ya will. Just go in there and show 'em what you're made of. They're gonna love ya. Who wouldn't?"

"Whatever, Tony. How about if you show me some love instead?"

Tony got chills when Kate ran her hand over his abdomen.

Tony flushed. "Yeah, I'm sorry 'bout all that."

"Why would you be sorry?"

"'Cause I ain't been able to make love to ya."

"You will. We're working through it together."

Tony pulled her closer. "I don't want ya to think that ya don't turn me on, 'cause ya do."

"I know I do. I've felt it...literally."

"Yeah, keepin' it that way is the problem. I'm good until I think about those motherfuckers in juvie. Ya know?"

"Well, we'll have to find a way so that you don't think about them. Like you did the first time we had sex," Kate said sadly.

Tony nodded. "It's hard. I get real into it wit' cha, and then one of their ugly mugs pops into my head. Makes me feel like a fuckin' freak."

Kate ran her hand through his hair. "You know what I'm going to do tomorrow?"

"What?"

"I'm going to the library to find some books that can help you. I'll read everything I can get my hands on, and then we'll work through it together. How's that sound?"

Tony kissed her forehead. "You'd do that for me?"

"I'd do anything for you," Kate said, laying her head on his chest.

Kate returned from the library the next day carrying three books. Tony was still out working with Salvatore and Vincent, so she took the books into the bedroom and read. Hours later, after going through each book, Kate had four pages of notes.

When Tony got home that evening, Kate met him at the door. He looked haggard and tired. "Bad day?"

"Nah. Just a lot of stuff goin' on wit' my job."

"Bad stuff?"

"No badder than when I was wit' the Slayers. It's just different is all. I gotta act more decent, ya know—can't say what I want, when I want. It's all right, though; I'll get used to it. Vincent told me today it took him a while too. When Mr. Morano is around, everybody is tense. Afraid to make a mistake. It's a pain in the ass."

"Is Salvatore different around his father?"

"Nope, he's the same. But that's his son, so he can say somethin' if he wants to. Anyway, it ain't nuttin'. How was your day?"

"Oooh," Kate squealed, "I'm happy you asked. I went to the library and got some books on...ya know...what happened to you in prison. Anyway, everything that's going on with you is perfectly normal. The nightmares and all the things you're feeling, ya know, and when we try to be together, you can't."

"There ain't nuttin' normal about losing your hard-on wit' the girl that ya love," he said sadly.

"That's not true. You've been through a traumatic experience. That makes everything get mixed up in your head. There are things that you can do to work through all of it," Kate said, wanting so badly to help him.

"What kinda things?"

"Well, for starters, when you and I are together, it's important to focus on things that make you happy."

"I know that, Kate. Don't cha think I try not to think about those ass licks? Come on. Get real," he barked.

Kate put her hands on her hips and pursed her lips. She glared at him. His eyes revealed the sadness that lay lodged in the center of his heart. Her arms dropped to her side, and she stepped closer to him. Kate put her arms around Tony's neck, and he bent in and kissed her.

"I'll try anything. OK?" he said.

"I will too. We'll figure this out. It's going to be fine. I have some other tricks up my sleeve that I read about," Kate said, giving him a sexy smile.

Tony stepped back and shook his head. "I feel like a fuckin' mutant. Let's just talk 'bout somethin' else."

"Sure. Let's talk about how you're going to help me make dinner," she said, flipping her hair over her shoulder and pulling the refrigerator door open.

Kate knew from all that she had read that when Tony was violated by the prison guards, he'd experienced a complete loss of control. One way for rape victims to regain a part of themselves was to gain control over some, if not all, of their life. She made it her mission to allow Tony to decide what he wanted to do, to give him control with her in the bedroom.

That night, as the couple lay in each other's arms, Kate spoke softly. "Will you kiss me?"

Tony pretended to think about it. "Yeah, I guess so." He put his hand on the side of her face and gently eased his tongue into her mouth.

They kissed for a while, and then Kate asked, "Do you want me to take my pajamas off?"

Tony cocked his head to the side. "Sure. That would be good."

Kate stood and undressed. She stood at the side of the bed naked.

"Do you want me to take your clothes off?"

Tony's erection was pushing his boxers out. "Yeah, I'd like that."

Kate pulled his shirt over his head and slid his boxers off. She lay down next to him again, and they gazed into each other's eyes.

"Do you want me to touch you?" she whispered.

Tony closed his eyes, savoring the tingling in his groin. He nodded.

Kate ran her hand down the top of his leg, all the way to his knee. She slowly brought her hand up the inside of his thigh, brushing past his erection. She repeated this until his breathing got heavy and she knew he was in a zone.

Tony reached between her legs to feel the warm place he wanted to call home. He wanted to be inside Kate. He wanted to satisfy her and let her feel the love she so deserved from him. He slid his fingers inside of her and she let out a sensual purr. He bent his head down to take one of her breasts into his mouth. Kate softly pushed him back.

"Can I go down on you?" she asked.

Kate hadn't done that to him yet. It was something that the guards hadn't done to him either, and that made him feel safe. A new experience.

"Yeah," he murmured.

Kate slowly made her way down to the foot of the bed. She took Tony's erect penis in her hand and took it into her mouth. Tony couldn't think about anything else except how good he felt. Before he came, he sat up and took Kate into his arms. He laid her on the bed and got on top of her. He slipped himself into her. Kate's back arched, and she let out a moan so beautiful it sounded like music to Tony's ears. She pushed her pelvis forward to meet his thrusts, and together they were one, in perfect harmony until they both came and collapsed on the bed.

"How'd ya do that?" he said, breathlessly.

"I read a lot today. I have my ways."

"Do you realize I just kept my hard-on the whole time?" he burst out, almost giddy.

"Yes, I was there, remember?"

Tony scooped Kate into his arms. "You're the only woman on the planet for me. Do ya think we can keep doin' that? I mean, do ya think I'm cured?"

"You're not sick, Tony, so there isn't anything to cure. You were traumatized. You just need time and practice to get over it. Trust me on this one," she said.

"I trust ya wit' my life," Tony said, nuzzling his face into her neck.

The tip of Kate's tongue peeked out from behind her lips as if it had a mind of its own. "Are you going to kiss me?"

Tony leaned over and put his lips to hers. He'd started slowly, with his lips together, waiting to feel the electricity. He nudged Kate's lips with his tongue, and they fell into a passionate rhythm. He had a ravenous urge for Kate again.

When they parted, Kate was smiling. "Not bad for an Italian fellow."

"What cha talkin' about, not bad? Ya ain't never been loved until you're loved by an Italian. Ya ain't got no idea how hard we love."

It was true. Kate had no indication of how hard Tony would love her.

As Tony moved into limbo, the state right before sleep, he saw Kate's face, and his body was weightless as he looked into the face of an angel, his angel.

Chapter Ninety-Six

One morning shortly after Halloween, Tony entered the Morano home at one o'clock after getting a call from Salvatore to come over. Johnny and Big Paulie were in the office. Alessandra was in the kitchen making coffee. She knew it would be a long night for the men.

When the three young men entered the godfather's office, Johnny stood. "Son, we just got word that Scary Joey was gunned down by the Bonanni family. Scary Joey was laundering money for several of their regular customers. The Bonanni family considers this stealing from their business. Scary Joey was sharing the profits with our family. As far as we're concerned, he was simply doing business. The family in New York doesn't agree, so they killed him tonight."

"What do you want us to do, Pop?" Salvatore asked.

"I want you all to take a trip to New York with me, Big Paulie, and Jackhammer. I've arranged for a sit-down with the Bonanni family. I'm going to tell them that by killing one of our brothers, they've gone too far."

"Mr. M., are ya sayin' we ain't gonna get revenge for what they done to Scary Joey?" Vincent said.

"No, Vincent, I'm not saying that at all. No one kills a family member and gets away with it. First, we get agreement from the Bonanni family that no other men die. Once we have established peace, our goal will be to find and kill the motherfucker who shot Scary Joey."

"Pop, why not just go to New York and blow their heads off?" Salvatore asked.

"Because that would be too obvious. It would raise suspicions with the cops. If we retaliate now, across state lines, we could put other families in jeopardy along the East Coast. No, this must be taken care of methodically. First we make peace; then we go to war."

Johnny turned to Tony. "You make sure that your shots are dead-on if we need you."

"Of course. I always do my best," Tony stated.

Big Paulie stepped closer to the boys. "You guys go get some clothes together. We'll be in New York for two or three days. We'll meet back here in an hour."

***

"I don't understand, Tony. Why do you have to leave? You've never had to leave overnight before," Kate cried.

"Like I told ya, Kate, I gotta go. Part of me workin' for Mr. Morano. I don't wanna leave ya. I wanna stay right here wit' cha. But it's what I gotta do. OK?"

"I guess." Kate pouted.

Kate followed Tony into the kitchen as he was leaving. While she wasn't privy to what Tony did every day, she knew enough to be afraid for him. Kate put her arms around his waist. "I saw on the news that Joey Scarfi, Scary Joey—whatever you call him—was killed. I'm scared, Tony. What if something awful happens to you?"

Tony squeezed Kate in a bear hug. "Ain't nothin' gonna happen to me. Scary Joey got on somebody's bad side, is all."

"How do you know nothing is going to happen to you? I'm sure Scary Joey didn't think he was going to die either. What am I supposed to think?"

Kate watched Tony pick up his overnight bag. She let her words linger between them, waiting for Tony to say something to ease her worries.

"Ya can't worry every time I leave ya, Kate. I'm real good at my job, and I know what I'm doin'. I also got Vincent and Salvatore wit' me most of the time. We take good care of each other."

Kate felt like there was nothing left in her. She started to openly cry again. "Oh Tony, my guts are twisted; I feel like there is barbed wire in my belly."

"Everything will be fine," Tony assured her. "I gotta get movin'—the guys are expectin' me."

Kate clung to Tony at the door to their apartment as he tried to leave. "Come on, Kate, let go. It's gettin' late. I love ya."

"Do you promise to call me?"

Tony released his breath from deep within. "I'll call ya. Stop worryin'."

Tony patted her shoulder and pulled the door closed behind him as Kate collapsed on the floor and cried until her sadness turned into anger.

Chapter Ninety-Seven

When the Morano family first arrived in New York, they immediately went to the restaurant where a sit-down had been arranged with the Bonanni family.

As Tony walked into the restaurant with the others, the private room in the back fell silent, and he could literally feel the temperature in the room shift. He looked at the members representing the Bonanni family. They looked just as mean and ruthless as men in his own group. Hatred bubbled up inside of him. One of these men had killed Scary Joey, forcing him to leave Kate alone to come to New York. There was nothing that pissed Tony off more than seeing Kate upset. It broke his heart that Kate was so distraught. Johnny noticed the rage behind Tony's eyes.

Johnny whispered, "Simmer down. All in good time."

Johnny approached the table, walking directly over to Harry Bonanni, the boss of the family. Harry stood and shook Johnny's hand and then invited him to sit.

As the higher-ranking men sat around the table, the lower-ranking members stood behind them, watching each other closely, waiting for someone to make a wrong move. The high-ranking men were relaxed. They knew that only a fool takes lives during a sit-down. Doing so would bring criticism and shunning from the other families up and down the East Coast.

"So tell me why you're here, Johnny," Harry said.

"I'm sure that you heard someone offed Scary Joey last night. I want to understand who did it and why," Johnny said.

Harry puffed on the thick cigar he was holding; then he picked up a glass of brandy and took a mouthful of the expensive liquid. He swirled the brandy around in his mouth before slowly swallowing. "I'd like to help ya, Johnny. I really would, but I ain't sure why you're here talkin' to me about Scary Joey. Are ya tryin' to say someone from the Bonanni family did this? Is that what this is about?"

"I'm trying to give you a chance, Harry. We know that some of your top customers flipped over to Scary Joey for their money laundering. They needed a good businessman, and your guys couldn't keep up with the growing demand.

It's no secret that the Morano family has a larger network. We can move more money, drugs, and goods than any other family on the coast. I'm asking you to talk to your men. I don't want any more casualties in either of our families. Capisce?"

Harry leaned forward, his index finger poking the air as he spoke in a gruff tone. "Johnny, what makes ya think ya can walk into my neighborhood and lay down laws? Ya been eatin' too many of those fuckin' cheesesteaks, and I think the fuckin' grease is cloggin' your fuckin' brain. Ya know what you're doin' right now is enough to start a fuckin' war. Is that what you want? A fuckin' war?"

"No, Harry, I want the opposite. I'm here for peace. Scary Joey took over some of your family business, and you killed him for it. I haven't forgotten that your father, God rest his soul, was the man who helped me make the Morano family what it is today. I was a loyal and dedicated servant to your father. He would have known how to handle this situation, as a gentleman. In fact, he would have welcomed doing business with my family. I'm trying to make it right between the two families. Remember, I once belonged to the Bonanni family. I was one of you. I don't want this to go any further. That's why I'm here, Harry." Johnny sat back in his chair and gave Harry a hateful smirk.

Harry thought about it for several seconds. "My father was a fuckin' fool for lettin' other families share in the business that belongs to us. I remember ya when I was a kid. Ya was always hangin' around the house, but I never saw why my father thought ya was so great."

"Your father was a good man. He cared about all of the families, not only his own family."

Johnny moved his gaze over to the Bonanni underboss. The man was picking his teeth with a toothpick and spitting food particles onto the floor. He looked like a brainless slob. Johnny visibly cringed. He had held the position of underboss in the Bonanni family many years prior, and it sickened him to see what the next generation had made of the Bonanni family.

"So here's what we're gonna do," Harry began. "The Morano family is gonna give the Bonanni family a cut of the money ya make on launderin' for the customers ya stole from us."

Johnny lit a cigarette and laid it in the ashtray. "Tell me, Harry. Why would my family do that?"

"'Cause ya just said ya want peace. Well, your family stole from my business, and ya oughta be payin' the Bonanni family somethin' for that. Don't cha think? It only seems right." Harry looked to his goons, who spontaneously nodded and grunted their agreement.

Johnny gestured toward Vincent, who walked over to the table and handed Johnny a large envelope. Johnny placed the envelope on the table in front of him. He looked around at the Bonanni family men: the underboss, captain, and others in high-ranking positions. An entire group of losers, Johnny thought. Then he placed his hand on top of the envelope.

"This is for the Bonanni family. It's a token of our generosity." Johnny pushed the envelope to the Bonanni family underboss, who flicked his toothpick on the floor and tore open the envelope to look inside. Satisfied, he gave Harry Bonanni a quick nod.

"I believe we got peace," Harry said, extending his hand to Johnny.

Johnny shook Harry's hand and stood up. "Big Paulie will make sure that you get a percentage of the profits moving forward." Both men sat down again. Johnny looked into Harry's eyes. "Just one other thing. I'd like to know who killed Scary Joey. Is he here with us today?"

Harry shook his index finger at Johnny and smiled a tobacco-stained, toothy smile that made Johnny want to rip Harry's head off and shit down his neck. "That's real good, Johnny. Nah, we don't know nobody who killed Scary Joey. It wasn't anyone from our family."

Johnny rose to his feet and turned to his family. "Let's go."

Chapter Ninety-Eight

T he next night, the Morano family enjoyed an early dinner in New York at one of Johnny's favorite restaurants. Afterward, they went back to the hotel and played cards, something they enjoyed doing together. At seven that evening, the men got into a rented car and drove to Brooklyn.

They entered the restaurant swiftly, and Tony moved to the front of the group. He positioned his gun expertly, and a bullet struck Harry Bonanni between the eyes. Tony turned the gun to Harry's underboss and shot him through the throat. Tony gestured to Vincent, who walked over and cut Harry's pants away. Just as Johnny had instructed, Tony reached into his pocket and rolled up three one hundred-dollar bills. Then he bent down and shoved the money up Harry's ass.

"There ya go, ya greedy prick...buy yourself somethin' real nice in hell." Tony sneered, thinking of Scary Joey.

The other two men who had been sitting with Harry stood off to the side of the room watching. These two men, trusted Bonanni family members, had easily turned on Harry and the underboss when Johnny promised them a chance at heading up the family. In fact, it was the two Bonanni mobsters who'd made sure Harry and the underboss were in the restaurant at the exact time Johnny had instructed.

Johnny stood over Harry's half-naked body, a lit cigar still dangling from his lifeless lips. He hacked up phlegm and spat on the younger man. Then Tony and the others walked out of the restaurant as casually as they had walked in. There were no other people dining there that evening, just as it had been planned. Johnny patted Tony on the back as they got into the rented car. Tony was oddly delighted and mildly irritated. It was the first time that Johnny had even acknowledged him in a positive way.

"You did very good tonight, Tony."

Feeling satisfied, Tony smiled. "I wish those dickheads were still alive so I could kill those fuckers all over again. I would've liked to torture that fuckin' Harry Bonanni to death."

"What about those two assholes we left alive in there that saw what Tony done, Mr. M.?" Vincent asked.

"They'll keep their mouths shut. Given that they helped set up the other two for us to kill, they have no choice. They'd be seen as traitors by the Bonanni family. There wouldn't be a place they could hide."

Johnny and Big Paulie knew there was always a chance that people could talk. However, they didn't let that slim chance of betrayal ruin their good feeling. The Bonanni family hadn't been upstanding since Harry had taken over as boss. Now, with Harry out of the way, Johnny and other bosses on the East Coast could help rebuild the Bonanni family. Harry Bonanni had been a renegade, void of charisma, sophistication, and all other qualities essential in a godfather of a crime family. Harry was going to the place that suited him most...a grave.

The men arrived back in Philadelphia just before midnight. Tony went straight to his apartment, the anticipation of seeing Kate gave him a warm feeling in his heart and his groin. When he entered the apartment, it was dark and quiet. He moved slowly to the bedroom, where he dropped his clothes onto the floor and crawled under the covers next to her.

Tony rubbed the back of her neck, moving his large hand down to her thighs. Kate moaned as she awakened to his soft caresses.

"I'm glad you're back. How come you didn't have to stay longer?" Kate rasped.

"We took care of business quicker than we thought."

Kate stretched, and her eyes closed.

Tony snuggled closer to Kate and listened to the steady rhythm of her breathing. He never in a million years would've thought he would find a woman like Kate. As Tony lay next to her, breathing in her sweet scent, his skin tingled, and his heart rate hurried. Tony knew, without a doubt, he'd found the love of his life. The only woman he'd ever love.

Chapter Ninety-Nine

The following week Tony heard Johnny in his office as he walked into the Morano house. "How the fuck did this happen? Find out who opened their fucking mouth!" Johnny yelled.

"We already know who told 'em," Big Paulie said. "Some of the boys heard one of the Bonanni captains is looking for revenge on whoever killed Harry."

Salvatore walked into his father's office with Tony and Vincent behind him. "What's going on with the Bonannis? Do you think the two assholes that help set up Harry turned?"

"No," Johnny said, "Big Paulie was just telling me it was the waiter who was working at the restaurant that night. One fucking waiter in the whole place, and he had to be the sonofabitch who would sing."

"Well, I understand they tortured the asshole before he told 'em what he knew. Now he's a one-handed prick." Big Paulie chuckled. "They cut his fuckin' lips off too for not comin' to 'em sooner with the information."

Big Paulie turned to Tony. "Look, ya gotta watch your back. One of those douchebags is gonna be lookin' for ya."

"The waiter don't even know who I am," Tony said, his stomach filled with iron butterflies.

"Big Paulie heard through some of his old friends that are still working in the Bonanni family. They know, Tony. The guy who wants revenge knows it was you. We're working with the two guys that set Harry up, trying to put this whole thing to bed," Johnny explained.

"So whata we do now?" Tony asked, worried about what would happen to Kate if he was killed.

"Johnny's got surveillance on ya. Ya ain't gonna be nowhere wit'out the family. Besides, Salvatore and Vincent are stickin' around ya too. Just to make sure you're OK," Big Paulie said.

The news put Tony in a dark mood. The veins in his forearms were pulsing, and his jaw was tightly clenched. He didn't like being threatened; he had given up fear a long time ago. He thought about how to kill the man out to get him.

For the next several weeks, Tony remained on high alert. Yet there were no attempts of violence against him. Shortly before Thanksgiving he ran into Big Paulie who was sitting outside of a small café in the Italian Market.

"Do we know anythin'? I'm tired of walkin' around waitin' for this asshole to find me," Tony said.

Big Paulie took a sip of his cappuccino. "Johnny's been talkin' to one of the Bonanni captains 'bout the whole revenge thing. Sounds like the Bonanni family is pretty fuckin' happy that those two assholes are gone. We don't think ya got nothin' to worry 'bout. They promised Johnny that if anythin' bubbled up over Harry's death, they'd take care of it."

Tony kicked at a small stone in the street. "And ya believe 'em?"

"Yeah, we think it's gonna be all right," Big Paulie said casually.

"Oh yeah? Would Johnny feel the same way if it was him bein' threatened instead of me?"

Big Paulie placed his cup on the table next to him and glared at Tony. "Listen, I told ya what I know. Ya don't wanna go 'round questionin' Johnny. Ya understand me?"

Tony drew a long breath. "Sure, I get it, but I don't feel so good 'bout all this shit."

"Stop worryin', will ya? I'll let ya know when ya gotta be concerned."

With the immediate threat avoided, Tony was cautiously optimistic. The information that Big Paulie had shared at least let him breathe a little easier. With a small sense of relief, he stopped at a flower stand on his way home and bought Kate a small bouquet of flowers. It had been a long, stressful couple of weeks, and he'd been very distant with Kate, and he knew his behavior had made her worry.

Tony walked into the apartment with a smile on his face. It was time for a small celebration as the dark veil of retaliation lifted.

Chapter One Hundred

Over the next month, Tony fell back into his normal routine but still kept up his guard. He lived two lives. It often made him feel like he was two people. He was madly in love with Kate, and they shared special, gentle times together. Then on the street, he was a mobster who worked for Johnny Morano performing horrible acts. His mixed emotions were always battling inside of him. It was his persistent struggle between good and evil.

Kate had been working at Osteria, and in early November, she trained as a waitress. The owner had cut a deal with Salvatore that he would let Kate start her training earlier than the normal six months he required of his workers. Part of the deal was that Kate must keep some of her kitchen duties. She had to stay after the restaurant closed to clean up. That she didn't mind, but taking out the trash at the end of the night was one pesky task that Kate hated the most, though she didn't dare complain.

It was a Saturday night, four days before Christmas. Kate had planned a romantic dinner for Tony. They had already accepted invitations to go to Donata and Ruth's on Christmas Eve and to attend a big party at the Moranos' on Christmas day. It was Kate's one night off before the holiday, and this was their last chance to share a quiet Christmas dinner.

Tony didn't get home until close to nine o'clock that evening. When he opened the apartment door, the aroma of turkey and mashed potatoes softly strummed his senses. He inhaled deeply, and his mouth watered. He walked into the living room looking for Kate, but she wasn't there, so he moved on to the bedroom. The bedroom door was closed, and he grabbed the knob. It was locked.

"Kate?" Tony said, in a hushed voice.

Kate slowly opened the door and gave him a bright smile. "Hello, handsome," she purred. "Would you like to come in?"

Tony smiled with his eyes and stepped forward. Kate took several steps backward into their bedroom. He took one long stride forward to erase the distance between them. He put his hands around her waist and pulled her to him, taking in a long whiff of her smell. "You're gorgeous." Tony closed his eyes to savor the warm feeling running through his core.

Kate put her arms around his neck. "Thank you. You're very handsome."

Tony bent his neck and met her lips. His fingertips skimmed over her jaw as he tried to control his urge to kiss her again. His hand reached out and softly followed along her curly, blond hair until it found Kate's shoulder. He gently drew her to him. He kissed her again as he ran his hand down the small of her back.

When they parted, Kate giggled. "We better eat. I know that look. No time for that right now; our dinner will burn."

Tony kissed Kate on the cheek. He looked deep into her eyes. He was immersed in the person he loved, the person he would die for, if necessary. Tony finally relented and followed Kate into the kitchen. Together they got everything set on the table, and when they were finished eating, they did the dishes.

Kate was scrubbing a pan that she'd cooked the turkey in. "Jingle bells, jingle bells..." she sang.

"Jingle all da way," Tony sang, joining in.

Together they finished cleaning as they sang Christmas carols. It was a perfect evening. Later that night, Tony and Kate walked into their bedroom. The room was dark. Kate crossed the room and plugged a cord into the outlet in the wall. The bedroom lit up with small white lights she had hung over their bed. It gave the room a romantic glow. Kate turned on soft music and went back to where Tony was standing.

"Would you like to dance?"

Tony took Kate into his arms, and they swayed to the soothing sound of the music. He leaned in and kissed her gently, and as he did, Tony slid his hand over her ass. Kate subtly pushed her pelvis closer to his.

"How do you like my Christmas lights?"

"Yeah, I like 'em real good. They make me horny."

"You're such a pig. Do you want to make love to me?"

Tony held Kate away so he could gaze into her face. "What's goin' on here? Ya tryin' to seduce me or somethin'?"

"Something like that. You know, a girl has needs."

Kate took Tony's hand and led him over to their bed. She unbuttoned his shirt, and as the fabric fell away inch by inch, she kissed his chest until she reached his navel. As Kate undid his belt buckle, Tony unzipped the back of her dress, which fell to the floor effortlessly. Kate stood before him in a soft pink bra, thong, and garter belt—something she had bought for the occasion with some of her tip money.

Kate's eyes begged him as he stepped out of his pants.

"You're beautiful, Kate."

Tony reached around and unsnapped her bra. As she slid it down her arms, Tony took one of her breasts in his hand and gently laid her on the bed. He kissed her passionately and then fluttered his tongue down her abdomen until he reached her thighs. Tony clenched the top of her thong with his teeth and slowly slid it past her thighs. He kissed the tops of her legs until he was gently licking her inner thighs—first the right inner thigh, then the left, and back again. His tongue grazed between her legs as he alternated his attention from leg to leg. His mouth finally settled in. His lips and tongue swayed gently between her legs. As his tongue floated over her flesh, as lightly as a feather, Tony softly eased his fingers inside of her. When he had Kate on the verge of orgasm, he stopped and moved back up to find her mouth. They shared a hungry, lust-induced kiss. Kate's hand found its way between Tony's legs, his erect penis waiting for her. Tony opened his eyes.

"Thanks for tonight, Kate. It was real special. Best Christmas ever."

She nodded and guided Tony inside of her. When it was over, they lay wrapped in each other's arms. Tony wished he could bottle his feelings of the evening so that later, when he needed them, he could use them to get through bad days.

Under the small lights that Kate had hung over their bed, the couple listened to mellow tunes on the radio. Kate snuggled in closer to Tony as she slid her hand across his inner thighs, again causing an instant stir in both of them.

"I love ya so much, Kate."

"Till the end," she murmured.

Chapter One Hundred One

T ony was sitting across from Salvatore and Vincent in the kitchen of the Morano house.

"What kinda work we got today?" Tony asked.

"Not sure," Salvatore began. "My father has been locked in his office all morning with Big Paulie and a couple of his captains. He said we need to stay here until they're finished."

"Someday I wanna be one of the guys in there makin' the decisions," Vincent said.

Tony nodded in agreement.

"I guess we'll see how it goes. I hope to take my father's place one day, and you two can be my bitches," Salvatore said, a cocky smile plastered on his face.

"That's real fuckin' funny, Sal," Tony said.

"Don't call me Sal."

"Oh hell, get a grip, Sally," Tony replied.

Salvatore gave Tony a grim look. "Keep that shit up and I'll tell Kate what an asshole you are."

At the mere mention of Kate's name, Tony smiled.

"Speakin' of broads," Vincent said, "we're makin' some decent money now. Me and Sal here need to go out and impress some ladies. Sweep them off of their feet. I wanna find myself a nice girl, get her knocked up, buy a house, and have her wait on me hand and foot."

"You're a Neanderthal," Salvatore chided.

"See, now why ya gotta talk so weird? Ya been talkin' weird since the day we met ya wit' all your fancy words and shit. Why can't ya just talk like a normal human bein'?" Tony said.

"I don't talk weird. Maybe if either of you actually read a book, you might know what I'm talking about..."

"Maybe we think you're a Neanderthal," Vincent joked.

"Oh yeah? So tell me then, what's a Neanderthal?"

Tony and Vincent looked at each other with blank expressions.

Salvatore took a bite of the toast sitting on the table in front of him. Then he picked up a napkin and wiped the crumbs from his mouth. "You're like a fucking caveman, Vincent...that's a Neanderthal."

"Oh, is that all it is? Why can't ya just say that, ya momma's boy?" Tony joked.

Johnny interrupted the banter when he opened his office door and called for the boys to join them in the office.

Tony entered the office last and stood with his back against the door.

"We found out that we have a drug dealer from West Philly pushing drugs on our streets. We have seen our profits drop; our dealers have been buying a lot less from us. We had a couple of our men investigate. Turns out that a dickhead named Ice thinks he can come into our neighborhood and squeeze in on a part of our business. He clearly doesn't understand who he is dealing with and that he will be stopped," Johnny growled. He paused for a moment to make eye contact with each of them. "Took us some time, but we know where this fucker lives. You three need to get a move on and take care of this asshole. I want you to do this the right way. This will be a message to the pushers who betrayed our trust in them and bought from another supplier."

Salvatore quickly acknowledged that they would handle the job. Tony was quite impressed this unknown Ice dude had the balls to try and steal from the mob.

In the early hours of the next morning, Vincent picked the lock on the back door of Ice's partially boarded-up row home. The stench of meth and alcohol smacked Tony in the face. The putrid aroma wedged into his sinuses. The boys crept through the house, guns aimed in front of them, and walked into the battered living room.

"What the fuck?" Ice said, awakened by the intrusion. The friend sitting next to him sat up on the edge of his chair with his hands slightly raised in the air.

"What the fuck is right," Tony said. "What the fuck were ya thinkin', ya dirt bag? Did ya really think ya could sell drugs to our dealers and get away wit' it?"

Ice smirked and jerked his arm out toward his gun sitting on the table next to him. Before he could grab hold of it, Tony fired the first shot into Ice's chest. Ice's body slammed against the back of the sofa, sending foam and blood flying through the air. Then Salvatore pointed his gun at Ice's friend and partner who was getting to his feet.

Salvatore shot a bullet into Coal's thigh and then he and Tony stepped closer. Tony took off his belt and turned his attention back to Ice, who was gasping for air. He slipped the belt around Ice's neck. Tony tightened and held the belt in place as Ice's eyes bulged from their sockets. The wound in his chest debilitated him, and he couldn't fight against Tony's overpowering strength. When Ice's body went limp and Tony had watched the life drain from his eyes, he released the belt. Salvatore walked over to Ice's partner, who was lying against the sofa. He bent over and pulled his knife from under his pant leg.

Salvatore glared at Coal with his teeth clenched together. "You two thought you'd get away with dicking around in Mafia business. You should've known better than that."

Salvatore plunged the knife into Coal's stomach and pulled upward until his guts spilled out. Before leaving, the boys searched the rest of the row home to make sure no one else was there. They left through the back door as calmly as they had come in.

In the silence of Salvatore's car, Tony looked at his two friends. "It's a good thing Big Paulie gave us those silencers. No tellin' who mighta heard the gun blasts without 'em."

Salvatore looked back at Tony.

"My pop said there would be a little something extra in our paycheck this week if we pulled this off."

"Really? Wow, man, that's great," Tony said, enthusiastically, "Kate and I can use the money. We're trying to save up, so one day we can buy our own house." Tony looked out the window as the dumpy neighborhood buzzed by in a blur. "Ya know, those two were defenseless against us. When I was young, I always wished I could protect myself against all the assholes in the world."

Tony gave Vincent a nudge.

"Hey, I told ya I was sorry a million times. I didn't know any better. If I knew ya was such an asshole, I woulda kicked your ass harder," Vincent teased.

"Yeah, well, I ain't never gonna forget how much I wanted to get even wit' people," Tony said.

"And what's your point?" Salvatore asked.

"My point is that now I'm in a place in my life where I can protect myself and the people I love. It ain't like killin' makes me happy, but it does help me get rid of some of the anger I got inside. Sometimes, though, I wonder if I'm gonna go to hell for the bad shit I've done. I mean, we do what we gotta do for the business, but does it ever get to ya?"

"Fuck no," Vincent said.

Salvatore hesitated. "I grew up with a father who did crazy shit all the time. I guess it became normal to me. I try not to think about it too much. You shouldn't either."

"Yeah, I know you're right," Tony mumbled.

"That's your pussy ass comin' out," Vincent teased.

Tony leaned over the backseat and punched Vincent lightly in the leg. Vincent curled up to avoid the punch. "Who's the pussy ass now?" Tony said.

***

Early that morning Johnny and his top men waited for the three boys to return.

"Everything taken care of?" Johnny asked.

Salvatore nodded.

"Follow us," Big Paulie said to the boys.

Tony's heart pattered as they followed the group of ten men into the basement. The men formed a circle around the boys.

Tony's eyes remained fixed on Johnny. Johnny's expression was dark, and his lips were pinched tightly together. Tony didn't know what to expect. The only comfort he had was that Salvatore stood in the circle beside him, and he thought, Surely Johnny won't hurt his own son, would he?

"You boys have shown great respect and loyalty to the family. You have been following the instructions we have given to you, without question. That is commendable. This has proven to us that you will do whatever is needed to ensure the success and safety of this family. As the head of the Morano family, I am offering you the opportunity to become a more formal member of our society," Johnny said.

In the middle of the circle of men, next to the boys, was a small table that held a knife and a gun.

"Salvatore, step forward."

Tony watched in fascination as Salvatore got close to his father.

"You see the gun and knife on that table?" Johnny said, looking over at them.

"Yes, Pop."

"Would you use either of those to protect any man in this room?"

"You know I would, Pop."

Johnny took his son's hands in his own and picked up the knife from the table. "Open your right hand, Salvatore."

Salvatore obeyed. Johnny sliced the tip of his son's trigger finger with the sharp blade. Then he took a small card with a picture of a saint on it, wiped Salvatore's blood with it, and laid it in his son's palm.

"I'm going to light this card on fire. As it's burning, I want you to juggle the card between both hands. As you do this, you are to say, 'May I burn like this card in hell if I ever betray this family.' You are to repeat those words until the card is nothing but ash."

Salvatore did as he was instructed, and when he was finished, Johnny put his hands over his son's hand and rubbed the ashes into his palms.

Tony's mouth hung open. He didn't know what all of it meant, but he knew he was about to become a part of something much bigger than himself. He felt weightless, and butterflies swooshed around in his belly. Then Johnny turned to him and performed the same ritual.

When it was all over, the three boys joined the circle of men.

"You are now a part of our family. This family has something much stronger than a bloodline. We have been cast together by our conviction to this society. Let me be clear, though—no matter what is happening in your life, you are expected to stop, turn your back on whatever it is, and come when this family calls you," Johnny explained.

Tony looked into Johnny's eyes and nodded. He finally felt like he was on his way to a much better life. A feeling of love and hate for Johnny ripped through him. Collecting himself, he pushed his feelings for Johnny aside, and a profound sense of allegiance to the family took root in his soul.

Chapter One Hundred Two

During the months that followed the initiation into the mob, Tony and Kate enjoyed a few more luxuries with his increased pay. They ate dinner out once a month and could even afford to buy nicer cuts of meat from the butcher. Before they knew it, summer had arrived, and it was the year they would both turn eighteen. Kate was still working at Osteria and had made herself valuable to the owner, who now trusted her to close the restaurant when he was busy. Kate liked that the owner trusted her and wished the new responsibility had come with more money than he had given to her. Life seemed to move along in a quiet pattern until the evening of June 4.

Tony walked into the apartment just before ten in the evening to find Kate sitting at the kitchen table hunched over a soda.

"Somethin' the matter?"

Kate looked up at him, the flesh around her eyes thick with worry. "You better sit down."

Tony pulled a chair next to Kate and sat. He put his arm over her shoulder. "What's wrong? Are ya sick or somethin'?" he said, thinking about how Kate's mother had died of cancer.

"No, I'm not sick," Kate's voice caught in her throat, and she shut her eyes hard for a moment. "I'm pregnant."

"Wait. What?" Tony said, pushing his chair back slightly.

Kate looked at him, unblinking. "I'm pregnant."

"I'm gonna be a father?" he asked in a tight voice.

Kate cried. "Yes, I'm sorry."

"Sorry? What the hell are ya sorry 'bout? I'm gonna be a father!" he yelled with joy.

Kate felt her tense muscles relax. "You're not mad?"

Tony shook his head feverishly. "I'm happy as a pig in shit. We're gonna have a baby."

Kate giggled. "But we're so young, and we don't have money for a baby."

"Who the fuck cares 'bout that? We'll figure it out," Tony assured her. He had another thought and approached his question carefully. "I thought bein' on the pregnancy pill stopped ya from gettin' pregnant?"

"It's a birth control pill, and it does stop me from getting pregnant. Remember last month when I had the flu, and I puked for a couple of days straight?"

"Yeah, that was nasty, and I was sure as shit happy that I didn't get it too. What's that gotta do wit' it?"

Kate sighed. "I stopped taking my birth control that whole week because I figured we weren't having sex anyway. I thought as soon as I started it again, I would be protected, but I found out that's not how it works. So here we are!"

Tony pulled Kate's chair out from the kitchen table and knelt on the floor in front of her. He rested his head on her belly. "Hello, baby, I'm your father. I swear I'm gonna be the best father in the world. I ain't gonna be nothin' like that rotten sonofabitch that's supposed to be my father. Anyway, I'm gonna take care of you and your mother. Ya ain't gotta worry about nothin'."

Kate lifted Tony's head from her abdomen. "You're really happy about this."

"Kate, I ain't never done nothin' good wit' my life so far. This here," he said patting her belly, "this is the first thing I've done right. I wanna be a good man, the kinda man that takes care of his family. Ya know, protects 'em and treats 'em like they're somethin'. I'm gonna teach my son how to do things, and I ain't never gonna let other kids pick on 'im either."

Kate's eyes were dreamy, almost glazed over. "What if it's a girl?"

"Oh man, if it's a girl, then look out. She ain't datin' till she's at least eighteen, and I don't want no boys knockin' at the door for her either. Boys are little fuckin' bastards, and all they wanna do is get into girls' pants. I'll make sure she's got all princess stuff and dolls to play wit'. You can take her to get her nails painted when she's older and teach her how to be girly. Look, Kate, I don't care if it's a girl or a boy—all I know is that I'm gonna love ya and love my kid forever. Gives me somethin' to feel good about after a hard day's work," he admitted.

Kate knew that Tony strong-armed people for Johnny Morano. She wasn't sure what extent he would go to nor whether he'd ever killed another human, but she was certain that Tony did things she would never have approved of. She asked him no questions, and he never volunteered what he was doing for the Moranos. Kate had decided long ago that the only way she could live with what Tony did on the streets was to never know about it.

"Hey!" Tony blurted.

Kate jumped in her chair.

"Sorry. But I was just thinkin' that we should get married. Ya know—make it all official and shit. Whata ya say? Will ya marry me?" Tony waited with anticipation.

Kate leaned in and kissed him on the lips. "Yes, I'll definitely marry you."

"Let the Tony Bruno family begin," he proclaimed.

That night as Kate lay sleeping next to him, Tony thought about all the things he'd do for his child. His joy and happiness grew with each passing thought. His life was turning out better than he ever could have expected.

Chapter One Hundred Three

K ate stood beside Tony as he knocked on the front door. His mother, Teresa, opened it slowly, peaking through her swollen eyes trying to adjust her sight so she could make out the large figure at her door.

"Ma?" Tony said and stepped into the house.

"Oh, Tony," Teresa cried, clinging to him.

"What happened to ya, Ma?"

They turned to the footsteps coming down the stairs from the second floor. Tony looked back at his mother, and she quickly looked away.

"What the fuck do ya want?" Carmen snapped.

Tony charged his father when he reached the bottom of the staircase, grabbing him around the neck and slamming Carmen into the plaster wall.

Tony's teeth were bared, like a German shepherd about to defend his owner. "This is the shit ya do to my mother, ya fuckin' loser. Only pussies hit women."

Carmen's fist came up and nailed Tony in the sternum. The breath gushed out of him, and he was bent over when his father kneed him in the face. Blood splattered as his nose broke. Tony went to his hands and knees. Carmen pulled back his right leg and shot it forward toward his son's gut, but Tony caught Carmen's leg in midair, and he flopped on his ass.

Tony pounced on him, sat on Carmen's chest, and punched him in the face. The sight of his father's blood fueled his rage and quenched his animal instincts. His desire to kill his father took hold of him like a drug. Tony kept punching him even after his father was unconscious. He only stopped when Kate put her hand on his shoulder, and he jerked around instinctively to go after his next victim. Kate jumped back, and Tony stared at her like a wild boar until she came into focus. Tony got up from the floor, straightened his shirt, and headed into the kitchen. The women followed.

Tony grabbed a handful of paper towels, holding the wad against his nose. Blood was running down his chin and onto his shirt. Teresa quickly moved around him, grabbed a dish towel, and stuffed it with ice. She approached Tony slowly.

363

"Sit down," she said.

Tony sat, watching his mother.

"Put your head back," Teresa said.

Teresa rested the dishtowel over Tony's nose and rushed back to the sink to fetch a wet rag to wipe away the blood drying on Tony's chin and neck.

Everything had happened so quickly. Tony watched Kate and then his mother. He took in the sight of Teresa. Her condition was sad...she was small and grim. Teresa's eyes were black and blue. She had bruises on the left side of her face. The neckline of her housecoat, which was several sizes too big, revealed the cuts and bruises on her collarbone. His eyes followed the neckline to her left arm, which was peppered with finger marks, dark purple tones that stood like ugly, menacing ghosts under her skin. Tony saw how much she'd aged over the years since he'd last seen her. His father's foul moods had taken a toll on her.

Tony lifted his head, holding the ice over his nose. "Ma, this is Kate. She's my girl."

As if noticing Kate for the first time, Teresa hurried over to her. "Kate, nice to meet ya, hon. Sorry it's under such bad conditions." Teresa turned back to Tony. "Ya grew a lot since I seen ya last. When was that?"

"When I turned fourteen, almost four years ago."

Teresa gasped and covered her mouth with her hand. "Sweet baby Jesus, I forgot you're gonna be eighteen soon."

"Yeah. That's why we came over. Kate and me are gettin' married. I need my birth certificate so I can get a license."

Teresa covered her face with her hands and wept.

"What's wrong wit' ya?"

"Oh, Tony. I ain't done right by ya. I put ya out when ya was just a boy. Your father...your father...he wouldn't let me help ya. Ya know?" she begged.

Tony went to his mother and put his arms around her. Teresa's body melted into him.

"I know, Ma. Ya did the best that ya could. I fuckin' hate that bastard. He's gonna rot in hell someday."

Teresa gently pulled away from Tony. "I shoulda been stronger. I shoulda told him ya weren't leavin'. I see that now, but back then...Macie was younger, and I didn't know where we would go. I'm sorry."

Tony patted his mother on the back. "It's all right, Ma. Hey, listen—I got some good news."

Tony walked over to Kate and put his arm over her shoulder. "Me and Kate here are gonna have a baby. You're gonna be a grandma," he said, trying to cheer her up.

"Wait. What? I'm gonna be a grandma? Oh, thank you, little baby Jesus. I've been prayin' that you'd be safe. Now here ya are, gettin' married and havin' a baby."

Teresa walked across the kitchen and stood next to Kate. "Can I touch your belly?"

"Sure."

"We're gonna be family now," Teresa said to Kate, tearfully.

Kate looked back to the front door when she heard Carmen stir. Her stomach felt like grasshoppers were inside. She was worried about Tony and his father having another fight. Tony followed the moaning sound coming from his father. Tony wanted to get Kate out of his parents' house quickly, before another fight broke out and he ended up killing his father.

Chapter One Hundred Four

"**M**a, can ya go get my birth certificate? We gotta get goin' before I have to kill that no-good asshole," he said, pointing at his father.

Once Carmen's head cleared, he pushed himself off of the floor and rose to his feet slowly. He shuffled to his reclining chair in front of the television.

"Teresa!" Carmen yelled. "Bring me a fuckin' beer."

Teresa wrapped ice in a clean towel, grabbed a beer from the refrigerator, and rushed into the living room. She handed the items to Carmen and quickly rushed toward the stairs for Tony's birth certificate. When Teresa was gone, Tony and Kate walked into the living room.

"You're nothin' but street trash," Carmen said. "Ya might fool that stupid bitch, but ya don't fool me." He lifted the beer can to his lips.

"Don't ever call my mother a bitch. Ya know, you're a real fuckin' loser. Ya always told me I was the pansy, the pixie, the pussy, but that's you. Ya don't give a shit about anybody but yourself. Why do ya bother stayin' around here? Why don't cha just slither off into some shithole bar where ya belong?" Tony said.

Carmen stood, and Tony stepped into his father's challenging stance. The two faced off, chest to puffy chest. Tony was a couple of inches bigger than Carmen now and had youth on his side. They stared each other down, each waiting for the other to make a move. Finally, Carmen turned away and walked back to his recliner.

"Yeah, that's what I thought," Tony said quietly.

Carmen looked away from the television to address Kate. He took a good long look at the girl. She was tall and slender. Her blond hair hung just below her shoulders in soft, silky ringlets. Her blue eyes sparkled with youth. Her plump, pink lips parted to reveal a dazzling smile as she nervously looked back at him.

"You're not Italian," Carmen stated.

"No, no, I'm not. That doesn't matter, though. Tony and I love each other, and we treat each other well," she answered sharply.

Carmen glared at Tony. "Ha! You got yourself a real winner here, ya stupid asshole. This girl ain't gonna be wit' ya long...she's too good for ya."

Kate was visibly rattled. Her lips puckered as she gave Carmen a hateful stare.

Tony let out a sharp laugh. "Ignore 'im, Kate. He's just a miserable old man. Ain't never did nothin' good wit' his life and is jealous of anyone who does. You should go find yourself a bottle of booze to drown in."

Tony's body was rigid, and his eyes were narrow as he waited for his father to respond.

"Tony, please stop it right now," Teresa interrupted. "I don't need any more shit." They all turned to look at Teresa, who was nervously twisting her hands together.

Kate put her hand on Tony's upper arm, and he flinched at the touch. When he looked over, Kate was smiling at him with adoration, which brought him out of his hate trance.

"Yeah, we gotta go anyway." Tony turned his attention to his mother. "Ma, I'll be back. I better not see a fuckin' mark on your body when I see ya again," he said and looked over at Carmen, who smirked at him.

"Don't cha worry; I'll be fine. Ya just make sure ya come back and see me," Teresa murmured.

"Who do ya think ya are, woman? Ya don't invite people into my house wit'out my permission."

Teresa flinched.

Kate felt the heat rise up in her chest. "Stop it, Mr. Bruno. You're so mean. Just stop picking on her."

"Listen, darlin'," Carmen replied, "don't go thinkin' you're a big shot 'cause your little boyfriend over there is a low-life mobster."

"Tony is not a lowlife—he is respected..."

"That's right. Tony only gets people to respect 'im 'cause they got to. He's a fuckin' mobster. Ya either respect 'im or he'll whack ya. Ain't that right, Tony?" Carmen slurred his words, making sloppy, drunk gestures.

Tony turned to Kate as her anger grew. Her beautiful ivory skin was splotched with red patches.

"We oughta go now," Tony said to Kate.

Kate remained motionless. Her brain was telling her legs to move, but her feet seemed glued to the floor. It took a few moments before she composed herself.

"We'll see ya soon?" Teresa asked them both hopefully.

"Sure," Kate said, noncommittally.

Tony's stomach was churning, and the bile burned at the lining of his belly. The visit had not gone as he had expected. For whatever reason, he'd built up a happy reunion in his mind. Tony gave his mother a quick hug and shot an agitated look at his father. As soon as the couple was outside, Tony turned to Kate.

"I'm sorry. Do ya still love me even though my father is a fuckin' dipshit, wife-beating, drunk, no-good piece of smelly garbage?"

Kate nuzzled against his chest. "I can care less about your father. He's not worth a pint of piss. Your mother is a very nice lady. We need to make sure to stay in touch with her. I'm afraid for her, Tony."

"Yeah, I know. He's gotten worse over the years, and my mother seems to be a lot weaker than she used to be."

"We need to help her," Kate said.

"Ya mean like she helped me when she let my father throw me outta the house five years ago? I was thirteen fuckin' years old, Kate. I didn't know how to survive on my own," he ranted.

"But you figured it out. You're stronger than anyone I know. Your mother is an empty woman. There's nothing in her eyes except sorrow and pain," she argued.

"So ya don't care that she threw me out?"

"Yes, I care. But I also believe in forgiveness—it's way more powerful than hate."

"See, there's another reason I love ya. Ya gotta real good heart."

Kate giggled. "Between the two of us, our baby is going to have the biggest heart of anyone who ever lived. We're gonna have the best kid ever."

Tony beamed with pride. He knew Kate was right. Their baby would be perfect.

Chapter One Hundred Five

T ony and Kate were married a month later in a small church. There were less than a dozen people present, including Teresa and Tony's sister, Macie. The couple had written their own vows.

The priest turned to Tony. "You can now say the wedding vows you wrote for Kate."

Tony pulled a small piece of paper from his pocket. He took Kate's hand in his own and looked into her eyes. "Kate, I promise to love ya more than I love anythin'. My life was real fucked up, and then I met ya. Ya made everything better and happier for me. I swear to take care of ya and our baby real good too. From this day forward, I will make sure I clean up my own dishes and make ya dinner once in a while. I will always be wit' cha, even after we have a fight 'cause I pissed ya off about stupid shit that ain't even worth fightin' about. You'll always be my best friend and my girl. I'll love ya till the end."

The couple looked at the priest, whose face was scrunched up for a second before he turned to Kate. "You can say your wedding vows to Tony now."

"Tony, you saved me from being alone in this world. You have given me joy and came through on all of your promises. I want to spend the rest of my life being by your side, taking trips to the ocean and walking hand in hand on the beach. You're my best friend, my only love, and my soul mate. I will always be there for you, when things are great and not so great. You mean the world to me, and I'm honored that you picked me to be your wife and mother of your child. Till the end."

The couple looked at the priest again. He looked down at the small mound hidden beneath the white dress she was wearing, and his eyes opened wide. "I see," he said.

After the ceremony they all went back to the bakery, where Donata was hosting the small group for the celebration. Salvatore and Vincent had paid for a buffet of hot pork sandwiches, roasted potatoes, and salad. Donata had made them a beautiful wedding cake that stood in the middle of the bakery floor. It was an intimate affair, exactly the way Tony and Kate had envisioned it.

The small group had brought the couple gifts. Even Teresa had managed to squirrel away fifty dollars to give to them. Tony was content. He'd never imagined finding a woman who would want to spend the rest of her life with him. Now he had two people, his wife and child.

After the small celebration, Tony drove Kate to Atlantic City in Salvatore's car. He and Kate were staying overnight in a small motel a few blocks from the ocean. The couple had made several day trips back to the sea whenever they could get away. It was their special place where they had peace and love in their hearts. Tony had saved just enough money for one night at the motel and a nice dinner at a beef-and-beer restaurant that Vincent recommended.

That night, after they made love in the candlelight of their motel room, Tony ran his fingers gently through Kate's hair.

"We're married," he said.

Kate giggled. "Yes, I know. I was there."

Tony sighed. "I really love ya. I mean, there ain't too many women who would sign up to be wit' someone like me. Havin' to wake me up from nightmares and all. Not to mention workin' wit' me so we can make love like normal people do."

Kate turned to him. "You saved me from my real-life nightmare. When my mom got sick and I knew she would die, I was so scared that I would be all alone. It was the worst feeling in the world. But you stayed with me and made sure that I was all right even when you were living with the Slayers."

Tony ran his index finger between her breasts. "That's different. You gotta put up wit' me yelling and cryin' in my sleep like a scared kid. Makes me feel bad sometimes. Ya know?"

Kate kissed the tip of his nose. "Well, you're forgetting that it happens less and less. So every day your head is getting better. That's how you have to look at it."

"That's the thing about cha. Ya see things all happy and shit. Ya always see the good."

Kate laid her head on Tony's bare chest. "What's the point of seeing the bad in things? I mean, it only makes us feel crummy. And you know what? Things aren't always as bad as they seem. At first, when shit goes wrong, it seems like the end of the world. When my mom died, I thought I would never be happy again. But over time, I realized that being unhappy is just a toxic feeling that latches on and never lets go of you—makes it so hard to live, to feel alive."

"You're right."

"I always am," she said, giggling.

"Good night, Mrs. Bruno."

"Good night, Mr. Bruno."

Tony fell asleep peacefully, grateful that he had Kate to love.

Chapter One Hundred Six

Kate was three months pregnant. She was in the apartment lying on the bed with her legs straight in front of her. She groaned and held on to the small ball in her belly. She was trying to focus on the television, hoping that her morning sickness would subside. Tony was sitting on the chair next to her when he heard a knock at the apartment door.

Tony pulled the door open for Salvatore and Vincent. "Wassup?" he said, his eyes squinted and nose wrinkled, surprised to see them.

"We got some business to take care of in New York. One of the families wants to have a sit-down. Families all the way down in Florida are coming up for this one. It's going to be big," Salvatore said.

"Kate isn't feeling too good. She's gotta go to work in a couple of hours. She's lying on the bed. Can it wait?"

Vincent pushed his way into the kitchen. "Kate's sick 'cause she's carrying your kid," he joked.

"Yeah, she's got some morning sickness thing. Except it always hits her in the afternoon, so I don't know why she calls it morning sickness," Tony explained.

"She'll feel better in a couple of hours, just like she always does," Salvatore reminded him.

"I know. I just hate to leave her when she ain't feelin' good. How long will we be gone?"

"Just a day or two," Salvatore assured him.

On his way into the bedroom, Tony contemplated what to tell Kate about going to New York.

He entered the room with Salvatore and Vincent following.

Kate looked at all of them with a slight scowl on her face. "What is it?"

"Nothin', Kate." Tony sat on the edge of the bed next to her. "Somethin's come up. I gotta go to New York wit' the boys."

Kate thought about protesting, even begging him to stay with her, but she knew that Tony was doing his best to make a living. She was already three months pregnant and could only work for four or five more months before she'd have to take off. Still, Kate pouted and hung her head.

"Come on, Kate. It'll be all right. I'm gonna go to New York for a day or two, and then I'll come right back. I want ya to have Billy walk ya home tonight after work 'cause I ain't gonna be there to come and get cha."

Kate stared into space, not so much because Tony had to leave, but because another wave of nausea had crept up on her.

Tony gently slid his index finger under her chin and lifted her head toward him. He kissed her softly on the lips.

"I wish you didn't have to go," Kate muttered.

Tony made the sign of an X over his chest. "I swear, cross my fuckin' heart, hope to die that I'll be back before you even notice I'm gone."

"He's right, Kate," Salvatore offered. "If we get done quicker, we'll bring him right back."

"OK. But the sooner you come back, the better," she said to all of them.

Tony wrapped his muscular arms around her. Then he loosened his grip, leaned back, and rubbed the tiny bulge of her belly. "I'm gonna miss ya too, little baby."

"Good, then that means you'll rush home faster because you'll miss us so much." Kate smiled when she spoke, but there was an icy edge to her voice.

"You got it. Till the end, Kate."

Kate always lit up when Tony said that to her. "Till the end," she said.

Kate looked at Salvatore and then Vincent. "You two owe me...big time."

Salvatore bent down and kissed Kate on the forehead. "Don't be upset, Kate. We wouldn't have come for Tony if it wasn't important."

"Yeah, I know."

Salvatore's face lit up with an insanely sexy smile. "You're the best. I hope someday I find a woman just like you."

Kate blushed. "Thanks, Salvatore."

Salvatore nodded.

"See ya later, Kate," Vincent said, pushing Salvatore out of the way as he leaned over and gave her a kiss on the cheek.

"OK, Vincent. The same goes for you. Take care of my husband, do whatever you have to do in New York, and get him back here fast."

Once in the car, Tony squirmed in his seat; he was feeling fidgety leaving Kate alone. He wanted to experience her entire pregnancy. "What's so important in New York anyway?" he finally asked.

"These six families can be the start of new business partnerships for our family. The three of us need to be there in case it's a setup and any of them try to do something stupid to my father. It's our job to protect him."

Kate had walked over to the kitchen window to watch as Tony and his friends drove off. As the car vanished from view, she asked God to bring Tony home safely.

Chapter One Hundred Seven

At the restaurant that night, Kate was still fighting bouts of nausea. She was relieved at midnight when the last customer was gone and she was finishing her shift. Just as Tony had instructed, Billy, one of the cooks at the restaurant, would walk Kate home.

"Billy, I'm going to run the trash out, and then we can leave," Kate said.

"Sounds good. I'm gonna finish prepping for tomorra," Billy said, looking up from the vegetables he was cutting. "Hey, ya feelin' all right? Ya look a little green."

"Yeah, I'm fine. My morning sickness is back. I'm really nauseous. It comes and goes. I'll have some ginger ale before we leave."

Kate grabbed one of the trash bags and went out the side door into the alley where the Dumpsters were lined up. As she walked to the end of the alley, she felt the contents of her belly begin a slow crawl upward. Her stomach was churning, and waves of bile rose and fell in her gorge. She scanned the alley and thought about running back inside to the ladies' room but knew she'd never make it in time.

"Come on, baby Bruno, knock it off," Kate said aloud, rubbing her belly.

Kate took a deep breath and lifted the trash bag but quickly dropped it to the ground and hurled her dinner onto the ground. Stepping over her own puke, she moved to the side of the Dumpster. She retched again, and the sound of thick liquid splattering over the blacktop drummed in her ears.

"Fuck," Kate breathed. "Come on, enough is enough."

Kate straightened up and leaned against the Dumpster. The nausea was slowly subsiding. Then she heard a man at the entrance to the alley groaning. At first glance, Kate thought he was drunk, but as she focused on him, she saw the man had collapsed onto the ground beside his car. She inched her way to the car to help.

Before reaching him, she stopped and leaned against the wall of the brick building. She stood motionless for a moment, hoping the nausea that bubbled up in her throat would end. Oh no, Kate thought as she leaned over and heaved again. The sour taste of bile clung to her tongue and she spat a few times to get rid of it. The man groaned.

"Are you OK?" Kate called out.

The man slumped against the side of his car. Kate edged closer to the sedan. She kneeled down and looked at the older man. His large warm-brown eyes looked up at her pleadingly.

"Are you OK?" Kate asked again.

"Yes, yes, I'm perfectly fine. I have low blood sugar. It came on me quickly. I'm just sitting here for a minute until I can get up and grab the bottle of orange juice from the cooler on my backseat. I noticed that you are a little ill yourself," the man stated.

"Yes, a little. I'm pregnant. It's just morning sickness that hits me at all times except the mornings," she chuckled.

The older man smiled. "I remember when my wife was pregnant with our first child. She puked for the first six months. I didn't think she'd have another baby after that, but she did. In fact, she blessed me with three more. My wife wasn't sick with the other three like she was with the first one."

Kate smiled. "Well, hopefully I'll have the same luck as your wife."

The man attempted to get up from the ground. He was holding on to the door handle of the car, trying his best to hoist himself up. Kate watched for a moment and then put her hand out to help him, but he was too heavy for her to lift.

Kate put her hands to the car window and looked into the backseat where the cooler was sitting. "If you unlock the car, I'll grab an orange juice for you."

"Oh, that would be splendid. It's very kind of you."

With the car unlocked, Kate opened the back door and shimmied across the backseat to the other side of the car where the cooler sat.

"Aren't you just a wonderful young lady," the man said.

Inside the car Kate smiled; she loved to help others. That was the last thing Kate remembered before she felt the prick of a needle being inserted into the back of her thigh.

Chapter One Hundred Eight

When Kate woke up, she was disoriented. She had lost track of all time and place. She was sitting in a wooden chair in the middle of a dreary room. As her mind cleared, she looked around. The room was large. To her left was a boarded-up window, and to her right, abandoned pieces of broken furniture, a dresser, a rocking chair, and a nightstand. Dust covered every nook of the room. The floral wallpaper was split and peeled where the plaster had cracked from the floor to the ceiling. Still groggy, she tried to focus her eyes, but everything was blurry. Her limbs were lifeless and heavy. Kate willed herself to move, but her body wouldn't respond.

Kate tried to remember how she'd gotten there. She'd been at the restaurant. She remembered puking. There was a nice old man that she'd helped. Then, nothing—she couldn't remember a thing. After several minutes the fog inside her head lifted. Kate tried to move off of the chair only to realize she was restrained. Her heart fluttered in her chest as her brain signaled to her body she was in danger. The adrenaline quickly forced away any remnants of the drug that still lingered in her body. She pulled against the ropes that held her wrists and ankles securely in place.

"Help," Kate screamed weakly. "Somebody help me, please."

The man Kate had helped in the alley of the restaurant entered the old bedroom. Her heart paused. She couldn't inhale. She couldn't exhale. Her whole respiratory system seized. Her mind rejected the realization of what had happened, and her body felt like it was hit by a surge of electricity, fried and torn to shreds.

"Who are you? Why am I here?" Kate screeched.

"You're a foolish woman. A foolish, pregnant woman that trusted a stranger. You made everything much easier than I expected. I thank you for that," the man said, bowing in front of her.

Kate's insides quivered. Her chin trembled, and her eyelids blinked in rapid succession. Kate wrapped her hands around the arms of the chair, holding tight, until her fingers were numb.

"Now, let's see...where do I start? You can call me Carnie. That's what my friends call me. Since you and I are going to be very close, I think we can consider each other friends now."

"Carnie?" Kate mumbled.

"Yes, that's right."

"My husband is going to be looking for me. You need to let me go before he finds you."

As Kate spoke, her voice broke in and out. She was bordering on hysterics.

"Yes, your husband, Tony Bruno. I know who he is. He is the man who turned on the Slayers. My good friend had his tongue cut out because of Tony. Poor guy sounds like a complete idiot when he tries to speak. So back to your husband: he is in New York. Imagine my delight when I saw him get into his friend's car and drive away yesterday. One can never be certain if a person will make the decision you want them to. But I was certain that Tony would do whatever the mob wanted, even if it meant turning his back on his wife. You know, it's amazing the information you can acquire when you are friends with the right people. And of course..." He stopped and cleared his throat theatrically. "I know all the right people."

"I don't know what you're talking about. Please just let me go. I'm sure Tony can tell you that you're mistaken. He didn't do anything to your friend."

Carnie rubbed his chin with his thumb and index finger. "Do you really think I would believe a word that came out of Tony Bruno's mouth? That man is nothing more than a two-bit criminal who knows how to shoot a gun. He's a fake, a dirty piece of street trash that the mob uses to do the work that no one else is willing to do. He would have been better off staying with the Slayers."

Kate locked eyes with Carnie. "I don't care what you think my husband did to your friend, but whatever it is, you need to talk to him about it. I don't have any information to give you. I don't know anything. If you have a problem, you need to talk to Tony about it."

"Ha. Well, then please, let me give you some information. I mean, you seem to be at a disadvantage. Clearly, a woman who hasn't earned her husband's trust yet. Your husband, Tony, got the Morano family to bust him out of the Slayers. Now, just in case you don't know, the Slayers are a very powerful gang in North Philly. Anyway, one night, your husband got the Morano family to attack the Slayers just so he could get away. Several of their men died, but the head of the gang, Razor, well, he had his tongue cut out. Like I said, he can't speak too well; he grunts a lot. Anyway, Razor got in touch with me—we have strong ties from past dealings. Razor helped me out once when I was in a real jam. I owe him my life. So here I am to help him get even with your dumb husband."

Carnie's dead, icy voice sent a shiver up Kate's spine.

"Do you want money? I'm sure Tony will find you money if you let me go."

"No, I have plenty of money. I need something..." Carnie looked up to the ceiling, tapping his index finger on his chin, as if searching for his words... "other than money. What I need, money can't buy."

Chapter One Hundred Nine

T ony and the others had arrived at an old warehouse where one of the major New York crime families kept their stolen goods.

"Stay alert," Johnny said before they entered the building.

"Johnny, good to see you. Please sit down," said one of the New York bosses. Johnny sat while Tony, Salvatore, and Vincent stood behind him.

"Let's talk business," Johnny said with a forced smile.

Two hours later, the mob families left the warehouse. Johnny took his men to eat at Umberto's in Manhattan for dinner. Tony was happy that everything had been handled in one sitting so he could get back to Kate the next morning.

Tony arrived back to an empty apartment. He figured that Kate had run to the store so he settled down in the living room and turned on the television. A few hours later, when Kate hadn't returned, Tony started to worry. By then, Salvatore and Vincent had come back to the apartment to pick up Tony.

"Wassup?" Vincent asked when he saw Tony's pale face.

"Kate wasn't here when I got home, and she ain't back yet."

"Maybe she went out shoppin' or somethin'," Vincent offered casually.

"Nah. Somethin' ain't right. When Kate goes out, she does what she's gotta do and comes home. She likes bein' home," Tony countered. "I was just gonna call the restaurant."

He picked up the phone and pressed in the numbers. "Billy, its Tony. Ya walked Kate home from work last night, right?"

Billy coughed nervously. "She took the trash out and never came back in. I wanted to call ya but didn't know how to reach cha."

Tony dropped the phone and walked over to the windowsill in the kitchen. He picked something up and turned to his friends. "Somethin' bad has happened to Kate."

"Why? What did Billy tell ya?" Vincent asked.

"Billy never walked Kate home, and this here..." he said, pushing the object forward. "This ring belonged to Kate's mother. She never takes it off, not even to shower. Someone was in my apartment. They left it here for me to find—it's a callin' card."

Chapter One Hundred Ten

Twenty-four hours later, Kate slumped over in the wooden chair where she remained captive. Her arms and legs were stiff, and her ass was numb. She had vomited on herself repeatedly, and the smell of the aging bile intensified her nausea. She was dehydrated, and her head had a searing, pulsating pain so overwhelming it made her captivity feel like a secondary problem.

When Carnie finally came back into the bedroom, he was a carrying a dish with food and a glass of water. Carnie held the glass of water to her lips. Kate slurped and gulped at the glass, bobbing her head down to get the water into her quickly. The water provided instant relief to her burning throat and her dry, vomit-crusted mouth. When Carnie finished feeding her, he untied Kate and took her at gunpoint downstairs into the kitchen.

"Get on the table," Carnie said.

"No. Why? Oh, please, don't hurt me. I'm pregnant," Kate said, sobbing.

"Yeah, I know that already. Now, be a good girl and do as I say: get up on the table. Otherwise, I'll have to hurt you, and I really don't want to do that."

Kate looked at the cold stainless-steel table that stood in contrast to the water-stained walls and chipped brown Formica countertop of the ancient kitchen. The top of the table consisted of a long sheet of metal with small holes. Getting a closer look, she realized the holes let liquid through, which would be caught in the under pan of the table. Then Kate saw the spots of dried-up blood around the edges of the table. Oh dear God, she thought, I need to find a way out of here. Kate considered trying to run for her life, but feared he'd shoot her before she made it out of the kitchen. Suddenly, Carnie whacked Kate across the face with an open hand. Kate reeled sideways and caught herself on the edge of the table before hitting the floor.

"The next one won't be so soft. Now, get on the table. I don't have all day."

Kate, still dazed, gingerly climbed up on the table.

"Hands above your head."

Kate was crying as she followed his instructions. When she felt the first metal handcuff fasten around her wrist, she instinctively jerked away from him. His fist came down hard on the side of her head. Kate was temporarily stunned, close to unconscious. Carnie finished locking her wrists and ankles in place to the legs of the table using handcuffs.

A moment later, Kate regained her wits, and Carnie cut her clothing away. Then he removed his own clothes. Kate screamed and thrust at her restraints.

"Don't do this. Oh, please don't do this," Kate cried, believing he was going to rape her.

Carnie became uncontrollably angry. He put his hand around Kate's throat and choked her. Kate tried to pull air into her lungs, but nothing could get through his thick hands, which clutched her neck as if he were squeezing juice from an orange. She felt the life begin to drain out of her. Kate thought about her baby, starved of oxygen. Just as she was fading into blackness, Carnie released his grip on her.

Then, with great precision, he pulled out his knife and cut off a piece of flesh from her forearm.

Half-conscious, Kate felt the knife going through the layers of skin. Her chest hitched off of the table, her eyelids were retracted and her teeth were clenched tightly together. Kate's senses became alert and went haywire.

Carnie watched her reaction, taking pleasure in the pain she revealed to him as though it was a present. He liked the way her chin jutted out and her upper body rose and fell from the table. He studied the piece of her flesh lying across the palm of his hand. He stared at Kate's forearm, where the warm red substance oozed from her open wound. The sight of her blood calmed his anger and awakened his taste buds. He bent down and licked the cut. He felt euphoric as he looked at the delicacy that lay before him. After his first taste of Kate, he forgot about Razor and his real reason for being there.

"I knew you'd be tasty," he tormented, with her blood dripping off his lower lip.

Kate squirmed. Her pulse quickened. Her mouth was so dry again that her lips stuck to her teeth. The sick, hopeless thoughts in her head were suffocating, and she began to hyperventilate. Carnie cut small slices into her legs and licked the cuts the same way a child licks an ice cream cone. Kate's outward fear escalated his desire to have more of her.

Carnie put his face close to hers. "You can blame your husband for everything that's happening to you. I bet you'll never look at him the same way again when I'm done with you."

Kate tried to remain calm and talk her way out of her situation. "I don't know what Tony did to your friend. I swear, if you let me go, I'll divorce Tony. I'll make him pay for hurting your friend."

"Yes, I like that, Kate," Carnie said, toying with her mind, playing on the hope he saw in her fake smile.

Kate's breathing slowed. *I'm getting through to him. I can talk my way out of this.*

"Please, I mean it. I'll divorce Tony, and he'll be devastated. I'll never let him see our child," Kate promised.

Carnie laughed. "Yes, I like the way you think. It's important that Tony suffers for all of the pain that he caused the Slayers. I'm happy that you agree with me."

Kate's breathing returned to normal. "Please, can I have some water?"

Carnie went to the sink and filled a glass. Then he took a spoon and dribbled the water into Kate's parched, hungry mouth. After only a few spoons of water, not enough to touch her scorching thirst, he put the glass back on the counter. Then he took out his knife again and passed it over her naked body. Kate's eyes grew in size. He wanted to see how far he could push her before she broke. He laid the knife on her leg. Kate's hips instinctively lifted off of the table. He pressed lightly on the blade and he inched the knife through layers of skin on her upper thigh, slicing off a three-inch piece of flesh.

Several minutes later, Kate lay on the table, staring blindly at the chipped plaster ceiling above her. She could feel the throbbing of the raw, open flesh on her arm and thigh. She heard Carnie rustling around and then the sound of her flesh sizzling as he fried it for his dinner. The smell of her own flesh burning made her stomach heave.

"Now, now, little Kate. You must remain calm and healthy if you wish to see your way out of this," Carnie taunted.

He walked over to Kate and grabbed a handful of her hair and pulled her face toward him. Kate looked into his demonic face.

"You see, Kate, you and I are only just getting to know each other. I need you to stay calm—otherwise, you'll ruin everything. Would you like some dinner?" he said with a sinister smile. "I made filet of Kate for our main entrée tonight."

Kate stared into Carnie's demented face. A roiling heat erupted in Kate's belly, and as it rose, her chest tightened. Kate had never felt pure hatred, and she prayed that Tony would come and kill the man who stared back at her with soulless eyes.

Chapter One Hundred Eleven

S ix days later, Tony sat in his kitchen. He hadn't shaved or showered in days. Salvatore had notified Johnny of Kate's disappearance, and the mob was looking for her. Tony was instructed by Johnny Morano to stay in the apartment in case she came home.

Salvatore and Vincent were sitting with Tony in his apartment.

"My father hasn't heard anything yet. Trust me—he and Big Paulie have lots of connections. They'll find someone who saw what happened to Kate. We're going to find her and bring her back," Salvatore assured him.

Tony rubbed his sloppy beard. "I appreciate it and all, but I gotta do more than sit here and wait for your father to hear somethin'. This ain't workin' for me. How 'bout ya drive me down to the restaurant. I wanna to talk to some of those people Kate works wit'.

The men left the apartment and walked toward Salvatore's car. Tony walked with his head down and shoulders slumped. He didn't see the man coming at him, but Salvatore did. Salvatore pulled his gun and aggressively charged the man. Vincent followed quickly behind Salvatore.

"Who the fuck are you?" Salvatore said, seething.

The man put his hands in the air. "I met yas before. At the market."

Slayers was embroidered across the chest of his leather jacket.

"Oh, yeah? Tony ain't got no more friends in the Slayers," Vincent said, jabbing the man in the side with his pistol.

It took Tony a moment to notice that his friends weren't walking behind him. He looked around him, and when he saw Salvatore and Vincent with their guns drawn, he ran to them.

"Smoke?"

"Yeah, hey Tony." Smoke looked from Salvatore to Vincent. "I told ya I was a friend of Tony's."

"Yeah, he's cool," Tony said. "What are ya doin' here, Smoke? If Razor catches ya, he'll fuckin' kill ya."

"I know that, but I had to come and warn ya."

"Warn me 'bout what?"

There were tight lines around Tony's mouth as he waited.

"It's Razor, man. He...well, he got this crazy fuck to go after the chick that you're wit'."

"What are ya talkin' about?"

"I'm talkin' about revenge. Razor wants to even the score. We lost eight guys that night when we was ambushed by the mob, and ya know what that guy did to Razor. He knows he can't wage war against the mob, so he's goin' after you. He's gonna hit ya where it hurts by sending some crazy fuck after your girl."

The blood in Tony's veins turned to ice. He spun and ran toward his apartment. Smoke, Salvatore, and Vincent trailed closely behind him.

Tony was still on the sidewalk when he spun on Smoke. "We gotta go. That motherfuckin', goddamn, no-good, useless prick has Kate. Where the fuck is she? Where'd he take her?"

"Let's take this into your apartment," Salvatore said, not wanting anyone to hear them.

Tony sat in the kitchen, his elbows cocked on the table and his hands balled into fists. "Tell me what the fuck ya know," he said to Smoke.

Smoke sat across from Tony. He breathed deeply. "Some guy named Carnie took her."

"How the fuck do we find this asshole?" Vincent growled and grabbed the collar of Smoke's leather jacket.

"Look, man, I didn't have to come here. I'm riskin' my fuckin' life bein' here." Smoke looked to Tony.

"He's right. If the Slayers find him here, they'll kill 'im."

Vincent let go of Smoke's jacket and took a step backward.

"The Slayers went to this creep's house a couple of summers ago. He's got this farm in western Pennsylvania...a couple of hours from here. I don't remember exactly how to get there, though. That's the only place I know where he might've taken her."

"Tell us about this guy," Tony demanded.

"Fuck man! I hate tellin' ya this shit," Smoke said.

Tony leaned into the center of the table. "Tell me everything ya know. This is my wife and kid that's missin'."

Smoke rubbed his forehead. "Look, this guy is a sick, twisted fuck. He gets his rocks off on torturing people. Razor calls 'im in to scare the fuck outta people sometimes."

"How so?" Tony asked, his face flushed with anger.

"He likes to control people. Ties 'em up, makes 'em suffer, not knowing what's gonna happen to 'em. He, ya know, mind-fucks 'em. Hopefully, Carnie will stay calm. I've seen 'im lose his shit wit' people—he can get real ugly," Smoke explained.

"He'll be calm when I put a fuckin' bullet up his ass," Tony said.

Salvatore hung up the phone and strode across the kitchen. "My father's getting some men together. Let's get on the road, and we'll let him know where we are going."

Of course, Johnny knew Carnie. Most of the hard-core criminals knew of him. Johnny shared all the things he knew about Carnie's history, but he instructed Salvatore to keep the details to himself. It was critical that Tony control his emotions.

Moments later, the four men got into Salvatore's car as they sped away from the City of Brotherly Love to find Kate.

The police on Johnny Morano's payroll hadn't been able to find any leads on Kate's disappearance. Because of this and the urging of his wife, Alessandra, Johnny Morano had pledged a ten-thousand-dollar reward for information regarding Kate's whereabouts. Johnny had also called upon several mob bosses in New York and New Jersey who were familiar with Carnie.

Johnny was sitting in his office when his phone rang. "Salvatore. Where are you now?"

Big Paulie pushed himself to the edge of his seat to listen.

"We stopped at a gas station. I'm inside the store," Salvatore said and told him their exact location.

Johnny jotted notes on the paper in front of him, hung up the phone, and threw his pen into the wall across the room. He turned to Big Paulie, his lips pressed together tight and his jawline prominent. "Get two cars together. We need to move."

Salvatore hung up the phone and walked back to his car. He bent into the open car window and looked at Smoke. "You sure this is the right place?"

"Yeah, I remember that broken-down tractor. See it over there in the field?" Smoke pointed.

"How ya know it's the same one?" Tony said.

"'Cause when the Slayers stopped here, we all went into the field across the street and took a picture standin' around the tractor. Just turn left outta this parkin' lot, and it's a couple of miles up the road on the right. You'll see a dirt road."

Salvatore pulled the car onto the road. Tony had a mixture of joy in his heart thinking about getting Kate back and violence pumping through his veins for the man who snagged her.

"The shit I'm gonna do to that mother fucker ain't gonna be pretty," Tony said, breaking the silence.

Vincent slapped Tony on the shoulder from the backseat of the car. "Correction, the shit we're gonna do. He'll wish he was never born. I ain't never felt this much hate in my whole life. I didn't even hate my own brother, Richie, that fuckin' asshole, as much as I hate this dude. Dickhead don't know how much we all love Kate."

Since Kate had gone missing. Tony hadn't been able to eat or sleep; he was sick with worry. Now that he was on his way to save his wife, he felt a rush of strength and angry courage. With a sincere lack of patience, he told Salvatore, "Speed it up. My wife and kid are waitin' for me."

Chapter One Hundred Twelve

K ate spent her time in captivity on the cold metal table in the kitchen of the old farmhouse. To her horror, Carnie wouldn't let her off of the table for a moment, not even to use the bathroom. The first time she had to pee, she pleaded with Carnie.

"Please. I have to pee. Just let me go to the bathroom."

Carnie giggled at her pleas. "Oh, sweet Kate. I like it when you beg; it looks very cute on you. However, you mustn't leave the table." He leaned in close to Kate's face. "Feel free to go right here on the table, and I'll clean you up when you're finished. It'll give us a chance to know each other better." He gave her a sickening, perverted smile, and Kate wanted to die. After that, she would hold her bladder until he left the kitchen, but he always noticed when he returned. He would put icy cold water in a bowl, and, using his bare hands, he would wash away the urine. Kate wanted to explode every time his hands touched her between the legs.

Throughout the endless days and nights, Carnie had sliced slabs of skin off of Kate's arms and legs. She had slipped in and out of consciousness from the pain and terror. When she awoke on the seventh morning of her captivity, she couldn't feel pain anymore; instead the pain of her torture had become as numb as her mind. The acidy burn remained, but the throbbing pain had passed. It was a part of her existence now, just like breathing air.

It was dawn. Kate looked around the kitchen, which was dimly lit from the rising sun. It was a soft, welcoming shade of orange, and in that moment she felt peaceful. She watched the green leaves rustle lightly in the soft breeze outside, and she longed to feel warm, silky air against her skin. She tried to remember what it felt like and closed her eyes to momentarily leave her torture. Then her thoughts settled on the baby inside of her. She willed Tony to find her, wishing she had magic powers she could use to bring him to her. Then reality settled in, and Kate began to weep.

"Well, we're up early," Carnie said. "Why are we crying so early in the morning, Sweet Kate? Is it because you missed me?" he taunted.

"Mister..." Kate began.

"I told you to call me Carnie," he growled. "I would have thought that over the last week you would have learned the basics, Kate. You call me what I tell you to call me. Aren't you curious where I got my name? Let me explain. There's nothing like the taste of human flesh. Of course I eat animals, like everyone does, but there is nothing as exceptional as the taste of a human. You, my dear, have proven to be the best human being I've ever tasted. I believe it has everything to do with the life growing inside of you. There is a splendid sweetness to your flesh and blood. You see, Carnie is a nickname that my friends gave to me—it's short for carnivore. So now, what were you trying to say?"

Kate lifted her head from the table to look at him. "Carnie," Kate choked out, "I'm begging you to let me go. I never did anything to hurt you, and neither did my child. I will never tell anyone about you. All you have to do is release me and let me walk out the door. I don't know how much more I can take...how much more my child can take," she cried.

"Oh, don't cry, sweet child—you're almost there. You're so close to being free; I promise you," he said.

Kate let her head drop over to the side facing away from him, and a wave of relief flashed through her core. He had gotten his revenge, and it was almost over. She let herself relax. Even the hard metal table under her seemed to soften as she thought about her freedom.

"Thank you," Kate muttered.

"The pleasure is all mine. Now, what shall we have for breakfast?" he said.

Carnie went to the other side of the kitchen and came back with a loaf of bread. Kate watched as he slathered butter over the white, spongy surface. He approached Kate and held the bread to her mouth. Kate took a big bite. Her eyes closed as she relished the taste of the sweet butter dancing over her taste buds. She opened her mouth again and took another large bite.

"See, that's a good girl. You must remain strong. It's important that you keep your wits about you leading up to your freedom. I'll want you to remember the last things we do together...be able to look back on these moments fondly," he said.

When Carnie finished feeding Kate, he retreated back to the bedroom on the second floor. Kate lay on the table, waiting, her heart brimming with hope. She had endured the worst, and all she could focus on was her pending freedom. Carnie had taken his revenge, and now he could move on, and she could pick up the pieces of her life and start over, putting this nightmare behind her.

Just before noon, Carnie came back into the kitchen. Kate had drifted off to sleep and was startled when he entered.

"I'm sorry, my dear. I didn't mean to frighten you."

Kate faked a small smile in his direction.

"Such a pretty smile. Tony Bruno sure does know how to pick a woman. He's one lucky man to have found you. I hope he realizes how lucky he has been," Carnie said, in a trancelike state.

"Tony is a good man. He treats me well," Kate said gently.

"Yes, I'm sure he does, and I'm certain he misses you right now," Carnie said. He shook his head like a dog coming out of water.

"Kate, I promised to set you free, and I'm a man of my word. The only thing a real man has is his word, and I think it's important that we are always truthful," he said.

Kate flexed her hands and feet in anticipation of being released.

Carnie stood over her at the metal table. As he absorbed her innocence and beauty, he heard the tires of a car crunching over the gravel of his long driveway. He had been expecting Tony to find him. After all, that was his ultimate goal, to destroy Tony. He tilted his head, and his eyes opened wide. Kate remembered those warm eyes, the same eyes that had made her trust him in the first place. He was finally going to free her.

"You want me to free you?" Carnie asked.

"Yes, please. More than anything, and I'll never tell anyone about you. I promise," Kate managed to say.

"You promise that you'll remember. Right?" he said.

Kate nodded and let her entire being relax. An instant later, Kate heard the car outside the house. It was coming closer. She lifted her head and pulled her arms and legs against the cuffs that kept her bound. They cut into her skin, but she didn't care anymore; she wanted whoever was coming toward the house to find her. She attempted to yell, but Carnie put his hand over her mouth.

"No, Kate. You don't want to scream. That wouldn't serve you well. I need you to be quiet. You want to be free, right?"

Kate's eyes widened and welled with tears. The car outside came to a stop near the front of the house. Carnie looked down at Kate, "Freedom at last, sweet Kate, freedom at last." He put a rag into Kate's mouth and covered it with thick tape.

Carnie scanned Kate's body and ran his hand over the tiny mound, her child. He covered his face with both hands and then spread his fingers to peek at her body again. He giggled and squirmed as he walked around the metal table taking in all of her. He inched closer to Kate, leaning over her body as his stomach fluttered with an excitement he'd not felt for quite some time.

Kate now knew that Carnie would hurt Tony. She tried to scream through the gag, to warn whoever was coming inside the house, but she knew it was Tony—her instincts told her this.

Kate heard voices coming toward the house. She recognized Salvatore's voice, his crisp and formal words. Kate's adrenaline raced, and she held up her head, looking with anticipation toward the doorway. She saw Tony coming through, his gun pointed in front of him. In the moment that Kate's and Tony's eyes met, Carnie lifted his knife and thrust it into Kate's abdomen.

Kate's scream, even through the gag, made Tony's blood run cold.

"Free at last, sweet child, free at last," Carnie chanted as he wedged the knife down to her pelvis.

Vincent tackled Carnie and put him in a headlock with his gun pressed against his skull.

Tony rushed to Kate and pulled at the metal cuffs. Her eyelids fluttered. "Tony?"

Carnie's insides felt like a festival. His joy at Tony's heartache gave him pure pleasure. He watched Tony rush over to Kate. Her eyes bulged, and her arms and legs flailed unnaturally against their restraints, the knife sticking out of her body.

"Kate! Oh, Kate!" Tony yelled.

While Vincent held on to Carnie, Salvatore fumbled through the despicable man's pants pockets. Finding the key, he rushed to unlock Kate's handcuffs. Finally, Tony lifted her off of the metal table and gently sat on the floor with her in his lap. When Kate finally opened her eyes, they were bloodshot. She studied Tony's face.

"You got here. I knew you would come," Kate whispered. "I want to go home now."

"Yeah, Kate. I'm here. I got ya now. Everything is gonna be OK. Ya need to hang on till we can get ya to the hospital."

Tony kept swallowing hard, trying to keep his emotions from scaring Kate more than she already was. He looked up at Salvatore and Smoke. "We gotta do somethin'."

Salvatore squatted on the floor next to Tony. He looked down at the knife inside of Kate. Her blood was spilling over the blade and down the sides of her body. Salvatore looked into Tony's eyes and solemnly shook his head. Tony rejected the quiet gesture. He shook his head and pulled Kate tighter into his arms.

"Kate, I'm so sorry," he choked.

Kate opened her eyes again. "I'm glad you found me," she murmured. "I was so scared."

"I know ya was scared. But I'm here now, and everything is gonna be fine."

"The baby," Kate mumbled. "Is our baby all right?"

Tony's lower lip quivered. He didn't want to lie to Kate, but he had no other choice. "The baby's fine. You're gonna be fine too, Kate. I love ya so much."

"Till the end," Kate whispered.

Kate moved her head, burrowing deeper into Tony's chest, soaking up the feeling of him, smelling his familiar scent. A stillness came over her, and Tony put his head to hers until her last breath pressed its way out.

Tony slumped over and began to rock. "Noooo, Kate, no. Ya can't leave me. I ain't got nobody else...I don't wanna be alone again. Ya gotta stay wit' me.

Remember, it was gonna be me and you and our baby. Oooh, Kate, please don't go. I ain't got nothin' if I ain't got you."

Wild animal sounds escaped from Tony's mouth. He looked up at his friends. Their faces were steeped in sadness. Neither knew what to say, their grief as real as Tony's. Smoke took over for Vincent, and he held his gun to Carnie's head.

Vincent got down on his knees and put his arms around Tony and Kate.

"This can't be happenin'," Tony said to Vincent, willing him to confirm it was all a big mistake.

Tony grabbed Vincent and pulled his face closer. The two cried like children as they clung to each other and Kate.

Vincent put his hand on the side of Tony's face. "Come on, buddy. Let's get you and Kate outta here."

Tony allowed Vincent to take Kate from his arms and carry her out to the front porch. On the front porch, Salvatore grabbed Tony and they held on to each other, while Vincent laid her body on the porch. They left Carnie inside with Smoke, who had handcuffed him to the metal table in the same way Kate had been restrained.

Outside, the sky was dark and cloudless, just a steady sea of gray. The air was thick with moisture, and the sunless space closed in on Tony. There was no longer a visible difference between the sky and the gray-colored dirt. The wind came in big billows of sizzling air. The tree branches with their long, bark-covered tentacles ebbed and flowed as if trying to snatch Tony's soul from his motionless body.

Tony sat on the porch next to Kate's body and took her in his arms as the sky began to weep. The rain came fast, turning the grassless ground into muddy pools of water. Tony put his hand on top of Kate's. His eyes washed over her body, taking in the large patches of missing flesh. The hellish red-brown wedges of exposed skin stared back at him, taunting him, making him face the torture she'd endured.

Tony scooped Kate up tighter into his arms and stroked her dirty, matted-down hair, rocking back and forth.

Salvatore retrieved a blanket from the trunk of his car and draped it over Kate's naked body. Then he sat next to Tony and put his arm over his friend's shoulder. He had never seen Tony more saddened. His own heart broke as he thought of Kate alone and tormented by the animal restrained inside the house. Salvatore could see, from the condition of her body, that Kate's suffering had been long and agonizing.

"Tony. I'm so sorry this happened. Vincent and I will be here for you—this is not something that you'll face alone. My father has a very special death planned for that pussy boy in there," Salvatore said, pointing to the front door. "Carnie will get the death that he deserves."

Tony's head hung, and then he let out a long, deep moan. He buried his face in his hands. The fear and isolation from his youth scratched and clawed its way into his body. He was alone again. He felt like the vulnerable second grader on the playground. Thoughts of a life without Kate kept slamming into his brain again and again. Normally, he would have swelled with raging anger, but now his regretful sadness overshadowed his anger. Facing a future without Kate was bleak and pointless. Tony lifted his head, and his tears flowed freely. He sobbed, and his chest heaved back and forth. He let out a groan that sounded like a wounded animal's and then finally spoke to his friends. "I shoulda been wit' her. It's my fault. Carnie killed her to get back at me."

Salvatore and Vincent locked eyes. Neither of them was equipped to deal with Tony's loss. Grief covered their faces. The pain and defeat was strangling the life out of Tony. His sorrow was so profound that they were not sure they'd be able to help him. Tony was inconsolable, a broken man.

Salvatore searched his own soul, willing himself to be strong for Tony. "We will destroy this barbarian, Tony. We will take the time to make sure that Kate and the baby didn't die in vain. We will make him suffer."

Tony felt like there was a black hole where his heart had been. The darkness of his reality closed in on him like a vice; it grabbed on to his soul, crushed it and ripped it from his body. "That ain't gonna bring her back, though. Ain't nothin' gonna bring back my beautiful Kate. I lost her for good, forever. I ain't never gonna see her again. When she needed me most, I wasn't there for her. I brought this to her. She paid for somethin' that was meant for me. Why didn't he just come after me? I'm the one who shoulda died, not Kate...not our baby."

Vincent sat next to Tony on the splintered wooden steps of the front porch. "Ya couldn't have known. None of us knew this bastard was gonna go after Kate. We woulda never let her be alone if any of us thought she was in danger. We all loved Kate. Ya can't blame yourself for this, Tony. It ain't gonna do ya no good—it'll ruin your life."

"My life is already ruined," Tony cried. "Ain't nothin' ever gonna be the same again. I lost the only woman who ever loved me for who I am. I can't get that again. I'd rather be dead then be wit'out Kate. I promised Kate she'd always be safe wit' me. I didn't protect her. Don't cha get it, Vincent?"

Salvatore and Vincent were silent, each remembering Kate's youth and beauty. Neither of them had the skills to soothe Tony's helplessness.

"We're gonna get through this, Tony," Vincent finally said.

Tony shook his head, and his heaving, gut-twisting sobs filled the country air. It was as if suddenly the wildlife, trees, and grass stood still. The only sound that could be heard was Tony's anguished cries of mourning and regret.

Tony sobbed. "Just let me be nothin'. That's what I am. Nothin'."

Salvatore and Vincent sat on either side of Tony, legs touching, squeezing him between them and trying to comfort him; it was all they knew how to do. Tony wailed relentlessly as his heart swam in a cesspool of bitter sadness. He cried for a long time, until his tears no longer fell.

A few hours later, two cars and a van pulled into the gravel driveway and slowly made their way toward the farmhouse. Two men from the Morano family got out and carried a long metal box into the barn as Tony sat on the porch, unable to move, paralyzed with remorse.

Chapter One Hundred Thirteen

Inside the farmhouse, two family soldiers watched over Carnie, waiting for orders from Salvatore. After Salvatore placed Kate's body in the back of his car, the three men went back inside the farmhouse.

Salvatore stood on the porch and looked at Tony. "I'm going inside. To see that motherfucker," Salvatore said.

Tony silently stood and opened the front door. He walked into the kitchen before Salvatore.

"Why would ya do this to my wife, ya fuckin' crazy fuck-ass?" Tony screamed.

Carnie smiled. "Your wife was delicious."

Vincent punched Carnie in the face. "He asked ya a question. Answer him."

Carnie held his eerie smile. He swirled his tongue over his bloody teeth in a menacing way. "Mmmm," he hummed. "There's nothing like the taste of blood from a woman with child."

Tony leaned in, his face twisted. "You fucked wit' the wrong person."

Carnie broke into a fit of psychotic laughter.

"You fucking, insane bitch," Salvatore screamed as he strode toward Carnie. He curled up his hand and smashed Carnie in the nose, breaking it on impact.

Tony stood by, watching. He was trapped between mourning his wife and child and a raging fire that burned inside of him. For a moment, Tony's anger won out over his sadness, and he stood directly over Carnie. Tony wrapped his large hands around his throat and strangled him.

Before it was too late, Vincent tugged Tony off of him. "No, Tony. We got other plans for this scum-suckin' pig."

Tony knew Vincent was right. He glared at Carnie. "Why would ya do this to an innocent girl? Why didn't ya come after me?"

"Because I could have never harmed you enough. The only way to get back at you for what happened to Razor was to hurt those that you love the most. Now you can see how clever I am, right? Besides, an eye for an eye, motherfucker," Carnie recited.

"You fuck. You rotten, dirty, woman-killin' fuck. You're gonna pay for this," Tony said, seething.

The family soldiers who had arrived earlier closed in around Carnie.

Salvatore turned to his soldiers. His eyes were like steel. "Cut his fucking clothes off."

When Carnie lay naked on the metal table, Salvatore grabbed his balls, strangling and twisting them in his large hand. Carnie squealed like a wild boar. Salvatore let the flesh roll from his hand. He turned and grabbed Tony by the arm and went back outside.

Two soldiers blindfolded Carnie as he lay upon the same cold steel table where Kate had lain being tortured and eaten alive.

Over two days, persuaded by violent measures, Carnie admitted to everything that he'd done to Kate. The details of what had happened to Kate further enraged Tony. Beyond disgusted and overwhelmed by his loss, he asked Salvatore to watch over Johnny's plan for Carnie's fate.

Tony stood to the side of the porch as the soldiers dragged Carnie out to a rotting, bug-infested barn, where buzzing flies multiplied by the minute. The mob soldiers did as they were instructed. They forced Carnie, still naked, into the long box they had brought with them. When he was inside, they screwed the lid on. The long metal box was shaped like a narrow coffin. The box had a lid that covered Carnie's whole body, leaving an opening just large enough to see his face.

The soldiers smeared a mixture of honey and milk on Carnie's face and stood back. The flies swarmed his face while he screamed. Carnie banged his arms on the sides of the box. The confined space left him barely any room to move.

The soldiers fed Carnie, promising that he would be let out of the box when he'd paid penance for his crime against Tony's wife and unborn child.

"You're lying. You guys aren't going to let me out of here," Carnie said, starting to lose his senses, rejecting the food they brought to him.

"Look, all we know is what we was told. That guy over there..." the solider said, pointing to Salvatore, "said ya gotta pay the price before we let ya outta here."

"Fine, I'll eat, but if you're lying to me, I'll find you and eat you," Carnie threatened.

Before long, Carnie was shitting and pissing inside the box from the food and drink the soldiers continued to give him. Besides the cuts on his face and chest left by the mobsters during their interrogation, sores developed from lying in his own waste. His urine and feces enticed the flies further, and they fed on Carnie's waste. Soon, the flies began to lay eggs, which hatched into maggots. The maggots fed on the open wounds that now covered much of Carnie's body. At first, the flies and maggots tickled his skin, making his desire to scratch verge on painful. Then he felt his flesh being eaten away, one tiny bite at a time. Losing all courage, he begged the soldiers to let him out of the box, insisting he'd paid for his crime. His pleas were ignored.

Johnny Morano arrived five days into the torture. He looked down on Carnie. "You're a sorry prick. What kind of man kills an innocent woman, let alone a woman who's pregnant? I'll tell you what kind of man that is—the kind that doesn't deserve to live."

"You can't kill me. The Slayers won't stand for it. Razor and his boys will hunt you down and kill you," Carnie threatened.

"Razor is dead. I saw to it myself. The Slayers—well, let's just say that they have been warned. I think I'll be safe," Johnny said with a sneer.

"Those guys over there said they were going to let me out of here," Carnie said, hearing the ridiculousness of his own words.

Johnny looked at the two soldiers, who smiled back at him. "What? You believed these guys? They were just messing with you. To be clear, you've reached the end. The more you suffer, the better we will all feel."

Johnny gave Carnie a grave, disapproving stare and walked away. When Johnny found Tony, he gave him a quick hug.

"I'm sorry for your loss, Tony."

"Yeah, thanks. She woulda never died if it weren't for me," Tony said for the hundredth time.

Johnny put his hand on Tony's shoulder. For the first time ever, his eyes softened as he looked at Tony. "Sometimes things go seriously wrong in our lives. This is one of those times. There is nothing more we can do but to execute that prick in the worst way possible. Once that is finished, you will come back and heal. I'll give you some time to do that, but you will need to get your shit together and move on from this devastating tragedy. We are all here to avenge Kate's death and the death of your child. That's the best we can do."

Tony looked at Johnny Morano and nodded halfheartedly.

Johnny patted Tony's arm. "Like I said, I will give you time to grieve and wallow in your misery. Then I will expect you to come back to the family as the man you were before all of this happened."

Tony's lower lip quivered, and tears streamed over his prominent cheekbones. "I ain't never gonna be that person again. Right now, I just don't know what I'm gonna do. I need time to think."

Johnny Morano stood. "Of course, Tony. That's what I just said: I'm giving you time to grieve."

Johnny walked away from Tony and went over to Salvatore. "You make sure he gets his head back on straight. Understand?"

Salvatore nodded and resisted the urge to tell his father to go fuck himself.

Tony, Salvatore, and Vincent stayed at the farm, checking in on Carnie often so they could absorb the pain and agony forced upon him. Over the next several days, other members of the Morano family came to gawk at the dying Carnie as a sign of respect to Tony and the family he'd lost.

Remaining alert for ten days, Carnie was slowly eaten alive by maggots, until he died.

Tony thought about Kate as he stepped closer to the metal box where Carnie lay floating in a thick, putrid liquid, a mixture of waste, flesh, and blood. The extended, cruel death that Carnie had suffered gave him a speck of solace for a moment. Then his thoughts reverted back to Kate, and he felt the guilt hammer away at his insides for not protecting her. He would never forgive himself; he had failed the only woman he'd ever loved and perhaps the only child he would ever have.

Chapter One Hundred Fourteen

A week after Carnie's slow and agonizing death, Tony had Kate and the baby cremated and held a small funeral at the same church they had used for Kate's mother. Only the mobsters knew how Kate had died, all of the barbaric acts Carnie had performed leading to her death.

Tony had told his mother and sister that Kate had been hit by a car and died instantly while they were in New York. His mother and sister attended the funeral along with Donata and Ruth. Too lost in his grief, Tony blamed Kate's death on himself. If only he had never been involved with the Slayers, Kate would still be alive.

"Here comes a couple of the Slayers. Have they lost their fuckin' minds?" Vincent whispered to Salvatore. Both got out of the church pew and stood behind Tony, who was sitting between his mother and sister in the front pew.

Three Slayers walked up to Tony but extended no gesture of comfort. "You got what cha deserved. Your little club here took Razor from us. Killed a bunch of our men, all because of you. You're a piece of shit. One day we'll get even wit' cha."

"Hey, fuck you! Don't talk to my son like that," Tony's mother said, moving closer to her son.

Vincent moved forward, but Salvatore grabbed his arm. "Let Tony's mother have her say."

Tony glared at the Slayers. He wasn't afraid to die, and he didn't care what anyone thought. He sat in the pew and remained eerily calm.

"Don't ya ever talk to my boy like that," Teresa said through clenched teeth. She looked up to the high ceiling of the church and made the sign of the cross. "I'll beat your fuckin' ass right here before the Lord our God, you no-good motherfuckers. God, forgive me for sayin' such things in your house. But if these no-good scabs say another nasty thing to my boy, I'm gonna lose my shit."

Tony was surprised at his mother's burst of anger. He wished she'd do the same to his father. "Ma, it's OK. Ya ain't gotta get involved in this." Tony gave Salvatore and Vincent a knowing look. They stepped in, guns under their suit jackets, and escorted the Slayers outside.

The Slayers got into their car, but before leaving the one in the passenger seat rolled down the window. "This ain't over. Ya tell your people we're comin' for 'em. Ya hear me?" he yelled as the car pulled out of the church lot.

Shortly after three o'clock the next morning, while Tony and Smoke sat at the kitchen table in Tony's apartment, the Slayers' house exploded. At Tony's request, Salvatore had convinced Johnny Morano to spare Smoke from dying with the other gang members.

"After all, Dad, Smoke is the only one of those assholes who tried to save Kate," Salvatore explained.

Salvatore and Vincent had sat in their car at a distance with the mob soldiers who'd planted the bombs. They watched the flames reach up high into the dark night, grabbing the Slayers' souls and pulling them into the blazing fires of the underworld, where lowlifes are tortured for all eternity. Then Salvatore started the car engine and drove to Tony's apartment, where he informed him that the Slayers were gone for good.

Early the next day, Tony lay restless in his bed, wondering how he would go on without Kate and how he would face his nightmares alone.

Till the End

Tony's life had become black. Not even the glaring sun shining in his face could penetrate the darkness inside of him. He stood at the edge of the water, the casinos of Atlantic City, New Jersey, stalking him from behind. Salvatore and Vincent stood several feet behind Tony, giving him the space he needed to say good-bye to Kate and his child. The ocean lapped toward his feet as he stood just out of its reach.

Tony put his hand over his heart as the water ebbed and flowed, soothing him, just as it had comforted Kate when she was alive. The sounds of the ocean made him feel safer somehow, not so alone in the world. The endless body of water provided solace—it didn't judge or demand anything from him. The ocean gave Tony the reassurance he longed for and quieted his aching soul.

Tony watched the waves in the far distance. He closed his eyes and imagined Kate standing next to him, holding his hand, and his loneliness drained away. Kate would always be a part of him, and he knew without a doubt she would live on through him. He opened the plastic bag nestled inside the cardboard box that housed her and their child's ashes.

Tony stepped into the water, and the waves welcomed him into their home. The cold of the ocean numbed him quickly. He liked being numb; it was better than feeling. He opened the bag and let the ashes pour into the water that hungrily jumped up and grabbed Kate and the baby, taking them to their final resting place.

Tony turned his head up to the sun. "I love ya, Kate. I'm sorry that I didn't protect you like I promised and that I let you die. I ain't never gonna forgive myself for your death. I suppose being alone is the least I deserve. I'd give my life if you and our baby could be here again. Ya ain't gotta worry 'bout me; I'm gonna be OK. I know what I gotta do, and I'm gonna make ya real proud. I swear. I ain't never gonna forget about cha. There ain't another girl in this whole world who can replace ya. Thanks for teachin' me how to love and be loved. I'll miss ya forever. Till the end."

Realizing, in that very moment, this was the end for Tony and Kate, he walked out of the water and fell to his knees. He covered his face with his hands as he wept, and his body shook with the racking sobs of a man in deep despair.

Salvatore and Vincent sprinted down to the water's edge and knelt beside Tony. Each embraced him for a moment and then helped Tony to his feet. They trudged through the sand together, supporting Tony along the way, like soldiers bringing their wounded to safety. They placed Tony into the car. The ride back to Philadelphia was quiet, as if their voices had been stolen, as if the silence would ease the pain and heal the wounds that losing Kate had left on each of their hearts.

That night in bed, Tony held on to the aquamarine ring that hung on a chain around his neck. Touching the ring made him feel as though Kate and their child were still with him. It was the only item that Kate had coveted, and now Tony would covet the ring for the rest of his days. When Tony finally fell asleep, he dreamed of Kate. She was alive again, and the couple was happy. It made Tony feel whole, and he woke in the morning joyful. It had been weeks since he'd felt happiness.

The next morning, as Tony ate breakfast alone in the kitchen, he embraced the only family that remained...the Mafia.

Six Months Later

Tony sat with Salvatore and Vincent in a black van used by the mob. They were parked in a lot at an old diner, a few hours' drive from South Philadelphia. Tony looked out the window intently. The gray morning matched Tony's mood. Then he saw an old Cadillac pull into the lot and park on the side. Officer Zody stepped out of the car. Tony held his breath, sitting still, watching…waiting. It had been over five years since he'd seen the pervert, but he'd never forget that rotten face.

Two doors swung open on the Cadillac. Officers Geltz and Nash got out, laughing.

"That's them. It's all of them," Tony said quietly.

"Let's wait until they go inside and sit down," Salvatore said.

Tony looked around him. The restaurant was quiet, and there were only two other cars in the lot besides theirs and Zody's. One car belonged to the waiter, the other to the cook. Johnny Morano had helped make all the arrangements at the diner to ensure they left no witnesses.

The officers were shown to a table at the back of the diner. Tony got out of the van. Salvatore and Vincent followed him. They lingered at the front of the restaurant for a moment. Zody looked right at Tony, but in the five years that passed, Tony had changed into a man and no longer looked like the boy they had ruined. Tony strode over to their table and stood looking from one to the other.

"You got a fucking problem?" Zody snapped.

Tony smiled. He slowly let them see the gun in his hand. The men at the table tried to stand, but they were stopped short when Salvatore and Vincent stepped closer, guns revealed.

Tony ran his hand through his thick black hair. "The problem wit' ya fuckin' pigs is that ya have no memory. Yas don't remember me, do ya?"

The men studied Tony a little closer.

Nash leaned forward. "No, we don't. Why don't you slither off and bother someone else. Maybe you haven't noticed the uniforms we're wearing. We're called the poh-lease, you idiot."

Tony scratched his chin. "Oh, I know what cha are. You're a pack of twisted pricks that get off on rapin' little boys."

Zody's face turned bright red. "I know who you are." He turned to Geltz and Nash. "He's that little greaseball. Yeah," he said, turning back to Tony, "you're one that's hard to forget. You made one of the best bitches we've ever had, Bruno."

Tony put his face inches from Zody's. "Well, today, you're my bitch."

Zody laughed. "I don't think so. Get lost, you prick."

Salvatore, who was standing quietly, pulled his knife out and jammed it into Zody's thigh.

Zody's pain-induced howl sounded like a siren and bounced off of the greasy walls of the old diner.

"Oh, man. Did that hurt?" Tony taunted. "It looked like it really hurt."

Nash and Geltz watched, and Tony turned to them next. "Here's what we're gonna do. We're gonna leave this nice establishment peacefully. You're comin' wit' us into that van over there. See it?" Tony said, pointing out the window.

Vincent got closer to the table. "Hey Tony, which of these assholes made ya eat your food and puke off the floor?"

Tony jabbed his gun against Nash's forehead. "This fuckin' cum licker."

Vincent pushed his gun into the side of Nash's neck. "Good, ya can be my little bitch. Get the fuck up."

Nash stood slowly, hands out to his sides. Geltz and Zody followed. As they were leaving, Salvatore turned to the waiter. "Thanks for your help. Johnny is very appreciative. Expect him to send a little extra money your way—I'll make sure of it. Sorry for the mess," he said, gesturing to the trail of blood on the floor from Zody's leg.

"No problem, man. They're three assholes. Think they're hot shit 'cause they work at the prison. Ya ain't such hot shit now, are yas?" the waiter yelled to the officers.

The six of them got into the van. Tony handcuffed the three prison guards to a pipe rigged down the back of the van. In their own way, each squirmed at being handcuffed. "Oh, yas don't like that so much, huh? Yeah, being handcuffed sucks." Tony turned to Zody. "Remember how ya handcuffed me to the pipe so ya could rape me?"

Zody shook his head in jerky movements. He was shaking uncontrollably and his eyelids fluttered rapidly.

"No? Well, I remember real good." Tony looked at each of them. "Still have nightmares 'bout ya three. I figure the only way to stop dreamin' 'bout cha is to make sure ya can't hurt nobody no more."

"You've lost your mind! We are employees of the state. You'll be sent to adult prison this time. Mark my words. It's all fun and games now, but it won't be when the law catches up with you," Nash stated.

"Ain't nobody comin' to get us. Ya got any idea who we are?" Vincent growled.

"Tell us—who are you?" Geltz said.

"We're the slaughter squad. If ya keep runnin' your mouth, we'll kill ya and your whole family," Vincent said.

Geltz smirked at Vincent, who got out of his seat, went to the back of the van, and kicked Geltz in the face.

The remainder of the drive, everyone was quiet. Then the mobsters took Zody, Geltz, and Nash into a dark warehouse, where their hands and feet were wrapped and tied with cord. The guards watched Tony with an intense, fevered stare.

It Ain't Over 'till It's Over . . .

G eltz looked at Tony, unblinking. "You motherfuckers don't have any idea what will be waiting for you when we get out of here."

Tony gave Geltz a slow, steady grin. He held Geltz's gaze, letting him know who was in control. Only when he was ready did Tony bend down and put his nose against Geltz's. "You inspire me to wanna hurt cha more. Ya remember how ya liked to hit me? Yeah, ya would hurt me real bad, left bruises all over me. Then, 'cause that wasn't enough for ya, you'd burn me wit' your cigarettes or lighter." Tony pushed up the sleeve of his shirt. "See, I still got the scars from the burns ya gave me. Ya made it real hard for me to forget."

Tony whispered something into Vincent's ear, his face emotionless. A few minutes later, Vincent came back carrying an axe. He stood over Geltz with a menacing glare. Geltz squinted his eyes, and the layers of skin crinkled around them. "Listen, man, I didn't really mean what I just said. I was trying to talk some sense into you. That's all," Geltz said. He looked over at Tony. "I'm sure we can make some kind of a deal between all of us."

Tony grabbed the axe from Vincent and lifted it into the air. He whacked Geltz in the face with it hard enough to cause serious injury, but not hard enough to kill him. The blood gushed from the deep gash down Geltz's face. He was stunned, but the excruciating pain kept him in the moment. Tony stepped away from him. Geltz let out a low, steady groan. After several minutes passed, and Geltz likely thought he was out of the woods, Vincent walked toward him carrying a can. Vincent lifted the can over Geltz's head, and gasoline flooded over his eyes, gushing into his open mouth. When the can was empty, Vincent stepped back.

"Please!" Geltz cried. "You don't have to do this. I get your point. I'm sorry for what I did to you."

Tony pulled a cigarette from his pocket and lit it. He looked at the orange glow on the tip of the cigarette and then into Geltz's face. The officer squirmed.

"Oh, you're thinkin' 'bout how much it hurts to get burned. Well," Tony said, taking a long drag of his cigarette and blowing the smoke out, "it hurts real fuckin' bad. I know, 'cause ya did it to me a lot. Do ya wanna see all the burn marks on my ass?"

"No, please, I shouldn't have done that to you." Geltz began to cry. "I have children."

"Oh, ya got children?" Tony said, acting surprised.

"Yeah, yeah, I have a boy and a girl," Geltz pleaded.

"That's nice. Do ya treat 'em good?"

Geltz nodded rapidly, clearly hoping for mercy.

"Yeah, that's real good. So ya don't tie 'em up and rape 'em like ya do to other people's kids in juvie?"

Geltz's head hung.

Salvatore stepped forward and stood over the bloodied, gas-soaked officer.

"What? Did you think that because you have kids that would change anything? You're a pathetic man. Looks to me like all the courage you had when Tony was a defenseless kid is gone."

Tony turned to Vincent. "Light 'im up."

Vincent struck a match and suspended it in the air over Geltz. Then he blew it out and did the same with another match. Geltz voiced his fear of burning to death with piercing screams of terror as Vincent kept lighting matches and blowing them out. Zody and Nash squirmed, obviously understanding the extent to which Tony would go to get even. When Vincent lit the sixth match, he grinned at Geltz right before he tossed it on him. They all watched as Geltz jerked around in eerie motions, burning to death. The smell of his blistering flesh left a pungent odor in the warehouse.

"Ewww, he smells nasty," Tony said to Zody and Nash. "Now what do ya suppose we should do wit' ya two?"

Zody and Nash were visibly rattled, their lives hanging in the balance.

Tony circled around the remaining two. "Now, we know who ya are: you're big bad guards of a juvenile detention center. Let me ask, do you have any idea who I am now? I mean, didn't ya ever think that someday I'd grow up and come after yas? Or that any one of the boys ya fucked wit' would come after yas?"

"Look, it was a long time ago. We're sorry," Zody ranted.

Tony squatted on the ground next to Zody. "You're sorry? Sometimes sorry ain't good enough. This is one of those times. Ya guys thought ya was all-powerful and shit five years ago. Seein' ya now, though, ya don't look so mean. I was real scared back then. Just a boy in jail for somethin' I didn't do. Ya guys hurt me. Like I told ya in the van, I still ain't completely over it. Sometimes I have nightmares about it, even when I'm wide awake. How many other kids have ya fucked up?"

"It . . . it . . . was just a one-time thing," Zody stammered. "We didn't do it to anyone else."

Tony laughed. "You're such a fuckin' liar. Everybody in juvie knew about the three of yas. I just wish I heard before I became one of the kitchen boys. You're a sick bastard." Tony unzipped his pants, pulled out his penis, and pissed all over Zody.

Tony turned to Salvatore and Vincent. "Do ya think we should let 'em go? He did say they were sorry."

"I don't know. Let me think about it." Vincent said. Silence followed for a full minute. "All right, I thought about it; I don't think we can let 'em go. They don't look sorry to me."

Salvatore grinned. "Yeah, me neither."

"That's what I thought," Tony remarked.

Tony turned back to Zody. "I got somethin' real special for ya. Somethin' I'm sure you'll like, given the kinda person ya are."

Zody didn't wince. His brow was furrowed and his jaw was set hard. Zody had murder in his eyes, and if he could have, he would have strangled the life out of Tony.

Tony stared back at Zody. He hated the man. He was nothing more than a low-life, scum-sucking rapist who had preyed on helpless victims, the kids he was supposed to protect.

"Now, let's see. You're Nash. Like Vincent said earlier, you made Tony do some awful shit with food in your cafeteria—is that right?" Salvatore asked.

Nash gave Salvatore a pained stare. The guard was sweating profusely, and he shook his head in denial.

Salvatore let out a chuckle. "Tony told us all about you. In fact, he said you were the kind of man that focused on food. I guess that's why you were the terror of the cafeteria, right?" Salvatore moved closer and stared at Nash with a deadpan expression. "We have something very special for you. One might even call it a delicacy."

Vincent stepped up next to Salvatore and put a gallon jug of turpentine on the floor next to Nash.

"Let me explain," Salvatore said. "This is turpentine. It is thick, and when you drink it, the liquid gets lodged in your lungs. Eventually, after a while, you'll suffocate to death."

Nash's whole body started to quiver. He jerked against his restraints. He shook his head and pulled against his bindings. Salvatore looked down on him. "It probably won't taste good as food mixed with puke, the meal you made Tony eat, but hopefully it'll go down easy. Open your mouth."

When Nash refused to open his mouth, Vincent moved forward with a large metal funnel. He bashed the funnel into Nash's mouth, breaking his front teeth. When they finished pouring the brownish-yellow liquid down his throat, they stood back and watched. To their delight, Nash began to vomit, coughing and gagging as the oil spewed from his mouth and filled his lungs.

"Ya liked watchin' me be scared," Tony said. "Ya stood there and smiled the whole time, no matter how bad it got for me. Where's your smile now?"

Nash stared at Tony with a look of disbelief. They all, including Zody, watched Nash battle against the contents forced down his throat. Nash was retching and gulping to pull air into his lungs; Tony watched, feeling a sense of justice. After several torturous minutes, Tony jammed an ice pick into Nash's throat. He stabbed him nine more times, each time screaming, "Die, motherfucker," until Nash was dead.

Salvatore turned to Zody. "See that? Tony still has a heart after all you assholes put him through. He could have easily let your friend suffocate to death, but instead he took him out of his misery. Personally, I would have let him suffocate. Oh well, this is Tony's show. Now, I was wondering, how did you manage to find yourself such a pretty young wife? I mean, you're a nasty old guy who rapes young boys. How did you meet Linda?"

Zody watched Salvatore closely but didn't respond.

"Oh well, Linda has a date with one of our associates. Don't worry—we'd never hurt her. She hasn't done anything to deserve punishment. I wanted you to know that your beautiful wife has other men on the side, that's all. Just in case you thought she'd miss you or something. Nope, I bet she's going to enjoy that life insurance policy you took out when you started working for the prison. I guess you thought you'd have children by now, but that wasn't Linda's plan at all. Linda used you for a place to live until she found someone better...and she did, and she told our associate all about her secret plans to leave you. I didn't want you to die thinking that the woman loves you—that wouldn't be right."

Zody's mouth dropped open. He closed his eyes and rested his chin on his chest.

"Don't look so worried; we're still here wit' ya," Tony said, savoring the noticeable stress on Zody's face. "We ain't forgot about ya. Have ya ever heard the old sayin' 'We're savin' the best for last'? That's what we've done here. Just to be certain ya get the best send-off, I'm gonna do it myself. Seein' that ya brought me into your twisted group, I feel like I should give ya more of my attention. Ya know, like ya gave me. I have this thing about men now, men who rape kids. Makes me want to rip 'em apart with my bare hands. I mean, I thought about doin' that, but that ain't sexy 'nough for ya."

Tony stood directly over Zody. "Anyhow, we all know you're an ass man, right? No need to answer me 'cause we both know I'm right. What we're gonna do is simple." Tony made eye contact with his friends. "Get 'im undressed for me."

Minutes later Zody lay naked on the floor, his wrists tied to his ankles in front of him. Tony moved close to him. From behind his back, he showed Zody the hacksaw he was holding. "Now, I need ya to bear wit' me. It's been a while since I used one of these things, so it might be a little rough at first."

Tony reached between Zody's thighs, grabbed his penis, and slowly sawed it from his body. Zody howled, pain gripping him at his core. The warehouse echoed with grunts and moans and a subhuman sound that made the air whirl with a creepy, sadistic energy.

"Get the sick fuck up on his knees," Tony instructed. Then Tony held Zody's sawed-off penis at the entrance of his rectum, and with a metal rod, he shoved it inside of him. "I figured since ya was an ass man, ya might enjoy that." Tony repositioned himself and looked Zody in the eyes; they were wide with terror. "Ya like it like that—I know that ya do. How's it feel? Huh! How's it feel!" Tony screamed, spittle spraying Zody's face.

Tony stood back and watched the blood spill out of Zody's groin from the stump where his penis had been severed. Tony eyes lingered for a moment longer; he took pleasure in watching the life drain out of Zody as he began his slow ride into hell. Then he took out his gun and waved it in Zody's face. Zody, aware enough to know it was over, closed his eyes, and Tony shot him in the chest. A single bullet tore through the empty space where Zody's heart should have been.

Tony stood and looked at the three dead bodies.

"Let's get going," Salvatore said. "I'll have our soldiers come in and clean up this trash."

Tony sat in the back of the van while Salvatore and Vincent sat in the front, talking about the next job that Johnny Morano had lined up for them. A sense of peace came over him. The men who had hurt him were finally gone. The beasts that had lived in his head since he'd left juvenile detention were finally dead, and he was finally set free.

***

That night, Tony ate dinner alone in his apartment. Tony thought about how good it was to have the guards dead and gone. He smiled. A lot had changed in his life over the past six months. He'd lost more than he'd gained, but he was still there, still living.

Tony went into the bathroom and grabbed a small towel. He put a drop of Kate's apricot-scented shampoo on it and laid the towel on his pillow. It was his nightly ritual, the way he eased himself to sleep. The scent reminded Tony of Kate, and smelling it next to him, he felt as though she were still there with him.

He thought of Kate as he waited for sleep to come. He remembered how they'd made love in that very spot. The room was warm then, cozy, a place that felt like a real home. Now, the same spot felt like he was lying on a bed of nails, and the room was an everlasting reminder that love had once lived there.

Kate's death had changed Tony. He had become a man of greater courage, and any fear that had remained inside of him was snuffed out. He would always know how to love, but that ability would stay idle inside of him, never to be seen again in the same way that Kate had experienced his love.

Tony's love for Kate was gradually replaced by his passion for the mobster life. The men he called his brothers were the closest thing to a family he had left.

Tony focused all of his energy on the mob. When he was working alongside Salvatore and Vincent, it was the only time he felt he had a home.

In the years that followed Kate's death, Tony would become one of the most feared Mafia men in Philadelphia and one of the most revered mobsters the Morano family had ever known.

The weak and vulnerable boy who'd once been the prime target of playground bullies had been transformed by the intense love and bottomless hate he'd experienced. Tony Bruno now had all the power he'd ever longed for, and he knew exactly how to use it.

Continue reading . . .

The New Family

Read about Joon, a friend of Tony Bruno's, in **Never Be Alone.** Joon is a homeless teenager surviving on the streets of Philadelphia. Joon chose homelessness over foster care. **Read a sample of Never Be Alone here . . .**

Jamie pulled up in front of a dilapidated house and parked. Eight-year-old Joon held her breath and looked around at her surroundings. Her insides felt weightless. The little girl hunkered down in her seat, determined to stay inside the confines of the metal-and-glass box that stood between her and this other, unknown life.

Joon peeked out the car window with unblinking, wide eyes. So much had changed since her parents had died. She had been ripped away from her friends and teachers, her sense of security torn away. She was reeling from the rapid changes in her life. She fought the urge to scream. Her anguish and loss overwhelmed her as her eyes roved over her new home.

The house was weathered. The small yard was neglected, with patches of overgrown weeds poking out of the dirt where grass refused to grow. Joon's gaze followed the broken walkway to the porch and the screen door hanging from a single hinge. She looked over at Jamie with apprehension, wishing she were back in the modest but well-maintained home where she'd lived with her parents, where she felt safest.

Hot tears stung her eyes. "Is this it?" Joon squeaked out.

"Yes." Jamie rested her hand on Joon's shoulder. "Now don't worry. It's going to be fine. Your foster mother, Aron Remmi, is excited for you to live with her. You have two foster brothers too. I think you'll love it here."

"But the house looks scary," Joon said, her bottom lip quivering.

"Well, I'll admit, it's a bit run-down on the outside, but Aron keeps her home very clean inside, I made sure of that," Jamie said proudly. "When I place a child in a clean home, that's when I know I'm doing my job right. Every child deserves a good family and a clean home. You'll have both of those things here, so don't worry."

Joon's eyes dropped to her lap, and she rubbed her sweaty palms on her thighs.

Jamie leaned toward the child. "I know this a big change for you, Joon. I'm sure it feels very scary, but I need you to trust me on this. Being in a single-family foster home is better than all the other places you could have been placed. You're one of the lucky kids. There are a lot of kids just like you that end up in group homes. Here, with Aron and her two sons, you get to have a real family." Jamie patted Joon's shoulder. "Now put on your best smile and let's go meet them."

As Jamie and Joon walked up the porch steps, Aron pulled the front door open. The woman wore a warm smile, and Joon noticed she had large teeth. They weren't unattractive, but they stood out against her blotchy, white skin, wide nose, and big ears. Her long, wiry, brown hair hung below her shoulders. She wore a beautiful yellow-and-white sundress and smelled of honeydew and cucumber lotion. The smell reminded Joon of her mother, Gwen, and sadness pressed in on her until she felt weighed down with it. She fought the urge to drop to the ground and cry.

Aron stooped and rested her fingers on Joon's shoulders. "You must be Joon. Welcome home, sweetheart."

The tears building in Joon's eyes spilled over. It didn't matter how nice Aron was—Joon feared her new home. Until now, she hadn't known where she would live, but she'd been comfortable at the temporary shelter. The people who worked at the shelter had told her it was temporary housing, but now that she was at her new "home," the reality, the permanence, of her situation was all too real. In the first days following her parents' deaths, she'd hoped they were still alive, that it was all a big mistake. As the shelter workers had waited for a foster home to become available for her, Joon had waited for her parents to come and rescue her.

Now, Joon looked at Aron, and her guts knotted. She wanted her mother and father. She didn't want to live with strangers.

Aron narrowed her eyes. "Are you gonna say hello, honey?"

Although Aron was smiling, Joon noticed the tightness in the woman's jaw, and her senses went berserk. The woman gave her the willies, and she instinctively stepped toward Jamie for protection.

"Come on, Joon. Say hello to Aron," Jamie urged. The social worker gently pushed her toward Aron again.

Joon looked up at Jamie, her eyes pleading for her to stop. The caseworker, feeling sorry for the girl, tried to comfort her, forcing a smile on her face again, and nodded in Aron's direction.

Joon turned to Aron. "Hi," she said in a small voice.

"Well, I see that you sent me a shy one," Aron said, her lips in a tight line.

Jamie stepped closer to Aron. "Joon has been through a traumatic experience, losing both parents suddenly. I think she needs some love and care. She's going to adjust just fine in your capable hands."

Aron bent, took Joon's hand, and moved toward the front door. Joon tried to dig her heels into the aged wood of the porch, but Aron steadily pulled her along.

"Let's go now," Aron said. "I want you to meet your new brothers."

For Joon, going inside the house meant closing the door on her old life—the life she'd loved. She had cherished being an only child, as her mother and father had given all of their attention to her. But her life was different now, and knowing she had foster brothers made her more nervous. Joon clenched her teeth, worrying that the boys would be mean to her or even hate her. She wasn't used to living with other children and all the changes about to happen overwhelmed her.

Aron tugged on Joon's hand, and her muscles tensed as she guardedly followed her new foster mom into the house. Just inside the door, Aron turned back to Jamie and stared into the other woman's eyes. "I can take it from here. I think it'll be easier for my new foster daughter," she said kindly.

Jamie nodded. "You're right. Bye, Joon. I'll be back to check on you in a month or so."

Joon's eyes grew double in size, and she clutched at her own neck to contain the bile burning the back of her throat. "Do you promise to come back and see me?"

Jamie nodded. "I'll see you real soon," she said, before turning and leaving the house.

Aron shut the door and pulled Joon into the living room. "Boys, this is your new foster sister. Her name is Joon," she said and cackled. "Such a stupid name. I don't really like it. In fact, I hate it. I'll have to think of another name for her. Anyway, this is Deen and that's Dobi," Aron said, pointing to one boy, then the other.

Deen, the older of the two, eyed Joon. "Yeah, Joon is a dumb name," he stated.

"I love my name," Joon mumbled, wrapping her arms over her chest and pressing her lips together. Her new foster family glared at her, and she felt the world around her darken—she could feel their coldness through their dead stares. She felt trapped, and fear rose from her stomach, pushing harder at the bile in her throat. Her body trembled.

Aron raised an eyebrow at the child. "Looks like we have a girl with no manners. I'll need to tame that if you're going fit in here. You need to tell Deen you're sorry."

Joon shook her head. She wasn't sorry. She didn't want to lie. Besides, he was the one who'd been mean. Shouldn't he apologize?

"Okay. I'll show you to your room, and you can sit in there until you're ready to tell Deen you're sorry for being rude to him."

Minutes later, Joon was sitting alone in her dingy bedroom. Aron had instructed her to sit on the edge of her mattress, feet flat on the floor and hands in her lap. So Joon sat still, her heart hammering away in her small chest, fear creeping up her spine and clenching tightly around her heart. Aron scared her. She was nothing like her own mother had been.

As she waited, Joon thought about her name. She had always loved it. She replayed a story her mother had told her often over the years: "Before you were born, your dad and I only had each other. Both of our parents were gone, and being only children, we had no one else...well, we had each other but we wanted a family. The doctor that delivered you laid you on my chest, and my heart filled with a love I had never known before, and I started to cry. Your father and I looked at each other, and he said, 'We finally have a family.' We were so excited to have you in our lives. The nurse gently touched the top of your head and asked what your name was. Your father and I felt silly because we hadn't decided on your name yet; we wanted to wait until we saw you. The nurse smiled at us and said, 'What about Joon? Joon means 'life.' That was it for us. The name settled into our hearts, and we knew we'd love you forever—our Joon, our life."

Joon's parents, Gwen and Rich, had met at a bowling alley when they were in their early twenties. They moved in together the following year and married six months later. They had a solid marriage and great love for each other. And they were good to Joon. Rich was a third-grade teacher and Gwen had quit her job as a secretary for an insurance company to stay home and raise Joon. Even though they had little money, they had an endless amount of love for their daughter. They always made certain she had decent clothes and plenty of food.

Joon's favorite memory was of Christmas morning when she was six-years-old, when her parents had given her a new bicycle. It was pink and purple, with a white basket on the front. For Joon, the bicycle represented fun and freedom. Over the summer, she had seen the other girls riding their bikes up and down the street. They had all looked so happy, riding along with their hair blowing in the wind as they raced to an invisible finish line. Now, Joon could zip through the streets too. Rich had taught Joon how to ride it as Gwen stood on the sidewalk and cheered her on. When she'd fallen off, her mother had taken her inside, made her a cup of hot cocoa, and told her to try again. After, Joon had rushed outside and climbed back on her bike. That night at dinner, Rich and Gwen told Joon how proud they were of her.

"Remember," Gwen had said, taking the child's hand, "you can do anything you want in life as long as you don't give up."

Chapter One

J oon's teeth were clenched and her lower lip trembled as she sat on the floor waiting for the pain to follow. She would have welcomed death, but instead, all she could do was cram herself farther into the corner of the kitchen, between the cold plaster wall and the wooden door that led to the dreaded basement. She wanted the hurt to stop. It had been three months since she'd been placed with her new foster family—three long months of terror and torture for anyone, let alone an eight-year-old.

"You rotten, ungrateful, little bitch. What did I tell you about stealing food?" Aron yelled. The woman pulled back her leg and kicked. The pointy toe of her shoe landed on Joon's thigh.

Joon let out a muffled yelp and scurried from the corner like a spider being chased by a broom. She scuttled under the kitchen table, hoping to find shelter beneath the pressed wood.

"I'm sorry. I'm hungry, Aron," Joon cried weakly.

"You don't know what hungry is, girl." Aron crouched, clamped her hand around Joon's ankle, and pulled the child out from under the table with one forceful yank.

Exposed in the middle of the kitchen floor, Joon curled up, knees and elbows pressed together, hands clasped behind her head, trying to protect herself from the fury brewing in Aron.

Aron opened the door to the dark, dank basement. "Get. Down. There."

Joon, willing to accept isolation in the darkness over another beating, quickly rose to her feet and stepped through the opened door. As she moved toward the first step, reaching for the railing, Aron elbowed her in the back. Joon tumbled down the wooden stairs and hit the bottom with a thud.

"You can stay down there and think about what you did. Ain't nobody gonna steal from me. I told you before—you get to eat when I say you can eat."

As the basement door banged closed, the cold blackness rushed in on Joon. She had sharp pain in her back. On her hands and knees, she dragged her aching body to the closest wall. She closed her eyes against the pain and the fear of being alone in the basement. Things moved around in the dark down there. There were rats and bugs. After moving in, she'd learned swiftly that Aron enjoyed punishing her. It made her foster mother feel important, powerful. Joon had also learned there would always be another punishment, no matter how much she tried to please Aron.

During the long hours of the night, Joon focused on her breathing to calm her frazzled nerves.

She must have eventually drifted off, because the sound of a toilet flushing above her brought Joon back into the moment. Tears dribbled from her chin at the fading memory of her parents. She sat in silence, hoping that someone would come and take her away from the hell she called home.

Chapter Two – Three Years Later

I n the early hours of the morning, the pain of Joon's cracked rib and sprained ankle gave way to a numbing disillusionment. Aron had pushed her down the basement steps again the night before. Joon was injured, but she no longer feared the dark space, the wet dirt floor of the basement, where the bugs and rodents crawled around her. In fact, the creepy-crawlies reminded her she was still alive. They made her feel like she wasn't alone.

Joon had slipped in and out of sleep all night. When the basement door was flung open later that morning, the light from the kitchen startled her. She squinted up at the shadow at the top of the steps until her eyes adjusted. Her thirteen-year-old foster brother Deen was staring down at her with a sickening smile. Deen was almost as mean as Aron—the boy thrived on the power his mother gave him over Joon.

"Mom said you gotta get up here now, maggot," Deen said, taunting her.

Joon got to her hands and knees, and used the old, wooden railing to hoist herself up. She limped up the stairs slowly.

Deen sneered as he watched her painful climb to the top. As Joon walked past, he whacked her on the side of the head with his open hand. "Mom said to get this kitchen cleaned up. She said it better be spotless."

Joon remained silent. She only spoke when given permission, a rule Aron established in the first few days after her arrival. The only time Joon broke this rule was when her hunger overpowered her fear.

With her body aching, Joon hurried to clear the dirty breakfast dishes from the kitchen table and put them on the counter next to the sink, then filled the sink with water and soap.

"The water needs to be hotter, scumbag," Deen growled. "Are you trying to get us sick?"

Joon turned the hot water higher and Deen shut off the cold water. The kitchen faucet spewed steamy water into the basin. When it was half-filled, Deen turned the water off.

"Get washin'," he demanded.

Joon studied the steam coming from the sink. She knew there was only one thing to do. The girl shoved her hands into the scalding water and washed the dishes. Her feet danced in place; her hands felt like they were on fire. Satisfied that Joon was being tortured properly, Deen spit on her and left the kitchen.

As soon as he was gone, Joon turned on the cold water and let it run over her hands, instantly relieving the throbbing burn. She hurried to finish cleaning the kitchen before Aron came in to inspect her work. Joon had just put the last dish away when Aron waltzed into the room followed by Deen and her twelve-year-old son, Dobi.

"Well, lookie here, boys. Pathetic, scruffy Joon looks a little hungry this morning," Aron said. "Should we give this animal something to eat?"

Joon's eyes grew bigger. The very thought of food, any food, made her hopes soar.

"Nah," Deen said. "I think she needs at least another day before she can eat."

Aron turned to her younger son. "How about you, Dobi? What do you think?"

Dobi squirmed. He pushed his hands into the front pockets of his jeans. "I think she looks real hungry, Ma. We should give her something now."

"Okay, Dobi, we'll do that then," Aron said, opening the cabinet under the sink.

She pulled out a bag of dry dog food and poured it into a bowl. Then she opened another cabinet and grabbed a bottle of Tabasco sauce. She drizzled it over the food before pulling the refrigerator open and grabbing a bottle of fish sauce she used to make seafood soup. The amber contents splashed onto the dog food. The smell made Deen and Dobi take a few steps back from the concoction. Aron mixed the three ingredients together and placed it on the kitchen table.

"You're hungry?" Aron sang, leaning into Joon. "Now you got food. I'm giving you two minutes to eat, starting now."

Joon stood over the bowl and looked at Aron.

Aron gave her a grave look, and Joon stared back, her eyes pleading for mercy. "Stop eyeballing me. You're hungry, and you wanted to eat, so eat. Who knows the next time you'll get food. Sooo, you better get to eating."

Joon looked down at the bowl, pinched her nose closed with her left hand, and grabbed a glob of the food with her fingers. She shoved it into her mouth and chewed. The Tabasco pierced her tongue and gums with fiery heat. She flung her mouth open and fanned at the garbage splayed over her tongue and lodged between her teeth.

"You got another minute left. You better hurry and eat up," Aron said, laughing.

Joon's eyes were watering. The heat was unbearable. The smell and taste of the fish sauce was strumming her gag reflex. Joon stepped away from the bowl and fell to the floor.

"Please," Joon pleaded, "I need water."

Aron put her hands on her hips and stared right through the child. She took a few steps and, with her foot, pushed the dog's water bowl over to the girl.

Joon cupped her hands and slurped the water. She was in too much pain to care about the food particles and thick, stringy saliva left by the dog that were floating in the bowl.

Aron stooped, so she could put her face close to Joon's. "You're a disgusting pig. Those mother fucking people that sent you here to live with me should be paying me way more money to keep you." She straightened up and turned to her two sons. "This here is what you call white trash. You remember what it looks like because you better never bring a little slut like this home as your girlfriend."

Deen snickered, grabbed a scoop of the rotten mixture from the bowl, and threw it onto the side of Joon's face. Most of it was in her hair, but a bit landed on her eyelid, and when Joon pushed it off her face, a small piece lodged in her eye. The Tabasco sauce scorched her eye, and as she rubbed it, the heat spread. Joon rolled around on the floor crying from the blazing agony.

Aron turned and left the kitchen. "Let's go, boys. Leave this piece of shit here for now. I'll deal with her later."

Joon flailed around, rubbing her face, but when Deen and Dobi obediently followed their mother, Joon got to her feet, grabbed a dish towel, soaked it with cold water, and pressed it against her eye. She dropped to her knees and trembled on the floor. Her heart felt like a lump of useless clay inside her chest, like it would continue to get heavier and heavier and, eventually, just stop beating.

Chapter Three

Joon rarely found relief from Aron's daily humiliations. It was almost the end of summer though, and she hoped that middle school would be better than her years in elementary school had been. Aron had stopped hitting Joon in the face weeks before school started, to avoid the bruises that had become as normal to Joon as her nose.

After the incident with the Tabasco sauce, Joon never felt hope again when being offered food by Aron. When Aron did feed her, it was only discarded scraps from the family's plates, and while it wasn't ever enough to satisfy her hunger, Joon at least knew the food was safe to eat.

Joon's bedroom was on the main floor of the house, the room that Aron had showed to Jamie before they placed Joon with her and when the social worker returned for visits, which was rare. But the small girl rarely slept in the bed. Most nights, she was sent into the basement and, on rare occasions, the family dog, Kensey, went into the darkness with her. When this happened, Joon and Kensey slept together, the dog providing her warmth through the night.

On the first day of middle school, Aron opened the basement door before the sun was up. "Get your ass up here," she demanded.

Joon ran up the steps and stood before Aron. Her head hung and her long, blond hair was matted and covered her face.

"Look at you. You're a disgrace. Today is your first day at a new school. There's a couple things you better not forget. Keep your fucking mouth shut. I don't want nobody knowing my business. The other thing is if anyone asks you how you like living here, the answer is that you love it. Understand?"

Joon raised her head to look at Aron and nodded.

"Then say it!" Aron yelled.

"I love living here," Joon repeated in a small voice.

Aron shook her head. "Let's go. You need to take a bath so you look human. It ain't gonna be easy for you in school given that you're so ugly."

Joon was so exhausted from the beating she'd taken from Aron the night prior, without thinking, she said, "My mom and dad thought I was pretty."

Aron spun on her. "Your mother was either a lying bitch, or as stupid as you. Besides, where's your precious mother now? I'll tell you where she is—she's dead, lying in the ground, rotting next to your loser father. Look around you. Do you see your wonderful parents here? Taking care of you? Making sure you're raised right?"

For a split second, Joon thought of protesting but knew it would only ignite Aron's fury further.

"No," Joon mumbled.

"That's right. Besides, they were too dumb to teach you how to act like a nice girl instead of a dirty pig. But I know how to raise you right. You ain't an easy one to help because you're the most stupid child I've ever known." Aron shook her head. "Get moving. I want you cleaned up before the bus comes."

Joon followed Aron into the bathroom and watched as her foster mom ran water into the tub. Her body tingled as she thought about cleaning off the grime caked on her skin. The buildup made her flesh feel too tight for her body.

Aron turned from the tub. She put her hands on her hips and scowled at Joon. "What are you waiting for? Get those filthy clothes off."

Joon undressed, and Aron's judging eyes bore through her, making the child feel self-conscious.

"Hurry up!" Aron screamed.

Joon removed the remainder of her dirty, worn clothing quickly and climbed into the tub. She hadn't taken a real bath in close to seven weeks. The warm water felt heavenly against her crusted flesh. Aron handed her a small bar of soap and placed shampoo next to the tub. Then she reached into the bathroom closet and tossed a washcloth into the water. "Make sure you wash up real good. Get that stink off of you." Aron put down the toilet lid and placed a thin bath towel on top. "That's for you to dry off with. Now get a move on. You ain't got a lot of time."

As soon as Aron left and closed the door behind her, Joon put her whole head under the water. She used the soap and washcloth to scrub her skin. Then she picked up the shampoo and washed her long, blond hair quickly and dunked her head under the water again. Joon felt released from the filth that had held her skin hostage. Being clean was a luxury that she yearned for in the long time between each bath. She leaned her head back against the tub and smiled, as she often did when she was allowed to bathe, and let herself get lost in the glorious moment. Then she heard footsteps coming toward the bathroom.

"Let's go," Aron yelled through the door. "Your time is up."

Joon hurried out of the tub and grabbed the thin towel, her sense of peace snuffed out by the crude sound of Aron's shrill voice. She dried herself and opened the bathroom door. Aron was waiting, staring down at her. Joon followed her foster mother into the bedroom. On the bed were a pair of secondhand jeans and a purple T-shirt.

"Get dressed, then get your ass into the kitchen. Breakfast needs to be cleaned up before you go to school," Aron barked. She glared at the child as Joon combed her tangled hair with her fingers. The older woman opened the top drawer and took out the brush that Joon's mother had gently ran through her hair. Aron stomped over to Joon and grabbed the top of her head. She raked through Joon's hair in long, hard strokes. Joon could feel the hair being pulled from her scalp. She squeezed her eyes closed, enduring the sting as her head jerked back and forth until Aron finished.

"There," Aron said, looking satisfied. "Now, hurry the hell up."

Joon finished dressing and paused in front of the mirror hanging on the back of the bedroom door. Her reflection was jarring. She had grown taller over the past seven weeks. Her jeans were two inches too short and her T-shirt was baggy. She was much thinner with dark circles under her eyes. Her once vibrant blue eyes were now faded to a dull gray. She no longer recognized the girl in the mirror—the person looking back was stripped of all humanity, a shell of the girl she once was. She only had access to a full-length mirror when she was in her supposed bedroom, and she was always curious to see what she looked like and hated to find the monster looking back at her. She pushed the wet strands of hair behind her ears, just like her mother had done for her when she was alive.

When Joon walked into the kitchen, Deen and Dobi were almost finished eating. Aron took a bite of her toast and motioned for Joon to sit in the empty chair at the table.

"You're ugly even when you're clean," Deen remarked.

Aron smirked and nodded.

Egged on by his mother's reaction, Deen continued. "All the kids are gonna pick on you. I already told my friends that you're a mutant, that there's something wrong with you. Everybody already hates you. Welcome to middle school."

Aron shoved the last of the toast into her mouth. "Okay. Finish your breakfast, boys."

Deen and Dobi finished eating while Joon was made to sit and watch. The smell of toast was glorious, and her mouth watered and her stomach gurgled thinking about taking a buttery bite or just one spoonful of the colorful, sugary cereal Deen and Dobi were eating. When the three were finished, Aron told the boys to get ready for school.

"You get this kitchen cleaned up. I want to see this place sparkle before you leave."

Alone in the kitchen, Joon cleared the dishes from the table. She thought for sure that Aron would have let her eat breakfast before going to school, as she had in the few years prior, even if it was just a banana or half a slice of dry toast. Joon considered drinking the milk left in the cereal bowls but knew if she was caught, the consequences would be severe.

A little later, at the bus stop, Joon stood far away from the other kids. The boys threw pebbles at her that stung, and the girls giggled and pointed at her clothes. Joon crossed her arms over her chest as the bus pulled up. Until now, school had been a short escape from her foster home, but nothing more. As the bus doors opened, she tried to be optimistic about her new school, hopeful that something would change for the better.

BUY NOW: Never Be Alone (Home Street Home Series: Book Five)

The HOME STREET HOME SERIES is a collection of novels that can be read in any order.

More books by Paige

Home Street Home Series:
Believe Like A Child
When Smiles Fade
One Among Us
Mean Little People
Never Be Alone
My Final Breath

Rainey Paxton Series:
A Little Pinprick
A Little High

A Note From Paige

Dear Dearth Reader,

I want to take a moment to thank you for reading and supporting my work. I appreciate you spreading the word about my books to family, friends and co-workers. If you enjoyed this book please go to Amazon and leave a short review so that other readers can determine if this is the right book for them . . . great reviews mean so much to me and keep me writing. Thank you!

~Paige

Made in the USA
Monee, IL
02 September 2023

42046834R00260